Madness Lies

Falkirk

Helen Forbes

TP

ThunderPoint Publishing Ltd.

First Published in Great Britain in 2017 by
ThunderPoint Publishing Limited
Summit House
4-5 Mitchell Street
Edinburgh
Scotland EH6 7BD

Front Cover Image © Cara Forbes
Rear Cover Image © Huw Francis
Cover Design © Huw Francis

ISBN: 978-1-910946-30-5 (Paperback)
ISBN: 978-1-910946-31-2 (eBook)

www.thunderpoint.scot

Acknowledgements

To all my family, friends and readers, thank you so much for your support and your patience. Grateful thanks to Detective Sergeant Stuart McNae for his kind help and invaluable procedural advice. Thank you to all at ThunderPoint for taking another chance on me. And finally, a special mention for Allan Goddard, who single-handedly boosted the sales of my last book by persuading everyone he knew, and quite a few that he didn't, to buy a copy. Thank you, pet – keep up the good work.

Dedication

For Cara and Nye, with so much love.

Chapter 1

The blood is dark. It surrounds and changes the patchwork of lichen on the rock, slipping down through cracks and fissures, seeking a return to the earth. The knife is sticky in his hand. He lets it drop to the ground. At his feet, the dead man's eyes are blank and open to the sky, all malice and vengeance gone.

What now? What price for taking a life? Even if the alternative was to lose your own? Even if there was never a choice, no other way? A mocking seabird flies overhead, its wanton cries echoing through him. And he knows. The price will be everything he has.

Joe Galbraith struggled to rise from the dream, but it kept pulling him back. The body. The blood. The price. When would it end? A beating noise, repetitive and strong, filled his head. He clung to it until the dream let him go.

Rain. On the window above his bed. He turned over and opened his eyes. Four thirty a.m. He'd be worth nothing if he didn't get back to sleep, at least for a couple of hours. But the man in his dream, the man he'd killed, was determined to keep him awake.

Not that he *had* killed anyone. The dream had distorted reality, so that Joe held the knife and used it on Stephen MacLaren, instead of the other way around. Was it regret that sculpted the dream? Did Joe wish he had killed Stephen?

No, though he'd have done anything at the time to save his sister. But as he and Stephen had fought on the rugged shore in Harris last year, Joe was stabbed, leaving him with a scar that itched whenever he remembered, and frequent haunting dreams in which the story played out a little differently each time.

Would the dreams end if Stephen's body was found? He was last seen jumping into the sea. Surely his remains must come ashore eventually. And maybe then the dreams would stop.

*

Five hours later, DS Joe Galbraith yawned as he took a call from his boss. A smell coming from a storage unit; surely that was

1

something for uniform? Aye, it was, DI Black agreed, but he'd be very grateful if Joe would just take a quick look.

When he'd transferred to the new Major Investigation Team, Joe had imagined something a little more challenging than checking up on smelly storage units. On the other side of the room, DC Jimmy Jackson was slouched over his desk, his clothes dishevelled and his hair lank and greasy. 'Jackson, you seen Roberts?'

No response. That was nothing new.

'Jackson?'

He sighed, looked up and put his hand on his chin. 'Eh… dunno…is he tall, dark hair, skinny long legs, a bit like a stick-insect?'

'Very funny. Have you seen him today?'

'Nuh.'

Joe would have liked to have taken someone with him, but when the choice was Jimmy Jackson or going it alone, there was no choice.

The smell was in unit 36, Duncan MacPhee told Joe. It had started two days ago, and if there wasn't something dead in there, he'd eat his broomstick putter. That explained it. MacPhee was a golfing pal of DI Black.

There was something dead all right; a whole barrel of something dead. MacPhee and Joe backed off, but the smell followed them. Joe picked up a stick and advanced on the barrel, his arm over his nose. He poked the lid off.

MacPhee gagged. 'Holy mackerel.'

Joe peered closer. 'Herring, actually.'

'There could be a body in there.'

Joe nodded. 'Let me know if you find anyone.' He backed out and pulled the door closed.

MacPhee's wee sharp chin was jutting out. 'What are you going to do about it?'

'Sweet Fanny Adams. There's no law against curing herring in a storage unit, no matter how badly it's done.'

'Clause 63 of the contract: no perishable food products.'

'Aye, your contract. It's not a police matter.'

'No?' A rush of colour surged from MacPhee's neck to his

cheeks. Flecks of spittle waited at the corners of his mouth, and Joe moved to the side, just in time. 'That's not very good. Thought you were here to keep law and order, see that people don't overstep the mark. That is what I call stepping well and truly over the mark.'

Joe shook his head. 'You really think I've got nothing better to do than chase up some numpty for breaching clause 63 of your contract? I've wasted enough time.'

'Suit yourself.' He wiped the spittle away, rubbing the back of his hand against his crumpled trousers. 'I'll maybe phone Brian Black again, see what he's got to say about it.'

'You do that.' Golfing chum or not, Joe knew his boss wouldn't expect him to take this any further.

*

The youth looked familiar but Joe couldn't place him, as he sprinted past the car. He was wearing a black puffer jacket, gleaming white trainers, and drop-crotch jeans. Not easy to run in them, but he was making a good effort. As Joe waited for the lights to change, he watched the youth in the mirror. Still running, a glance over his shoulder, starting to cross the road, and jumping back as a jeep just missed him. The vehicle pulled up behind Joe, and the driver opened his window and shouted abuse. Joe wondered. Had he had dealings with the boy before? Maybe he should turn and go after him.

But something was happening up ahead. Someone screaming. Someone crying. People gathering. Lights changing and cars going nowhere. At times like these Joe wished he'd stuck to being a joiner. He'd have turned the car and driven away without another thought. He'd have read about it later in the newspapers and wondered what Inverness was coming to. He'd have talked about it on the job, speculated with his workmates about who had done it and why. And then he'd have forgotten about it.

But he'd become a policeman, which meant he had to investigate. And it meant he'd keep seeing the body over and over in his head, whenever he closed his eyes. And he'd have that smell of blood and the subtle hint of gun smoke stuck in his nose for days. And that sinking feeling, wondering how long it was going to take to find out who did it, how many more might die while they tried to figure it out, and when the hell he would next get a day off.

*

DC Nigel Roberts was not happy. He'd come back from a union meeting and been sent straight out with Jimmy Jackson to a sneak theft in the Crown. An old dear, went upstairs to hoover. Came down and found the back door burst open and her TV, purse and laptop gone. Jackson had been a sarcastic pig. Why weren't her laptop and purse out of sight, instead of sitting on a table in the living room? And why did she need a laptop anyway? Online gambling?

The old dear had been fit for him. Skype was much easier than bush telegraph when it came to contacting her family in Australia, she'd said. Jackson looked puzzled. He probably didn't even know what Skype was.

While Jackson was dusting the kitchen for prints, the old dear told Roberts to take a seat in the living room. 'Is he your superior?'

Roberts winked. 'What do you think?'

She laughed. 'Coffee?'

'Yes please.'

There was a shout from the kitchen. 'Milk and two sugars.'

She rolled her eyes. 'Don't remember offering him anything. Chocolate biscuit?'

Roberts nodded.

Proper coffee and a couple of decent biscuits. If only they were all like that. She'd never see the goods again, but hopefully her insurance would pay out. Roberts tried to let her down gently.

She shook her head. 'Don't worry about me. The laptop was playing up. I was thinking of getting rid of it for a tablet. iPad Air 2, maybe. Fingerprint recognition – no need to bother with a passcode. Weighs less than half a kilo. What do you think, son?'

Roberts hadn't a clue. He might try and give Joe Galbraith the impression he was a technical whizz kid, but it wasn't hard to impress Joe. There would be no fooling this old bird.

'And see that FaceTime? Far better than Skype. My grandkids in Sydney have their own iPhones. I'll just contact them direct. Bypass the scowling parents sitting like stooges in front of the family PC. I've been thinking about it for ages – this has given me the shove I needed. Every cloud, son; every cloud. And speaking

4

of clouds, plenty of space on the iCloud for the photos and music.'

Roberts smiled, and kept quiet. She looked at her watch and nodded towards the kitchen. 'Himself's taking his time. If he'd hurry up, I could get a taxi to Argos. There's a cracking deal on a 42 inch Wi-Fi enabled smart Sony. I saw it in Which? You can even talk to the thing. Tell it what films you want to watch and it'll come up with a list.'

Roberts smiled. 'Aye? I shout at mine all the time, but it's not that obliging. You'll need to get the door fixed before you go anywhere. And definitely before you bring any new technology into the house.'

'Aye, son; you're right. I'll get hold of a joiner when you leave.'

Roberts thought of Joe Galbraith. He used to be a joiner. He'd probably offer to repair the door in his own time. He was a bit of a softy, though he hid it well. Roberts' phone rang. It was Joe Galbraith.

The old dear smiled when Roberts ended the call. 'That fair brightened you up. What is it? A gun battle down the High Street?'

She wasn't far off the mark, only it wasn't down the High Street.

Chapter 2

As she passed through the women's clothing in Debenhams, Sharon MacRae saw herself in the mirror and smiled. What was it her mother used to say about a pig's ear and a silk purse? Or was it a sow's ear? Whatever it was, turns out the old cow was wrong. You could do it, if you had money. You could do anything with enough money. Should she worry where the money was coming from? Aye, right. She was doing nothing wrong. Someone had fallen for her. Someone rich. Why would she worry about that?

A smiling sales assistant approached. 'Can I help?'

'No, just looking.' But why not? Just because she'd never asked for help before, it didn't mean she couldn't now. 'Eh...aye, you can help, please. I was looking for one of those bras, the ones that push you up.' She pushed her hands further down in her pockets, just to stop herself from showing the girl what she meant. She waited for the shop assistant's scorn. It must be coming. In fact, was that not the bird that had caught her in the home department two years ago, with a frying pan up her jumper? The frying pan had pushed her boobs up, all right. And made a hell of a mark on the side of the assistant's face. She peered closer. No mark on the girl's face, and she was still smiling, waiting to help.

Sharon left with three bras. She wore one of them, the pink balcony bra with black edging, and she felt fabulous. In M&S, she checked the recipe from the Tesco magazine. Spinach, ricotta, fresh pasta and crème fraiche. A year ago, she wouldn't have set foot in M&S, and she certainly wouldn't have got excited over finding organic spinach.

She decided to stop by Linda's for a quick cookery lesson, if her friend was home. Linda was a cook on an oil rig, and there had been a time when her schedule was imprinted on Sharon's brain. She'd count the days until her friend came home, so she could tap her for a tenner.

Linda was home. They hadn't seen each other for a while. She looked Sharon up and down. 'Looking good, Shar. Your hair's gorgeous.'

Sharon smiled. 'Cheers.'

'And check the teeth. Is that crowns?'

'Bridges.'

'Must be going well with Christopher.'

'Not bad, Lind; not bad at all.'

They drank coffee while Linda talked Sharon through the recipe.

'Thanks, Linda. You're a pal. When are you away again?'

'Next week.' She dipped a biscuit in her coffee. 'How are the boys doing?'

'Sound. Liam's a wee darling, and Ryan's still a big gobby shite.'

'No change there, then.'

As Sharon walked down Grant Street, she wondered if it was time to ask the Council for a move. Kinmylies, maybe. Dalneigh? Raigmore? Not that any of these areas were perfect, but there was no escaping the stigma of living 'down the Ferry'. It didn't seem to have put Christopher off, but still. Maybe it was time for a change.

But how would Ryan feel about a move? Liam would be fine no matter where they went. Nine years old and still talking about being a copper. He wouldn't mind, as long as he was with his mum. But Ryan was different. He scared Sharon sometimes. That look, as if he might be thinking of hitting her. Maybe she was mistaken. Maybe it was the memory of her brother battering her mother that time, before they took him away. A memory that had scarred her and scared her and fucked her right up. Ryan wouldn't do that; he wouldn't. Maybe she'd best just stay where she was.

*

She had no idea she was being watched. Too busy gloating over her hair and her new teeth, her designer gear and her shopping bags. Smug bitch. Did she really think any of that cosmetic shit could change what she was? First time he'd seen her, about a year ago, she was such a mess. No way did he think she'd ever be a threat to him, that she'd take what was his. Look at her, thinking she was something special, as she walked down to the Ferry. Down the fucking Ferry? Bitch. If he had his way, she'd be six feet under, along with everyone else that had crossed him.

But he couldn't stick around here. The town would be crawling with cops by now. As he drove away, he smiled. He might not be able to bury her yet, but the shit was about to hit the fan in her smug little world. Big style.

*

Life might be looking up, but Sharon didn't half miss her fags. It wasn't the same drinking coffee and watching TV without a proper fag. Christopher had bought her a fancy e-cigarette, but it didn't really hit the spot. It stopped Ryan nicking her fags, though; that was one plus.

As she sat down with a coffee and the remote control, she heard a key in the door; Ryan must be home early. She winced as the door slammed and the walls shook. And again when he slammed his bedroom door. Why was he always so noisy and aggressive and bloody annoying? And why wasn't he at school? At least when she'd skived off school, she hadn't the barefaced cheek to come home. She used to hang out in the park or down the canal. Not that her mother would have given a shit whether she went to school or not; she just wouldn't have wanted Sharon around any longer than absolutely necessary, cramping her style.

Style? Aye, right. Scared one of her paedo boyfriends might fancy trying his hand with Sharon or her sister. It didn't work, did it? Not when you left said paedos to babysit so you could go out with your mates. Old bitch. If Sharon ever came across her again, she'd kill her.

Her hands shaking, Sharon rummaged in her bag for the e-cig. What she wouldn't give for a good lungful of carcinogenic compounds and toxins, a healthy dose of formaldehyde, ammonia and arsenic. They couldn't be that bad for you, could they? Arsenic? Christopher was probably making it up. Gullible cow, she'd taken his word for it. She could look it up on her new pink Acer netbook, if she wasn't a) terrified of the damn thing, and b) terrified he'd check what she'd been looking at, and hammer her.

Sharon's mood plummeted. A rich boyfriend didn't change anything. She would always be a useless junkie, and he would never be anything but a man. Nothing good had ever come from a man that showed interest in her. He needed his head examined, and so did she. Just 'cos he'd never hit her, it didn't mean a thing. Maybe he was reeling her in, just like her dead husband, Peter MacRae, had done. Treating her like a princess until she was hooked. Then it would start.

This was no use. She had to do something to change her way of thinking. Nip to the shop for fags and a half-bottle? It was tempting. Nah; she'd try the abdominal breathing exercises Christopher had taught her when she started reducing her methadone. She lay on the couch, one hand on her chest, the other on her belly. As she inhaled, she imagined her diaphragm contracting and her lungs stretching. She was getting better at this; her chest hadn't risen at all. She held her breath, then she tightened her tummy muscles, forcing the air out through pursed lips. Three or four times, and her mind was quieter, her body relaxing into the sofa. This shit worked.

Or it might have, if the living-room door hadn't opened with a kick that almost took it off its hinges. Sharon sat up, her head spinning as the calm evaporated. Ryan dashed past with a pile of clothes in his arms, heading for the kitchen.

'What are you doing?'

No answer. Ignorant wee shit.

'I said, what the fuck are you doing?'

Nothing.

She counted to forty, before she went through to the kitchen. The air was thick with the scent of lotus flower and jasmine, and Ryan was standing watching his clothes immersing and turning darker in the washing machine, a look of sheer terror on his face.

'Ryan, what is it? What's wrong?'

He often ignored her, but not like this, like he didn't even know she was there. She wanted to touch him, to hold him. She reached out a timid hand. A thump stopped her. And another.

It was his new trainers, thumping round in the washing machine. And was that his jeans and his new jacket? She'd lived with his father long enough to know what this meant. 'Get to the shower.'

And still he stood there, watching his circling clothes. She shoved him as hard as she could. 'In the shower. Go.'

He went. There was something white under the table. A sock, with a splatter of small red specks down one side. The phone was shaking in her hand. 'Christopher, I need you. Now.'

Chapter 3

The victim had looked quite serene for someone who'd taken a bullet through the chest. Probably hadn't a clue it was coming. He'd been shot in the back, through the car seat. Maybe he'd been chatting about something pleasant, completely unaware that his back-seat passenger was about to cut the conversation in the most drastic of ways.

Joe was back at the station now, a map of Inverness spread out on the table. Had the sprinting youth been in the car with the murder victim? The timing was right. The victim's car had been stopped on Kenneth Street near Central School, heading towards Tomnahurich Street. The driver of the next car that came along hadn't seen anyone leave the abandoned car. When he came up behind it, the front passenger door and the door behind the driver were open. He'd signalled, pulled out, glanced to his left to give the driver a glare for stopping in such a stupid place. And freaked out.

He'd swerved onto the pavement, embedding his car in a wall, as an oncoming car crunched into his passenger side. The road was well and truly blocked. Minutes later, Joe was on the scene. When he'd called in the incident, he'd mentioned the boy and the direction in which he was running. A patrol car had a look, but no luck. Joe checked his watch. Almost two hours had passed; plenty of time to destroy any evidence.

But was the boy the shooter? If he'd been in the back seat behind the driver, surely he'd have been on the other side of the road when he bolted past Joe, several cars further back, just before the lights at the top of Fairfield Road.

Though he hadn't seen the boy's face, Joe was certain he knew him: the build, the way he ran, the hair. The more he tried to think, the cloudier his head became. The lack of sleep wasn't helping. On cue, he felt his scar start to itch. Bloody Stephen MacLaren.

But wait. There was something, a vague shadow flitting through Joe's head. He tried to grasp it, but it evaded him. Something about Stephen MacLaren and the youth. A connection. A slim one.

Instead of trying to follow the shadow, he traced his finger down Kenneth Street. The guys in the patrol car had concentrated on Dalneigh and the Carse. Joe looked for routes on the other side of Kenneth Street. The boy could have gone down Celt Street or Wells Street and along the riverside to Grant Street. There were any number of streets and lanes he could have taken to stay off the main roads. And from Grant Street? Did he cross the Black Bridge towards the town, or turn left towards the Ferry?

The scar was itching again. No surprise. Stephen MacLaren had murdered Moira Jacobs down the Ferry last year. That was where it all began. And MacLaren had befriended Moira Jacobs' neighbour, Sharon MacRae, to get access to his victim.

Sharon MacRae. Joe smiled. Of course. Much as he'd have liked to challenge Sharon's son, Ryan, as soon as possible, Joe knew he couldn't go near him. Not after being at the scene. The possibility of cross-contamination would give Ryan's lawyer a field day, if it ever came to that.

*

Sharon wanted to hammer Ryan. Cocky wee shit, eyeballing the Filth like an American gangster, just like his father would have done.

'What the fuck's he doing here?' Ryan looked Roberts up and down, then he smirked at Jackson. 'And who's that ugly numpty?'

Sharon saw rage in the older policeman's eyes. If she wasn't here, he wouldn't think twice about hitting Ryan. Roberts smiled. 'Come to see you, Ryan. Me and Detective Constable Jackson. What you been up to today?'

'Nice of you to show an interest. This and that. Nothing much.'

'Why are you not at school?'

Sharon wanted to give him an alibi, tell them he was sick or something, but she'd never been good at lying, so she kept her mouth shut.

'Wasn't feeling well, so I came home.'

Roberts nodded. 'Is that what you were wearing today?'

Ryan glanced down at his white t-shirt and black trackie bottoms. 'Looks like it.'

'So you weren't down on Kenneth Street a couple of hours ago, in white trainers, drop-crotch jeans and a puffer jacket?'

Sharon could have sworn there was a hint of fear in her son's eyes. Just for a moment. A blink and it was gone. She'd probably imagined it. She knew she hadn't.

The thumping grew louder. Sharon and Ryan both glanced at the kitchen door. The officers ran. Roberts banged on the washing machine. 'Stop this thing. Now!'

Sharon hadn't a clue how to stop it. It was brand new, all flashing lights and annoying jingles. When the cycle was finished, it played Schubert's 'Trout'. Why play a tune? What was wrong with a beep or a blinking red light?

'Where's the plug?'

She had no idea. Christopher had had it installed while she was out. She came home to find her thirty year old third-hand Hotpoint gone, and this shining streamlined Samsung in its place.

Roberts lunged at three switches on the wall. The first two put the oven and the fridge off. The third stopped the washing machine, with a whining reluctance and a sad little tune.

Jackson crouched before the machine. 'Looks like a puffer jacket, jeans and trainers to me. Son, you're nicked, and so is this monstrosity'.

*

'You?' Jackson's face was contorted into a sneer. 'Sitting in while we question Ryan? I don't think so. For all we know, it was you that put the washing on, trying to destroy evidence.'

Sharon shook her head. 'But Ryan's told you it was him. And the boys don't have a social worker now. I'm clean. I have been for ages.'

'Aye, as clean as your son's clothes. Might look all right on the surface, but go any deeper and it's all there, all the shite of the day, just waiting to come out. Shame your fancy new machine doesn't have a DNA removal cycle, a special programme for dealers, pimps and general scum.'

Sharon's fear turned to rage. She pointed at Jackson. 'Who the fuck are you calling scum?'

As Jackson laughed, Roberts stepped between them. He frowned at Sharon. 'I really don't want to have to arrest you, but I will if you don't calm down.'

Jackson shook his head. 'Mental bitch.'

12

*

Sharon was glad it was Galbraith that questioned her at the station. He seemed to believe her when she said she hadn't put the washing on. The female cop that accompanied him wasn't quite so accepting. How many fourteen year old boys knew how to work a washing machine?

Sharon shrugged. 'Just the ones with a retard for a mother. I hadn't a clue how to use it. He read the book and showed me. He often puts his own washing on.'

'And where does someone on benefits get a top of the range machine like that?'

Sharon hesitated. She didn't want them knowing anything about Christopher. 'Eh…a friend.'

'What kind of friends buy – '

Galbraith stopped her. 'Sharon, Ryan was in school first thing this morning, but he didn't come back after the morning break. He's been taking a lot of time off lately, and showing up the next day with a note from you.'

Shit. What was Ryan up to? 'He goes off every morning and tells me he's going to school. What can I do if he leaves during the day?'

The woman screwed up her wee red face. 'It's your job to see that he goes to school and stays there. Not a lot to ask, is it? Not as if you're working yourself.'

Stuck up bitch. Bet she didn't have any kids. Sharon didn't say what she was thinking. If it wasn't for Roberts, she'd have gone for Jackson earlier, and she'd be in custody now too. She told them Ryan had gone to school as usual. She didn't know what he was wearing; she'd been in the bathroom when he left. He went early, probably to avoid having to walk Liam to school. She didn't know who he'd been hanging about with. His best mate was Sean Anderson, but there were others at school. 'He doesn't tell me much, but I know he'd never have anything to do with a shooting, with a murder. You must have got it wrong.'

The female cop sneered. 'You're the one that's been getting it wrong, for the last fourteen years.'

Sharon didn't know how to answer that. The bitch was probably right. 'Can I wait for Ryan?'

The officer laughed. 'Your concern is so touching.'

Galbraith frowned at his colleague, then he smiled at Sharon. 'There's no point waiting. I don't think Ryan's going anywhere any time soon. We'll call you if there's any change.'

Sharon crossed to the petrol station and bought a bottle of water. Time was, she wouldn't have paid for water. Even this stuff in plastic bottles wasn't good for her, Christopher said, but it was better than a fizzy drink. She'd a bit of a thirst after last night. They'd been out for a meal and a few drinks, and she'd overdone the wine. It was the happiness that did it. Aye, right. Happy, sad, excited, down – was there a state of mind that didn't make her want to drink? But she had been happy, and it wasn't just the money Christopher had given her; it was knowing that someone liked her enough to want to spend time with her, to listen and learn about her. He wanted to know her favourite colour, favourite singer, favourite designer, favourite vegetable. No one else had ever given a shit about whether she had a favourite anything.

He'd come straight away when she'd phoned him earlier. He hadn't asked any questions and he hadn't seen Ryan. He just listened to Sharon, then he put the sock in a plastic sandwich bag, as if he was a scene of crime officer. Stuffed it in his pocket and said he'd take care of it. She'd rung him again from the station, and he'd offered to arrange and pay for a solicitor for Ryan. The best. She didn't ask how he knew the best criminal solicitors.

Christopher came across as a decent guy. His father had died two years earlier and he'd inherited money. He'd moved up from London, bought property in Inverness and started a letting business called Brent Properties. It all seemed on the level, but really? No decent guy was going to fancy her. Decent or not, she didn't want to lose him.

Please, please, please. Not now. If she repeated it often enough, maybe he wouldn't finish with her.

Chapter 4

The shooting victim was Gordon Sutherland, a local SNP councillor, DI Black told the officers gathered for the briefing. Married with two grown up kids, he'd left the council offices about an hour before he was found dead. He'd been expected at a constituency meeting that afternoon. His wife, Roz Sutherland, was at the opening of an art exhibition at a gallery near Beauly when her husband was killed. She'd been interviewed by DI Black and Joe Galbraith. She wasn't being considered a suspect for now. Door to door enquiries were ongoing, but there was nothing of interest so far. The post mortem would take place in the morning.

Roberts updated them on Ryan MacRae. He couldn't remember where he'd been after leaving school. Just wandering about. Nowhere near Kenneth Street, of course, and DS Galbraith could really do with a trip to Specsavers. That got Roberts a laugh.

Ryan had no alibi. A partial print on the inside handle of the front passenger door of the victim's car might be a match for his thumbprint, but it wasn't conclusive. The contents of the washing machine had gone for analysis. One black puffer jacket, a black sweat-shirt, white t-shirt, a pair of drop-crotch jeans, boxer shorts, white trainers and one white sock. They had turned Sharon MacRae's flat upside down, but there was no sign of the other sock.

Ryan was still in custody. It was unusual to keep a child of fourteen in a cell at the police station, but the severity of the crime and Ryan's likely association with criminals gave the police the authority they needed. The situation had to be reviewed every few hours, and Social Work was closely involved. The other alternative was a secure unit, but there were none in the Highlands. Hopefully they'd get something from Ryan's mobile phone and his clothes. If they didn't get anything, Ryan would walk. For now.

As Joe left the briefing and headed for the canteen, he wondered about Ryan. Chances were he'd inherited more than a surname from his late father. He fitted a profile that had been mapped out for him long before he was old enough to talk.

Dysfunctional family. Mother an addict. Abusive drug-dealing father, that he probably now idolised. He'd been referred to the Children's Reporter before for his behaviour. And yet, his little brother seemed so different. Liam was cheerful and friendly. And Sharon was okay; she'd had her problems, but she'd never been in trouble with the police.

Who knew? One thing Joe did know was that he wouldn't be seeing Carla tonight.

*

PC Carla MacKenzie was at her third call in as many hours. Another shop in Nairn targeted by a group of shop-lifters. Her colleague was taking a statement from the manager when Carla saw herself in the mirror. Thank God for the hat. She couldn't remember when she'd last washed her hair. It was hard to distinguish one morning from another. Nausea, aching, greyness. So tired, the thought of even turning the shower on made her want to crawl back into bed. She'd forced herself into the shower each morning, but a quick scrub was as much as she'd managed this week, followed by a dusting of dry shampoo.

She was supposed to be seeing Joe later. The very thought was exhausting. Another shower. A hair wash. Attempt at cheeriness. Something more. No way. Maybe she'd call it off, crawl into bed as soon as she got home. She glanced in the mirror again, and saw her face turning grey. Her eyes looked so dull, and were her cheeks starting to sink? She heard her colleague say her name. And then the grey in her head turned to black.

Carla dreamed of a North Uist summer. Walking with her father down the track towards the beach. She wanted to run ahead. She wanted to pluck the dancing poppies that peeped out of the whispering crops, take them home to her aunt. She wanted to chase the rabbits that bolted this way and that, everywhere she looked. But she couldn't. To do that, she would have to let go of her father's hand. She couldn't.

When they reached the tickling marram grass, he let go of her hand. For a moment there was panic in her heart, and then he lifted her. She felt his body sink with each step into the soft sand. 'Do your legs not get scratched, Daddy?'

16

He didn't answer. He was gazing through the gap, to a sea as blue as the stone in her mother's ring. The water was bright with diamonds that danced on the shifting ocean like fairy lights.

On the summit of the dune, he put her down. They held hands and ran down the slope to the stretching white sands, right to the edge of the sea. She giggled as the foamy water tickled her toes. A strand of seaweed tried to get her. It would have dragged her in if she hadn't jumped. It would have taken her all the way to America.

'Daddy, the seaweed's not getting me.'

There was no answer. She turned and he was gone. The lonely sands stretched all around her.

Her head was as light as air, her body like stone. There were people surrounding her, but she couldn't make out their features. Maybe they weren't real; just shadows, dancing and mumbling, caressing her arm with the lightest of touch, then the sharpest of pricks. Something looming closer, a brilliant white light searing into her eyes and forcing them to close. Her body getting lighter, rising, floating. The sky over the beach a deep turquoise. Her dad is hiding. He must be, just on the other side of the dunes.

*

Joe had just started on the Gordon Sutherland report when the custody officer at Nairn called. Carla was in Accident and Emergency at Raigmore Hospital. Joe phoned the hospital and was told there was no point in coming up to see her. She was drifting in and out of consciousness, and they were doing tests. Had she been ill recently? Could she be pregnant? His throat constricting with something that felt like fear, but could have been shame, Joe told the nurse he hadn't seen Carla for a week. She hadn't felt well at the weekend. He'd offered to go round, but she'd said she was too tired; she was going to bed. He didn't tell the nurse he'd offered to join her there. Nice try, Carla had said, her voice weary. He'd wondered then if she'd had enough of him. It was only a matter of time; he knew that. But then she'd suggested doing something tonight – she was sure she'd be better by then.

Pregnant? No way. She'd have told him. Just 'cos they didn't see each other as often as they'd have liked, she'd have told him. The nurse asked about her next of kin. They wouldn't do that if it wasn't serious, would they? He told her Carla's mother lived in South Carolina. She had no siblings and no other close family. That made him the first point of contact. They'd call him as soon as they had any news.

*

Carla scrambled up the sand dunes, shouting for her father. At the top, she scanned the view. Across the machair, there were tiny houses in a ragged row. The white one was her aunt and uncle's, between the tallest and the smallest. Maybe her dad had gone back. But why would he leave her here all alone?

There were voices. Insistent annoying voices. Making her head sore. Carla, they said; Carla, wake up.

No way. She couldn't leave the beach without her dad. What if she never found him again? And suddenly, he was there, standing on the track, smiling. 'Go. They're waiting for you.'

'But I want to stay with you.'

'I'll be here. Come and find me.'

'But, Daddy; I can't go on my own. I'm too wee.'

He was shaking his head. Blowing a kiss. Fading.

'Carla.' A harsh voice. The smell of cheap body spray and antiseptic. Two uneven rows of yellow teeth.

'Daddy…'

The nurse's words made little sense to Carla. She couldn't grasp them. Something about her blood cell count. She just wanted to sleep. But that wasn't going to happen. Clanging metal. Shrieking nurses. Gossiping patients. It was torture. Exhaustion was pouring over her in waves, but every time she dropped off, some bugger would start again. She opened her eyes and the curtains round the bed were closed. Maybe they thought that was enough to keep the noise out.

Her eyes were open when the curtains shook and shifted. And he was there. Not her dad, but someone just as solid and sure. And just as loved. Joe's face was as grey as the face she'd glimpsed earlier in the mirror, his blue eyes worried and his forehead frowning.

Her hand in his felt so good, until the dizziness came. He

pushed her hair back from her damp forehead and wiped her face with a soft towel. He smiled and kissed her hand. 'You gave me a fright.'

'Now you know how it feels.' Her voice was weak and croaky. 'Same hospital too.'

Joe smiled and moved his hand towards his scar. She'd sat by his bed in Raigmore last year, waiting for him to come round. It was the first time she'd met his parents, as they dotted back and fore between him and his sister, Lucy, who was recovering from pneumonia after jumping into the sea to escape Stephen MacLaren.

'Will I phone your mum?'

Carla shook her head. 'I'll do it later. Listen, there's someone else you could call for me. I don't have his number in my mobile phone. It's in my address book at home, in the drawer in the hall table. It's my cousin in North Uist: Ronald MacKenzie.'

'No problem. I might be quite late home though. Do they know what it is yet?'

Carla shook her head. She saw him glance at his watch. 'Go.'

'I don't have to.'

'You do. I understand.'

Chapter 5

Roz Sutherland put the phone down and waited. She got about five seconds silence before it rang again. When would it stop? Would she ever get a chance to mourn her husband in peace? 'Councillor Davis. Thank you for calling; I appreciate it. No, I don't know what happened; I've been told very little. I don't think the police know much. It's very early days. Yes. A shooting. Yes. Kenneth Street. No, I don't know who was with him.'

The same questions. The same answers. The same comments. Over and over. She left the phone off the hook after the call. The kids knew to call her mobile. They'd both be home tomorrow with their partners. She was glad they were in relationships. It was much easier for her to cope with their grief.

But how and when was she going to cope with her own grief? She made a pot of tea and reached for two mugs. As she put one back, she realised she'd never pour him another cup of tea. Never. It was so hard to take in. How could he be here this morning, drinking his tea, irritating her by dropping crumbs of toast on the floor, and then just be gone? He'd looked so peaceful when she'd identified him. No sign on his face of the violence that had taken him.

As her lips had brushed his waxen cheek, she'd tried to remember if she'd kissed him goodbye that morning. Thirty years of marriage. Had they kissed every morning? She really didn't know. And she bet he wouldn't have known either.

She sat in the conservatory and watched the sky darken. As she gazed into the gloom, she wondered if she might just sleep here, on the sagging sofa. She couldn't imagine going up to bed alone. How often had she wished for the bed to herself, for a night's sleep uninterrupted by his snoring and restlessness? It hadn't happened often during their marriage.

She put the mug of tea on the floor and wrapped her arms around herself. She didn't want to cry. If she started now, she might never stop, and that wouldn't do. She could keep the tears at bay, but not the questions. A shooting? The irony wasn't lost on her. He'd been the most vocal of the local councillors when the story broke about armed police attending routine calls. In Inverness? It had really shaken him.

And who had he been with today? And what was he doing? She tried to remember what he'd said in the morning about his day ahead. Was she going senile or had she just stopped listening? He'd taken early retirement from his job as an English teacher ten years ago. His father had died shortly before that, his mother years earlier. No one had been more surprised than Gordon to find out just how wealthy his elderly parents had been. They didn't give away much in their lifetime, but they left enough to pay off the mortgage and see the kids through university. And quite a bit more. Roz had been worried about him giving up work, and becoming a councillor. They'd manage, he'd always said, and she'd taken his word for it. Was that wise? She had friends that wouldn't trust a man to put the bin out, far less take control of everything. And it was everything. Well, everything that mattered. She'd had her say on holidays and children and where they would live, but she'd taken nothing to do with their finances. She'd earned a little over the years as an art therapist, and spent it all.

There was no support in the old sofa, and Roz's back started to protest. She didn't expect to sleep, but she might as well lie in a comfortable bed. She checked her phone. Nothing from the kids. How would they cope with this violent intrusion into their steady lives? They'd always been so sheltered. Inverness might be the capital of the Highlands, but it wasn't exactly crime central. They'd lived in Glasgow for a while when the kids were young, but Gordon had hated it. He'd said he never felt safe there, not like he did in Inverness. Safe?

She reached for the cup of tea, and felt her hand brush against something soft. His slippers. How often had she told him not to leave them under a chair or the table, in the bathroom or the garden shed? If he was out, they should be in the porch waiting for his return. Simple.

She left his slippers, and took the cup through to the kitchen. As she passed the front door, she saw a long white envelope on the mat. The first written condolences, no doubt.

There were no condolences in the envelope. Just a photograph. One that would keep Roz awake all night.

Joe wanted to stay in Carla's flat and lie in her king-size bed, enfolded in the softness of her tasteful Egyptian cotton bedding, breathing in her fragrance. Pervert.

Back in his own cottage in Nairn's Fishertown, he wondered if it was too late to phone the cousin that Carla had never mentioned before. He knew her grandparents had come from North Uist, but he'd never known her to be in touch with anyone there. Maybe he'd leave it until tomorrow. Fit it in somewhere during the day. Aye, right. He'd forget all about it, until he visited Carla and saw the disappointment in her eyes.

Joe wanted to tell this Ronald MacKenzie that he and Carla were more than just colleagues; they were a couple, and had been for ages. So why did he feel like a dry characterless cop breaking bad news?

'Tell her…tell her I'm here,' Ronald said.

I think she knows where you are, Joe thought.

'I'm here, whenever she needs me.'

Joe felt like an arse.

As soon as he put the phone down, it rang. It was his sister, Lucy. She was studying law and doing a placement at a law centre in Inverness. Joe had meant to call in to see her at their parents' home after work, but that was before the shooting. Lucy sounded tired. She wasn't sure if social welfare law was for her. She'd had a hard day and the only positive thing was that their parents were in Lanzarote and she had the house to herself.

She asked him how his day was. Not good, he told her. A fatal shooting and a girlfriend in hospital. That really cheered her up.

*

On North Uist, Ronald MacKenzie pulled the barn door over and turned to the sea. The sun had almost set. It would be another good day tomorrow. Overhead, a crow was harassing a falcon. It always made him smile to watch the brave clumsy crow attack the sleek bird that could kill it with so little effort. The falcon gave in, as if it really couldn't be bothered with the hassle. Ronald watched it fly towards the west. Maybe over on the Committee Road it would find its prey, with no interference from the crows.

His thoughts were with Carla as he sank into the old chair in the kitchen, a muddy trail of footsteps leading from the back door to the chair. When had he last forgotten to leave his boots at the door? Taking them off had become as natural to him as taking his clothes off before bed. But when had he last had to worry about anyone else? Carla was the last of the line, ten years younger than him, and he hadn't seen her since her father's funeral.

Who was Joe Galbraith? Was he a colleague or something more? Sounded like something more. Carla hadn't mentioned him, but then her calls were short. Regular enough, but never very detailed. All she wanted to hear about was the croft or the weather or the beach. She should come and see for herself, he'd told her often enough. One day, she kept saying; one day she'd come home.

As he rinsed his mug, he saw Will's shambling figure down at the shore. The tide was out. He must be searching for cockles or winkles. Both, probably. And seaweed. Was that what he lived on? Sometimes Ronald left food near Will's caravan. A few carrots and potatoes, and a piece of meat occasionally. Nothing much. He'd get a wave as thanks, and that was enough.

His tea made, Ronald buttered himself a scone and sat by the stove. On cue, a wet black nose poked out from under the chair. He ate the scone slowly, and the nose waited. He laughed as her head appeared, mouth open. The last bit of scone was always Bessie's.

Chapter 6

Christopher lay awake until he was certain Sharon was sleeping. He eased himself away from her and out of the bed, careful to ensure that his left leg took his weight. He reached to the chair for his stick. Ah, he'd left the passion killer downstairs. Seemed the best place for it at the time. Maybe he should rethink the layout of his home, change the downstairs study to a bedroom. He probably shouldn't have bought a house on two levels, but he was reluctant to give in to his injured leg. These were things you expected to consider when you reached seventy or eighty, not before you turned forty.

As he tackled the stairs in the dark, he remembered Dr Griffiths' warnings. There were things he should never do, and going downstairs without his stick was one of them. Doing it in the dark was another. He made it in one piece.

As he waited for his laptop to start, he considered getting a new one. This was taking longer every day. He could have used his phone, but he found it easier to type on the laptop. There was an email waiting for him, as he knew there would be. It had been sent at 10:30pm, as usual. Did Todd sit and wait for 10:30 before he pressed 'send'?

> *Mate, how's the leg now? Hope it's better. I did that bit of business for you, so no need to worry about it. Strange day. Good to get things sorted out.*
> *Can you believe it'll soon be ten years? It's mental. Don't know where the time has gone. We have to do something special.*
> *Sleep well. Yours always. T*

Christopher's shoulders felt heavy as he typed his reply.

> *Cheers for that, mate. Leg much better now. Nothing new. Heading off to bed. Will be in touch. C*

It was half twelve. Todd wouldn't like that. Two hours was a long time to wait for a reply. And the reply was too short. Too impersonal. There was a time when Christopher would have sat for ages trying to think of something suitable to say. Anything to appease Todd. Now it felt like a burden he could do without.

*

Unbelievable. Two hours waiting for a reply, and that was all Chris could manage. Who did he think he was? He was really taking the piss now. Heading off to bed? He'd been in bed for two and a half hours with that fucking tart. Their nonsense on the couch before they went upstairs had nearly turned Todd's stomach. All that fuss about a new bra. And those kind of contortions were not good for Chris's leg. Then, when they stood up, still wrapped around each other like a couple of mating stick insects, the clumsy tart knocked against the DAB radio, turning it the wrong way round. All he could see then was the wall. He could still hear them, though. Made him shudder.

Bastard. After all he'd done for him today, not to mention over the last ten years. And Chris hadn't even bothered to acknowledge that. It was the tart. Wasn't like that before she came along. He could count on a response to his email within minutes then. What was going on? As far as he knew, and he was certain he knew everything that went on in Chris's house, she'd never been there before today, far less stayed over.

He wasn't having this. No fucking way. He slammed down the lid of the laptop. Someone was going to pay.

Chapter 7

Sharon reached out and pulled the curtain back. Looked like a good day. It had rained in the night. She'd heard it bouncing off the skylight on the landing, as she'd lain awake worrying about Ryan. He'd never have anything to do with a shooting. No matter how dour and unpleasant he could be, he wasn't evil. Was he?

In the column of light streaming through the gap in the curtains, she saw a shimmering spider's web in the corner of the ceiling. Who did Christopher's cleaning? Should she offer? Pay him back for all he'd done?

She couldn't believe she was here. Instead of finishing with her yesterday, Christopher had asked her to come and stay with him until she was allowed back into her house. Liam too, but she'd already arranged for him to stay with his Auntie Gillian. That offer was only open to Liam. No surprise there.

Sharon had never been to his house before. It was beautiful, an old cottage in the woods at Ness Castle. No television. Books everywhere. Like a library. Why would anyone need so many books on so many subjects? Was that what he did with himself on the evenings she didn't see him?

They'd met in the Phoenix Bar not long after he left London and moved to Inverness. She'd been out with Linda one Friday night. Christopher was on the other side of the bar, drinking on his own. Linda said he kept looking at Sharon. Aye, right, Sharon had said. Probably couldn't believe she had the nerve to be out in public, looking the way she did.

Linda shook her head. 'Stop putting yourself down. You've got a beautiful smile and a fantastic figure. I'm telling you; he's eyeing you up.'

'Look at him. Sexy as fuck. I'm sure he's into birds with no teeth, and skin like orange peel.'

'You've got most of your teeth. More than my mam has. At least your gaps aren't right at the front. And there's nothing wrong with your skin. Well, nothing that a bit of slap doesn't hide. If I wasn't as straight as your hair, I'd fancy you myself.'

Sharon pushed her friend. 'I wouldn't fancy you, you tight bitch.

It's your round. Get them in.'

'Cool the jets, will you? We've a long night ahead of us. I'm going for a pee.'

'I'm going for a fag.'

When she came back in, he smiled at her. She looked over her shoulder. No one else there; it was definitely meant for her. She smiled back and kept her mouth shut. He was there again the next Friday and the next, though he didn't stay long. And it seemed Linda was right; he was watching Sharon. By the fourth Friday, Linda was off-shore. Sharon thought of asking someone else to go out with her, but the rest of her pals looked worse than she did.

So she went to the Phoenix by herself, and sat at the bar with a drink, constantly checking her watch as if she was waiting for someone. She was. And if he didn't come by the time she finished her drink, she'd leave. She was just draining the glass when he came in. Their eyes met and she didn't look away. Neither did he. He ordered a pint and whatever she was having, then he came over. His accent was posh, like a newsreader, but he was kind and funny, and interested in her. She spent the evening with her elbow on the bar, her hand hiding as much of her mouth as possible. He paid for her taxi home, but not before he had her phone number. She didn't think she'd hear from him again, but he'd called the next day, and every day since.

After a shower, she stood in front of the bedroom mirror and pulled the black bathrobe tighter. Looking not too bad, despite everything. As she stretched her arms upwards to let her hair down, the sleeves fell back, exposing an ugly map of scars and marks on her lower arms, the legacy of several years of self-harm and a year or two of heroin. She'd tried to hide her arms from Christopher, but it was impossible. A shiver ran through her as she remembered the night he'd kissed each scar and told her they only made her more beautiful. Maybe he'd pay for plastic surgery, or a tattoo. She turned away from the mirror. Who was she kidding? A solicitor for Ryan was probably the last thing he'd pay for. Why would he bother sticking with her after all this shit? He could have anyone.

When she was dressed, she went to the kitchen for a drink of water. She forgot to use the wee filter tap, but it tasted fine. A bit of chlorine wasn't going to kill her. But there was more than

27

chlorine in drinking water, according to Christopher. She wasn't bothered. If she lived in a house like this, the last thing she'd worry about would be a few chemicals.

He was in the garden, talking on his mobile phone, leaning on his stick. His leg must be playing up. She had no idea what he'd done to his leg. They'd been going out for a while before he used the stick in front of her. One day he'd picked her up at the retail park. He'd limped out of the car to put her shopping in the boot, and she'd seen the stick. She'd lifted it. 'I'm presuming this is supposed to be used when your leg's sore?'

He'd nodded. 'I hate it. Makes me feel old and unattractive.'

'Hardly. It's cool. Quite sexy.' The stick was black, and the handle was an intricately carved dragon's head in silver. 'If you need it, you need it. At least you've got all your teeth. How do you think it feels to look like me?'

Of course he'd assured her she looked great, but if she felt that bad about her teeth, he'd pay for dental work. She'd thought about it for five seconds, then she'd bitten his hand off.

It was only recently he'd stayed the night with her. Before that, he'd dress in the dark and leave. Even now, he kept the lights off, then he got up really early, like today, or he waited until she was out of the room before he got up. She didn't know why he didn't want her to see his leg. Couldn't be worse than her arms.

He came in from the garden, made her tea and toast, and asked if she wanted to go for a run in the car. It would be good for her to get out, he said. No point sitting waiting for news of Ryan. They'd get her on her mobile if they wanted her. She didn't need much persuading.

*

Through a gap in the trees, Todd watched them leave. He still couldn't believe Chris had let that slapper stay the night. And they were off for a run in the car now. Why the fuck was she looking so happy? Her son in the jail and she looked like she'd just won the lottery. And that smug smile on Chris's face. This had to be a joke. It was one thing banging the tart when he felt the urge, but inviting her to his house, letting her stay? She'd be moving in next with her brats. The thought made him feel sick. Maybe he should follow them. Run them off the road. Bastards.

He walked up the lane to his car, waited five minutes, then drove into Chris's drive. As he turned the key in the front door, he thanked Chris for being such a trusting friend. Made it so much easier for him to come and go as he pleased.

He turned the radio round the right way, then he took his iPhone from his pocket to check the live stream. Saw his own face and gave himself the thumbs up. He felt like gluing the damn thing to the shelf so her arse couldn't shift it again.

The camera in the kitchen was still in place. No surprise, really; she'd have to be some kind of monster to reach the heat alarm and knock it off course. Maybe he should have put a camera in the smoke alarm in the living room, instead of buying that radio. It had cost him a fortune, but Chris had appreciated it. What was not to like about a new DAB radio, courtesy of your best friend?

Everything else was as orderly as ever, but the house was stinking of her. Fucking tart. She hadn't left anything. Nothing he could destroy. No toothbrush he could use to clean the toilet bowl. That was a good sign. She hadn't moved in. Yet.

He sat down at the desk in the study and switched on the laptop. Useless piece of crap. He should offer Chris his expertise, help him get something decent, but how was he going to broach that subject? See the last time I was sitting in your leather chair at your antique oak desk, checking your laptop to see what you'd been up to, as I do on a regular basis, I noticed it was running slowly. Would you like me to recommend a replacement? It would make life so much easier for me.

A noise in the hall startled him. Shit. He fixed on a smile and went to investigate. It was only the postman. Nothing interesting, but who used snail mail these days? Certainly not their mutual contacts in London. If he was going to find any communication between them and Chris, it was going to be electronic.

The laptop was ready. A quick check. Nothing. For a year, he'd been checking, and found nothing. He'd left a mess behind him in London. Last thing he wanted was for anyone to know where he was. It would be easy for Chris to let it slip, but, as far as he knew, Chris wasn't in touch with them either.

Nothing new in the desk drawers and filing cabinet, except a couple of receipts. Fuck's sake. Did Chris really pay that for a bracelet for the skank? He needed his head seen to.

Chapter 8

Jackson smirked. They had no leads in the murder of Gordon Sutherland. Nobody in the Council had a bad word to say about the victim. He hadn't fallen out with anyone. Everyone loved him. His wife had no idea why anyone would target him. Nothing had come from the prints they found in and on the car. Wee Ryan MacRae was saying nothing, and the DNA results weren't back yet.

So Wonderboy Galbraith hadn't got it all sewn up yet? Oh dear. No one had a clue what was going on. Just the way Jackson liked it.

The DI gave out some tasks. Galbraith and his wee lap dog Roberts, were off to the Council to see some SNP councillor. This one was to go and do that, and that one was to go and do this. Jackson switched off until he heard his name mentioned. He was to work his way through some boxes from the Council's Education Committee. The victim had been chair of the committee for a few years. Simples.

*

A tiny woman with thinning curly hair and bad breath, Alice McGarvie had such a lot to say. Gordon Sutherland was a family man with impeccable morals and a brain the size of a planet. They'd had high hopes for him. He'd refused to put himself forward as a candidate for the 2015 Westminster election, but they'd hoped to talk him into standing for Holyrood in 2016. He'd said he was too old. At sixty four, he was hoping for a quieter life, wanted to spend some time with his wife. At least, that's what he'd said, but Alice had got the feeling he was interested in Holyrood.

She dabbed at her eyes with a hankie every so often, though Joe couldn't see any sign of tears. 'I was hoping to get a chance to talk to him at our constituency meeting yesterday afternoon. Someone had contacted him about making a donation to the party, some business man. Gordon was hoping to bring him along to the meeting.'

Joe nodded. 'Did he tell you who this man was?'

'No. I thought it would all become clear at the meeting.'

'Does he have any enemies within the council or the party? Any rivalries?'

She shook her head. 'Not within the council or the party.'

'Anywhere?'

Alice McGarvie was quiet. She sighed and looked beyond Joe and Roberts.

Joe leaned towards her. 'Well?'

'I really didn't want to have to say anything. He's dead, after all. It doesn't seem right to cast aspersions.'

'You haven't, but if you know something, please tell us.' Why couldn't she just spit it out?

She reached to the drawer on the right of her desk. Of course, the drawer was locked, and could she find the key? Three plant pots and one waste paper bin. No luck. It was under the second pencil caddy. Joe reckoned she knew where it was all along, but she couldn't resist hamming it up.

Another tortuous wait for the key to turn, then another, while she rifled through some papers. A white envelope. She slid it across the desk as if she was offering Joe a bribe.

He took a pen from her caddy and pushed it back. 'Could you please open it?'

She looked surprised, but she pulled a single folded piece of paper from the envelope and slid that across to him. He pushed it back, his eyebrows raised.

'Ah, I see. Prints.' She opened it up and turned it towards him. One sentence on the page:

Councillor Gordon Sutherland is a coward and a killer

'Do you have any idea why someone would say that?'

'No. Gordon was so easy going. Except when it came to gun-carrying police. He'd been het up about that. We all were. It was ridiculous in the Highlands. We don't have the sort of criminals you get in the Central Belt.'

Joe raised his eyebrows. 'Roz Sutherland might disagree.'

Alice McGarvie nodded. A wee dab at her eyes. 'Quite, but you know what I mean. Gun crime's pretty rare up here. Not every day someone gets blasted through the chest, sitting in their car on Kenneth Street.'

Joe stared at her. How exactly did Alice McGarvie know her colleague had been shot in the chest?

*

Christopher's words weren't reaching Sharon. She had a lump in her throat, and it was growing, as memories rushed through her head. She tried to stop them, but it was hopeless. She left Christopher in the shade of the tree, his brow creased as he tried to decipher the hidden ancient words beneath the lichen and moss.

Everything in Dunlichity Cemetery was just as it had been the last time Sharon was here, as a teenager. The birdsong and the rustling breeze, the faint barking of dogs and the hum of a tractor's engine. The stories on the grave stones, the words that had made her jealous. Would she ever be anyone's beloved wife or mother? Would anyone even miss her? She hadn't voiced her thoughts that day. She'd boxed them away in her mind, along with all the other emotions and memories she didn't know to deal with, and she had smiled. It had been a perfect day, the best ever. Before long, it too was boxed away, a little deeper than the rest, where it should have stayed.

Christopher was behind her. He put his arms round her and held her tight, his breath on her ear making her shiver. 'Are you okay, love?'

That word. People said it to each other all the time; it didn't mean anything. But now, in this place, with her heart a little sore and her defences low, it was more than she could take. She didn't make any noise as she cried, for she had learned long ago that noisy crying alerted people. They reported it. There were consequences.

Christopher guided her to the low wall behind the church. He sat beside her and took a hankie from his pocket. He wiped her tears, then he stroked her hair. 'Is it Ryan?'

She took the hankie from him and shook her head. 'It's nothing.'

'Must be something.'

She looked out over the drystone wall to the sloping field, where a cluster of cows lazed in the shadow of the trees. The wind was whispering to her. Or maybe it was Alison, letting her know it was safe to remember. She took a deep breath, and she told him.

Alison was a writer. Her children's books were the most beautiful books Sharon had ever seen. Her husband, Mark, was a doctor. They lived in a house in the Crown, a huge house with stained glass windows on the stairway and marble tiles in the hall. It was the only foster placement Sharon ever had to herself, and the only foster parents that made her feel safe. It couldn't last. She told herself that every day of the five months she was with them.

She'd always done her best to wind her foster parents up, even the nicest ones. Safest to hurt them before they could hurt her. But not Alison and Mark. She'd have done anything for them, anything to stay with them.

For five wonderful months, Alison and Mark encouraged her to think, to have an opinion, to believe in herself. They made her feel like she was equal to them, like she mattered. They knew what she had been through, but they never criticised her mother, never tried to turn her against her own family, as so many of the others had done.

Alison took her to a Children's Panel once. Sharon's mother was there, all tarted up and showing off, with her latest creep on her arm. Sharon was mortified. What would Alison think?

She'd watched in awe as Alison took her mother's hand, stared into her eyes and told her not to worry, that Sharon was doing really well. Her mother was gobsmacked, the old boot. Never had any social worker, foster carer or Children's Panel member treated her like that. Not a kind word or the slightest morsel of understanding for the fact that she was a useless slut. Sharon had been jealous. She didn't want to share Alison with her mother. And yet, she'd seen a new look in her mother's eyes; helplessness and a hint of hope. And maybe even a tear. Was that all it might have taken to make her a better mother? A bit of understanding?

Sharon closed her eyes. She'd told the tale so fast, it belied the impact of Alison and Mark upon her young life. She wanted to rewind, to tell Christopher again, tell him more, just in case he didn't get it.

*

Christopher got it. Until he met Sharon, he hadn't appreciated the safety and security of his own childhood, with an abundance of

33

food and warmth and love, with parents that wanted the best for him, no matter how hard he had tried to push them away. Now, the sun was shining on her hair. The breeze lifted a strand of gold and whipped it across her pale, beautiful face. He reached for it, but she got there first and pushed away. He followed her gaze to the faded plastic flower that skipped across the cemetery, going this way and that, searching for the right grave, just as he searched for the right words. But she wasn't finished.

'Alison took me here. We spent ages reading the grave stones, seeing who could find the oldest one. I hated cemeteries before that. They creeped me right out. But it's different here, isn't it?'

He nodded. He'd discovered it shortly after moving to Inverness. He couldn't count how many times he'd driven up here and sat on his own, thinking, remembering, wondering.

'We went for a walk in the forest, beside the reservoir. I'd never gone for a walk before. Not without a reason, like to the shop, or town, or school. It was amazing. The trees and the birds, and someone listening to me, as if I had something really important to say.

'On the way home, she stopped at Essich Farm so I could see the ponies. One of them seemed to take to me, a little black and white Shetland pony. I was scared to touch it, but Alison showed me what to do. I scratched its neck, and it nuzzled into me. That smell.' She closed her eyes and smiled. 'Alison said we could go pony trekking at Drumnadrochit. I was so excited.'

Christopher had ridden as a child. He'd loved it, and often thought of trying it again, if his leg would let him. 'Did you like it?'

She made a noise. It sounded like a groan. She stood, her shoulders tense. The plastic flower was back. It circled her feet, and she stamped on it, pinning it to the ground. When she turned, her eyes were narrowed, her face full of spite. 'Didn't happen, did it? Alison went and died. Brain haemorrhage. There in the morning when I went to school; gone when I came home. It shouldn't have surprised me. Everyone I ever cared for deserted me. But Alison seemed different. I really trusted her.'

Christopher felt as if his body had been plunged into icy water. She really believed Alison had died just to get at her.

'Mark fell to pieces. I've no idea what happened to him. I barely had time to pack my things before I was off to the next placement and a foster father that couldn't keep his hands to himself.' She shrugged again. 'That's life, I guess.'

No, Sharon, he wanted to say. That is not life; not for most of us. But no words came.

Sharon smiled. 'Forget it. I don't know where that came from. It's all in the past. Fuck's sake; that's not the worst thing that ever happened to me.'

But Christopher knew it was. The crap mother, the brother and sister she'd lost touch with, the violent husband, the drugs – she had expected no less. But to have foster parents that loved her and wanted the best for her, that was something so unexpected and wonderful, the loss of it must have had a devastating effect. He stood up and put his arm round her shoulders. 'Why don't we go horse riding soon?'

Her eyes sparkled. 'Really?'

'Yeah.'

'Sound.' She blew her nose, shrugged and smiled. Business as usual. 'Are we going for lunch? I'm starving.'

Chapter 9

A single shot from a handgun had severed his spinal column and sliced through Gordon Sutherland's heart. He would have died in seconds, according to the interim post mortem report. The killer was either very experienced or he'd got lucky. They'd get a detailed report on the ballistics in due course.

Today there was no eye contact from the victim's wife. Roz Sutherland was distracted and fidgeting, short answers forced through a clenched jaw. Not surprising, really; she probably hadn't slept. Still, Joe wondered. She'd been in shock yesterday, without a doubt, but she'd been much more together than this.

She confirmed she'd spoken to several of her late husband's council colleagues yesterday, but she hadn't given them any details, and no one had been unduly persistent in seeking information. She listed those she'd spoken to, including Alice McGarvie. Was that a shudder when she mentioned McGarvie's name? Definitely not Roz Sutherland's favourite person.

Roberts took a call on his mobile. He went out into the hall. Joe decided to push her. 'Mrs Sutherland, I know this is a terrible time for you, for all the family.'

She nodded.

'Is there anything you want to tell me? Anything new since we spoke yesterday?'

There were tears in her eyes as she nodded again, and took the envelope from down the side of the sofa.

*

Bio-bloody-logical washing powder. Whoever thought that was a good idea clearly wasn't a copper. They got nothing from Ryan MacRae's clothes, not a scrap of evidence. And his phone was squeaky clean. Well, the parents of one Natasha Scott might not be too happy if they knew the content of certain text messages between her and MacRae, but not a bloody thing they could use against him. And see the way the arrogant little shite had smirked when they let him go? If he wasn't back inside within a day or two, there was no justice in this world.

Joe nodded and waited for DI Black to finish ranting, then he told him about Alice McGarvie's note. The DI almost smiled. 'That's more like it. And what did Ms McGarvie do about this?'

'Nothing. Sat on it for six months. She said it was nonsense and she saw no point in mentioning it to Gordon Sutherland or anyone else. I've got this too, Sir. It was put through Roz Sutherland's door last night.'

There was a hint of a smile playing at the corners of the DI's mouth as he looked at the photograph. 'Doesn't really look as if he's enjoying himself, does he?'

The victim, Gordon Sutherland, did not look happy. He was seated between two attractive young women. One of them had her arm draped over his shoulders, while the other had her hand on his leg. She looked as if she was moving in for a kiss. 'Do you think those girls are foreign?'

Joe shrugged. 'Hard to say. Could be.' Both were dark haired and tanned.

'And did his missus suspect anything?'

'No. He's been his usual self.'

'I think my missus would notice something was up, or not, if I was giving it to those two.'

Joe's stomach turned a little at the thought. The DI's dirty laughter followed him down the corridor.

He phoned the hospital, but they couldn't tell him anything, except that Carla was still in. He tried her mobile, but it was switched off. He looked at his watch. Maybe he could sneak off now. The phone on his desk rang. It was the custody officer. Joe listened and sighed. 'Not again. What is it this time?'

'Out of his head in the Eastgate Centre. He's better now, and he's asking for you.'

Ali the Bampot made a habit of asking for Joe. Sometimes he had something worthwhile, a valuable wee snippet, but usually he talked a heap of shit. Living on the streets, he was regularly lifted when the drugs or the alcohol, or both, got the better of him. He didn't really cause trouble. He just insisted on debating life's mysteries with passers-by, to their alarm. More often than not, he was lifted for his own safety.

Ali was hunched up on the bench, the cell as fragrant as ever. He looked up and smiled. 'Detective Sergeant Galbraith, you're a gentleman.'

Joe nodded. 'I'm a very busy gentleman.'

'Surely you've time for a wee word?' He shifted along the bench. 'A wee seat?'

Though he'd rather not get too close, Joe sat. He noticed a grubby plaster cast on Ali's right arm. 'How did you get that?'

'Lovely nurse up at Raigmore. She made my day. Gave me new clothes and a fiver. I can't remember her name, but I'm sure they'll tell you up at the hospital.'

'I'm more interested in why you needed a plaster cast. What happened to your arm?'

Ali shook his head. 'Sergeant, I can't say.'

'Do you remember?'

'Remember? I'll never forget. If I was twenty years younger, it wouldn't have happened. No one messed with Ali the Bampot. Trouble is, the pots are all way more bammy these days than I ever was. Anyway, forget that. Have you found Sally?'

Joe shook his head. 'We haven't got much to go on, have we? No one at the council has heard of a homeless girl matching your friend's description. No one has reported her missing. We don't have a surname. Is there anything else you can tell me?'

Ali frowned. 'Not really. A wee beauty she was when she first showed up. Her looks didn't last long once she started on the smack. Last time I saw her, at least three months back, I was trying to sleep in a bin store round by the flats where the old La Scala was. I'm not a minger, mind; they'd emptied the bins that day. Anyway, I'd told her not to be offering blow…I mean, services for a couple of quid, but she wouldn't listen. There's some bad people out there, Sergeant. Some bad bastards.'

'Aye, you're right. Did you see her with someone that night?'

Ali shrugged. He avoided Joe's eyes. 'It was dark. I couldn't see properly.'

'What could you see?'

He started scratching at the top of the cast. 'Bloody itch. Ach, I saw nothing. Just hoped you might have found her.'

Joe drove to the hospital, Ali's missing girl on his mind. He took it seriously, but without more information, what could he do? He was certain Ali knew more than he was letting on.

Chapter 10

'Duck!' Spittle flew from Graeme Freel's mouth as he shouted across the room.

Really? Like Lucy might not have worked that one out for herself? Graeme hadn't. The first used incontinence pad had caught him on the chin, and Lucy had stifled a laugh as the pad clung to his designer stubble, then slid downwards over his chubby belly and his pin-striped knees, landing with a squelch on his polished brogues.

His client, Mary, must have been saving the pads up for some time. They'd gone to see her in New Craigs, the psychiatric hospital in Inverness. She had a Mental Health Tribunal pending, and she'd asked for a solicitor. She didn't like what she got, and Lucy wasn't too impressed either.

Another pad hit Graeme in the face. Was Mary aiming for him and deliberately avoiding Lucy? It seemed so. At last, two nurses restrained Mary. She laughed as they led her away. 'Useless numpty; that'll teach you.'

Graeme scrubbed at his face with a hankie. That was never going to work. Lucy nodded at a dispenser of hand sanitiser. 'Try that.'

He slapped it on like aftershave. It improved the smell a little, but Lucy was certain she could still detect the lingering odour of stale urine, as Graeme told the nurse he really couldn't be expected to take instructions from such an unwilling client. Though she didn't know much about dealing with psychiatric patients, Lucy felt he could have tried harder. A little forethought, and he might have avoided winding the client up in the first place by asking her if she'd really tried to choke her neighbour's cat with a set of jump leads. Or he could have waited until she calmed down. But he hadn't, and now they were leaving, with no instructions and one very ruffled solicitor.

The nurse apologised. Mary was like that sometimes, until her medication kicked in. Maybe they could phone again when she was feeling better. Graeme looked aghast. He patted his pockets. No. He didn't have his work phone with him, and he couldn't remember the number off the top of his head.

Arse, Lucy thought. 'I'll give you my number. Just call early next week if Mary's doing better.'

Graeme Freel looked at Lucy as if she was nuts.

*

Betty MacLaren was sitting in the corner of the communal area, wearing a coral pink twin set, and a double row of pearls. She'd seen the solicitors arrive and she'd admired the young woman's suit and high heels, her confident, but humble, manner. She'd seen the way the woman looked around her, with kind eyes. She wasn't judging the patients, as did so many visitors to the ward. She looked interested and interesting. She looked quite beautiful.

Betty had clocked all that went on. Mary and her flying incontinence pads, the terrified male solicitor, and the amusement of his assistant. All the while, a little bell was ringing in Betty's head. Did she know the young woman?

And then the woman gave her name, and Betty knew. She gave her phone number, and Betty was ready. She always had a pen in her pocket for the crossword. Today, she had the Press and Journal on her lap. It was simple to write Lucy Galbraith's phone number on her paper. And no one saw her do it.

*

Joe hated playing the cop card, but there was nothing else for it. He couldn't wait until later. He told the nurse he was working on the shooting – not a lie – and he didn't know when he'd get away. This was really the only time he could see Carla; he didn't want to disappoint her. The nurse gave in, with a knowing smile. He'd have to go if the consultant came round. And it was almost lunch time.

Carla was curled up, face to the wall. He didn't want to wake her, so he sat on a chair at the end of the bed. It wasn't long before she moved, turned, and tried to smile. Her forehead glistened with sweat, her face was grey, her hair flat and dull, and Joe had never loved her more. He got a hankie and wiped her forehead, then he stroked her hair.

She frowned. 'Don't. I'm disgusting.'

'You're beautiful.'

40

There were tears in her eyes. 'I'm an idiot. Why didn't I go to the doctor? I've been feeling crap for ages. The glands in my neck are swollen and I didn't even notice. And now this.'

Joe's stomach lurched. 'What is it?'

'There's something wrong with my blood count. Too many of some kind of white blood cell. They're waiting for more results and talking about bone marrow tests. One nurse mentioned leukaemia.'

'No.' Joe shook his head. 'No, it can't be.'

Carla wiped at her eyes. 'If there's one thing we both know, it's that crap can happen to anyone. We see it every day. And there's nothing we can do about it.'

She was right, but he couldn't bear to admit it. 'I spoke to your cousin last night.'

'Thanks. He's sound, Ronald; we've always been close. I don't suppose he said he'd come and visit?'

'No. He didn't say much. He sounded worried.'

'Do you have his number?'

Joe took the piece of paper from his pocket and placed it on the locker.

'Cheers. I'll call him later. Try a bit of emotional blackmail; might get him off the croft and onto the ferry. I'm likely to be off work for a while. How's the investigation?'

When he repeated DI Black's comments about the girls in the photo, Carla groaned and asked for the sick bucket. Joe jumped up. 'Where is it?' He looked under the bed, in the locker, at Carla. She was smiling. 'Ah, you're joking.'

'Only just. The nausea is never far away, and thinking about DI Black *in flagrante*…' She shivered. 'Anyway, you have to get back.'

'I don't.'

'You do – not that I don't appreciate the visit, and the fact that you haven't looked at your watch once.'

He nodded at the clock on the wall beside the bed. 'Didn't have to.'

Joe kissed her and held her. But he didn't tell her. He wanted to. He wanted to say the words that echoed in his head, in his heart, whenever he held her, made love to her, even just watched her. Why was it so hard to say he loved her? Because she'd never said it? Idiot. Someone else would say it to her one day, and he'd

41

lose her. And he knew then why he couldn't say it. He was just a staging post, temporary. She was way too good for him.

As he drove back to the station, Joe thought of a colleague he'd had in traffic. He was only thirty two when he died of bowel cancer. Nice guy. Couldn't remember his name. He'd gone to see him in the hospice with a couple of the boys. He'd been a big guy, played football, didn't drink. Joe shook his head, trying to clear the image of the nameless cop in the hospice bed, but it wouldn't go. Cancer had turned him into a shadow, wrinkled and grey, his hair gone and his arms like twigs. That couldn't happen to Carla. He wouldn't let it.

Fool, he told himself; as if he could stop it from happening. No wonder Jimmy Jackson thought him a conceited git. He'd overheard Jackson saying as much to someone in the locker room the previous week. He hadn't let on he'd heard – if there was one thing Jackson wanted, it was a reaction. He'd not forget it, though. Just add it to the list of things he had on Jackson, and take his subtle revenge whenever he could.

Chapter 11

Drew Easter nodded, his face serious as he commiserated with Graeme Freel over his treatment at New Craigs. He told Graeme not to worry about it; he'd tried his best, couldn't have done any more. Why not go home and get changed? Maybe have a shower? Graeme wiped his sweaty brow with a hand that was still shaking, and thanked Drew. He'd do that, and he'd be back soon.

As Graeme's fat footsteps stamped down the stairs, Drew looked at Lucy. He put his hand over his mouth and shook his head. With his other hand, he clutched at a filing cabinet as if to steady himself, as a strange strangled sound tried to force its way out.

Downstairs, the front door opened and closed, and Drew erupted. The noise he was making, two of the secretaries came from the main office to check that everything was all right. He waved his hand at them, but he couldn't speak.

Before she started at the law centre, Lucy had envisaged the boss as an older man, someone with peppered grey hair, a beard and an encyclopaedic knowledge of the law. Drew certainly had a good grasp of the law, and there was a touch of grey in his dark hair. He was older than her, but not as old as her imagination had imagined. He was tall and slim, with laughing eyes, and a way of looking at Lucy that made butterflies dance in her stomach. Not that he was looking too cool right now. Yes, it had been funny, but really?

He straightened up and wiped at his eyes. 'I'm sorry; I've waited such a long time.'

She didn't have to ask him what he'd waited for. Anyone that knew Graeme Freel would be gagging to see the tosser brought down. She smiled. He swallowed and straightened his face. 'I'm going up to see two clients in the prison this afternoon. Do you want to come?'

'Definitely.' Lucy tried not to look too keen.

He nodded. 'Great. About ten to two? There'll be no dirty protests, I promise.' He went into his room and closed the door, and she could still hear him laughing.

The clients in prison couldn't have been more different. Donny had learning difficulties and he was in for an assault on his wife, perpetrated in front of his two children. He and his wife had significant support to enable them to parent. Lucy watched in awe as Drew calmed his client down. He had to stop worrying. Settle down and wait for the court case. Drew would speak to Social Work, find out how the children were.

Donny was grateful. 'I'll just ignore the others when they laugh at me. And I'll not let them spit in my food again. They're just jealous, these guys; they don't have kids like mine.'

The next client was probably the one spitting in Donny's food. Rough as. He'd been convicted of growing cannabis in his loft, he was two thousand pounds in arrears of rent, and the council had raised a court action to have him evicted. He wanted to know if there was any chance of keeping his tenancy while he was inside.

Drew shook his head. 'That'll be a no. You'll not get Housing Benefit now you're off remand, so you've no chance.'

Fair enough, the guy said. He stood and shook Drew's hand. He hadn't expected there'd be anything Drew could do, but there was no harm in asking.

As they walked down the hill back to the office, it was the second guy Drew talked about. He'd get out of jail eventually and have nowhere to go but a B&B or an HMO in the town, with access to every drug you could imagine. Not that Drew thought the Council should keep his tenancy for him. How could they, when no one was paying the rent? Even if the rent was paid, they'd probably evict him for the drug dealing. It was just the revolving door that got Drew down. With nowhere to go and nothing to do, the guy would be back inside before long. 'Still, it's people like him that keep me in work, I guess.'

*

It was shite being back home in this tip. And Sharon was a shite mother, wishing Ryan had been kept in longer. And he was a shite son, giving her nothing more than a grunt when she tried to speak to him. She should have sent him to school, even though there wasn't much of the afternoon left. Instead, he was sitting in his room, gabbing to his pals. But how was he able to speak to anyone when the police still had his phone?

Sharon hesitated at the bedroom door, and then she lifted her hand to knock. What was she doing? It wasn't a hotel. As she reached for the handle, she heard Ryan raise his voice, and she knew he was terrified. 'I told them fuck all. Honest. Fuck all.' In the silence that followed, she knew every line and frown on his worried face. She wanted to kiss them away, to hold him and rock him. It was a long time since he'd let her do that. 'I'm not a grass, and my clothes were clean; they found nothing.' Another pause. 'Okay.' Trepidation in his voice. 'See you there.'

Back in the living room, Sharon remembered the sock. It wasn't clean. As far as she was aware, Ryan didn't know he'd dropped it. She hadn't wanted to worry him, and he hadn't mentioned it. Had Christopher really got rid of it? Maybe she should have done it herself, made absolutely sure.

Shit. What kind of monster was she, tampering with evidence to protect her son, when a man was dead? Her shaking hands reached for the e-cig. She pulled on it, desperate for some calm. All she got was the taste of blueberries. Useless. Fucking useless. The e-cig bounced off the small coffee table, before hitting the TV and falling to the floor. She heard the bedroom door open, and Ryan's feet thundering down the hall. As the front door slammed, she grabbed her jacket.

Ryan's head was down as he hurried along Thornbush Road. On Grant Street, he met a group of youths. He nodded at them and carried on, but they called him back. Sharon ducked into a doorway and wiped sweat off her brow. The youths were jostling and shoving each other like little kids. Were they the Glendoe Gadgies that Ryan was hanging about with last year? She'd pulled Ryan's leg about them so many times. Gadgies in Inverness? Gadgies were from Dingwall. She knew nothing, Ryan had told her; the gang leader was a gadgie. His family were evicted from their house in Dingwall, and came to live in Glendoe Terrace in the Carse.

Gadgies or not, they were a shower of wee shites, laughing at a disabled man with a stick on the other side of the road. Ryan didn't join in, but Sharon wasn't about to congratulate herself for that. It wasn't his good upbringing that stopped him; it was fear of whoever he was meeting.

He left the boys and hurried on. Sharon followed him half way across the Black Bridge. When he crossed over to Portland Place car park, and got into a car, she stopped. Although she couldn't make the driver out, he looked big and bald. She didn't think she knew him. She wanted to run across the road and pull her son from the car, but he wouldn't thank her for it. Besides, it was almost time to collect Liam from school.

Chapter 12

Jackson looked at the photo of the shooting victim and the two girls, and shook his head. No, he didn't know them; hadn't seen them before. He could hardly say otherwise, could he? He'd just have to make sure he was nowhere near the station if the girls were identified and brought in. Maybe it was time for another bout of 'work-related stress'. He hadn't pulled that one for a while.

DI Black was staring at him. 'You sure you don't know them? I haven't seen you smile like that since Wee Mary gave you one round the back of the Legion in '89.'

Bastard. To think they had once been friends. That was before the two-faced chancer, Brian Black, had walked all over Jackson, all the way to the top. How Jackson would love to bring Black down. One of these days. Him and Galbraith. Just wait. 'Never seen them in my life, Sir.' And he kept on smiling.

*

Jackson was up to something; Joe was certain of it. They should have got rid of him years ago. He hadn't done a decent day's work in all the time Joe had known him. More interested in withholding information and jeopardising investigations. Nothing major. He wasn't clever enough for that.

Joe was going to meet a source. He had cropped images of the girls from the photo with Gordon Sutherland. If they were on the game and working locally, Ricky Shaw would know them.

'Give me a shout when you get back,' DI Black said. Behind him, Jackson was staring. Grinning. Arse.

The older bird was Lithuanian, Ricky Shaw told Joe; the other was from Shetland. At the higher end of the 'escort' market, a fascinating cultural experience awaited those brave and well-off enough to venture into their abode on Carlton Terrace. No, Ricky didn't know who was working them. Could be freelance.

Joe called the DI and updated him. He asked for someone to accompany him to see the girls. A female, preferably. He'd meet her at Carlton Terrace.

The road layout didn't allow Joe to park in front of the flats, so he parked outside the Chieftain Hotel. He clocked the right flat, then he waited at the corner. There was a guy walking back and fore past the flat. Joe felt a little sorry for him. He clearly couldn't make up his mind if this was how he wanted to spend his afternoon, or a good chunk of his wages. He stopped close to the door, looked at his watch, took a deep breath and stepped towards it.

'I wouldn't if I were you.'

The guy turned. 'What are you on, creeping up on people like that? You looking for trouble? Tosser.' He didn't look so nervous now, as he took a step towards Joe, his breath rich with alcohol. He was unshaven, with blood-shot eyes and a hairy belly-button peeping out of a gap in his checked shirt. Not quite the type of punter Joe had imagined finding here. Just off the rigs, probably.

Joe nodded towards the door. 'Not as much trouble as you'll be in if you go in there.'

'That right? Who's going to stop me? You?'

Joe shrugged. 'Suit yourself.'

'Aye, you're not so brave now, are you, wee man?'

Joe laughed and ducked as a flabby fist sailed over his head. More chance of being knocked out by the guy's BO than a punch. As the drunk squared up for another attempt, Joe's back-up arrived in a marked police car. They pulled in as close as they could get, blocking the hotel entrance. There were two uniformed officers in the front. They stayed where they were, both smirking as they watched the drunk advance on Joe again. He really should try to make some friends in uniform.

The back door of the car opened and a long pin-striped leg emerged. Joe felt a tightening in his stomach. He wished DI Black had sent someone else. Even Jackson.

DC Tina Lewis was trying not to smile, but the laughter in her green eyes gave her away. Her face was pale, with flawless skin and just a hint of colour on her high cheekbones. There wasn't a blonde hair out of place.

The drunk whistled. 'Are you a police woman, gorgeous?'

Tina nodded. 'I am. And you are...?'

'I am just on my way home, minding my own business. I see this guy about to go in there. I try to stop him but he won't listen. The wee shite tried to hit me.'

'And why would you want to stop him going in there?'

'It's a whore-house. And a bloody expensive one. Just doing my good deed for the day. Wouldn't want him ripped off.'

Smiling, Tina turned to Joe. 'And what you have got to say for yourself, sir?'

Joe raised his eyebrows, and her smile disappeared. Her face reddened. 'Sorry, Sarge; I couldn't resist it.'

The drunk looked from Tina to Joe. 'Sarge? Oh shit.' He rubbed his hand on his jeans, offered it to Joe. 'No offence, officer; I'm just a bit – '

'Do one,' Joe said. 'Now.'

'Thank you; you're an officer and a gentleman. Thank you.' He backed off, his hands together in prayer, bowing and scraping his way along the road.

Joe pressed the buzzer and waited. And waited. Nothing. He held it down. Her poise regained, Tina grinned. '*Coitus interruptus.* Nothing worse, except maybe *limpus dickus*.'

'I wouldn't know.' Shit. Had he really just said that?

Tina's eyes sparkled. 'I quite believe it.'

He felt his face flush as he pressed the buzzer again. 'This place is not as upmarket as I expected. Looks right grotty.'

At last someone answered. An Eastern European with a serious strop. 'What your problem?'

'Police.'

'You fucking having on me?'

'No, I fucking not having on you. Open the door. Now.'

'That Jimmy?'

'It is not Jimmy. Open the door or we'll open it.'

Nothing. Tina looked towards the patrol car. 'Will I get the guys?'

'Nah. Give them a minute to get their togs on. Do you think there's a back door?'

'Will I go and see?'

Joe shook his head. Last thing he wanted was to get caught up with a couple of punters. Easier just to let them slip out the back door and crawl back to respectability.

As someone buzzed them into the close, the back door at the other end of the passage swung closed.

On the first floor landing there was a single, expensive shoe. Tina laughed. 'How I'd love to hear him explain that to his missus.'

Joe looked at his watch. 'Or his secretary.'

Keeping her composure in a foreign language was no trouble at all to the Lithuanian, Katya Birze. They were escorts. High-class. They escorted people. No funny business.

Joe nodded. 'So, the man that just left by your back door, dropping a shoe on the stair, he was being escorted to…?'

'Man? Shoe? I see no man. I see no shoe.' She turned to her fellow escort. 'You see shoe?'

Eighteen year old Danielle Smith wasn't quite as poised, but she did her best. 'I don't know what man or shoe you're talking about.' Her accent sounded almost as foreign as the Lithuanian's. They were both in dressing gowns, and Joe knew he could catch them out. There was evidence in the bedrooms, he was certain of it. And the patrol car had probably seen the shoeless punter making his escape. But that wasn't what they were here for. Not yet.

Katya was good. Not a flicker when she was shown a picture of the victim. Meant nothing to her; never seen him before. Danielle tried to copy Katya, but the slight flush on her neck gave her away. Time to separate them, and bring out the picture of them with Gordon Sutherland.

Katya first. 'Okay.' A slight nod. 'I see him different now. I remember. We invited to special charity evening for special people. He there. We speak. That all.'

'You speak very closely,' Tina said. 'Why him?'

She shrugged. 'He was there.'

'And was he interested?'

She shrugged again. 'No.'

'Did you escort him anywhere else? Into a hotel room, perhaps?'

'No.'

'Did you try?'

'No.'

'Why not?'

'Is simple. He was not interested.'

'You say you were invited – who invited you?'

She stared into the distance, as if trying to remember. 'I forget.'

Aye, right.

Danielle Smith was a pushover. There was a man with an English accent. His name was Todd. She hadn't met him and she didn't know his surname, but he and Katya were close, and he'd put a lot of clients their way. He usually dealt with Katya, but this time he'd phoned Danielle about a local charity event and told her to show Councillor Sutherland special attention. If things went the way he hoped, there was a room waiting for them in a hotel nearby.

Things had not gone as Todd had hoped. Councillor Sutherland was polite, but completely uninterested. Danielle wasn't sure he even understood what was on offer. He was just like her father, she said. Kind and respectable. And completely incorruptible.

'You sound disappointed,' Joe said.

She shrugged. 'I was offered good money. I could have done with it.'

'Are you using?' He didn't think so, but he might as well wind her up.

'No. I…I'm going to university.'

'Aye? No tuition fees in Scotland; student loans. Do you really have to do this?'

Though her face was red, her look was defiant. 'I'm going to Oxford.'

'Better class of punter there?'

Joe saw the blow hit home. Had he been too harsh? No, he hadn't. No amount of ambition justified doing this to herself. Tina Lewis stepped in. Probably just as well. Her voice was firm but kind. 'Will you come down to the station to look at some pictures?'

Danielle's voice rose to the verge of hysteria. 'I told you, I haven't seen Todd. I wouldn't know him. I can't help you.' She was picking at the sleeve of her dressing gown, her hands shaking.

'You don't know that.' Tina leaned towards her. 'We're investigating a murder. You've been pictured with the victim. You can come voluntarily. Or…'

'Can I make my own way down?' Danielle looked at the clock on the wall. 'In an hour or so? I have to go to the bank before it closes.'

Tina nodded. 'That's fine. See you around five.'

Katya's English had deteriorated remarkably. She no understand anything. Who is this Todd with English voice? What is Councillor? What this mean?

The improvement in her English was equally remarkable after they left the flat. A shout from behind the door made them pause on the landing. 'Stupid fucking bitch. What you tell them for?'

They couldn't make out Danielle's response. She was crying, incoherent. A door slammed and there was silence.

Chapter 13

Ryan couldn't remember ever feeling this fear. Not even the many times he'd hidden under his bed while his father battered his mother. He'd fantasised about killing his father. There were so many possible ways, and his father had shown every one of them to him. A heavy arm round his little shoulders, the smell of beer, carnage on the television.

Fate beat him to it, his father killed in a car crash on the A9. He took three others with him when he smashed head-on into their car. In the days following the funeral, while his mother reclined in drugged oblivion, his Aunt Gillian recreated his father for Ryan. Peter MacRae was a good man. He'd looked after his kids and tried to keep Sharon out of trouble. And that wasn't easy. Not that Sharon was a bad mother, his aunt said. She just didn't make things easy for her man. And his dad was a good man.

There hadn't been any fear since then. Just resentment against his mother, the police, the world. And a slow burning anger, accompanied by an overwhelming desire to know everything he could about his father. His mother wouldn't help him. Best not to ask, she'd say; she didn't want to speak ill of the dead, but that fucker...well, enough said. Only it wasn't enough, and when the opportunity arose to find out more about his father, from someone who really knew him, someone who appreciated him, Ryan had jumped at the chance.

And now, Ryan was trying to keep his fear from Todd. His hands were deep in his pockets so they wouldn't shake, and his feet were braced hard against the back of the foot well.

Todd didn't like it. 'Look at you, slouching like a sloth when I'm talking to you. This is serious shit.'

Ryan straightened up and pulled his knees in. 'Sorry.'

'That's better. Show a bit of respect; that's what your father would have done. He knew the game.'

Ryan wasn't even convinced that Todd had known his father. Just 'cos he had a few photos. Anyone could get photos. He should have walked away that first day. He'd been to his Aunt Gillian's house in Wyvis Place, but there was no one home. He was just closing the gate when a big black car had pulled up. The driver got out. 'Gillian MacRae live here?'

This big bald git could be anyone. Ryan shrugged.

'You don't know? You're coming out the gate, but you don't know who lives here? You a Jehovah's Witness or what?'

Ryan shrugged again. The guy had stared at him with eyes full of malice. 'Idiot.'

Ryan's heart had been hammering as the guy drove away. It took him the walk to his own flat before he calmed down. And guess what? The same car was outside his block of flats, and it was empty. Though he wanted to turn and run, Ryan couldn't leave his mother to deal with the guy he'd seen at Gillian's. He took the stairs two at a time, his head down.

'Careful,' a voice said as he reached the top of the second set of stairs. He looked up into the eyes of the bald giant. He was smiling. 'I don't suppose you know if Sharon MacRae lives here either?'

His mother must be out. Ryan shrugged and turned away.

'Listen, son, I'm not here for trouble. I'm figuring you must be related to Gillian and Sharon. Are you Ryan, Peter's son? I've heard a lot about you. You look just like your dad.'

And that was all it had taken to reel Ryan in. He hadn't told his mother. She was still a mess at that time, and mentioning his father would only make her worse. Todd gave him a phone so they could keep in touch. He said Ryan could text any time and he'd pick him up at school.

Ryan guessed Todd was into all sorts. Money lending, drugs maybe, and worse. He'd get phone calls that would make him angry, then he'd drive to a house and leave Ryan in the car. He'd come out all hyped up and even more arrogant than before. He wouldn't say much. Just the odd comment about people that crossed him, and how Ryan's father would have handled them just the same. He gave Ryan money and told him not to let on to his mother. And Ryan had thought he was it. He'd arrived. Idiot.

Now Todd leaned towards him. 'You know, son, no one would blame you if you had told them. You're young. It's not easy to keep quiet under that kind of pressure. I'd understand.'

Despite his fear, Todd's attempt at cunning pissed Ryan right off. He'd understand? That would be right. He hadn't spilled; he hadn't given a thing away, and here was Todd trying to pull one over on him, trying to trick him into confessing. Bastard.

Todd laughed. 'You've seen through me. I guess we both know what would happen if you talked. But it's not over. They could have you back in any day.'

Ryan shrugged. 'I can't see what they'd have on me. Nothing on my phone. Nothing on my clothes. They've got fuck all.'

'They've got an officer that saw you fleeing the scene. I'd say that counts for quite a lot. Listen, this is not just about me. Chris…I mean, Christopher, is involved too. You really don't want to cross him or his associates. Have you said anything to your mother?'

'About?'

'Me. The shooting.'

Ryan shook his head. As if he'd tell his mother anything.

Todd nodded. 'That's good. Christopher wouldn't want her to know about this.'

He took his phone from his pocket and fiddled with it, then he passed it to Ryan. 'Look. Cute or what?'

As Ryan looked at the photo, he felt sick. He tried to keep his hand steady.

'Move it on,' Todd said.

Ryan swiped though a series of photos of his wee brother. The first few were taken in the school playground. Then the swing park near the flats. Liam looked so innocent and happy.

A phone rang. It wasn't the one Ryan was holding. Wherever it was, the call must have connected automatically through Todd's Bluetooth earpiece. Ryan saw Todd's hands tighten on the wheel, the knuckles turning white, his face and thick neck turning red. 'No way.' He shook his bald head. 'No fucking way. Where is she?' He thumped his hand on the wheel. 'Tell me where she is. Right. Keep her there – don't let her out of your sight.'

His face contorted with rage, Todd started up the car. Just as well the roads were quiet. Ryan wouldn't have fancied the chances of anyone that crossed Todd's path as he raced towards the Longman, passing the police station and the college, then turning right onto Harbour Road.

'What the fuck are they stopped for?' Todd thumped the steering wheel again as they approached the railway bridge and a row of cars.

'A train?' There was a level crossing just after the bridge.

'Fuck's sake. Fucking train. The traffic in this place is a fucking joke.'

Ryan saw his chance. 'I'll just get out here. I can get myself home.'

Todd pressed a button and Ryan heard the doors lock. 'No chance. You need to see what happens to people that grass me up.'

Chapter 14

Todd was staring at the cars ahead as if he could will them to move. Ryan willed them not to move. Maybe the train would break down on the level crossing and the road would be closed for hours. Maybe the poor cow that had grassed Todd up would be long gone by the time they got wherever they were going.

'Fuck this,' Todd said, 'I'm going to turn.' But he couldn't. The traffic was backed up on the other side of the road too. As he stared ahead, a low growling noise filled the car, and chilly fingers caressed their way down Ryan's spine.

At last the traffic started to move, and soon they were on Millburn Road, heading back towards the town. Todd turned left and pulled up in front of the Chieftain Hotel. 'Come on. Hurry up.'

Ryan got out of the car and he could hear two women shouting. He followed Todd to a row of tenement flats. One of the doors opened and a teenage girl came out. Her dark hair was pinned up and her short skirt showed off long tanned legs. There were tears in her big eyes as she teetered out the gate in high-heeled sandals, shouting: 'Leave me alone.'

Behind her, another female, older, with fury in her eyes. She was wearing a thin robe that might have been see-through, but Ryan didn't dare look too closely.

When they saw Todd, they both fell silent. Ryan glanced up, and saw that Todd was transformed. He was smiling. 'Hey girls, no need for that shouting. What will people think? You must be Danielle,' he said to the younger one. 'I'm Todd. Where you going, honey?'

Her eyes were filled with fear. 'To the bank.'

'In town?'

She nodded.

'I'll take you along. I'm going that way myself.'

Ryan saw Danielle glance over her shoulder. Run, he wanted to shout. Just run! But she was following Todd to the car. There were locks of hair cascading down her slender neck. Todd held the back door open and she got in. Ryan reached for the handle of the passenger door.

'In the back, Ryan,' Todd said. 'Shift over, honey.'

Ryan should have run then. He should have made for the hotel, told them to call the police. He could have stopped whatever was going to happen to Danielle. He would have told the police everything, even if it meant going away himself.

Could've. Should've. Would've. Didn't.

Todd locked the doors, and Danielle looked at Ryan, her eyes huge.

'I thought you were going to town,' she said, when Todd took a left turn into Victoria Drive. Ryan had never heard an accent like it before.

Todd looked in his mirror. 'I am. Just trying to avoid the traffic.'

Ryan stared at the back of Todd's thick neck, and wished he had a weapon. He'd like to strangle him with that thick chavvy gold chain he always wore, but it would take some strength.

Todd took a right turn before the top of the road, and right again. He passed a row of tall posh terraced houses. Ryan glanced at Danielle. The colour was gone from her face. 'This isn't the way to the town. It isn't.'

Ahead, Ryan could see the road coming to an end. No more houses, just trees on both sides. He felt the car leave the road and bounce on to the wide track. Todd pulled in to the side. When Ryan looked back, he saw they were out of sight of the houses. On his right, he could see the land sloping downwards. They hadn't come far. If he could run down that wooded embankment, he'd almost be back at Danielle's flat.

Beside him, Danielle was crying. 'I'm sorry, Todd.' Her voice was soft. 'I didn't tell them much.'

Todd didn't look round. Ryan saw a hint of red creeping up his neck. 'You didn't tell them much?' His voice sent shivers of ice through Ryan. 'You didn't fucking tell them much? You told them my name, and you said I told you to target Gordon fucking Sutherland. You offered to go and look at photographs. You stupid bitch.'

'I'm sorry. I didn't know what to say.'

He turned and his eyes were like lasers, boring into Danielle's. 'Fucking little tart.'

'I'll tell them I was wrong. I'll…I'll give them someone else's name. Please…'

'Please.' His voice was high and terrifying. 'Please don't hurt me. Please don't make me pay for my fucking stupidity. Please…'

She was crying. 'I'll do anything.'

'You're good at doing anything, I hear. I did everything for you. I moved out so you could get set up in that flat. I sent the best of punters your way. Kept you off the streets. And I didn't even try the goods for myself first.'

'You…you can now.' The words were forced through her sobbing.

'I can do whatever I want. But I'm going to be a gentleman and let my friend go first.' There was excitement on Todd's face as he stared at Ryan. 'How about it? You been with anyone yet?'

Ryan shook his head. He couldn't speak.

'What better place to start?' He opened the glove compartment and took something out. Tossed it over the seat and it landed on Ryan's knee. A condom. 'Tell you what, I'll not watch. In fact, like the gent I am, I'll even get out of the car while you fill your boots. Take your time, son; savour it. And remember, she'll do anything.'

*

Carla and Ronald didn't talk often but when they did, he always left her feeling better. Safe, somehow. He was her only link to her father, and he reminded her of him. The same quiet certainty, the shared mannerisms and phrases. Though her father wasn't brought up on Uist, and though her grandparents hadn't passed their native language to him, he had used the odd Gaelic word here and there. When she was very young, it fascinated her, and when she was a teenager, it bugged the shit out of her. And now, when Ronald said the words in his soft island accent, she regretted every time she'd criticised her father. What she wouldn't give to hear him speak now, to have him hold her and reassure her, tell her everything would be all right.

Despite Ronald's obvious concern for her, Carla couldn't entice him away from the island. He had too much to do, but he had a suggestion. 'Why don't you come here? You can fly from Inverness.'

Carla didn't even know how she'd manage to get back home, far less make the trip to Uist.

'Keep it in mind. I'd love to have you here. Sorry, I'm going to have to go. The sheep are making another bid for freedom. We'll speak soon. *Tiorraidh ma-tha.*'

She wanted to repeat the words her father used to say. Instead, she used the English equivalent. 'Bye, then.'

She lay on her back and watched the clock. Her friend, Louise, had promised to bring in some food, and she'd expected her hours ago. A hint of nausea rose in her throat at the thought. Typical. After only managing half a slice of toast for breakfast, she'd spent the morning craving prawn sandwiches, grapes and carrot cake from M&S. She probably wouldn't be able to eat it. Maybe it wasn't the thought of the hospital food that had turned her stomach at lunch time; maybe her stomach was riddled with cancer, no room left for more than half a slice of toast.

Get a grip, she told herself, as tears threatened. If Louise didn't hurry up, they might not let her in. She couldn't expect them to keep making allowances for the police. Another five minutes and Louise appeared, in uniform. Grateful that she'd had time to recover her composure, Carla tried to smile. She could see Louise wasn't fooled. 'You look like shit.'

'Cheers.' At least she was more honest than Joe.

She put a bag down on the bed. 'Last prawn sandwich. I had to fight off a pensioner with a zimmer and a death wish. My ankles are black and blue. No respect for the police these days.'

*

Tina Lewis was pacing. Joe looked up at her. 'You're giving me a headache. Haven't you got work to do?'

She stopped by his desk. Raising her hands, she ran her fingers through her hair. Her top lifted and he saw a glimpse of taut ivory skin, and a flash of silver. A pierced navel? Joe felt his face flush again as he looked away.

'Sarge, our little northern friend is taking the piss. We should have brought her in. Both of them. What do you think?'

Joe thought. What was there to link them to Sutherland's death? They'd had their photo taken with him weeks ago. Someone had seen fit to deliver that photo to his wife. It certainly wasn't one of them. There wasn't enough. Not yet. 'Give her half an hour.'

'If you say so. Coffee?'

He nodded.

Chapter 15

If Sharon had been worried about Ryan before he went out, she was terrified when she saw him return. She was coming out of the bathroom as he came into the flat. His face was grey, his eyes wide and scared. 'Hi, son. You all right?'

It wasn't that unusual for him to ignore her, but it was the first time he'd ever pushed her. She crashed against the wall and almost fell. The bathroom door was slammed and locked. Sharon kicked it. 'Ryan, open the door, you little bastard. I'm so sick of you!'

There was no answer; just the sound of choking and crying, gasping and retching. It went on for a minute or more, then she heard the shower start. She slumped to the floor and sat with her back against the bathroom door. There was no way he was getting past her without an explanation.

'Mam, what's wrong?' It was Liam. 'What was that banging noise?'

'Nothing, son. Ryan's just a wee bit sick; I'm going to wait here for him.'

'Will I get him some ice cream?' His wee face was so serious.

Sharon smiled. 'No, he won't feel like anything. He'll be…' She heard the shower stop, the toilet flush. 'Go on, son; you go and watch the rest of the film. I'll be through in a minute.'

Liam gave her a hug and left, just as Ryan unlocked the door. She got to her feet and stood in the doorway. 'You're not getting past until you tell me what's going on. And don't even think of pushing me again, or you're dead.'

He looked half-dead already, his face washed out, like someone going cold turkey. He had a towel wrapped around his waist, and there were scratches and marks on his neck. Looked like someone had grabbed him. Was that a hickey? He stared at her, but there was no fight in him. He sat on the edge of the bath.

'Well?'

He shook his head. 'I can't tell you anything, Mam; I just can't.'

'Have you done something? Is it to do with that shooting? I know you went…' She couldn't tell him she'd followed him. 'You can trust me. I'd do anything to help you, son; anything.'

'I know. It's nothing to do with that. And I haven't done anything. I just...just...' He put his hands up to face and started to cry. As she reached for him, she noticed scratches on the back of his hands.

'Who did that to your hands, son?'

There was no answer. She held him tight and whispered that everything would be all right. When the crying stopped, she wiped his eyes with a bit of toilet roll. 'Why don't you get dressed and come and watch the Lion King with me and Liam? You used to love the Lion King.'

He sniffed. 'Aye, when I was about five.'

'I'm thirty three and I still like it.'

'Okay.' Ryan tried to smile. 'Are you going out tonight? Are you seeing...seeing Christopher?'

'No. We'll have a night in, just the three of us. We'll get fish and chips.'

Ryan nodded. 'Mam, I'm sorry for pushing you. I really am.'

'I know, son. I know.'

*

There was no answer at the flat on Carlton Terrace. When Joe looked through the letterbox, there was a dark emptiness. Had they gone already? He knocked on a neighbour's door. A middle-aged woman answered. She looked Joe and Tina up and down. 'You'll be the police, then.'

Joe showed her his warrant card. 'We're just making some enquiries about – '

'About them next door. Bloody tarts. Ever since that young one arrived, they've been at it day and night. I complained to that other policeman, but nothing was done.'

'What policeman?'

'Smallish, dark hair, moustache. And bad breath. That was ages ago.'

'Did you go to the station?'

She shook her head. 'He was hanging about in the stairs. I thought he looked suspicious, so I said I was going to call the police. He told me not to bother 'cos he was the police. He showed me his card, but I can't remember his name. The bugger did nothing.'

'Did you hear anything today?'

She shook her head. 'I've been out at work, and I'm not long home. What are you going to do about it? It's not fair on the rest of us, men back and fore day and night. The things I've heard have given me nightmares. Or they would, if I could get any sleep. It's no wonder I've turned grey. It wasn't so bad when the big bald guy was there. He and the older tart moved in at the same time, but he left just before the young one came. I was terrified when I first saw him, he looked that fierce, but there was no trouble from him.'

'Do you know his name?'

She shook her head. 'I didn't want to encourage them. Just nodded on the stairs, that sort of thing.'

'Did you see his car?'

'I saw him with a couple of different cars. Big dark things mostly. I've no idea what make. If my man was still here, he'd be able to tell you, but he buggered off with another tart four years back. I told you, it's no wonder I'm grey. I've got the landlord's number. He lives in Perth. I phone him every time I get disturbed. He doesn't answer now, not if it's the middle of the night. Just wait there and I'll get it for you.'

She returned with the number scrawled on a piece of paper. 'Good luck with him. He's a cheeky wee shite, so he is. It's little wonder I'm grey.'

The landlord hadn't met Katya Birze. She'd signed the lease through a letting agent. She had a partner, but she didn't want his name on the lease. He didn't really know anything else about her. The letting agent had done all the checks. He'd been about to terminate the lease anyway, sick of the neighbour phoning him at all hours.

Joe had just started up the engine when they got the call. A body in the lane between Victoria Terrace and Auldcastle Road. Young female. Late teens or early twenties. Dark hair.

'Yes.' Tina beat her hands on the dashboard. 'Bugger this running around after a pair of skanky tarts. Some real police work. Where is that? Can we get there quick?'

Joe stared at her and shook his head, then he took off. She clutched at the dashboard with her manicured hands as he pulled into Victoria Drive, sped past Millburn Academy, and took a sharp right into Victoria Terrace. He drove past the terraced houses and on to the muddy track between the tall trees. He pulled to a halt a few yards into the track. They'd left the flat on Carlton Terrace about a minute earlier. 'Quick enough for you?'

'Jesus, Sarge…what's going on?'

'Ask her, why don't you? See how exciting she finds it?'

There was a woman standing on the track, with a black dog on a lead. Her face was ashen. Joe called the station to tell them he was there. As he and Tina got out of the car, a patrol car pulled up behind them, lights flashing.

They stood and looked down the wooded slope, and Joe heard Tina gasp. He felt a little bad. He should have remembered how he was at first. A long night in traffic; nothing happening; the excitement of a call. It hadn't taken too many calls to rid him of the idea that there was anything exciting about a road accident. And now, although he'd known as soon as he got the call, he should have realised that Tina had no idea. She hadn't been in Inverness for long, and didn't know the lay of the land. She had no idea that Victoria Terrace was just above Carlton Terrace, and that the chances of this dark-haired young corpse being anyone other than Danielle Smith were slim.

Danielle's body was lodged between two trees on a wooded slope. Her dead face was looking upwards, eyes wide. She'd been thrown down there after death; didn't need a SOCO to tell Joe that. As Joe stared down at her body, he felt his world tilt. The marks on her throat spoke of strangulation; the skirt up around her waist spoke of sexual assault. She looked so young.

The Senior Investigating Officer was DCI Archie MacBain. His eyes widened when Joe told him he knew the victim. His bushy eyebrows lifted when he heard that Joe and Tina Lewis had spoken to her less than a couple of hours ago. He didn't say much. He didn't have to. Joe felt like shit. Though he wasn't about to admit it to anyone else, he lived with the certainty that he'd be found out one of these days. He was good enough at the job, better than many of his colleagues, but that didn't stop the little voice inside that told him he was useless, always would be. He could have done his job differently, and if he had, this beautiful girl would be alive.

That was nonsense, Tina Lewis told him, before he could even voice it. They'd had no way of knowing Danielle was in danger. She was barely linked to Gordon Sutherland. They couldn't have arrested her; they couldn't even have forced her to come in for questioning; they'd done the right thing.

Words, words, words.

*

Katya Birze was gone, and it looked like she'd left in a hurry, clothes discarded on her wardrobe floor, a cold cup of tea and two bits of toast on the bedside table. In Danielle's room, some cheap jewellery, a map of Shetland, and some clothes. No phone, laptop or tablet. Had Katya taken everything, or was Danielle on the run when she was caught? And if she was, where was her bag?

They found the sock later that night. It was lying close to the body, just a small flash of white reflecting off the bright lights brought in to counteract the fall of dusk. The first thought of the SOCO that found it was that it was unconnected to the murder. But wait. Was that a splatter of blood spots along the edge of the sock? No blood at the scene, so probably still unconnected, but odd. She bagged it and passed it to a colleague for logging.

*

It was 10:40 when Christopher sat at his desk. The email was waiting.

> *Howdie mate. Leg okay? Another strange day. Got a lot on my mind. I'm going away for a while but will try to keep in touch.*
> *Any ideas for our ten years? We have to do something. I'm leaving it with you. Take care. Yours always. T*

Christopher thought for a while, then he typed.

> *Leg's fine, ta. Didn't do much today. Busy tomorrow with house inspections. A couple of tenants are for the chop if there's no improvement. Maybe I should take you with me more often for the initial meeting. All those that met you are*

model tenants. I wonder why…
Where you off to? Take care. C

Christopher knew he wouldn't get an answer to the question of where Todd was going. Not that he really wanted to know, but he had to ask. There were unspoken rules and consequences. He was breaking the rules by not acknowledging the ten year thing. The consequences would be a huff and a couple of jibes, usually about Sharon. He wondered what he'd have to do before his pal would decide not to send the 10:30 email. That had never happened.

He was about to turn the laptop off when the first of the jibes came in.

How's the tart? Joke!! Night night mate.

He didn't answer.

*

Todd watched as Chris looked at the clock on his desk. Smile: you're on camera. The quality of the image and sound from the study camera was almost as good as the DAB radio. Not that there had been much to see or hear from any of the cameras tonight. Chris had been in and out of the house a couple of times. He must have been working out on the gym equipment in his garage. Came in all sweaty and panting. And limping.

A shower, then food. A bit of Radio Four and a quick call to the tart. She hadn't wanted to speak for long. Worried about Ryan, by the sound of Chris's responses. At least she wasn't at his house. At home with her boys. She should make the most of them for now.

He laughed at the scowl on Chris's face as he read the second email. Good. He needed to learn some respect, some gratitude for all Todd had done for him, was still doing for him. Ten years was a big deal. They were doing something special. Just the two of them. The sooner that tart was out of the picture, the better.

66

Chapter 16

When Sharon woke and felt a small body curled up beside her, she thought of Ryan. He wasn't in her bed; that would be well obscene, but it didn't seem that long since he'd regularly crept in beside her, his cheeks wet from a bad dream. She'd tried talking to him again last night, but he wouldn't say a thing. He'd hugged her at bed time, held her tight. Not like him at all. He'd looked so scared.

She couldn't see Liam's face, and she didn't want to move and disturb him. It wouldn't be that long until he was too big to creep into her bed. The thought gutted her. Much as she loved Ryan, she'd always known the distance between them. He remembered his father and resented his mother. Sharon blamed Peter's sister, Gillian. They'd never really got on. Gillian had looked after the boys for long spells when Sharon was out of it on drugs, or in hospital or rehab. Given half a chance, she would have kept the boys for good. And Sharon hated her for it. And for messing with Ryan's head and telling him his father was a decent human being, when he was nothing but an animal. Sharon had put a stop to that. She'd warned Gillian not to start that with Liam, if she wanted to stay in the boys' lives. She knew she was chancing it. It wouldn't have taken much for Gillian to poison the social workers against Sharon, make sure the boys were taken off her for good. But for some reason, it had worked, and Gillian had stopped talking about Peter to the boys. She'd hardly give Sharon the time of day now, but at least she wasn't poisoning Liam.

And Liam was different. It wasn't just his age. He was soft and kind, and absolutely devoted to his mum. She looked at the clock and saw it was almost time to get up. As her heart swelled with love, Sharon pulled him close. He turned and smiled, and then their front door exploded.

'What the –?'

Liam screamed as heavy footsteps thundered down the hall towards the bedroom. The door was thrown open and several dark figures with guns rushed in. 'Police! Where's Ryan? Where the fuck's Ryan?'

'No one in the living room or kitchen,' she heard someone shout.

'Bathroom's empty.' Another voice. 'So is the other bedroom.'

She could hear them opening cupboards and drawers and scattering furniture. The policeman grabbed her arm and hauled her from the bed. 'There's a boy here,' he shouted. 'Too young for Ryan.' One of his colleagues pulled the wardrobe doors open, grabbed her clothes from the rails and scattered them on the floor. He checked under the bed.

'Mummy!' Liam hadn't called her that for years. Sharon pulled against the man that held her. 'Get your hands off me, you bastard. Let me get my boy.'

'Let her go.' It was Galbraith.

'Fucking bastard.' Sharon rubbed her arm and got back onto the bed, holding Liam tight, rocking him. 'It's okay, son. It's just a game. It's okay.'

Galbraith told his colleagues to leave them. 'There's no one else here.'

When they'd gone, Sharon pulled the quilt up around her and Liam. 'What the fuck?'

Galbraith sat on the edge of her bed. 'Where's Ryan?'

'Last time I checked, about quarter past midnight, he was fast asleep in his bed.'

'He's not there now. What's going on, Sharon?'

Sharon shrugged. 'He didn't shoot that man; I know he didn't. I thought youse had nothing on him. I thought he was in the clear.'

Galbraith shouted Roberts. His lanky frame appeared at the door. He nodded his curly head. 'Sharon.'

Liam pulled away from her and scrambled out of the bed. 'Roberts, I remember you. I'm definitely going to be a copper. I want to play games like this. It's exciting.'

Galbraith told Roberts to take Liam through to his room. Sharon nodded. 'Aye, son. Show him what you and Ryan made with your Lego last night.'

Roberts looked a bit shame-faced. 'Eh, there's a bit of a problem with that...'

'Bastards broke his castle? There's no need for that.'

'Come on,' Roberts said. 'You can show me what other toys you've got.'

Liam hesitated. 'Will you be all right, Mam?'

'I'll be fine.'

*

Sharon MacRae hadn't half changed since last year. Even first thing in the morning she was looking pretty good. Skin much better than it had been, decent hair, new teeth. Where had the money come from? Her arms were a state, though. She saw Joe looking at her scars.

'You going to pass me my dressing gown?' She nodded at the back of the door.

Joe passed it to her. 'Sharon, you've got to tell us everything you know. Who's Ryan hanging about with?'

'Just his mates from school. Mostly Sean; he lives in Hawthorn Drive. Ryan tells me nothing.'

'Has he mentioned someone called Todd?'

Sharon shook her head. 'I'd remember that.'

'Did you see him last night?'

'Aye; he came in before tea time, and he was in all night. We watched telly, then he played with Liam. Hasn't done that for years. What's going on?'

'Someone matching Ryan's description was seen leaving the scene of another murder yesterday afternoon, and there's evidence that suggests he was there.'

Sharon's face was the colour of putty. She shook her head. 'Another murder? No way was that anything to do with Ryan.' There were tears in her eyes. 'He wouldn't kill anyone; I know he wouldn't.'

'What was he doing yesterday afternoon? Did he go to school?'

Sharon sniffed and shook her head. 'No. By the time he got home, there was no point in sending him. He was here, with me.'

'All the time?'

Sharon nodded, then it turned into a shrug. She'd been a hopeless liar last year when they'd questioned her about Stephen MacLaren, and nothing had changed.

'Sharon?'

'I heard him speaking on the phone yesterday and I wondered how he could do that when youse had his phone. He sounded really scared. He went out, and I followed him. He got into a car on Portland Place.'

'What kind of car?'

Sharon shrugged. 'Just a big dark thing. I couldn't see the number. Big bald guy driving. I didn't go too close. Ryan came home at tea time, and I didn't let on I'd followed him.'

'How was he?'

She shook her head. 'I…I can't…'

No wonder she was struggling. Joe put his hand on her arm. 'I understand how difficult this is, Sharon, but it's serious.'

She nodded, and said nothing.

He moved off the bed, and crouched in front of her. 'We need to find him, to help him.'

She wiped a tear from her cheek. 'I can't grass on my own son.'

Joe nodded. 'I get that, but it's for his own good. He could be in danger.'

Her eyes met his and she took a deep breath. 'He was…he was a mess when he got home. Throwing up in the toilet and crying. He looked terrified. He had these scratches and marks on his neck and his hands. It looked like he'd been grabbed by the throat. I tried to find out what was going on, but he wouldn't tell me anything. You don't believe he'd kill someone, do you? Was it another councillor?'

Joe shook his head. 'Danielle Smith. Eighteen years old. Murdered yesterday afternoon.'

Sharon's eyes were wide and scared. She shook her head. 'No way. No fucking way. Not Ryan.'

The clothes Ryan had been wearing yesterday were gone. He'd taken a black rucksack, more clothes, and £100 from his mother's purse. 'Wee shite,' Sharon said. 'Bet he didn't expect to get more than a fiver. Must have made his day.'

Joe didn't ask her where she got the money. It wasn't just Sharon that had changed since last year. As well as the fancy washing machine, there was new furniture, a couple of nice pictures. Something was going on. On the game? Wouldn't have surprised him last year, but there was something different about her now. She was stronger, more confident. That kind of change usually came from sorting your life out, not from turning to prostitution.

'Are you lot done?' Sharon asked. 'Liam's going on a trip with the Cubs. I've got to take him soon.'

'No, and we won't be for a while. SOCO are on their way.'

'Again? Fuck's sake. Neighbours will think I've got a drug factory here.'

He hadn't thought of that.

Chapter 17

Looking into the grief-filled eyes of Danielle Smith's parents, listening to their questions, and answering them honestly, while trying to maintain the precious dignity of their only beloved child, was harder than anything Joe had done for a long time. Tina Lewis did it well. Much better than Joe. He had compassion, far too much of the stuff. Maybe even more than Tina, when it came down to it, but it was perception that counted. She had a way of putting it across that seemed really genuine.

This couple, Andy and Aileen Smith, they thought their daughter was working in a sports shop in Inverness, saving money to go to Oxford. She was going to study law, become a barrister. They'd been so proud of her. Brilliant at sports and top of the class in everything. She'd left school last summer and worked in Shetland for a while, then she'd moved to Inverness. They hadn't worried. Inverness wasn't that far. It must be safer than Oxford.

An escort? They looked confused. What did that mean? Was it something to do with taking disabled people out? Danielle had always been so kind.

That just about did it for Joe. Maybe he didn't have as much compassion as Tina after all. He certainly couldn't have handled the escort explanation as well as she did. Their faces. Their little girl? Was that like a…a prostitute?

*

A life on the ocean wave. That had been Ryan's dream, ever since he was a young boy. He'd spend hours down the canal, watching the yachts and barges come and go. He'd sit at the harbour too, as the ships arrived with their loads of timber and oil, frozen fish and salt. He'd marvel at the tiny tug vessels, pushing the great, lumbering cargo boats into place. Imagine sailing away, leaving everything behind.

Maybe that's what he'd thought he'd do when he'd crawled into the old boat at the canal marina early this morning, not long after the gates were opened. He'd been keeping an eye on the boat, and no one had been near it for months. How hard could it be to get the boat going and just disappear? Impossible. That was the answer. He hadn't a clue. Didn't know where to start, and if he messed about with it for too long, someone would notice.

Still, it gave him somewhere to hide. At least his head had stopped spinning, but he couldn't banish Danielle's face, especially in the dark beneath the tarpaulin. The terror in her eyes as he'd started to open her zip. The silent, desperate pleading. She hadn't said a word. Just watched him with those eyes, her leg pressed against his, the short skirt rising up her thigh, her perfume filling his nostrils and turning his head. She was a whore, Todd had said; a dirty little whore. There was nothing Ryan couldn't do to her if he wanted. No limits.

He had to get out of here, get some food, though he wasn't sure he would be able to eat. The Co-op wasn't far. But what if he was seen? He'd heard voices at the marina earlier, people moving around, boat motors starting up. It would be much harder to sneak back onto the boat now. Shit, he had to get a plan together, find a way out of Inverness. Ryan lifted the tarpaulin. There was no one around.

In no time at all he was back on the canal bank. He decided to stay in the bushes for a while, instead of lying beneath that tarpaulin. A couple of sausage rolls, three packets of crisps and some Irn Bru, and he felt more human. Maybe he'd make for the town later, get a bus to Glasgow.

Through the bushes he saw a blonde woman and a dog. He thought of his mum, and how tight she'd held him yesterday. Made him feel safe for a while, until he was alone in his room, and the darkness came. And with it, Danielle's eyes, and the knowledge that it wouldn't be long before everyone, including his mum, would know what he'd been involved in. She'd never hold him like that again.

His hands shaking, Ryan took his phone from his pocket. He'd phone her one last time. She wouldn't recognise the number; maybe she wouldn't answer. She answered straight away. Her voice made his stomach churn. He almost hung up; best just to leave, get out of town. But she knew. Without him saying a word, she knew. 'Ryan, son? Is that you? Where are you? I'm worried sick.'

'Mum. I'm…'

'Son, tell me where you are. I'll come and get you.'

'I can't.'

'Aye, you can. We'll sort everything out. Come home, son. It'll be all right.'

God, he was tempted.

'Liam's missing you. Said it wasn't the same without you nicking his toast this morning.'

Ryan would have given anything just to see that annoying wee shit, Liam, now. 'Mum, I want to come back, but I don't know if I can.'

'You can. You just need to tell them everything. Son, I know you didn't kill that girl.'

He dropped the phone. He could hear his mother's tinny little voice shouting, begging. He wanted to stand on the phone, stamp it into the ground. But he needed it, so he picked it up, cut the call, and threw up in the grass.

Chapter 18

Sharon had never ignored Christopher's calls and texts before. She'd relied on him for almost a year, told him everything. But this was different. A dead teenager, just a young girl. There was no way Ryan had anything to do with that, but it could be enough to put Christopher right off. And who could blame him?

Maybe if she hadn't fallen so fast and so hard, Ryan wouldn't be in this trouble now. He'd never been easy, but over the last few months, he'd been more arrogant, rougher with Liam, and disdainful of Sharon. She'd wondered if he was jealous of her relationship with Christopher, but she hadn't done anything to try and find out. Too busy enjoying her new life.

Where the hell was he? Her phone rang and she snatched it up, hoping it was Ryan. It was Christopher. She hesitated, but couldn't stop herself. 'Hi Christopher.'

'Hi honey. What are you up to?'

Honey. Just one word and her legs felt like rubber. 'Nothing much. I was…I was a bit busy earlier. Sorry I missed your calls.'

'Yeah? What were you doing?'

She hesitated. 'Eh…it's Ryan. He left early this morning, before we were up. The cops are looking for him.'

'Cops? Do they still think he had something to do with that shooting?'

'I guess. I think there's something else too, but I'm not sure.' She couldn't tell him.

'I've got to take a run round a few of my properties, sort out a couple of problems. Do you want to come with me? It'll take your mind off things.'

She should stay at home in case Ryan came back. But what if he didn't? She'd waste the day. Liam was going to Gillian's after the trip, and she was to pick him up later. 'Do you need a heavy to duff up your tenants?'

He laughed. 'I'll give them one last chance, but I might have to take you up on that offer if things don't improve. Are you coming?'

Of course she was.

*

See that sick leave Jackson had been considering? Now was probably the time to take it. DI Black had pulled him up about the neighbour in Carlton Terrace. There were only three moustaches in the station, and one of those belonged to PC Rona Lennon. Jackson had talked his way out of it, for now. He'd never been called to that block of flats, he'd said. It could have been anyone. The guy probably wasn't even a cop. Just because the old bird thought she'd seen a warrant card, that didn't mean a thing.

But that wasn't what was making Jackson sick to his stomach. It was the thought of wee Danielle lying on the slab in the mortuary, waiting to be cut open. It was all Galbraith's fault. If he'd taken her in yesterday, she'd still be alive.

Jackson tried to ignore the wee voice that whispered in his head, telling him he could have done something. He could have contacted Danielle as soon as he saw that photo, told her the police were coming to see her. He could have gone for her himself, taken her to his house until this blew over.

But he didn't know, he told the wee voice; he didn't know what was going to happen. And then the wee voice reminded him that Galbraith didn't know either. Fuck that voice. Galbraith was an arrogant shit-head. Didn't give a damn about Danielle or anyone but himself.

She was a wee sweetheart. So young and beautiful. He'd almost been scared to touch her. She was far too good for a sad loser like him. But she seemed to enjoy herself all right. Happy enough to take his money, sit on his knee, and all the rest.

And Katya? Where was that bitch now? A born whore if ever there was one, she'd have taken off without a thought for Danielle, left her to whatever sick bastard had done this. Was it Ryan MacRae? He'd love some time alone with the boy to beat it out of him. And that bald guy, the one mentioned by Katya's neighbour and Sharon MacRae, was he their pimp? Was he the Todd that Danielle had spoken of? Who the hell was he?

Jackson had tried to find out who was working Danielle and Katya. Best to know his enemy. It wouldn't take much for their pimp to find out he was a cop and use it against him. He'd tried to coax it out of Danielle, but she was giving nothing away. She'd met Katya online; that was all she would say. He'd persisted, but she had ways of distracting him.

*

Enfolded in Councillor Alice McGarvie's embrace, Roz Sutherland wanted to throw up. That smell. A mix of cheap rose scent, hair spray and halitosis. Roz pulled away. 'Come through. Mairi and Philip are upstairs. They're sick of visitors.'

Alice's eyes narrowed. She took a pristine white cotton hankie from her sleeve and dabbed until the annoyance was gone. Roz didn't care that Alice had taken her words as a rebuke. She didn't ever have to be nice to her again. No more council ceremonies or lunches or dinner parties. No more watching Alice fawning over her husband, laughing and preening herself.

Gordon hadn't seen it. He couldn't believe Roz thought Alice fancied him. She was just a colleague. A good councillor. She wasn't like that. And anyway, even if she was, he wasn't like that, so Roz had nothing to worry about.

She hadn't worried about it. She might not have looked after herself as well as she could have, but she was certain her husband wouldn't be attracted to Alice McGarvie. The thought made her shiver. But was he attracted to the two girls in the photo? Who were they? And who had put that envelope through her door?

'Roz, dear, how have you been?' Alice held her hands up. 'I know. I know. Stupid question. Forgive me. It's so very difficult to know what to say. I just wanted you to know I'm here for you. Anything you want, any time of day or night, you know where to find me.'

That'd be right. Roz nodded, smiled, and thanked Alice. 'I'll make tea.' The thought of another cup of tea made her nauseous, but that was what people expected. As she went into the kitchen, the front doorbell rang. It was DS Galbraith.

Roz showed him into the kitchen and closed the door. She shouted up the stairs for Mairi. When her daughter came down, Roz saw she'd been crying again. She hugged her, then asked her to go into the living room and talk to Alice.

Mairi grimaced. 'McGarvie?'

'Yes. Sorry. There's a detective here to speak to me. I won't be long.'

Joe looked around the kitchen. About a dozen cups waiting to be washed, and another dozen on the draining board. It was a homely kitchen. Warm. Lived-in. Lots of family pictures on the wall. Roz Sutherland came in and closed the door.

'Detective Galbraith, what can I do for you today? Have a seat.' She gestured to the chairs round the dining table. The table was covered with boxes of cakes and biscuits, and at least three bunches of flowers. There were cards too, lying on top of their envelopes. Joe sat at one side of the table, Roz at the other. She looked worn out. Sounded it too. 'I wish people would stop bringing stuff. I should put the flowers in water, but I can't even face that.'

'Are the family home now?'

She nodded. 'Mairi and Philip and their partners came yesterday. I'm expecting Gordon's brother and his wife later. I'm hoping they've got an appetite.' She tried to smile.

'Mrs Sutherland, something else has come up. Did you hear about the murder yesterday?'

Her eyes widened. 'Another one? I haven't listened to the news or looked at the papers; I can't bear it.'

He nodded. 'I'm sorry to have to tell you this, but we think the murders are connected.' He took the photo from his pocket, and he saw her recoil.

'It was this girl.'

*

Roz knew the girls' faces. They were imprinted on her brain. The slightly hard-looking older one, with her arm round Gordon. And the other one – so young and pretty, leaning towards Gordon as if she was about to kiss him. It was all so improbable, and Gordon looked so uncomfortable. And now one of them was dead. She was just a child. 'Who was she?'

'Danielle Smith. She was from Shetland. She was a – '

'A prostitute.'

DS Galbraith nodded. 'It might help you to know both girls told me Gordon wasn't remotely interested in what they were offering.'

Roz thought she was going to laugh, but it was tears that came.

As DS Galbraith passed her a hankie, she wished she hadn't let herself cry. It seemed so important to hold herself together for everyone else. But the relief. Gordon wasn't interested in them. She wanted to shout it out for everyone to hear. Instead she sniffed and apologised.

'Don't apologise, Mrs Sutherland. You said you hadn't noticed anything unusual about Gordon recently. Are you sure? We think someone might have been trying to set him up. These girls were told to target him.'

Everything was all jumbled in her head. It had been a difficult and strange time recently. The independence referendum result had been such a blow for Gordon, for all his colleagues. Then the surge in support for the Scottish National Party lifted their spirits, and soon it was all go for the general election, and then the euphoria of the party's success nationally. Just when everything was looking up, it all went wrong in the Council, and the Independents had seized power from the SNP. He'd been annoyed about that, but he was philosophical. It might not do the party any harm to be out of the spotlight for a while. He took it all in his stride. It was all part of the ups and downs of political life. Things would settle down.

She tried to explain it all, and it sounded stupid. What did the referendum and the election have to do with anything? Yet she couldn't separate her husband from these events. The party, the cause, those were his very reasons for being. Always had been. She and the family had taken second place for as long as she could remember. And she didn't mind. They'd met at an SNP conference when they were both students. She'd never met anyone as solid and dependable as him. And nothing had ever changed that.

Galbraith nodded. 'I know I've asked you this already, but please think again. Is there anyone that would have it in for your husband?'

'I've gone over and over that in my head. I just can't think of anyone that might have wanted to harm him.'

'Was he interested in standing for election to Holyrood?'

'Not at all. Alice McGarvie liked to think so, but he was winding down, feeling too old for a challenge like that.'

There was a knock on the kitchen door. Alice popped her head round the door. 'Roz, I'll have to…oh, I am sorry, Detective Sergeant Galbraith. I had no idea it was you. I have to go to a meeting. I'll come again, soon.'

Roz nodded, and said nothing. Alice raised a hand and backed away.

'You don't like her much, do you?'

Roz felt herself blushing. 'Is it that obvious?'

Galbraith smiled. 'The curse of being a detective. I can't switch it off. Even in the queue at Tesco, I'm sensing all the tensions and traumas in the lives of those around me. Not that I'm always right, but I noticed it the first time you mentioned her. Anything I should know?'

'I guess it's not a crime to fancy someone else's husband, but most people manage to keep it hidden. She didn't bother. Not that Gordon could see it. He thought I was paranoid, imagining it. I wasn't. Ach, it wasn't really that; I trusted Gordon. There's just something about her. I can't explain it.'

Joe shrugged. 'It's important to go with your instinct. Listen, we've gone through all the paperwork you gave us and there's nothing that helps us with the investigation. Might he have kept paperwork anywhere else?'

Roz shook her head. 'I don't think so, but I'll have a look. You really think someone was targeting him?'

'It looks like it. Let me know if you find anything.'

Chapter 19

The afternoon briefing was a dismal affair. DI Black put it in a nutshell for the troops. 'We've got two bodies, a runaway whore, a missing school boy whose thumb print is on the murder victim's zip, a bald man, and a slightly dodgy and unattractive SNP councillor. Have I forgotten anything?' No one answered. 'Oh, aye – we have a sock.'

DCI MacBain was more upbeat. 'That sock might be just what we need. A combination of Gordon Sutherland's blood and Ryan MacRae's DNA – pretty powerful stuff. And we also have the partial fingerprint from MacRae.'

'Aye, and for all we know, if Ryan MacRae's not the killer, he and Katya Birze might already be victims. The sock won't get us very far if that's the case.'

MacBain nodded. 'Still, got to stay positive. Chins up.'

DI Black rolled his eyes, and his three chins rolled too. 'Fat lot of good that'll do us.'

One of the admin assistants stood at the open door with a piece of paper in her hand. She looked from one senior detective to the other. DCI MacBain smiled as DI Black snatched the paper from her hand. 'Tell me this is good news.'

She shrugged, blushed, and left.

DI Black studied the missive while everyone in the room held their breath. With a smirk, he passed it to MacBain. 'What say you, Sir? One for the two of us?'

MacBain didn't look quite so impressed. 'My ulcer's playing up today; I think I'll leave him to you.'

'Galbraith,' Black said. 'This one's down to you. Come on.'

Bemused, Joe followed DI Black from the room.

*

Mikey Morrison might have been screwing up his face, but it was always hard to tell. An ugly little shrew, he'd made a fortune selling home-made porn. He leaned forward. 'Metropolitan Derby? I haven't a clue what you're talking about.'

DI Black looked under the table. 'Trainers with a suit? A bit common even for you, Mikey Boy. You not got a decent pair of shoes to match the suit? Luis Vuitton maybe?'

A flush started to creep up Mikey's short neck.

'The penny's dropping, DS Galbraith. So, Mikey, what exactly made you leave a Luis Vuitton Metropolitan Derby in a stairway in Carlton Terrace? Lucky for you, my sergeant here just happened to find it.'

Joe nodded. 'Not every day I find such a fine specimen. You wouldn't have had much change from £600. You'd think you'd be a bit more careful.'

'Who says it's mine?' Mikey's face was beetroot now.

'Our database.' Joe tapped his fingers on the table. 'Unless there are things about your sordid little love life we don't know. Maybe you're in the habit of handling other men's shoes. Is that your thing, Mikey? A foot fetish? A male foot fetish?'

It was so easy to wind him up. 'That's disgusting. What do you think I am?'

DI Black laughed. 'If DS Galbraith was to answer that question, we'd be here all day. We know exactly what you are, so stop wasting our time and tell us what you were doing at that flat on Carlton Terrace yesterday.'

Mikey sighed. 'I was just visiting some friends.'

'Friends with benefits?' Joe said.

'Eh?'

'What are your friends' names?'

'Eh…Kat and…do you know, I can't remember the other one's name.'

'Danielle Smith?'

'Danni – that's her.'

'And would these be good friends?'

He shrugged. 'Quite good. I've known Kat for a while, and I just met Danni recently.'

'And what did you do with these friends yesterday afternoon?'

'Watched a DVD; can't remember what it was called.'

Joe shook his head. 'I'm not even going to ask what it was about. The last time we watched one of your DVDs, our colleague was off sick for a week.'

'They weren't mine.' The anger was back. 'The Sheriff threw that case out. DI Black, is he allowed to do that? Winding me up with lies? I was innocent.'

'Innocent?' DI Black nodded. 'Mikey, you're as slippery as an eel. You've got the cunning of the subnormal.'

Mikey looked quite pleased with that, until he thought about it. He narrowed his weasily eyes. 'You saying I'm subnormal? What the fuck does that mean?'

Joe straightened up. Leaned across the table. 'Let's get back to Kat and Danni. You watched a DVD. What else?'

'Nothing. Had a cup of tea, then left.'

'Carrying your shoes?'

'Aye. Kat won't let anyone in with their shoes on. New carpets, I think.'

'No carpets in that flat, Mikey.'

Mikey shrugged. 'Germs, then; she's fussy like that.'

'Cut the crap, Mikey. We know what you were there for. We know your afternoon of pleasure was interrupted, and you had to leave suddenly. I expect you hid in the back garden for a while until one of your low-life friends could come and rescue you, with a spare pair of shoes.'

'But – '

'Don't even think of denying it. You've wasted enough of our time. It wasn't just the shoe that was covered in your prints. They were on the bedroom door and the headboard in one of the bedrooms. This is a murder enquiry. You were one of the last people to see the victim alive.'

Mikey's face paled. 'A murder enquiry? That body that was found in the Crown? I need my brief.'

'Why do you think you need a solicitor?'

'I'll hold my hands up. I was with Kat yesterday. I had sex with her, but I didn't kill her.'

'Are you working those girls?'

'Me? Hardly. That's not my game.'

'Then who is?'

Mikey was silent.

The DI stood up. 'You'll be wanting that brief then?'

'Wait…I…you've no idea. Oh fuck. He's nuts. He'll kill me if he knows. I bet he killed Kat. Bastard.'

'Who is he, Mikey?'

A phone rang. Mikey patted his pockets, took out his phone.

He stared at the screen, then at the detectives. 'But...she's not dead...what are youse on?'

'Answer it,' DI Black said. 'And put it on loudspeaker.'

Katya's voice spat from the phone. 'Mikey? Listen you. You don't tell police you with me yesterday. You don't tell them you ever with me, or you be fucking dead. Todd say he cut your balls off and feed you to them. Understand?'

Mikey stared at the phone.

'Mikey? You fucking understand?'

Joe gestured to Mikey to speak.

'Eh...em...yes, Kat.'

'This is good.' The line went dead.

Mikey slumped in his chair. 'I don't know what you guys are trying to do to me. Why did you say she was dead?'

'We didn't. Who's Todd?'

'Some Londoner. Moved here last year with Kat. I don't know his surname, but he's mental. You think I've got a temper? He broke Ali the Bampot's arm last week with his bare hands. Poor bastard hadn't even done anything. That was just to show him in advance what would happen if he didn't pay for his gear.'

'So this Todd's pimping and dealing? What else?'

Mikey shrugged. 'Money lending, maybe. I don't know. Honest; I don't want to know.'

'Where can we find him?'

'Haven't a clue. Drives a big dark motor sometimes. Often has a boy with him. No idea who that is – his son, maybe.'

'Were you with Danielle Smith yesterday?'

He shook his head. 'I thought about it. She's gorgeous, but she doesn't have Kat's experience, and the two of them together – well, you'd need a bank loan. She was there. I didn't see her, but I heard her in the bathroom; I think she was having a shower when the buzzer went, so Kat had to answer the door. Pissed off, Kat was too. Threw me out before I could get all my clothes on.' He smiled and shook his head. 'Mental bitch. And she's not dead.' He frowned. 'But I will be, if Todd finds out I'm here. Fuck's sake. What are you lot on? Who was killed?'

Joe and DI Black stared at him until he got it.

'Man, youse are kidding me? That wee girl? What sick fucker would do that?'

Chapter 20

Light streamed in the big window, illuminating Kat as she huddled in the corner of the sofa in a towelling dressing-gown. Her hair was damp and she looked haggard without make-up. She was clutching her phone. When Todd reached for it, she looked as if she might be thinking of saying no. Cheeky whore. He held his hand out. 'I'll have that, love. Cheers. You did well. I like the idea of feeding Mikey Morrison to his balls.' He was laughing as he took the phone from her. He switched it off and took out the sim card. 'Your hands are shaking. What's up?'

Kat shook her head and pulled her dressing gown tight. 'I cold.'

'You cold? I put heating on. You soon warm up.'

Her eyes narrowed. 'You take piss?'

He laughed. It was loud and it made her jump. 'Relax, honey. I not take piss.'

Kat wasn't going to relax, and that was just the way he liked it.

'Why you tell me hide here?'

'Because the police are onto you.'

'I do nothing.'

'You've been running a brothel. That's illegal and you could go to prison, thanks to that stupid little cow, Danielle.'

'Where is Danni?'

He shrugged. 'Dunno. Last time I saw her, she was with Ryan MacRae. They were getting to know each other.' He winked. 'Know what I mean?'

She didn't. 'Why she not phone me? Why she not ask for her things? Why we have to leave the flat?'

He leaned towards her and she shrank back into the sofa. 'Enough with the questions, all right? I'm looking out for you. I've always looked out for you. If it wasn't for me, you'd still be in that skanky whorehouse in London, making videos and God knows what else. You should show more gratitude, more respect.'

'Okay. You want fuck?'

'I take it you mean, do I want to fuck?'

'Two fucks? Okay. Here?'

He laughed and shook his head. 'Nah. You're all right.' Tart. As if he was going to shag her after Mikey Morrison and God knows how many others.

She glared at him. 'What you want?'

'I'm trying to help you.'

'I go home.'

'You said. A million times. And I told you, I'll take you to Edinburgh or Glasgow in a day or two.'

'I fly Glasgow to Vilnius, Monday.' She leaned towards him, her dressing gown gaping at the neck. 'You take me tomorrow. I need phone or laptop. I must book flight.'

'I'll do it. Give me your passport.'

He could see how torn she was. Give him her passport and get home, maybe. Or refuse to give it to him, and have no chance whatsoever of ever getting home. Mmm. Not much of a choice. He smiled as she took her passport from the pocket of her dressing gown and handed it to him.

*

No, Mikey Morrison was not a suspect. Yes, DI Black was certain of it. You'd have to have been there to understand, he told Jackson. Fat chance of that happening, Jackson thought; as if Brian Black would let him in on the real action in a major enquiry. That pleasure was always reserved for Galbraith. Not that Jackson usually cared. Staying in the background suited him fine. Only another three years and he'd be out of here, with a good pension and freedom to do the things that really mattered to him. But Danielle had really mattered to him, and he'd do anything to bring her killer to justice. Mikey Morrison was a skanky low-life. Jackson had almost got him over those DVDs, but he'd wriggled out of it, as he always did, leaving Jackson looking stupid. The bugger had been in the flat shortly before Danielle was killed. Just 'cos he said he wasn't with her, didn't mean anything. He was a liar; always had been. Galbraith didn't know Morrison the way Jackson did. He and Black could be mistaken.

'I'm telling you, Jackson, we're not mistaken.' DI Black looked down at a document on his desk. 'Shut the door on your way out.'

'There's something else...Sir.'

Brian Black always looked at Jackson as if he was simple, but when he heard what Jackson had to say, he looked as if he might be about to have a heart attack. Veins were bulging in his neck, as he leaned across the desk. 'Don't be such a fucking twat, Jackson.'

Jackson shrugged and leaned back in the chair. 'Whatever. I've heard it from a few sources.'

'Galbraith and Sharon MacRae? Having it off? What a load of shit. Have you seen Carla MacKenzie?'

Seen her? He'd tried his hand before she started going with Galbraith. She'd been amused but not unkind. Next thing he knew, she was going with Golden Balls. The perfect couple. They'd no doubt marry and have 2.4 children, a nice house, and a good social life. All the things he'd never have.

He nodded. 'So what? They don't even live together. What's to stop him playing around?'

'With Sharon MacRae? Do one, Jackson. You're talking shite.'

Jackson did one, smirking as he pulled the door shut. Even though Black knew it was a load of crap, he'd still have to investigate.

*

The house was surrounded by trees on three sides, the front close to the single-track road. It looked like a fine house, but it gave Sharon the creeps. Was it because it was isolated, with no other houses in sight? She wasn't sure. They'd been to Culloden and Nairn, then several properties in Inverness. They were all tenanted, so Sharon had waited in the car. When she wasn't worrying about Ryan, she was considering asking Christopher if she could rent a property from him. Maybe she'd still get Housing Benefit, if she didn't let on she was in a relationship with her landlord. But this house outside Evanton was the only empty property he had, and there was no way she would live in it.

They went upstairs first. The three large bedrooms were clean and tidy. There was a fourth door on the landing. 'Is that the loo? Can I use it?'

'Of course you can.'

As she heard his footsteps go down the stairs, she looked around the bathroom. Manky or what? She wasn't sitting on that. And the sink was no better. She'd wait.

In the kitchen, Christopher was frowning. 'I think I'm going senile. The house has been empty for two months. I did the exit check when the last tenant left, and it was spotless. I'm sure of it, but the kitchen's a mess now. There's rubbish in the bins and dirty dishes in the sink. I've got someone coming to see it next week. I'll have to have it cleaned.'

'Bathroom's manky too. You've just got too many properties. You're probably mixing them up.'

'I've got the paperwork at home. I'll check later.'

Sharon shivered again as Christopher locked the door. He held the car door open for her. 'Do you like it? I considered living here myself, before I viewed the house at Ness Castle.'

Sharon hesitated. 'It's nice, but…you made the right choice.'

'Have we got time for a walk? I want to show you something.'

She checked her phone. 'Aye, an hour until I have to pick Liam up.'

'This won't take long.'

Christopher turned right, and Sharon saw a sign for Black Rock Gorge – 500m. 'Is that where we're going? Sounds creepy.'

'Dead creepy. The ideal place to dispose of a nagging wife.'

'Anything you want to tell me?'

It was just a wee wooden bridge, the kind that might cross a stream or a narrow river. There was no warning of what lay below, other than the distant sound of gushing water. Sharon looked over the side and felt her stomach rising. The narrow gorge was dark and deep, the rugged walls sloping inwards towards the bottom, so that only a fast-flowing sliver of water could be seen forcing its way through the broken cleft. The gorge was surrounded by trees and branches of all shapes and sizes. They stretched from side to side, branches meeting and mingling in the middle. The walls were coated in mosses and ferns, but the greenery did nothing to soften the impact. It was terrifying and fascinating. Sharon shivered and turned to the other side. It was much the same. As she gazed downwards, there was a whisper from behind. 'Can you hear her?'

She thumped Christopher's arm. 'I thought you'd gone for a pee.'

'I did. You've been standing there for ages. I was certain you could hear her.'

'Who?'

'A noblewoman, the Lady of Balconie. Lured into the gorge by the devil, she's held in a cave at the bottom, guarded by two hounds. Her cries are still heard to this day.'

'You'll be crying in a minute, creeping up on me. I don't think I like this.' She peered downwards again. 'But I can't stop looking. Imagine falling in there.' She shuddered.

'They filmed part of a Harry Potter movie here. There's another bridge, just along a bit. You get an even better view from there.'

Sharon shivered. 'I'll give it a miss.'

'I'll keep you safe.' He put his arms round her and kissed her. They were standing in the centre of the bridge, in a shaft of sunlight, yet Sharon didn't know when she had last felt so cold.

He was holding the car door open for her when his phone rang. He looked at the screen. 'Sorry, love; I'd better take this.'

He closed her door before he answered, and she felt that familiar dread. Must be another woman. She saw him smile, and a wee shard of envy stabbed her in the heart. No matter how good he was to her, he was still a bloke. And then she watched the smile disappear. He put his hand up to his head, frowning as the colour drained from his face. He didn't speak for long. When he got into the car, Sharon asked him what was wrong. He stared ahead as if she hadn't spoken. Eventually, he shook his head. 'I'm sorry.' His voice was a little shaky. 'That was my sister, Isobel. Mother's had a heart attack.'

'Is she – ?'

'She's in hospital. I'll have to see if I can get a flight to London in the morning.'

'Of course.'

He took her hand. 'Sharon, will you come with me?'

Chapter 21

Sharon and Gillian eyed each other like two cats in an alley. 'Where does someone like you meet someone like him?' Gillian nodded at Christopher's car. 'You on the game?'

Sharon felt her temper rising. She quashed it. Wasn't worth it. 'Nah. Ten years of your brother was enough to put me off men and sex for a good long time.'

'Put you off? So all those guys after Peter died, the ones that the Social deemed unfit to be around your kids, who, let me remind you, were with me more than you – what was that all about?'

'That, Gillian, was all about the drugs, the shit your brother got me and thousands of others hooked on. It had nothing to do with sex. I was raped so often by your brother, I couldn't let any guy touch me. Until him.' She turned and pointed at Christopher. He wasn't looking; he was staring ahead. 'So don't try and make me and him into something dirty just to suit your warped fantasies.'

A window creaked shut in the house next door.

Gillian shook her head. 'Another floor show for the neighbours. Well done. They'll have plenty to keep them talking. Police were at my door today, looking for Ryan. You can hang out with all the rich guys you want, but it doesn't change what you are. See if you hadn't been so caught up with your fancy man, you might have noticed what was going on with Ryan. Typical; whatever you want has always come first, before those boys.'

All Sharon's fight was gone. Gillian was right.

'Hi Mam.' Liam darted out from behind his aunt and hugged Sharon. He smiled up at her. 'Are you not coming in?'

'No, son; listen, I have to go away for a couple of days. It's Christopher's mum. She's not well.' She looked at Gillian. 'I was wondering if you could stay with Gillian for a couple of nights.' Gillian shook her head, and Sharon couldn't blame her. It should have been the first thing she asked, instead of rising to the bait.

Liam shrugged. 'Okay.' He looked up at Gillian. 'We can go and see that film.'

'Film?'

'Yes, silly. The Jurassic one. You said you were going to ask

Mam if I could stay with you tonight or tomorrow night and we'd go. Now we can.'

Gillian was stumped. She smiled at Liam. 'Why don't you run upstairs and waken Mick? Do it gently, mind. Tell him he has to get up for work.' She watched Liam run upstairs, then she turned back to Sharon, her face like thunder.

Sharon put her hands up. 'Gillian, I know I'm taking liberties, but his mother's ill and he says he needs me. I'll only be away a day or two. I can get back quickly if Ryan turns up. Gillian, please promise me you'll let me know if he comes back, or if he phones you.'

Gillian rolled her eyes, sighed and nodded. And nearly passed out when Sharon hugged her.

*

As Joe turned into Church Street, he saw a pile of dirty bedding. It was hard to tell if there was anyone there, then he saw Ali's dark head. The plaster cast hadn't softened people's hearts; there were only three pennies in the grubby Costa cup that supported a tattered cardboard sign - *Hungrie and Howmless.*

Ali winked a glazed eye at Joe. 'Sergeant, what can I do for you?'

'Maybe we could go somewhere for a cup of tea?'

'I'd like nothing better, but really?' He pushed the blanket away, revealing filthy jeans and a torn jumper. 'I'm not quite dressed for the occasion.'

'I'll get you a coffee or tea when we've chatted. Something to eat?'

Ali's face lit up. 'Sound. You're a gentleman. Is it about that wee toe rag with the missing fingers? I didn't mean to hit him with the stookie, but the bugger was trying to steal my takings.'

Joe shook his head. 'No, Ali. It is to do with the stookie, though. I'm going to ask you again; how did you get it?'

'I don't like talking about it, Sergeant. There's not that many evil people about, but…' He shivered.

Joe crouched down beside him. 'Is his name Todd?'

Ali's eyes were wide as he nodded.

'We're trying to find him before he hurts anyone else. Can you help?'

Ali looked around. 'He could be anywhere. Watching. Waiting

to get me again.'

'I think you might be the least of his worries right now. I'm not looking for you to press charges against him, unless you want to. I'm just trying to find out his surname, where he lives and where we might find him. Before he hurts someone else.'

Ali was staring into space, frowning. 'I don't know any of that, but...there is something...' He shook his head. 'Oh, shit.'

'What is it, Ali?'

'I'm worried he did for that wee lassie.'

'Sally? The one you've been asking about?'

'Aye. I think it was him she was with that night, the last time I saw her. Him and another man; a bloke with a walking stick. They didn't see me, but I heard her make them an offer. Todd shouted at her. All the names under the sun. Slut. Skank. Tramp. She was just a wee lassie.' There were tears in his eyes. He wiped them away and sniffed. 'Worthless shit. That's what he called her. Worthless shit? How could he call anyone that?'

'Ali, we need to find him. What about the guy with the stick? Had you seen him before?'

Ali shook his head. 'I didn't see his face. If I tell you someone who might know where Todd lives, and a bit more about that girl, you won't say you heard it from me, will you?'

The deal was struck, and sealed with two bacon rolls, a large coffee and a tenner.

*

Davie Dobbs was a local lowlife with a lucky streak and a permanent smirk that Joe ached to wipe off, with steel wool. There was no way he was going to see Dobbs on his own, so he went back to the station for Roberts.

'Sound, Sarge.' Roberts caressed the muscles of his lower back and stretched his legs. 'This is mind-numbing stuff, going through these boxes. There's not a thing of interest here. Not even a letter of complaint from a constituent. Hundreds of letters of thanks. The man's a saint. Will we take the e-fit?'

Roberts was trained to use the computer programme to produce an impression of a suspect. He'd worked with Mikey Morrison on the picture of Todd, but he didn't have a lot to go on. The essence of Morrison's description had been 'he's a great big bald fucker in his thirties'. There were strict guidelines to ensure that the programme operator did not influence the witness in any way. Roberts had done his best, but it wasn't great. Joe shrugged. 'Might as well. It's all we've got.'

In the drive of Dobbs's semi in Scorguie, there was a blue convertible Audi with a personalised number plate. Roberts whistled. 'We're in the wrong job.'

Davie Dobbs didn't disappoint Joe. The arrogant grin, the tossing of his long hair, the contempt in his cunning eyes. He knew lots of people. Didn't think he knew a Todd, though. When he saw the e-fit, he almost doubled up with laughter. 'Saw someone like that on TV. Shrek, I think his name was. No, officers, I definitely don't know him.'

Joe bristled. 'Heard you have a lock-up, Davie. Bruce Gardens, isn't it?'

Dobbs's smile was gone. 'That's shite.'

Joe smiled. 'I guess we better get off. Where to next, DC Roberts?'

'Eh…Bruce Gardens, I think, Sarge.'

'Excellent. Call in back up, will you?'

Roberts took his phone out of his pocket.

Dobbs reached for the picture. 'Can I see that again?' He scratched his head and played for time. 'Mmm. Todd, you say?'

'Uh huh.'

'He might live down Millburn Road way.'

Joe nodded. 'Carlton Terrace?'

Dobbs smiled and pushed his hair back from his face. 'Aye, that's the place. The terraced flats. Don't know the number.'

'You're behind the times; he moved from there months ago. We'll be off then.'

'Moved from there? Is that right? I didn't know that.' There was sweat on Davie Dobbs's brow. 'Eh…there's another guy; a Londoner. James something? They call him Jimmy Spaz. Big scar down his face. Stays in the luxury flats with the balconies up at Castle Heather. I've never been there, but I've heard.' He wiped his brow with his sleeve. 'You won't mention my name, will you?'

'That depends. What's Todd's surname?'

'I have no idea. Never heard him called anything other than

Todd.'

'What can you tell us about a homeless girl called Sally? She went missing from the town after offering Todd some services.'

Joe could almost feel the nausea radiating from Dobbs. 'Oh, fuck.' He shook his head. 'I swear I don't know anything for certain. There was talk. He was boasting she wouldn't be offering herself to anyone again. No one's seen her since.'

'Talk? Who was talking?'

He shrugged. 'Just people in the pub. I can't even remember now. He's not someone you want to be caught talking about.'

'And the girl? Where was she staying?'

He shook his head. 'I don't know. She could have been sleeping rough, or in one of the homeless hostels in the town centre; there's plenty of them to choose from. I know you think I'm scum, but I have standards, and mixing with the homeless isn't really my thing. I'm not sure I even saw this girl. Just heard about her.'

'Do you know of anyone with a walking stick that hangs about with Todd?'

'Definitely not.'

Joe gave him a card. 'If you hear or remember anything else, call me.'

Chapter 22

Castlefield Apartments consisted of three blocks of glass-fronted luxury flats built on a north-facing slope that had once been part of Castle Heather Farm. There wasn't much farm land left in the area, with new housing schemes extending the city ever outwards. 'Must be some view from upstairs,' Roberts said. 'Right across to the Black Isle.'

Joe nodded and pulled away from the flats. The last thing they needed was Todd or Jimmy Spaz getting wind of them before they'd discovered the right flat and got a warrant and an armed response unit. Was Todd's pal the Jimmy that Katya Birze had mentioned the day Tina Lewis and Joe went to the flat on Carlton Terrace?

It was going to take a while to get mobile phone records to show where Katya Birze had phoned Mikey from, but they had her previous address in London. The Met were looking into that. Her photo was about to be circulated to the press, and there was a flag on her passport. In the meantime, Joe wondered if she too was in danger.

At the station, Joe asked Roberts to see what he could find out about the occupants of Castlefield Apartments. 'I'll be back shortly; I've just remembered something.'

He had just remembered he had a girlfriend in hospital, possibly with a life-threatening condition, and he hadn't texted, called or visited her today. He hadn't even looked at his phone. It was on silent in his pocket. There were three texts from Carla and two missed calls. One of the texts said she might be getting home tomorrow. A bit late to be calling her now, but he tried anyway. Her phone was off. He left a grovelling message and sent her a text saying he could take her home tomorrow, of course he could.

There were two texts from Lucy asking if he had time to call round before he went home. He replied and told her he'd have to work late, but he'd see her soon. Well, soonish. He was making his way back to see how Roberts was getting on, when DI Black asked him into his office. He told Joe to sit down. 'Awaiting a call.

Could be interesting.'

The call came and DI Black managed to disconnect the caller twice. Joe took over. It was a DCI from Manchester. The prints on the back door handles of Sutherland's car, and on the envelope and photo delivered to Roz Sutherland matched those found at the scene of a murder in Manchester in 2008.

'Nancy Connor,' the Mancunian DCI said. 'Fifty year old prostitute in Cheetham Hill. A heroin addict, she was bipolar. Mad as a box of snakes, by all accounts. She was found in an alley close to her flat, strangled with a leather belt. His fingerprints were all over it.'

'Any leads?' DI Black asked. 'Did you have a suspect?'

'Big bald bloke in his early thirties had been asking questions about her. He'd paid two toms for information about her earlier that week. He wasn't local. London, maybe. We got nowhere. I'll get the file copied to you, and we can discuss it further.'

Fifteen minutes later, Joe found Roberts on the phone. He was grovelling. Must be Jill. A veterinary nurse, he'd met her when they were working on the Moira Jacobs case last year. She looked like butter wouldn't melt, but it sounded like she was giving him hell.

'Okay. Yeah. Okay. Bye.' He cut the call, his face red. 'Sorry Sarge. I thought I better take the call. Forgot to let her know I wouldn't be round tonight. She's not happy.'

Joe tried to smile, but nothing came.

'What's wrong, Sarge?'

He shook his head. 'Nothing. There's been a development, actually.' He told Roberts about the murder of Nancy Connor.

'So why are you looking so miserable?'

'Just a bit tired. You seen Jackson?'

'No. He probably sloped off hours ago. In his kip, lazy bugger. What do you want with him, Sarge?'

'I don't. I'd be more than happy if I never set eyes on him again, but see if he pushes it tomorrow, I might just have to kill him.'

*

Ryan's body felt like it was made of stone. Maybe he was so heavy, he'd sink the boat. Might not be a bad thing. Slip into the water, into unconsciousness, oblivion. What else was there for him? The police would have the bus and train stations covered. He peeped out from under the tarpaulin. It was almost dark. He couldn't stay here. He'd go mad.

He slipped from the boat, his feet light on the walkway so he wouldn't alert anyone. Shit. The gate was locked with a dirty great padlock, and there was no way he could get over the high fence with three rows of barbed wire at the top. Idiot. Of course it would be locked at night to keep people like him out. He should have sneaked off the boat earlier, but there was too much activity going on. There was no way he was going back in that boat. Maybe he could find one with more facilities, a comfy bunk and some food. He turned to go and look, and then he heard the rattle of a chain.

The guy on the other side of the fence was trying to get the key in the padlock, with no luck. Pink jumper, polo shirt, cream chinos and soft black deck shoes. Definitely a yachtie. He peered through the fence at Ryan. 'Evening.' The smell of booze nearly knocked Ryan over.

'Good evening.' Ryan used the posh voice he kept for taking the piss out of his teachers. 'Have you had a good night?'

'Excellent. Too good.' He winked. 'You wouldn't have a torch, would you?'

Ryan used the torch on his phone to light up the padlock. It took a while, but at last the guy opened it.

Ryan smiled. 'Excellent. Don't worry; I'll lock it behind you. Take care getting on your boat.'

'Cheers, mate. Have a good one.'

Ryan left it open; he might be back. He crossed the main road, and made his way along the canal bank. Up the slope, down the steps, and along the path at the back of his pal's house. Despite the light in Sean's bedroom, it took several handfuls of small stones to alert him. He came to the window, headphones round his neck. 'Ryan? Is that you? Police were here looking for you.'

'Tell the world about it, why don't you? You going to let me in?'

Sean held out his hand. 'Respect, man. Pigs everywhere. Put it there.'

'Piss off.' Ryan pushed past Sean into the kitchen. It was the usual stinking mess. 'I need water, something to eat. Where's your mother?'

'Who knows? Haven't seen her for a couple of days. Probably with that Pole she's been seeing. Junkie bastard. Anyway, enough about my mother. What you been up to? Is it something to do with that bald guy that picks you up from school? I didn't mention him to the pigs. Who is he?'

'The less you know the better. Food? Water? Then I'll be on my way.'

'Plenty water.' Sean filled a pint glass. Ryan held it up to the light, studying the faint remnants of Sean's mother's lipstick. 'Too much to ask for a clean glass?'

'You're on the run. Can't expect silver service. Turn it round, mate; that side's clean. Now, food.'

'Is that a lip and eye pie?' Ryan poked the cold pie with his fork. 'And what the hell's that?' Slices of something red and slimy, swimming in a pink juice.

'Beetroot. Can't beat it – get it? Can't beet it? Never mind. It's the dog's bollocks, that – meat pie and beetroot. Why d'you call it lip and eye pie?'

Ryan smiled. 'Just something my auntie's man says. He works in a bakery. Turned vegetarian after seeing what they put in these pies.'

The tanginess of the beetroot went well with the pie. Ryan washed it down with a second pint of water.

'Jeez, you're thirsty. Where you been hiding?'

'If I tell you, I'll have to kill you.'

There was a hint of fear in Sean's eyes. How much had the police told him?

'Sorry, mate. I'm joking. I was down the canal in an old boat. Listen, it is that bald bastard that's got me into trouble, but you're better not knowing the details. Any chance I could use your laptop before I get off?'

While Sean played the PlayStation, Ryan fired up the laptop. He didn't dare check his email or Facebook, just googled his name. Shit; he was on the BBC news website. Police were worried about a missing child in Inverness. Aw, not that photo. First time his mother had the money to pay for a school photo, so he'd ruined it. Dark greasy hair and a scowling, dour, spotty face. A frightening face; he'd never seen anyone look guiltier. At least they hadn't linked him to the next story – two people wanted in connection with two murders in Inverness. A woman, Katya Birze, the dark haired woman that was arguing with Danielle. Must be the Kat that Todd often spoke to on the phone. There was no photo of Todd, and no name. Just a description – bald, well-built, about six foot, in his late thirties. And extremely dangerous. And below it, a photo of Danielle in her school uniform. So young and fresh-faced. And beautiful. Ryan wanted to cry.

Ryan hadn't expected to ever laugh again, but when he saw himself in Sean's bathroom mirror with his hair bleached almost white, and his eyebrows as dark as coal, he collapsed into a fit of giggles. Sean poked the back of Ryan's head. 'Shit, there's a big dark patch at the back. What a mess. I think you can well and truly kiss Natasha Scott goodbye now.'

Ryan nodded. 'Probably. Keep your hands off her, though. I might be back…well, doubt it, but you never know. It'll get me on a bus to Glasgow. Shame I can't grow a beard overnight.'

'You wish.' Sean stroked the dark shadow on his own chin.

'Mate, would you go and buy the ticket tomorrow morning at the station? I can just slip on the bus at the last minute. Less likely to be seen that way.'

Sean shrugged. 'Aye. Whatever. You going to stay here tonight?'

Ryan hadn't intended to, but he suddenly felt exhausted, and he had no better plan. 'Might as well.'

'Sound. You have my bed; I'll sleep in my mother's room. Just hope the old cow and her Pole don't decide to come home tonight. I'm going to snib the doors, just in case.'

While Sean was downstairs, Ryan checked his phone. Three texts from his mother, and two calls. In the last text, she mentioned London and Christopher's sick mum. He swithered before replying. Should he tell her Christopher was involved with Todd? Did he even believe Todd? He wasn't sure. Christopher had been good for his mother. Sorted her out. Expensive presents, private dentistry, anything she wanted. Helped her reduce her methadone. Stopped her smoking. No more temper tantrums, vodka binges or drugs. Why burst her bubble now? He sent a text, then he switched off the phone.

Chapter 23

Christopher had been quiet all evening. Sharon understood. He was worried about his mum, and his leg was playing up. Not that he'd said anything. Just kept rubbing it, when he thought she wasn't looking. She checked her phone again. Nothing from Ryan. Christopher took her hand. 'No word?'

She shook her head.

'What are we like?' He stroked her face. 'It'll get better, I promise. Will we go up?'

His progress on the stairs was slow. He was only half way up when he stopped. He leaned against the wall and turned. 'Sorry, honey. This might take a bit of time. You go up. I'll get there.'

His face was so pale. 'Can I get you something? Your stick? Pain killers? A drink?'

'Thank you, but no.' He tried to smile. 'It'll pass.'

'What about a bath?'

He nodded. 'Thanks, love. That might help.'

Christopher came into the bathroom in his dressing gown. He thanked Sharon, and hugged her. She smiled. 'Go on; it'll get cold. Shout me if you need a hand to get in. You know me; always keen to help you get your leg over.'

They both laughed. She pulled away, but he didn't let her go. 'Will you come in with me?'

'Yeah. Will I put the light off?'

He shook his head.

It took all Sharon's self-control not to gasp when he took his dressing gown off. It looked like the muscle of his upper right leg had been mangled and twisted, deforming the shape of the leg. There was a great hollow in his inner thigh, where the skin sagged and puckered. The front of his leg was like a jigsaw, with scars from the knee to the hip. Some were criss-crossed, and others were long and straight and red.

He looked embarrassed, apologetic, as if he was worried the state of his leg might offend her. It was all she could do not to cry, as she turned away to take her clothes off. When she turned round, he was in the huge roll-top bath. He lay stretched out and Sharon knelt between his legs, covered her hands in soap, and massaged his leg. He lay with his eyes closed and she saw his body relax as the pain eased.

'Better?'

He nodded. 'Thank you.'

The taps were in the middle of the bath, so they lay facing each other, their bodies side by side. Christopher's eyes were still closed, and it felt safe for Sharon to ask. 'How? Will you tell me?' She could hear the soft whirring noise of the fan on the roof. Christopher was staring over her head, as if he could see something horrible. He looked as if he might cry. 'You don't have to. I shouldn't have asked.'

He nodded. 'I should have told you ages ago. I'm sorry; I'm not very good at relationships. The last one was nine years and eleven months ago.'

That hurt. Fool. Of course there had been others. He just hadn't mentioned them. She tried to keep her voice steady. 'She must have been special, if you're still counting.'

He shook his head. 'Not really. It's not about her. It was the night before the…the accident. If we hadn't split up that night, I wouldn't have moved out. I wouldn't have been on that train the next morning.'

'You were in a train accident? In London?'

He nodded.

She did a calculation in her head. 'July 2005?'

'Yes.'

As the memories of that day flooded her, she felt sick. It wasn't just the television images of the London bombings. It was where she was at the time. A hospital bed after another 'fall', courtesy of Peter. Another miscarriage, the third in less than two years. She'd seen the news and she'd turned her face to the wall. Her life was so full of misery, there was no room for the misery of others.

She wiped tears from her eyes. 'It must have been awful. All those people that died.'

'Fifty two. And countless lost limbs and horrific injuries. I was fortunate, Sharon. I didn't appreciate it for the first few years, with more operations than I can count, and indescribable pain. You wouldn't think so to look at it, but a lot of time and money went into making my leg this good. My parents and I weren't always close, but they did everything they could for me, and I'll never be able to repay them. I wasn't easy to be around, and I regret so much. Especially the way I was to my father. Too late now to do anything about that, but I can still be there for my mother.' He sat up and took her hand. 'It's so long since I've been home; I didn't want to go alone, but it was selfish of me to ask you, with Ryan missing. I'd understand if you changed your mind.'

Sharon had changed her mind several times; she just hadn't told him. She might have looked like she was reading that magazine earlier, but what she was really doing was dithering back and fore between her responsibilities to her man and to her boy. She had to put Ryan first, there was no doubt about that. But he wasn't here, and she could sit around for days waiting for him. She owed Christopher. He'd do the same for her. But what if...

'No need to thank me. But you know I'll have to come straight back if Ryan shows up, or if he needs me?'

'Of course, love; I wouldn't expect anything else.'

There it was again. That word. Sharon had never loved anyone but her boys. Peter had known it. No matter how often he used physical or mental force to make her say those three words, they both knew she didn't mean it. She didn't feel it. She never would. And as for feeling loved, the only time she'd ever felt that was for the short time she'd been with Alison and Mark, and even then she hadn't been sure. They were paid to be good to her. That didn't make it love.

But the way Christopher was looking at her now, his eyes, his smile. The way her heart and her stomach were melting. The way she felt when she looked at his leg. It felt a lot like she imagined love should feel.

Later, she lay in the dark and waited for her heart and her stomach to calm down. She told herself not to be stupid. She was temporary; she had to be. No matter how good he was to her, he wasn't going to fall in love with her. It just didn't happen like that. Beside her, Christopher's breathing settled into sleep. She checked her phone, one last time. There was a text from Ryan.

*

Christopher wasn't sleeping. Just focussing on his breathing, rather than the pain and the memories. And the worry that his mother might die before he got there. He should have gone home before now. His mother had asked him often enough and his excuse was always the same; his leg was playing up, and he didn't feel up to the journey. And every time, she accepted it, though she probably knew it was only an hour and a half in the plane.

His sister hadn't been so understanding. He was a selfish pig, she told him regularly. And he was. But London had taken on the proportions of a monster in his head. The accident and the pain, the shame of all he'd done and been since. It had been with him constantly, growing and growing, until he couldn't breathe, and he had to leave. He'd come to the Highlands just over a year ago on Todd's recommendation, and every new day felt like a reprieve.

At the thought of his friend, he remembered he hadn't checked his email. His phone was beside the bed, but he couldn't face it. And he wasn't going downstairs. As he turned over and moulded his body against Sharon's, he felt a sense of relief and release. Maybe it was time to let go, to move on.

*

Looked like all was not rosy in paradise. Chris had his head in a book all evening, and she was reading a gossip magazine. They'd seemed close enough, but Chris was looking really down. Good.

Speaking of down, if Chris didn't come down those fucking stairs soon, bad leg or not, and reply to his email, there was going to be trouble. This was not the deal. He wasn't having it. Chris had been slipping for a while now. No respect, no gratitude. No fucking way.

Todd thumped the table, toppling his mug of lukewarm coffee. It missed the laptop, spilling across his thighs. As the coffee soaked into his jeans, it took all the self-control he had not to hurl the laptop at the window. No fucking email. Someone was going to pay for this. That skank, Sharon MacRae. And his so-called mate.

A few taps on the keyboard and he saw that Ryan was still

missing. And he and Kat were the top headline on the Scottish news. No picture of him. No name. Good picture of Kat. And look. Wee Danielle in her school uniform. Bless.

He looked at the time again. Bastard. He'd go for a shower and hope, for everyone's sake, there was an email waiting for him when he came out.

*

Katya heard the sound of the shower in Todd's en-suite. She waited a bit, then she crept out of her room. She checked the living room first. No sign of her phone or her passport. She pushed open his bedroom door. He always took ages in the shower, so she must have a bit of time. She'd hoped to see his clothes lying on the floor or the bed, with her things in his pocket, but there was nothing. He must have taken them off in the shower room. She checked the drawers and under his pillow. Nothing.

Maybe she'd have time to log in to her email. She could contact someone, ask them to come and get her. But who? She only knew Todd, Danielle and her clients. There were plenty clients that would like to hear from her, but none that she wanted to contact. And what could she do without her passport?

The shower was still running. She kept the living room door open, so she'd hear when it stopped. She switched on the laptop, her heart racing. It only took seconds to open at the last page he'd been looking at.

She took a step back. What? Why was her picture on here? And Danni? Her English wasn't great, but she knew it was a news website. And she knew what murder meant.

Katya pulled her jacket on as she ran down the road. She could hear the coins jingling in the pocket of her jeans. She'd found them in a dish in Todd's room. She didn't know where she was and she didn't know where she was going. Anywhere away from him. She prayed as she ran. Please please please don't let him look into the bedroom. And if he does, make him think the two pillows she'd shoved under the quilt were her. And may God and the priest and her mama forgive her for turning her back on them.

Old Edinburgh Road. She knew what this Edinburgh was, but why was it here? There was a young couple walking on the other side of the road. She could stop them, but what would she say? If she asked for the police, she would go to prison.

She reached a junction. Balloan Road. A phone box; the first she'd seen. Even as she ran towards it, she had no idea who she would phone. Inside, she breathed in the stench of urine and scrabbled for the coins in her pocket. A number came to her. She hadn't consciously remembered it. Indeed, she had probably hoped she'd never have to use it again. Now, it seemed like her only hope.

Chapter 24

The breathing exercises didn't work. Christopher felt hot and uncomfortable, and his head wouldn't stop. Sharon had been sleeping for a while. How he envied her. He turned onto his back and stared at the ceiling. Not that he could see much. One of the things that had attracted him to Ness Castle was the privacy and the lack of street lights. The trees surrounding his house ensured he couldn't see any of his neighbours. Although it wasn't far to the nearest housing estate, it felt like the countryside.

He thought of Todd. Was he sitting waiting for an email? He'd not be pleased, but he was sick of thinking of Todd's feelings. There was no point lying here awake; he might as well get up and have some tea. As he reached for his dressing gown, he saw his phone flashing. At least he'd remembered to put it on silent. Was it Todd? It wasn't. Though the number wasn't stored on his phone, he knew it. They hadn't spoken in a long time. The deal was there would be no more contact. He was free. He'd really wanted to keep it that way.

*

There had been no surprises in the interim report of Danielle Smith's post mortem. Her body temperature confirmed what they already knew; she'd died not long before her body was found. The cause of death was manual strangulation, the skin of her neck showing typical contusions and abrasions left by her assailant's fingers and nails. Beneath the skin, there was massive bleeding in the muscles, and damage to the tiny bones in the front of the throat. Her assailant had faced her as he killed her, using much more force than was needed. There was recent genital bruising consistent with rape, although her occupation made it difficult to be conclusive. No semen. There were traces of skin under her nails, and a badly sprained right ankle. Her clothes and other samples had been sent for analysis.

'Sarge,' Roberts said. 'The sprained ankle is interesting. Remember SOCO found a hair clasp and signs of a possible struggle further round in the lane?'

Joe nodded. 'She ran from him or them, and fell.'

It had rained the night before Danielle died, leaving the ground soft and ideal for capturing shoe marks and other signs. There were two areas identified by SOCO that suggested a struggle may have taken place. One of them was further along the lane, with marks that looked to match Danielle's sandals, and larger footmarks. The same larger marks and another set of smaller ones were found in the flat area above the slope where Danielle's body was found.

As Joe drove home, he wondered. Two struggles. Two men and Danielle. Todd and Ryan MacRae? Had Ryan helped Todd to throw the body down the slope after they were done with her?

*

When Sharon woke, Christopher was gone. Must be his leg. She put the light on. It was four o'clock. Not long until they had to be up. As she stretched to get her phone, she noticed the bottom drawer on the bed-side table on her side was slightly open and there was something sticking out. Looked like a photo.

She pulled it out and her stomach lurched. Who was she, this gorgeous bird in expensive underwear? Was she the one from nine years and eleven months ago? It didn't look like an old photo. There were more. They weren't porn shots; everything was covered up, just. Maybe porn would have troubled Sharon less.

She heard the front door open and close. She put the pictures back, the corner of the first one sticking out of the drawer, then she switched the light off. She heard him flush the toilet downstairs before he came up. He didn't come into the room. Sharon got out of bed and crept to the door. She could hear him talking, but she couldn't make out the words. When the talking stopped, she went back to bed.

Christopher joined her, and his skin felt cold. She didn't turn. 'Where have you been?'

He was silent for ages. 'I...I went for a drive.'

'You what?'

'A drive.' His voice sounded strange. 'Sometimes I have to do that, if I can't sleep.'

'Was it your leg?'

'Yeah.'

She knew he was lying. He wouldn't choose to drive if his leg was sore. She didn't ask who he'd been speaking to, though she would have loved to know. 'Can I get you anything?'

He put his hand on her arm. 'No. Thank you. I took some tablets. Should help me get a bit of sleep now.'

Lucky him.

Chapter 25

Ryan drifted in and out of troubled sleep until the alarm on his phone went off. Sean was snoring next door. Ryan was supposed to wake his friend and get the plan in motion. He listened for a while, then he decided. What was the point in involving Sean? Might end up getting him into trouble too. He'd do this by himself. Almost.

He looked in the mirror and laughed. His mother wouldn't recognise him with this hair and these clothes: skinny jeans, a flowery shirt, and a rainbow-striped back pack. There were bruises on his throat; they'd attract attention. He rummaged in Sean's bottom drawer and found a scarf. A great, long maroon thing; it didn't exactly go with the image, but he had no choice. He wrote a note for Sean. *'Gay Boy, I've taken your homo gear. I'm doing you a favour, leaving you some decent clobber. If you come to your senses, maybe you'll get a look in with Natasha. Cheers. You're a good mate. Will be in touch.'*

There were cops at the bus station, but they didn't give him a second glance. He bought a ticket for the Glasgow bus, then he sat at the stance and waited. He was feeling okay. This might just work. He felt the phone vibrate in his pocket. Probably his mother.

It was Todd on Snapchat. A photo of a white sport sock with a splattering of red spots, lying in a pile of leaves. And a caption: *'Cheers Sharon'*.

Ryan watched the image until it disappeared, then he called his mother. Her phone was switched off.

*

There was a lot of faffing about with this flying malarkey. Turbulence. Expensive plastic food. No toilet while the seat-belt signs were on. A bumpy landing, then crammed into a bus at Gatwick. Even when you got off the bus, there was miles to walk. Christopher took Sharon's hand. 'Come on; this way for the shuttle.'

'Shuttle?'

'To the South Terminal; that's where we get the train.'

'This isn't easy, is it?'

He laughed. 'You get used to it.'

She never would. And see those lines on the ground in the South Terminal to show where you should walk? She couldn't make any sense of them. And the lane system for buying rail tickets was completely overwhelming.

'Just as well you've got me, then,' he said.

Was that right? Sharon couldn't get the photos, or his trip in the middle of the night, out of her head. But she couldn't find a way to ask him about them that didn't sound like she was snooping. She shouldn't have come, no matter what Ryan had said in his text. It was too far away.

On the station platform, while Christopher watched the board for the next train to East Croydon, Sharon searched his face. There was no sign of fear, and there had been none in the shuttle. Had he been having her on? If she'd experienced what he said he had, she'd never go near another train.

He saw her looking. 'I know what you're thinking.'

'You don't.'

'I do. And you're right to wonder. It was all down to a friend.' He hesitated. 'There's more to tell you another time, Sharon. Much more. Let's just say it wasn't easy. There was a lot of crying, swearing, biting, kicking, threats of arrest…'

'You or him?'

'Both. Here we go.'

*

Pinching herself had once been Sharon's speciality. She had the marks to prove it. You could do a lot of damage by pinching, as a self-harm method of last resort when there was nothing sharper around. While Christopher paid the taxi driver, she stood before his family's Gothic villa, her nails digging into her arm as she counted the floors. There were four, and bay windows that gleamed in the morning sun, a couple of spires, and a small turret. The garden was huge, a lawn stretching out the back as far as she could see. She felt Christopher's hand on her arm, stopping her nails before they broke the skin. 'You okay?'

She shook her head. 'I could have stayed in a hotel.'

109

He smiled. 'Hardly.'

The door opened into a massive entrance hallway with dark wood panelling and a tiled floor. Through an archway, she could see a huge staircase, masses of paintings and a sparkling chandelier. It was like Downton Abbey.

A blur of shouting children descended on them. 'Uncle Chris, Uncle Chris!' Three boys and a girl.

'Children, give Uncle Chris a break, will you?' Isobel had long dark hair, and eyes just like his. She hugged Christopher, then she put her arm round Sharon's shoulders. 'You've no idea how pleased I am to meet you. I've heard a lot about you. It's such a surprise.'

Aye, for you and me both, doll.

Sharon felt a hand in hers. It was too small to be Christopher's. It was the youngest, a wee girl with Frozen pyjamas and a lisp. 'Would you like to see our spaceship?'

Her mother shook her head. 'Ruby, not now. Uncle Chris and I are going to visit Grandma in hospital. You're going to Nanny's with the boys. Go and get dressed.'

'I don't want to go to Nanny's. She just talks to the boys about football all the time and I get bored.'

'That's too bad.'

'Sharon can look after me.'

That would do Sharon nicely. They hadn't discussed whether she'd go to the hospital with Christopher. She'd hoped not. It was one thing bringing your girlfriend home for the first time, and quite another introducing her to your mother in intensive care. One look at Sharon and the mother might peg it.

As Ruby led Sharon up the never-ending stairs, she got a glimpse into several rooms with deep pile carpets, satin bed-linen and antique furniture. This was mental. Why would someone like Christopher, born with half a dozen silver spoons in his mouth, want anything to do with her? And why was Ruby insisting on taking her to the attic?

Ruby ran ahead of Sharon up the last few steps, and threw the door open. Though she was trying hard to watch her mouth, Sharon was unable to stop herself. 'Bloody hell'. Ruby giggled.

The attic was a spaceship. Two old car seats were fixed in front of rows of monitors and a huge control panel. There were wheels and dials and lights, buttons and cables and speakers. Ruby pressed a button, and music from Star Wars came bursting out of the speakers, accompanied by flashing lights. 'Look up,' Ruby said.

Stars and planets drifted across the roof in a mass of colours and lights.

'That's the solar system. I can teach you the planets, but first I'll go and get dressed, then you can read me a story in my room.'

Ruby's room was huge, with shelves of books, an intricate doll's house, and a rocking horse. The décor was white and pale lilac. She'd wanted pink, she told Sharon, but her Grandma said pink was common. 'What's common, Sharon?'

You're looking at it, kiddo. 'It just means lots of people have it. This is much nicer than pink.'

'I like you,' Ruby said, when Sharon finished reading *Emily Brown and The Elephant Emergency*.

Sharon smiled. 'I like you too.'

'Are you a mummy?'

Sharon nodded. 'I've got two sons, Ryan and Liam. They would love to see the spaceship.'

'Then you'll just have to bring them for a holiday. Are the boys with their daddy?'

'Eh, no; they're…they're with their aunt. Their daddy died.'

'That's sad. Our dog died once. My daddy's away somewhere. Probably work.'

Christopher had told Sharon that Isobel's husband had run off with their au pair, three years ago. Clearly, no one had told Ruby.

'Sharon, do you fuss like the elephant's mummy in the story? My mummy does.'

Fuss? She hadn't even switched her phone on since they arrived at Gatwick over an hour ago. She was a shit mum.

'Ruby, I'm just going to run down and get my phone. I need to call the boys and check they're all right.'

Four missed calls from Ryan. She called him back and the phone rang once before he answered it, and started shouting.

'Calm down, Ryan. I can't understand you. What is it?'

'You tell me. That bastard, Todd; he's sent me a picture of a sock on Snapchat with 'Thanks Sharon' written on it. What's he on about?'

Sharon's heart started to race. 'A sock?'

'A white sports sock with something red on it – spots of blood, maybe. What's going on, Mam?'

Sharon felt as if her legs were going to give way. She sat on the stairs. 'The day of the shooting, you dropped a sock in the kitchen. I…I got rid of it.'

Ryan's roar nearly deafened her. 'And Todd's got it? How the fuck did that happen?'

'I don't know. I…I gave it to Christopher before the cops arrived.'

'Christopher? He's in this with Todd. They're both involved in the shooting. It's all to do with Dad; I know it. They're getting their own back for something he did.'

'Christopher's involved in the shooting? He knew your father?'

'I don't know. Todd did. I'm fucked, Mum. Totally fucked.'

*

The bus came in. And it left. Ryan watched it go, then he picked up Sean's back pack and left the bus station. On Academy Street, he heard another text.

> *Ryan, darling, where r u? I'm coming home. We'll get this sorted.*

He walked towards the car at the top of the taxi rank. Just before he reached it, he replied to his mother.

> *Sorting it. Sorry. Luv u xx*

He switched the phone off and took out the sim. As he opened the back door of the taxi, he dropped the phone and sim through the metal grate in the road.

The driver looked over his shoulder. 'Where to, mate?'

Ryan took the scarf off and shoved it under the seat in front. 'Stadium Road, please.'

Chapter 26

Carla had kept Joe awake most of the night, but not in the way he'd have liked. She must be feeling like shit waiting for her results, and he hadn't even remembered to call her. He was a tosser and he didn't deserve her. She hadn't answered his texts. Maybe that was it over. And who could blame her?

And when he'd managed to put Carla out of his head, Danielle Smith and Gordon Sutherland replaced her. And hundreds of questions. It was starting to get light when he slept. There was still no rest for him. Another struggle and a stabbing on the rocks in South Harris, only this time Lucy lay dead, while Stephen MacLaren's laughter echoed through Joe's head.

Joe slept in. He should have been in the station early. There was so much to be done. A video-link with Manchester to discuss the Nancy Connor file; an undercover operation to coordinate at Castlefield Apartments; a meeting with the homeless services to discuss women that might have disappeared over the last few months; find out from Roz Sutherland if Gordon had any money problems, and might he have borrowed from this Todd? Maybe they'd have the results from Katya's phone, or even an arrest at an airport somewhere. So much to do. But first, he had to see Carla.

He was at the Tesco roundabout on the outskirts of Inverness when a call came over his radio. A jumper on the Kessock Bridge. 'Can someone else take this?' he asked control. 'I'm busy.'

'There's been a fire in a hotel on Loch Ness side, a road accident in Hilton and another at Daviot. DI Black says you've done a negotiator course.'

'A half day, five years ago.'

'He's trying to get someone else, but you're it for now.'

Great. 'Which side of the bridge?'

'Northbound. Near the middle. Young guy.'

At the first lay-by on approach to the bridge, he swithered. He could park here and run, or he could stop on the bridge. He decided on the lay-by. The bridge was too busy and the traffic too fast. There would be no way to give adequate warning of a stationary car to approaching drivers. Hopefully, he'd have backup before too long, and they could close the bridge.

It was a good half mile to the centre of the bridge. As he ran, he noticed the tide was in. That was a plus. There had been jumpers that hadn't thought to take account of the tides. Messy.

Joe was out of breath and he wasn't even quarter of the way across. Nothing to see so far. Maybe the guy had jumped or gone home. The weight of the central section of the bridge was carried by four towers, with steel cables stretching down to the road deck. There were caged platforms with ladders for maintenance at intervals across the length of the bridge. As Joe approached the first of the towers, he saw someone standing in the adjacent caged platform. Messy dyed blond hair and a bright flowery shirt. Poor bugger. There had been so many of them in recent years. Young Highland men that had chosen suicide as the only way to solve their problems.

Joe stopped a few feet from the jumper. He breathed deeply and centred himself. Tried to remember what he'd learned on that distant course. Nothing came to him. Before he could speak, the guy turned. As he looked beyond the blond hair and the odd assortment of clothes, Joe felt as if he'd been punched in the stomach. 'Ryan?'

There was fear in the boy's eyes. He backed off. 'Don't even think about coming any closer.'

Joe held his hands up. 'I won't.'

'Why the fuck did they send you? Haven't you got two murders to solve?'

He almost told Ryan the truth; he just happened to be passing and no one else was available. Probably not the best way to start. He smiled. 'I have, but you're more important.'

Ryan shook his head. 'Aye, right.'

'You are.' Joe stayed to the left of the cage. He leaned on the metal barrier and looked out across the Beauly Firth. 'What's up, Ryan?'

'As if you care. You're only interested 'cos you think I can help you solve your murders. Otherwise, I'm nothing. Completely insignificant. I'm never going to be anything.'

Joe smiled. 'That's not true.'

'Aye it is, I've spent my whole life watching everyone else know what they're doing. God knows how they know, or where they get it from. Probably their parents. Maybe they're brought up knowing they belong. I just don't.'

'Not belonging.' Joe nodded. 'I know what you mean. It's tough.'

'You?' Ryan's voice was scornful. 'Mr Super Cool Detective, with your fancy suits and your tan? Not belonging?'

Joe shrugged. 'Appearances can be deceptive. I've had my problems; still have.'

'What? Getting stabbed?'

Though his instinct was to rub at his scar, Joe kept his hands on the rail. He nodded. 'That's one of them.'

'Why did MacLaren do that?'

'Long story, Ryan. A whole catalogue of disasters and trauma that could have been avoided if our parents had handled things differently. Parents don't always get it right. None of us do.'

There was a long pause. Joe was tempted to fill the space, but he didn't. Embrace the power of the pause – one of the few things he remembered from the negotiation course.

'Have you…have you seen my mum?' Ryan's voice was weak.

'Yes. I saw her yesterday morning at the flat. We were looking for you. She was really upset you'd gone.'

'She's got Christopher now; she doesn't need me. I've only ever caused her trouble. She's always been closer to Liam.'

Christopher? Joe didn't dare ask, much as he'd like to know. 'Her worry seemed genuine to me.'

'What did she tell you?'

Joe saw the marks on Ryan's neck and the backs of his hands. 'Nothing much.' The lie made his heart race. But what would the truth have done to Ryan? 'I don't think she knew anything.'

'She'll hate me now.' There were tears in his eyes. 'Everyone will.'

'She could never hate you. She doesn't believe you've done anything wrong; she just thinks you're scared to come home.'

'What about you?' His voice was shaky. 'Do you think I killed them?'

Joe shook his head. 'I think you've been dragged into it by someone. Maybe you had no idea what was going to happen, no idea what he was really like.'

Ryan nodded. 'He came looking for me. Reeled me right in. Bastard.'

'Looking for you?'

Ryan rubbed his eyes. 'Said he was a friend of my dad. You've no idea what that meant.'

Joe knew exactly what that meant. The memories, the wishing, the fantasising. He'd been fortunate to have the best step-father he could ever have asked for, but still. 'It's tough to lose your dad, especially when you're wee. Believe me, I know.'

There was confusion and despair on the boy's face. 'But…my father was such a bastard. I hated him.'

Joe nodded. 'Doesn't matter, does it? Doesn't stop you convincing yourself that everything in your life would be different if he was still around.'

'Yeah. And Todd Curtis played on that. I've been such a fucking idiot.'

Yes. A surname, at last.

'I'm fucked. Whatever I do, I'm fucked.'

'You're not, Ryan. I'll make sure of that.'

He laughed, but there was no humour in it. 'You going to promise I won't go inside? Like on TV?'

'I can't promise that. But I can make sure the court knows you helped.'

There was a hint of hope in Ryan's eyes. He might just be taking Joe seriously. A breeze blew in from the north, and Joe saw Ryan shiver. He looked down to the water. There was a yacht approaching the bridge, its white sail catching the wind. 'You ever been on one of those?' Ryan asked.

'Many times. This is not really a tan; I'm just weather-beaten from sailing.'

'Do you think that's Swedish? Vindo 45, maybe?'

'Could be.' Joe nodded. 'How do you know that?'

Ryan shrugged. 'There's one for sale in the Inverness Marina. Not that they'd let me anywhere near the place. I saw it online.'

'You're interested in sailing?'

Ryan almost smiled. 'Yeah. What's it like?'

Joe had been asked that before, usually when he'd chosen a sailing trip over a girlfriend. He'd never found a way to adequately describe the exhilaration and freedom, but now was the time to try, and he had to do it justice.

He leaned his elbows on the metal rail and looked out over the water. 'It's like a different world, Ryan. Even after the shittiest of days, when my brain is crammed with all kinds of crap, I step on-board and it all starts to slip away. Excitement comes. Doesn't matter if it's a routine evening club sail, or a long trip, that excitement is always there. When I'm on land, the water is something that separates me from other people and places, but as soon as I step on-board it becomes this amazing thing that connects. The possibilities are endless.'

Was he overdoing it? He glanced at Ryan, expecting disdain or mockery. Ryan was side-on, gazing at the yacht, the merest hint of a smile on his lips. Joe's pause made him turn. His look was impatient. He wanted to hear more. He had to.

'This is going to sound a bit odd, but it almost feels like every boat is a living thing, with a personality of its own. And it's not really about mastering the boat; you almost want to blend together, to create something new. And if you do it right, and if everything else works out, it's amazing. Like flying.'

Joe was sweating. Time to bring it down a bit. 'It's bloody hard work, physically and mentally. So much to learn, and so many things to take account of. The boat, the tide, the currents, the wind, the crew. You have to learn how to read them all, and yourself. It's a game of chance. No two outings are the same, and it doesn't always go well. But when the wind and the water are right, there's nothing else like it. That sense of confidence when you succeed.' He smiled at Ryan. 'I've never found anything I enjoy as much. And after each trip, I feel as if I come back a little different.'

Ryan smiled. The transformation shocked Joe. This was the boy that Sharon loved, the one she knew and believed in, no matter what anyone said. He looked so young and earnest. 'I knew it would be like that. I knew it.'

'Would you like to learn?'

He nodded, but his smile faded. 'It's not for the likes of me. Just a dream. I used to go down the canal and watch the boats, imagine myself sailing away. No looking back.'

'I could teach you if you want. When this is all over.'

Ryan looked just as surprised as Joe felt. And no wonder. What the hell was he saying? But it wasn't just about trying to build a rapport with Ryan, trying to stop him from jumping. Joe really would like to help the boy if he could. He knew just how easy it was to take the wrong road, and if he could help to stop Ryan doing that, he would. There was hope in Ryan's eyes. It was so alien, yet so welcome.

'Really?'

Joe nodded. 'I hope to have my own boat before long.'

He knew Ryan understood. He'd have his own boat by the time Ryan got out. 'So, do you think you might come out of there? I promise I'll do my best for you.'

Ryan nodded. He took a couple of steps forward. Joe smiled. And then Ryan's eyes widened, and the glimmering light of hope was gone. There was nothing but bitterness and disdain. 'What the fuck is he doing here?'

When Joe turned and saw Jackson, he knew the last twenty minutes had been wasted.

Chapter 27

Ruby's voice made Sharon jump. She wiped tears from her eyes before she turned. The little girl sat beside her on the step. 'Are you sad about your boys' daddy?'

Sharon shook her head. 'No, I'm just missing my boys.'

'I'm missing my mummy. Can I have a hug?'

As Sharon felt Ruby's arms wrap around her neck, she breathed in the smell and thought of her miscarriages. Surely one of them was a girl? She'd have loved a girl.

Ruby pulled away. 'Do you think you and Uncle Chris will have a baby? I'd like a cousin.'

She'd fantasised about having a baby with Christopher. Her rock. Her saviour. Her two-faced, lying bastard.

'I love Uncle Chris, but I don't like Todd. He looks mean.'

Sharon's stomach lurched. 'You know Todd?'

Ruby nodded. 'He comes here sometimes.'

'Has he been here recently?'

'Sometimes.' Ruby shrugged. 'Not too long ago. He always has dinner with us and stays downstairs in the servants' quarters. We don't actually have any servants. Not really. Just Aneta, the cleaner.'

'And she lives downstairs?'

'No, silly. No one lives there now, except Todd, when he comes.' Her face serious, she whispered: 'Sometimes there's funny noises from down there. I think I heard noises today.'

Sharon nodded. 'I've just got one more call to make, Ruby. It's quite important.'

Ruby sighed. 'Mummy makes important calls all the time and I have to leave the room. I'll go to the den and watch telly.'

The den was tiny, with bean bags and an old television. Board games, jigsaws and boxes of Lego were piled on shelves. Ruby sat on a bean bag. 'Can I watch a DVD? Postman Pat, please.'

The theme tune of Postman Pat brought mixed memories for Sharon. The good ones were of Liam, snuggling into her on the couch. The bad ones were of Peter mocking Ryan for watching children's TV. What had that warped bastard done to her wee boy? And why had she let him do it?

She could hear Ruby laughing as she sat in the next room, a massive lounge that looked to be bigger than her flat. As she waited to be connected to Joe Galbraith, she repeated what she was going to tell him, for the tenth time:

Ryan has another phone; this is the number.

I spoke to him yesterday and today.

I tampered with evidence and gave Ryan's sock to Christopher Brent the day of the shooting.

Christopher gave the sock to Todd.

Todd has sent pictures of the sock to Ryan.

Christopher and Todd are in this together.

Christopher lives at Ness Castle. This is his phone number.

DI Galbraith wasn't available. No, she didn't want to speak to anyone else. She left her number for him to return her call. Then she tried Ryan again.

*

It wasn't the first time Joe had suspected Jackson was on something. He wasn't stupid enough to drink at work, but there were times when he seemed to be verging on the type of hysteria that usually came in a small tab. Like now. His hair was all over the place, and he was unshaven, eyes wired to the moon.

Jackson's mouth was twisted with mockery. 'MacRae, bad hair day or what? You look like a right poofter. What you doing in there?'

'What does it look like?'

'You're the jumper? Ha ha ha. The hair's not that bad. And there's easier ways of doing it. You could have got an overdose of smack from your junkie mother, or your dealer pal, Todd.'

Ryan's eyes narrowed. 'Fuck off. You're such a tosser.'

'And you are one cheeky wee shite. I can't think of anyone I'd rather see in there. Do the world a favour, why don't you, and jump.'

'Jackson,' Joe said. 'Go to the station. Now.'

'That'll be right. You think you're going to tell me what to do, Golden Balls Galbraith? Why don't you just get in there beside him? This world would be a whole lot better without you too.'

'Jackson. The station. Now.'

Jackson threw his head back and laughed. 'Yes, Sir. D'you want me to crawl on my knees?'

'No. I just want you to go.' He turned back to the boy. 'Ryan, you were going to come out of there.'

Ryan shook his head. 'There's no point. I'm fucked.'

'Think of your mum, Ryan.'

Ryan shrugged. 'She's survived worse. Her useless mother; a whole succession of step-fathers that couldn't keep their hands to themselves; my father. She doesn't expect things to work out for her. That's just the way it is.'

Jackson's laughter was loud and nasty. 'Careful. My heart strings can't take any more. Poor Sharon MacRae. Doesn't give a shit about you, though. She spilled her guts to Golden Balls yesterday – told him she saw you getting into a big dark car with a bald driver in the Portland Street car park. Not long before Danielle was murdered. And the state you came home in – crying and throwing up. I see the scratches she mentioned on your hands, the bruising on your throat. Imagine stealing a hundred quid from your own mother. Tut tut.'

Ryan stared at Joe. 'Is that true? My mother told you all that?'

Joe hesitated, then he nodded. 'She was worried about you.'

Jackson laughed. 'Worried? Aye, right. Do you know what, MacRae? They're shagging, him and her.'

Last night, DI Black wouldn't say which of Joe's colleagues had reported a relationship between him and Sharon MacRae, but he'd known it could only be Jackson.

Ryan leaned over the side of the cage, pointing his finger at Jackson. 'Shut the fuck up, you prick. They are not shagging. He's not that stupid, but he is a lying bastard. You all are.'

Jackson nodded. 'Such insight. For a rapist. A murderer.'

Ryan shook his head and backed off. 'I never raped or murdered anyone.' He hitched himself up so he was sitting on the edge of the cage, with his back to the water.

'So how did you get those marks? And who did that to my Danielle?'

Joe stared at Jackson. His Danielle? Was he the Jimmy that Katya had mentioned? The policeman on the stairs with the moustache? Shit. Why hadn't he thought of that?

'I loved that girl.' There were tears in Jackson's eyes as he turned to Joe. 'She'd still be here if you'd done your job properly. You should have taken her in straight away. Saved her from this fucking wee shite.'

'I didn't kill her.' Ryan's voice was shaking. 'It wasn't me.'

'Wasn't you? Your sock was there. Your fingerprints were on her zip. You killed her, you little shit.' Jackson lunged for the cage and starting clambering over the metal barrier.

Joe leapt forward and grabbed Jackson's arm. His colleague was straddling the barrier, and he kicked out at Joe. 'Fuck off, you bastard. You can't stop me.'

His foot caught Joe in the centre of his chest, and he staggered backwards against the metal rail that separated the path from the road. By the time he'd righted himself, Jackson was in the cage.

Ryan's face was ashen. He raised his hands, trying to ward Jackson off. 'Keep away from me.'

Jackson laughed. 'Let's go for it together. There's no future for me either. We're both fucked.' He hitched himself up so he was sitting beside Ryan. 'Come on.' He held out his hand.

Joe leaned towards Ryan. 'You were coming out of there – you still can. Please.'

Ryan looked uncertain. He pulled his hand away from Jackson. Wobbled, and steadied himself against the tower with his other hand. Beside him Jackson was laughing. Leaning back, looking over his shoulder. 'This is something else. Want to join us, Galbraith? Do the world a favour. Who needs an arrogant shithead like you?'

'Get out of there, both of you.' Joe noticed the road had gone quiet. No passing cars. His colleagues must be on their way.

'Fuck this.' Ryan eased himself off the edge of the cage and took a step towards Joe.

Jackson reached for him. 'No way. You're coming too. A life for a life.' He grabbed Ryan's shirt. Both hands, holding on. Pulling. Joe leaned into the cage. He took Ryan's arm and held it tight. He reached out his other hand to Jackson. 'Jimmy, come on…don't do this. Please.'

Jackson stared into Joe's eyes. 'You and him, you've taken the only thing I ever loved. She'd have loved me too, given the chance. I'd have…we'd have married, if it wasn't for you and him.' His voice broke. 'I'd have had everything you have.

Everything. I'd have had a future.' His eyes filled with tears.

Joe shook his head, his hand still outstretched. 'I'm sorry, Jimmy; I really am. Please give me your hand. We can sort this.'

Jackson let go of Ryan. His hand moved towards Joe's. Their eyes met, and Joe saw a frenzy of questions and misgivings and aching deep in Jackson's gaze. Had Joe misjudged him? Could they start again, and sort things out? Joe was willing to try. He felt a smile hovering on his lips. Jackson saw that smile, and his lips curved upwards in response. There was only an inch between their hands. Almost there, and then Jackson laughed. The sound was cruel and bleak and without any hope. Jackson's eyes narrowed as he snatched his hand away, his body tilting backwards. And then he was gone.

As the water swallowed Jackson, Ryan climbed out of the cage. Joe heard cars stopping, doors opening and closing. Two uniformed cops, Roberts, Tina Lewis and Anne Morrison, Ryan's previous Social Worker.

'Sarge,' Roberts said. 'You talked him down. Well done.'

Ryan nodded. 'Too right he's done well. He's just pushed Jackson off the bridge.'

Chapter 28

That skanky lying wee shite, Ryan MacRae, should be in the station, where DI Black could wring the truth out of him. No chance of that now. He was in New Craigs, and it would be all risk assessments, protective factors, empathising and supporting, drawing up care plans and general molly-coddling. It could be days before they'd get a chance to question him, especially if MacRae milked it for all it was worth. Not that DI Black would get anywhere near him. They had to keep this clean. There could be no room for doubt, not with that brief of MacRae's. Who was paying for her anyway? There were far too many unanswered questions.

And Jackson? Where and when would his body show up? No sign of him so far, although the Life Boat and Coastguard rescue helicopter were out within minutes. Could be weeks before he surfaced. Poor bastard. They hadn't always detested each other. They'd worked together and got on okay at first. That was in the days when officers could dispense their own kind of justice. He'd never been happy with that sort of thing, but Jackson had. And it was his gung-ho attitude, his pettiness and bitterness that had kept him where he was. Jackson rarely spoke of his family. There were brothers somewhere, two maybe. Parents dead. Who were they going to tell? Would anyone give a damn?

And what about Galbraith? Poor sod. He hadn't said a word when MacBain took his warrant card and his phone. Sitting there waiting for the officers from the Professional Standards Unit in Aberdeen to arrive, and none of them could go near him. It was bloody ridiculous. His best officer off the case. Damn.

*

Would he? Wouldn't he? Joe tapped his fingers on the table and considered. He wouldn't like to put money on either scenario. Roberts was turning into a good detective, and he did everything by the book. He'd have to tell. And so he should. If Joe was working with a detective that threatened to kill a colleague, who then died in suspicious circumstances the next day, he'd tell.

But Roberts' loyalty to Joe was embarrassing. Everyone in the station had noticed, and taken the piss. Roberts didn't seem to care. He'd decided he was going to learn all he could, and for some reason, he thought Joe was the best person to teach him. Poor misguided idiot.

It was impossible to know what Roberts would do. Or Carla. She hadn't answered his texts from last night, and now his phone was gone. No way would he be taking her home from the hospital. Maybe he could get a message to her pal, Louise. But no one was going to come near him before his interrogators arrived. No one was going to risk speaking to him.

*

Roberts phoned Sharon, and she picked up straight away. She didn't give him a chance to speak. 'DS Galbraith? Thank fuck...I mean, thank you for calling me back. It's just that – '

'Sharon, it's Roberts. Galbraith's not available.' There was silence. 'Sharon?'

'I'm only speaking to Galbraith.'

'You might have to wait a while. What was it you wanted?' More silence. 'You still there? I was going to call you or come and see you anyway. We've got Ryan.'

'Got him where?'

'New Craigs. He was on the Kessock Bridge, threatening to jump.' He heard a sharp intake of breath, then there was silence. 'Sharon, are you there?'

'Yeah.' Her voice was shaky. 'Is he...is he all right?'

'He seemed quite all right when I saw him, minutes after Galbraith talked him down, but we have to go through the usual procedure where there's a suicide risk. He's being assessed now, evaluated. If he gets discharged, he'll be back here for questioning, but I doubt that'll be today.'

'You sound angry with him.'

Roberts was bloody angry with him, but he shouldn't have let Sharon know that. 'Sorry. We're a bit overwhelmed right now. Will you be arranging that brief for him again? He's going to need her.'

'Aye, of course.'

'So, Sharon, what were you going to tell Galbraith?'

*

Sharon couldn't think straight. They had Ryan now. Did they need to know about the sock, or that she'd heard from Ryan and not told them? She couldn't afford to get into trouble. She had to be there for the boys. 'It's not much. I heard Ryan's been hanging about with someone called Todd, and he knew Peter MacRae. I wondered if Ryan was with Todd the day of the shooting, and in the car park.'

'Where did you hear this?'

Sharon hesitated. 'Just word on the street.'

'Is that it?'

'Aye, that's it. So, what'll happen to Ryan? Will he go back to the Children's Hearing?'

Roberts made a noise that might have been a laugh. 'The Children's Hearing? I very much doubt it. Ryan is facing serious charges. He can't be sent home as he's likely to associate with a criminal if he's released.'

'I'm not a criminal.'

'Not you. This Todd and anyone else that might be involved. When Ryan comes back to the station, we have to review his custody every few hours. We'll try to find a safe place for him, but it's not always possible. With these charges, we're looking at a secure unit. There are none in the Highlands, and most secure units are unlikely to take a high risk suicidal child.'

A suicidal child? Sharon shivered. 'When can I see him?'

'That's not a decision for me. He might not want to see you. The doctor or the DI might feel it's not appropriate for the time being.'

'Surely I've got a right to see him?'

'Ordinarily, yes, if that's what he wants, unless there are exceptional circumstances, and we're still considering that. I'll let you know. Try not to worry, Sharon; he's okay. Anne Morrison's at the hospital with him.'

That made Sharon feel a little better. Anne, their previous social worker, had always done her best for the boys. 'Will you tell him...tell him I'm sending my love.'

'I'll pass that on. We'll be in touch when we have more news.'

Sharon didn't tell him she was in London. They already thought she was a shit mother. And so did she.

Chapter 29

Carla sent Joe two texts as soon as the doctor had been round. There was no response, so she tried Louise. Her friend's phone was off, and there was no answer on her landline. All her other friends were either on duty or they had nine to five jobs, and wouldn't be able to get away. She wasn't staying at the hospital a minute longer than necessary, so she ordered a taxi.

At home, she tried not to get herself worked up about Joe's lack of contact. It didn't work. She'd never complained about his unavailability or that he rarely switched off when there was something big going on. It had been worse since he'd transferred to the MIT, and sometimes had to travel to incidents in other areas. She'd understood. But there was no excuse for this. She knew there had been a second murder; she'd seen it in a newspaper, but still. He had to pee, didn't he? Surely it wasn't that difficult to send her a quick text from the loo?

She was always the one to get in touch, always the one to suggest they might actually do something other than walk on the beach or go to bed. He hadn't asked her if she wanted to go sailing last weekend. She'd felt like shit and wouldn't have gone anyway, but that wasn't the point. They'd both been off, and his priority was sailing with his mates.

And the time before that, it was football. He didn't even like football, but going to the match with the boys was preferable to spending the day with her. He was happy enough for her to come to Inverness and pick him up later, of course, stinking of beer and meat pies, with only one thing on his mind.

She got the calendar out and started trying to remember what they'd done over the last few months. Very little. Why had she not noticed this long ago, and dealt with it? What a mug.

Her head was aching, and her chest was tender at the site of the bone marrow aspiration. The doctor had decided against a bone marrow biopsy, for now, but it might become necessary, depending on the results of the sample. She was tempted to go on the computer, and google the life out of leukaemia and white blood cell abnormalities. But that would be silly.

So she lay on the couch and listened to Runrig. Her father had loved the band, especially as two of the founding members had family connections in North Uist. She remembered herself and her father in the car, singing at the top of their voices. Single track roads and curving passing places marked by diamond-shaped signs. Waving to everyone. Rabbits everywhere. Tumbling lapwings and busy oystercatchers. Stray sheep stuck in fences, and her dad stopping to release them and reunite them with their bleating lambs. Ronald, awkward and gangling, saying nothing as she followed him around the croft asking endless questions.

Her mother had never liked Uist. Too many flies and not enough shops. Although it broke her dad's heart when her mum left him for Rudy, a salesman from South Carolina, they'd never had anything in common other than Carla. Her father had spent his last years with Ronald and his mother in North Uist. Not long before he died, Carla's mother married Rudy and moved to South Carolina. Maybe that was the final straw for her dad; he'd died just a few months later.

That was the last time Carla had been in North Uist. She remembered the cemetery, and how the raised mounds at each grave had haunted her dreams, so much so that she didn't go back a year later for Ronald's mother's funeral. She felt as if she'd abandoned her father there, left him all alone. She should have gone back and tended his grave. Maybe then she wouldn't have those dreams of losing him in the sand dunes. The dreams had been so vivid lately. Was he trying to tell her something? She listened to *Flower of the West*, and she knew what she should do. She'd have to wait a couple of weeks for the results of all her tests. Why not wait in Uist? And why bother telling Joe she was going?

She rang the airline, then Ronald. 'I'll be over tomorrow.'

'That's brilliant,' he said. 'But I've no television. Will I get one?'

'No. I hardly watch it anyway.'

'And there's not much in the way of shops.'

'That's fine; I'm not that keen on shopping.'

'And I don't know how the weather will be, though it's been good lately. It could change.'

'Ronald, are you trying to talk me out of coming?'

'Heavens, no. That's the last thing I'd do. I just don't want you to hate it here.'

'No way. I can't wait.'

*

A year ago, when Sharon had no control over anything, she wouldn't have been able to stop herself from punching Christopher's smug face. He was looking so chuffed with himself, so full of it. His mother was out of danger. Isobel was still with her, but the doctors were really pleased at her progress.

Sharon tried to smile. He frowned. 'Are you all right?'

'Not really.' At least she had a good excuse for not being all right. 'Ryan's in New Craigs. He tried to kill himself on the Kessock Bridge.'

'No? I'm so sorry, Sharon.'

He was good, really good. If she didn't know better, she'd even believe he was upset by the news. 'Will you get that solicitor for him again? I'll pay you back, I swear.'

'I'll do it now. And you're not paying me back.' He smiled. 'Don't be silly.'

'We'll see. I need to go home as soon as possible.' And the first thing she was going to do was find a Legal Aid solicitor for Ryan.

After Christopher had spoken to the solicitor, he tried the airline. The soonest they could get seats was midday tomorrow. 'Could try the overnight sleeper. That would get you in early tomorrow morning.'

A train from London to Inverness? The thought exhausted her. Probably wouldn't take as long as his bloody laptop. Sharon waited. And waited. At this rate, there'd be no berths available. There weren't. 'I could hire a car. Leave now.'

With his leg? That'd be right. Might be nice to watch him suffer, but she wasn't putting her life at risk. She shook her head. 'Tomorrow's fine.'

He called the airline and booked the seats. 'Give me a minute to check my emails, love.'

She sat across the table and waited. He looked apprehensive as he studied the screen. Then he looked worried.

'Uncle Chris, will you come and play computer games with us in the attic?' It was Robert, the oldest of his nephews.

'Okay.' He closed the laptop and smiled at Sharon. 'Are you coming up?'

'No, thanks; I'll sit out on the patio.'

Sharon stared at the laptop on the kitchen table. Other than those photos, she'd never spied on Christopher. Never looked at his phone, though she'd often had the opportunity and the inclination. It had been hard, but she couldn't let herself. Every time she'd looked at her late husband's phone, she'd found something she didn't want to see. She'd told herself Christopher was different. He wouldn't cheat on her.

She had no such qualms now. Only fear of what she might see. Probably nothing, she told herself, as she waited for the lap top to crank itself up again. Unless there was a great big icon saying 'EMAIL THIS WAY', she was unlikely to be able to find her way around his laptop. She didn't have to. He'd left his email open at the last message. It had been sent at two in the morning from *universalsaviour@mail.com*

> *Mate, are you all right? No email tonight. Worried about you. I'm heading south. Bit of bother. Don't believe what you hear. Yours always. T*

T for Todd. Yours always? Were they lovers? Nothing would surprise Sharon. She closed the laptop and went out to the patio. Tall trees surrounded the garden, casting dark, moving shadows on the flawless striped lawn. They were regimented trees. Straight and green and identical. Nothing like the old wizened trees in Christopher's garden, the ones that reminded her of endless summer days when she'd curl up in the branches of the trees on the canal banks and pretend home was somewhere far away, somewhere safe. There would be no climbing these buggers, with their flimsy pine-scented needles and their skinny trunks. They looked like giant toilet brushes.

The bushes and plants were in bloom, their scent strong and heady. A painted wooden well sat in the middle of the lawn, the grass around it cropped to perfection. There wasn't a thing out of place. Not a weed or a stone or a leaf. It was stifling.

The only thing that interested Sharon, apart from the stairs leading down to the servants' quarters, was a small white lodge at the bottom of the garden. It was tiny compared to the house, but to her it looked like a palace.

No time to investigate the lodge; she had to find out if Todd was in the servants' quarters. He could have been on his way to London when he sent the email this morning. He could have arrived before them. She looked around before going down the steps. There was a window by the door, but the curtains were shut. The door was locked.

Sharon had seen another set of steps earlier, leading down from the kitchen. In the entrance hall, she listened. There was no sound. She tip-toed to the kitchen and down the stairs. Another door, with a key.

The way her heart pounded as she opened the door reminded her of coming home to the flat when Peter was alive. She'd creep in, hoping he'd be in bed, or in a good mood, or with a friend. He never hurt her in front of his friends. He put her down often enough, laughed at her, but he couldn't be seen to be hitting a lassie in front of his mates. That wouldn't do at all.

Sharon gave the hall cupboard a wide berth. She still did that at home. Peter used to hide in the cupboard and jump out on her. Terrified her every time. Not knowing if it was a joke or an attack. And if it wasn't a joke, was he going to batter her or lock her in? Or both?

Although the rooms were dark and gloomy, the servants' quarters were almost as posh as the house. Three bedrooms, a big kitchen and a bathroom. There was no food in the kitchen cupboards or fridge, and nothing in any of the waste-paper bins. The bed in the largest room was made up. She considered turning the quilt back and smelling the sheets, but maybe that was going a bit far. It didn't look as if it had been slept in, and there were no signs that anyone had been there recently.

And yet. As she pulled the bedroom door closed, Sharon shivered and wondered if she was imagining a lingering hint of evil in the air. She had a sudden memory of the way she'd felt in Christopher's house near Evanton. Had Todd been living there?

The only place she hadn't looked was in the cupboard by the door. As it creaked open, she shivered. There were boxes on each of the shelves. She looked in a couple. Old toys and shoes. On the top shelf, there was a plastic document wallet. Sharon's heart hammered as she stretched up for it.

There were photos at the front of the wallet. A younger Christopher, looking miserable, sitting in a chair on the patio, and a big guy with dark curly hair and a huge smile standing beside him. The date on the back was July 2007. She slipped the photo into her pocket and reached for another.

She heard a noise behind her. Footsteps. A door creaking. Before she could turn, something hit her on the back of the head.

Chapter 30

No, Joe didn't like Jimmy Jackson. No, they'd never got on. Yes, he'd go so far as to say he hated him. Yes, Jackson had tried to humiliate him, and not just once or twice. Yes, Jackson had said yesterday that Joe was having it off with Ryan MacRae's mother. No, he wasn't. Yes, he'd sat on her bed during the recent raid. No, he hadn't been touching her up. Yes, he'd have been more than happy to see Jackson off the Force. No, he wouldn't want to see Jackson dead. And no, he didn't push anyone off the Kessock Bridge.

The wee bald PSU guy looked bored. The taller one had a steely glare as he leaned back in his chair. Joe would have loved to see the chair give way. It had happened before. A touch too much arrogance, or a little boredom, and the chair was likely to go flying. More often than not it happened to the accused, rather than the interviewer. Most of the Inverness detectives were wise to it. These guys weren't.

Would Joe say he had a good relationship with Ryan MacRae? No, they had no relationship at all, but that didn't stop him understanding the boy and realising what made him the way he was.

And what would that be?

He wasn't about to give these numpties a lesson in psychology. But he had things to say; things they needed to know, though they probably wouldn't believe him. 'Jackson was out of his head on something.'

'That's convenient for you, isn't it?'

'Not really. He'd probably be here now if he hadn't been high as a kite.'

'Time will tell. Anything else?'

'He was having it off with Danielle Smith.'

The taller one laughed. 'Aye, right.'

'We've seen her picture,' the wee one said. 'As if she'd be interested in Jackson.'

Joe stared at him. 'We're not talking romance here, other than in Jackson's head. She was a prostitute. In case you're not familiar with the concept, men paid her for sex. She wasn't fussy. Wasn't about to turn Jackson away because he was an ugly rancid bastard.'

The big one leaned forward. 'You sound quite resentful towards him.'

Joe sighed. 'I thought we'd already established my resentment towards Jackson. I wouldn't get too excited about it, if I were you. And if I was going to murder him, do you really think I'd do it with Ryan MacRae looking on, and any number of cars passing by?'

'So you've thought about it?'

'No, I haven't thought about it. Why don't you go and see how many people you can find in the station that actually liked Jackson. As for those that disliked him, ask how many of them have thought about murdering him. I think you'll find there aren't too many in either category.'

'Tell us again what Ryan MacRae said.'

Joe told them again.

*

'Is that helping?'

Sharon shook her head and winced. Christopher put the bag of ice on the kitchen table. 'Maybe I should take you to A&E. I can use Isobel's car – she's just come back. She's upstairs with the kids.'

'I'll be fine. What was it?'

'An axe on the hook on the back of the door. The string broke when I banged the outer door against the cupboard door. You're lucky it didn't break the skin or knock you out.'

'An axe? Why?'

He smiled. 'It was for chopping wood for the fires. It's been there for a very long time.'

She wondered. Had he hit her with it to stop her finding something? What was he doing down there anyway, sneaking up on her? The fact that he was more entitled than she was to sneak around his family home wasn't lost on her. Nor were his manners. He'd helped her up to the kitchen, found some ice for her head, made her a cup of tea, and he hadn't even asked. Yet.

'Sharon?'

'Yeah.' Here it was.

'Were you looking for something in particular? Something I can help you with?'

He was so polite, for a lying bastard. Sharon didn't hold back. 'Aye, there is something you can help me with. How about telling me where your fucking mate, Todd, is? You do know a Todd? Stays here sometimes. The Todd that's been hanging about with my boy. The Todd that knew Peter. The Todd the police want to question. The Todd you've never mentioned.'

His eyes wouldn't meet hers, but he tried to take her hand. She pulled it away. 'How did you know Peter?'

Christopher shook his head. 'I didn't know him. Todd did. He was Peter's…his supplier. They were together the day Peter died. They'd met in Glasgow for the handover. Peter wanted to sample the goods. Todd didn't realise he was going to drive back that day. He tried to stop him, but Peter wouldn't listen. Todd was gutted when he heard about the crash.'

'So why isn't he targeting the relatives of the three people Peter killed? What about the woman that lost her young child and her elderly parents? That's who he should be feeling guilty about. Not Ryan.'

'I don't think it's about guilt. I think Todd feels some kind of duty towards Ryan, now that Peter's gone.'

'A fucking duty towards him? So he gets him involved in two murders?'

That was definitely shock on his face. Probably shocked that she knew. 'Two murders?'

'The shooting, and a young girl, just the other day.'

Christopher shook his head. 'No way was Todd involved. No way. I'm sorry I didn't tell you about Todd and Peter. I figured Ryan would tell you himself about Todd. I didn't really want to talk about that part of my life. My relationship with him is complicated, and a bit odd. To be honest, I've been trying to distance myself from him for a while.'

Aye, right. What about the sock? And Ryan saying you were both involved in the shooting? Though it was hard not to blurt everything out, Sharon knew she had to watch herself. If Todd and Christopher were killers, she could be in danger. All she wanted was to get home to her boys. But there was something she had to ask. 'Did you know who I was when you saw me in the Phoenix?'

He nodded, and she felt a shaft of pain shooting through her heart.

'Not long after I moved up north, Todd and I were parked on Grant Street, when you and the boys passed. Todd told me who you were. Liam fell and cut his knee, and you were so loving towards him. I thought you were beautiful, and I couldn't stop thinking about you. I couldn't believe my luck when I saw you with your friend in the Phoenix a couple of weeks later. I was desperate to get to know you, and it had nothing to do with Peter or Todd or anyone else.'

She almost felt better when he said that, but it was too late. 'So where does this Todd live?'

'Carlton Terrace, off Millburn Road, I think. I don't see that much of him, and I don't ask.'

'Will you go to the police?'

Christopher stared into the distance. 'He didn't kill anyone.' His voice was firm. 'I know he didn't, but I think he might be in some trouble. I was going to go out after dinner. There's some people I need to see. They might know where he is.'

'Good. Where are we going?'

He stared at her. 'You can't come. Your head – you should rest.'

Was that a reason for hitting her? To keep her from coming with him? 'No way. My son's in deep shit because of this Todd. If you're going looking for him, I'm coming.'

'It might not be pleasant.'

'I'm a big girl. I can handle it.'

Chapter 31

Joe was suspended while the investigation was on-going. He was free to go, they said, for now. They didn't give him his phone back, so he couldn't call Carla. He sat in the car and wondered if she was home, if she was okay. He couldn't wait to see her. Probably best to go to the hospital first, and take it from there.

He started up the engine. Before he could pull out, Roberts and Tina Lewis drew in beside him. He knew he couldn't speak to them; it wouldn't be right. He should just ignore them, drive away. But when Tina Lewis opened his passenger door and whispered the name of a pub, he decided he'd join them for one drink, then he'd go to the hospital.

*

In the Clachnaharry Inn, Joe ordered a half-pint. He was looking forward to seeing Roberts. He had no intention of discussing today's events. All he wanted was a friendly face, and a bit of inane chat. Maybe a game of pool. That would be enough. But Roberts didn't come. Just Tina Lewis, with way too much lipstick and a beguiling smile. The clang of warning bells almost deafened Joe. He was used to them by now; he heard them every time she was near, but tonight he was past the point of listening.

Tina bought two drams and pointed him towards a table in the corner. She said nothing about Jackson or Ryan MacRae or the investigation, until Joe asked how they'd got on at Castlefield Apartments.

Tina shrugged. 'We didn't get much. There's a James Allingham lives on the first floor. Apparently, he has a scar on his face. Hasn't been there for a while, but it's not unusual for him to be away for long periods. Someone else has been staying there recently, and he fits Todd Curtis's description. Allingham has a black Lexus. We've got the registration and it's logged on ANPR. When I left tonight, the DI was considering what to do next. He wanted to talk it through with DCI MacBain.'

Tina always looked good, but with each dram, her looks and her wit were enhanced until Joe could hardly take his eyes off her. She laughed and teased and made him forget. They played pool and she beat him hands down. When some ugly wee bastard tried to charm Tina, Joe felt his hackles rising and his hand tightening on the pool cue. It reminded him of a night in a pub in Perth, before he'd even turned twenty. He was playing pool with his pal, Matt, when these two girls started coming on to them. He and Matt hadn't even argued over which one they preferred; they were both gorgeous. The night was going so well, until their Neanderthal boyfriends turned up. Matt wasn't a fighter. He'd talked the pool cue out of Joe's hands, persuaded him that, gorgeous though the girls were, they really weren't worth fighting over. 'That kind of anger's bad,' Matt had told him, as they walked back to their flat.

Joe knew he was right. Several double vodkas inside him, and he'd felt invincible, as if he could have taken both guys and half a dozen more. And for what? He'd given up spirits then. Stuck to beer and the odd glass of wine. Until Tina Lewis decided she knew what was best for him.

She knew what was best now, as she took the pool cue from Joe's hands, winked at the other guy, and led Joe out of the pub.

Back at her house, she opened a bottle of wine, and put on some music. She sat beside Joe on the sofa. Close, too close. She passed him a glass.

'Thanks. D'you think I killed him?'

She shook her head.

'I told Roberts last night I'd like to.'

'Yeah? He didn't say.'

'I hated him.'

'You weren't alone there.' Her voice was soft. She reached a hand towards his leg, touched his knee. 'You're not alone now.'

She was much closer. Her blonde hair brushed his face as she leaned towards him. Her breath smelled of toothpaste, and her neck of perfume. He felt her lips on his, the slide of her lipstick, and the gentle biting of her teeth.

*

Sharon knew evil. And she knew it wasn't always obvious. Peter MacRae had been a good looking guy, with a broad smile and beautiful blue eyes. He was a bit overweight, and it made him look cuddly. For a long time, she hadn't seen the evil. His temper and cold sarcasm were never far away, but the evil was buried deep, waiting. And when it came, and stayed, she knew she was to blame. If she hadn't spoken back to him, if she hadn't given so much love to Ryan and Liam, if she hadn't wanted so much, the evil wouldn't have come. She was convinced it must be her fault. Her mother had told her often enough just how evil she was. Her mother's boyfriends and their beatings, their wandering hands; none of that would have happened if Sharon and her siblings hadn't been evil.

Aye, right. Sharon knew now that neither she nor her siblings were evil. But this guy was. It was in his eyes, and it was dark and strong, and if she looked too long, she might drown in the fear that was washing over her. She wanted to reach for Christopher's hand, but that wasn't an option now.

They'd entered the club through a back door in a filthy alley. Sharon hadn't heard what Christopher muttered to the thug on the door, but the way the bugger had looked at her made her shiver.

They followed the thug down a corridor. To her right, behind a wall, she could hear music, talking and laughter, bottles clinking. They climbed a rickety stair to a landing with two doors and another stair.

'Stay here.' The thug knocked on the nearest door and went in.

Christopher tried to smile at Sharon, but his mouth was having none of it. There was sweat on his brow. Behind them, a door opened. Sharon turned and saw a blonde girl, her head down as she slid past. She was wearing a towel, and she ran up the next stair. She looked about fourteen. The door was still open. As someone hurried to close it, Sharon saw a mirrored wall, bright lights, a bed, two naked men. And that smell. 'Oh fuck.'

'What?' Christopher's eyes had been on the other door, waiting for it to open.

'Nothing. A bit nervous, that's all.'

It was like something she'd seen on screen, so many times. The back alley, the thug, the stairs, and the doors, hiding secrets and shame. She expected the vice squad to burst in at any moment.

And now the door was opening and the thug was beckoning them into the room.

At least you could see what the thug was. Not like these two, in their designer suits and shiny shoes, Rolex watches and soft undercut hairstyles. Smart as fuck, and probably twice as evil. They made Sharon's skin crawl. Christopher seemed happy enough to see them. The older of the two, a swarthy mafia type in his late forties, stood and reached for his hand. 'Chris, my man. Put it there.'

The younger one, a skinny guy with red hair, followed suit. 'Chris, dude. What's kickin'?'

Dude what's kickin'? His arse needed kicking.

'Same old, same old. Guys, this is Sharon. Sharon, Dino and Lucas.'

Dino took her hand first. She thought he was going to kiss it, but he didn't. Just held onto it and stared into her eyes until she had to look away. It wasn't any easier with Lucas. His hand was sweating, slimy, disgusting. She avoided his eyes.

'How is life in Scotland?' Dino asked.

Before Christopher could answer, Lucas laughed. 'Fucking Jockland? Fuck's sake. Fucking Sturgeon. Fucking ball-breaker, man. Fucking Jocks'll have us all fucking bankrupt.'

Sharon stared at him. The language. Lack of vocabulary or what? And who did he think he was, slagging off Nicola like that?

Christopher smiled. 'It's good. I like it.'

'And Todd Curtis?' Dino's voice was cold. 'Does he like it?'

The camaraderie was gone. There was silence. Steely eyes.

Christopher's face paled. He shrugged. 'I'm a bit worried about him. He said he was heading down south. I wondered if you'd seen him.'

Dino picked something up off the desk. It looked like a letter opener, but sharper, deadly. He turned it over in his hands. 'I haven't seen him, but I'd very much like to.' Sharon jumped as he drove the thing into the desk.

'Sharon, doll,' Lucas said. 'How about you go with the ape and leave us men to talk?'

'I don't think so.' Go with 'the ape'? That'd be right. Was that his nickname or just a very fitting description? She felt a hand on her arm. 'Don't fucking touch me, ape.'

The ape laughed, a high-pitched sound that echoed round the room. 'Pardon me, Ma'am. But you're leaving one way or another.

What's it to be? On your own two feet or over my shoulder?'

Christopher gave her a weak smile. 'Go on, Sharon; I won't be long.'

'Run along, doll,' Dino said. 'And ape, no touching.'

As the door was closing, Sharon was certain she heard Dino mention the name Katya.

They were standing in the downstairs corridor and the way the ape was looking at her was winding her up. She glared at him. 'Less of the drooling, eh?'

'What's that, Jock?'

Fucking Jock? See if he touched her, she'd rip his balls off. Sharon hadn't felt this hyped up since…she couldn't remember when. This ape might have evil in his eyes, but she'd die rather than let him touch. 'Think you're smart with the comments, do you?'

He laughed and moved closer. Sharon was right up against the wall in a very narrow corridor. And he was huge. As her bravado slipped away, she could smell his excitement.

'I like a bird with a bit of fighting spirit. Turns me on.'

'I expect most of your birds have no choice but to fight back.'

He winked. 'You've got the picture. No excitement if they're willing, is there?' He cupped his crotch.

'You're giving me the dry boak.'

'Eh? I know what I'd like to give you.'

'Dream on.'

His hand shot out and grabbed her throat, forcing the back of her head into the wall. 'Fucking Jock bitch. You want to learn some proper English and some manners.' His breath was hot on her neck. With his other hand, he grabbed her breast. 'Nice.' He squeezed, and laughed when the pain made her groan. She felt his knee forcing her legs apart. She looked into his eyes and they were cold, dead. 'No,' she tried to say, as his hand on her throat squeezed tighter. 'Please.'

Chapter 32

Lucy had been trying to contact Joe all day. She'd seen on the BBC website that an officer had fallen from the Kessock Bridge. He was in his forties, so she knew it wasn't Joe, but it still worried her. In the early evening, she'd given up. She'd read up on Permanence Orders for one of Drew's cases, then she'd watched telly. She was rinsing some dishes in the kitchen when she heard her phone ping. At last. But it wasn't Joe.

> *Lucy. Constantly on my mind. With love and apologies and hope that life is all you want it to be. Yours always xx*

What? Who? She didn't recognise the number, and she wasn't sure she knew anyone except Joe that wrote texts in proper English. It wasn't Graeme Freel, was it? He had her number, and a creepy way of looking at her. No, it couldn't be. The only thing he had to apologise for was his utter incompetence as a solicitor.

Sebastian Moore? No way would her last boyfriend be contacting her. Too scared she'd wreck the precious marriage he'd forgotten to mention while they were going out together. He wasn't going to risk opening the can of worms that had resulted from their relationship, was he? Unless his marriage had ended. He certainly owed her an apology. Several hundred apologies. And he was posh enough to write like this. But why wouldn't he put his name on the text?

She could ignore it. She could delete it and block the number. She could reply. She replied.

> *S?*

A few seconds of dread while she waited.

> *Yes*

Bloody hell. A car engine was running outside. Lucy went through to the living room. She peeped through the curtains. A taxi. She watched as the back door opened and someone fell onto the pavement.

Lucy helped Joe up. There was drool running from the corner of his mouth and he had the eyes of a dead cod. She pushed him against the garden wall, rifled through his pocket, found some cash, and paid the driver.

He thanked her. 'Do you want a hand to get him in, love?'

'Should be okay, ta.' Was that the neighbour's curtains twitching? 'Where did you pick him up?'

The driver shrugged and said nothing.

'I appreciate you probably feel duty bound to adhere to some misguided Cabbies' Code of Conduct for the Protection of the Meandering Male, but he's not my husband or my boyfriend; he's my brother. Does that make a difference?'

'What are you – a lawyer?'

Recognition at last. Lucy smiled. 'Could be.'

'Leachkin Drive.'

That meant nothing. 'Thanks.'

Lucy prodded Joe up the drive and into the house. It wasn't easy. His legs were like rubber and his arms like the blades of a windmill. And at least two of the neighbours' curtains had progressed from twitching to wide open.

When she'd shoved Joe through the front door, and laughed as he tripped over her mother's 'welcome' mat, Lucy waved to the taxi driver, then both neighbours.

*

If Sharon could get him in the balls, he'd let go. She tried to lift her knee. The ape laughed. 'No fucking chance, bitch.' He pressed his full weight against her, his hand thrust between her legs.

At the end of the corridor, the outside door opened. Footsteps. Stilettos. A squeal, and Sharon was released. She gasped for breath, and saw a manicured hand twisting the ape's right ear.

'Ape, you bastard.' A posh voice with a hint of a foreign accent. 'You are an animal.'

The woman was older than Sharon, tanned and beautiful. She was wearing a tight red dress and black stilettos, and carrying a soft black leather tote that would have made Sharon's mouth water, if she wasn't half choked.

Ape was trying to prise the woman's hand off his ear. 'Please, stop.' He sounded as if he was about to cry. 'Dino said – '

'Whatever Dino said, he certainly didn't say, 'Choke this woman and sexually assault her'.'

'He told me to keep an eye on her.'

She let him go. 'You had more than an eye on her.' She turned to Sharon. 'Do you want to press charges? I'd be happy to be a witness.'

Sharon shook her head. She just wanted Christopher to hurry up so they could get out of here.

'Ape, it's your lucky day. Upstairs. Now.'

The ape backed off, his right ear beaming, his eyes full of resentment, and more. His feet were slow on the steps, and when he reached half-way, he turned and glared at them both.

'You better watch your back,' Sharon said, the words scratching and croaking as she forced them out. 'He didn't like that.'

The woman smiled. 'I will not lose any sleep over it. I'm sorry you had to go through that.'

'Thank f…I mean, thank you for coming along when you did.'

'Are you here about a job?'

Sharon shook her head. 'I'd have to be desperate to work in this shit-hole. Are you?'

The woman's laughter was loud. She took a while to compose herself. It wasn't that funny, was it? 'I wouldn't work in this shit-hole either.'

'I'm waiting for my…for a friend. He's with two dodgy cu…customers upstairs. Probably nailed both his hands to the desk by now.'

The woman was still smiling. 'Has there been any screaming?'

'No, but I was a bit preoccupied for a few minutes there. Might have missed it.'

'Is he in trouble with these dodgy cu…customers?'

Sharon shrugged. 'Dunno. Old pals of Christopher's, I think. I was just tagging along.'

'Christopher?' Her smile broadened. 'Chris Brent? He came?'

Sharon nodded and wondered. The woman offered her right hand to Sharon. 'Elena Conti.'

Cool name. Her nails were shellacked, her skin soft, and her handshake strong. 'Sharon MacRae.'

'MacRae? We knew a Peter MacRae. He was Scottish too.'

'Another animal. I was stupid enough to marry him.'

There was compassion in her eyes. 'You need a drink.'

'Aye, I did, and more than just drink for several years, but I'm over it. Coffee would do fine for now.' A drink would have been just the thing, but the back of her head was throbbing again, and she couldn't risk letting her guard down with Christopher.

Elena nodded and shouted: 'Ape, tell Chris we're in the lounge when he's ready.'

There was a grunt from upstairs.

The club was no shit-hole. They sat in a quiet corner with low lighting, but Sharon still felt conspicuous. Though her jeans cost more than she got in Child Benefit for a month, there was no way anyone in denim would normally be sitting here. Even the staff were in dresses and suits. The handbag had a chair to itself, and it didn't half deserve it. Elena noticed Sharon's envy. 'Beautiful, isn't it? Givenchy. Dino chose it all by himself. It has only taken him twenty years to know what I like.'

Sharon spluttered into her coffee. 'Dino? Oh fuck.' She put the cup down and wiped her mouth. 'I'm sorry. I had no idea.'

Elena laughed and patted Sharon's arm. 'Don't be. You made me laugh. They are dodgy customers, but I'm certain they're not nailing Chris's hands to the desk. He's a good friend.'

'I'm not even going to ask. The less I know, the better.'

Elena's hand tightened on Sharon's arm. 'You should know that he is a decent man, a good man. Don't doubt him.'

Aye, right.

Sharon's stomach lurched when she saw the way Christopher and Elena looked at each other. Then the grasp of hands, a slow melt against each other, a lengthy embrace. Don't be so stupid, she told herself. You don't care about him; you can't. Dino didn't look too happy about it either, his arms crossed, dark eyes glued to his wife. Christopher was first to let go, but not before Sharon heard him apologise to Elena. And something about Katya.

Chapter 33

'Carla, I really really really love you.' The words were croaked through dry lips.

'I'm not Carla. Get up, will you?' Lucy hauled at his arm until he scrambled to his feet. What a state, and was that lipstick on his face? Leaning against the wall, he started scrabbling in his pockets.

'You looking for your phone?'

He nodded. Lucy tried his pockets. 'Looks like you've lost it. You might have to actually go and buy yourself one at last.' His phone had been her old iPhone 4.

His face turned the colour of chalk, and Lucy ran for a basin.

When Joe was done throwing up, Lucy helped him through to the kitchen, then she rinsed out the basin and brought it back, just in case. He was sitting at the table with his head in his hands, groaning. 'I need to speak to her.'

'Joe, it's too late, even if you had your phone. Is she still in hospital?'

He shrugged. 'Dunno.'

'Why don't you just go to bed? You can get in touch with her in the morning.'

He looked like a wee lost boy. 'I just need...I just want her to know.'

'I'm sure she does. Come on, I'll help you to the spare room. You're taking your own clothes off, though.'

He looked like he might be trying to smile, then he threw up again.

*

The late train was packed. Christopher kept his voice low. 'I'm sorry for taking you into my sordid past, especially when it didn't lead anywhere. They're seriously pissed off with Todd. Something about him running off with one of their best girls.'

'Why would he do that?'

Christopher shook his head. 'I...I think he's involved in prostitution. Sharon, are you okay? Are we okay?'

'Chris…is it all right if I call you that? Everyone else does.'

'No, it's not all right. I like the way you say my name, my proper name.'

'Okay, Christopher; no, I'm not okay. While you were chewing the fat with the Cosa Nostra, their hired ape groped and hurt me with one hand, while trying to choke me with the other. If Elena hadn't arrived, I'd have been raped. I suppose it's no big deal when you move in these circles.'

For the first time since they'd met, she saw fury in his eyes. 'Of course it's a big deal. I had no idea. I'm going back there. I'm going to have it out with…with Ape.'

'Don't talk shit. What do you expect if you leave me in the care of something called 'Ape', in a dodgy, albeit posh, club run by serious criminals that are filming underage porn? Anyway, it's not the first time it's happened to me. Probably won't be the last.'

'Don't say that, Sharon. It will be the last.' He took her hand, half-smiled. 'Are we having our first argument?'

Hardly. This was full-on final death throes, only she couldn't tell him yet. A little goading might make her feel better. 'Does Dino know how you and Elena feel about each other?'

He looked uncomfortable. 'It's not like that. She's just a friend.'

'A sexy, gorgeous, elegant friend, with the hots for you.'

'No way. She's just a friend. I promise.'

She nodded. 'Probably best to keep it that way. Wouldn't fancy your chances if Dino thought there was anything going on.'

He took her hand and stared into her eyes. 'I just want to focus on the future, on us.'

She looked away.

Isobel had suggested they sleep in the green room on the second floor, but Christopher wanted to stay in the lodge. It had one bedroom, a living room and kitchen, and a bathroom. And it was still posh.

As he locked the door, Sharon wondered if he was going to do away with her in the night. Maybe Todd was here. Maybe Ryan was right; this had all been an elaborate plan to get back at Peter MacRae for something. If it was, she was too tired to worry about it. She spent ages in the shower, trying to scrub away the memory of the ape. It didn't work.

While Christopher was in the shower, she picked up his phone. There was a slight feeling of guilt as she swiped across the screen, but she couldn't think like that. They had no future. She needed to find anything that might help her son. She heard the shower stop. She didn't have much time. She went to his recent calls. He'd taken a call from someone just after midnight last night. And he'd called that number back at two, and again at four in the morning. Was it Todd?

As they lay in bed, Christopher told Sharon he'd stayed in the lodge for a while after his accident. 'I couldn't bear to be in the house with my parents fussing over me, but I needed them. My father had not long retired and he was in my face all the time. At least I could lock the door of the lodge and ignore them when I wanted to.' He put his arms round her and kissed her neck.

She moved away from him. 'I'm sorry, Christopher.'

'No, I'm sorry.' He stroked her face. 'You're worried about Ryan.'

'Not to mention feeling disgusting after that bastard pawing me.'

'He's disgusting, not you. I'm so angry about that; I'll never sleep. Can I…can I tell you something?'

'If you want.'

The curtains weren't pulled properly. She could see the moon in a cloudless sky, the shadows of the tall trees waving. Christopher was lying on his back. He took a deep breath. 'Sharon, we may have more in common than you know. I…I used to take drugs too.'

'You what?' Sharon got up on her elbow and stared at him. 'Do you mean prescription drugs?'

He shook his head. 'Cannabis. It was the only thing that helped the pain.'

Sharon wanted to laugh, but that was too cruel. 'Cannabis isn't such a big deal.'

'It was for me, the amount I was using. And I wasn't just using.'

'You were dealing?'

'For a while. I was sick of living off my parents and I couldn't work. It seemed an easy way to make money. I wasn't into anything harder. I hate that stuff; you know that. And eventually

I hated the worry about getting caught, and the people I had to mix with.'

'Dino and Lucas?'

He nodded. 'I'm sorry, Sharon. I haven't done right by you. And I don't just mean with Todd and Peter. I mean not telling you about my past, about the accident, not taking you to my house until recently, not introducing you to friends and family.'

Sharon shrugged. 'I wouldn't introduce someone like me to my family either, if I was you. It's no big deal.'

'No, Sharon.' He ran his hand up her arm, making her skin tingle. 'Don't say that. I would never be ashamed of you.'

'Not now you've cleaned me up. You wouldn't have been taking me home last summer when we met, would you? You wouldn't even have taken me now, if your mother hadn't been ill.'

'I haven't been home since before we met. I don't like London and all its memories, but I've never been ashamed of you. Never.'

He was probably telling the truth. He hadn't shown any sign of being ashamed of her, even before she'd been done up. It didn't really matter now.

'So why have you never introduced me to Todd?'

He was silent for ages. 'I…he…I don't like the way he treats women. And he's probably still dealing.'

'In Inverness?'

'I think so, but I don't ask.'

'Does he know you're seeing me?'

'He…he knows there's someone.'

Liar. Todd couldn't have got his hands on the sock without Christopher telling him where he'd got it.

*

Todd didn't put on any lights in Chris's house. Though no houses overlooked this one, or the garden, you never knew who might be out and about. Chris could come home even. Unlikely. There hadn't been any movement in the house since he and the tart left with suitcases early in the morning, and his car wasn't down the Ferry. Where the hell were they? Off for a romantic break?

Things didn't always turn out as planned. Maybe they were on their way back now. His pulse quickened at the thought. What would he do? Hide under the desk and slip out when they were asleep? Confront them and see his friend squirm, see the slapper crapping it? Hide under the bed and…? So many possibilities.

His head torch did the job. He yawned as he waited for the laptop to start. This heap of junk just wasn't good enough; it had to be sorted. When all this was over, and everything had quietened down, he'd bring it up. New laptop? Leave it with me. Anything for a mate.

At last he was in. Flights to London? He felt an unfamiliar shiver of fear in his belly. Was Chris meeting Dino and Lucas? Would he tell them where Todd was? He should have confided in Chris before now. Told him that he didn't want to be found by anyone, and certainly not by Dino and Lucas. Trouble was, he didn't trust anyone, not even Chris.

And he had taken the tart? What was that all about? Not exactly the type you take home to mother. Meet Sharon. She's a junkie. Mother of teenage killer, Ryan MacRae. Widow of junkie loser, Peter MacRae. *Jesus.*

Calm. Centre yourself. Deep breathing. She will not win. She cannot.

Chapter 34

There was music. Arms around Joe's neck. The smell of perfume and peppermint. He was trying to shake the arms off, but he couldn't. The face was shadowy, indistinct, as the lips tried to kiss his face, his neck, tried to get to his mouth. Carla? Wrong perfume.

The smell changed. It was tweed and after-shave, sea-salt and cut grass. And still he couldn't see the face. There were hands on his little childhood shoulders, a mouth whispering in an ancient tongue that calmed his heart. Tears on his face and a hand wiping them away, the skin rough but the touch gentle.

And then it was Carla, and her face was clear. He tried to say the words, to tell her how sorry he was, but nothing would come out. And she stared at him, her dark brown eyes brimming with hurt.

Joe pushed the covers away and tried to get up. His spinning head had him flat out again in seconds. But he had to pee; he had to get something to drink. Slowly. Gently. He tried again, and made it to his feet. The journey to the toilet was a blast, his head as light as a balloon, his legs like jelly, and his stomach threatening to leap out of his mouth.

As he retched over the toilet he tried to remember what had happened after Tina's lips closed in on him. There was nothing. Only Lucy rifling through his pockets in the street as the taxi engine idled. And then a desperate search for his mobile phone, and a longing to speak to Carla and tell her how much he loved her.

How often had he scoffed at people that claimed to have been too drunk to remember what they'd done the night before? Too often. But there was much to remember earlier in the day. Mostly eyes. The betrayal in Ryan MacRae's eyes when he discovered Joe had lied; Jimmy Jackson's drugged, mental eyes before his backward flip into the Beauly Firth; the earnest but dead eyes of the numpties from the PSU as they asked yet another series of mindless questions that he'd already answered; and the predatory, cunning eyes of Tina Lewis.

The clock in the kitchen said ten past seven; Lucy would be up soon. A pint of water and a couple of paracetamol would be good, but he doubted he could keep anything down. Perhaps a walk to the Clachnaharry Inn to get his car, but it was a long way, and he was probably still over the limit. Was it too early to phone the hospital?

He decided to wait until eight. After a small glass of water and two paracetamol, he went back to bed. As his head hit the pillow, he remembered something, and he wished he hadn't. Tina Lewis might well have been manipulative, but look how he had reacted when another guy came on to her. What was that all about?

As if he didn't know. Every guy in the station fancied Tina Lewis. She was gorgeous, and whenever she looked at him, Joe felt as if she could read his thoughts. It was easier not to look at her, to avoid her. He had known deep down just how easy it would be to fall for her. But how far had he fallen last night?

At eight, he heard Lucy in the bathroom, then the kitchen. The smell of toast almost started him retching again. He could hardly bear to face his sister, far less her breakfast, but there was no point lying in bed going over and over last night, beating himself up, and dissing Tina Lewis.

'Toast?' Lucy offered him her plate with two slices of toast. Was that marmalade? It turned his stomach at the best of times. He made the sign of the cross and shook his head.

'Coffee?'

Another shake.

'A bullet?'

'Aye, that would do it. Do you think it'd be all right to phone the hospital now?'

Lucy shrugged. 'Should be. Any idea what you did with your phone?'

It would be so easy to say he'd lost it, along with Carla and his self-respect. 'Aye, I know exactly what I did with it.' And he told her.

Lucy pushed her toast away. 'I read about that, but I didn't think for a minute you'd been involved. I was trying to contact you all day. No wonder you were in such a state last night.'

'How bad was I?'

'You want the truth?'

He shook his head. It hurt. 'No thanks. I'll just go and phone the hospital.'

Carla wasn't there. She'd gone home yesterday, in a taxi. He phoned a florist and ordered a bouquet. No, he didn't have a clue what flowers she might like. Anything, the bigger the better. And a grovelling message of apology.

*

Sharon had been in some rough places in her life, but they were palatial compared to this squat. Have a seat? That'd be right. She'd just stay where she was, thank you very much, close to the door, ready for a quick exit when the smell overwhelmed her. Christopher sat, though he didn't look too comfortable. Across from him, on an ancient threadbare sofa, Banger was rolling a joint with military precision, using a rolling block and a pair of tweezers. Would Christopher take a smoke? She wouldn't mind a wee toke herself, in the right circumstances, but these were definitely not the right circumstances. Christopher asked Banger if he'd seen Todd recently.

'Todd the sod?' Banger's accent was straight out of Eastenders. No surprise, really; they were in Hackney in north east London, checking out another contact of Todd's. 'Haven't see him in ages, mate. Thought you two were closer than my arse cheeks.'

Christopher hesitated. 'I'm worried about him. He's…he might be in a bit of trouble.'

Banger laughed. 'Not before time, mate. Never known anyone dodge the Old Bill for so long.'

'When did you last see him?'

He shrugged. 'Few months.' He held the joint up, turning it in his fingers. 'You taught me that, mate. Never forgotten it. Here.'

Sharon watched the struggle on Christopher's face. She knew what he was feeling, probably better than he did.

'No thanks.'

Banger shrugged and looked at Sharon. 'She doesn't approve? That's posh birds for you. Come back without her, mate.'

Sharon laughed and considered pulling up her sleeves so he could see just how posh she was. But he'd mistaken her for someone decent, someone with morals. What a score.

Christopher stood. There was something stuck to his arse. Looked like a bit of mouldy sausage roll. It fell off before he reached the door, leaving a blue and grey smear on his trousers.

Sharon didn't look into the other rooms as they negotiated their passage to the front door, stepping over paint tins and bricks, and circling round an old twin-tub and a cracked toilet pan. The toilet pan nearly did for her, when she glanced in and saw an enormous turd, fresh as. Backing away from it, she almost fell over the cistern lid, perched against the wall. 'Fuck's sake.'

Her shout aroused something in the last room, and movement caught her eye. Impossible to tell what was beneath the pile of filthy bedding, in a room with a half bricked-up window. Enough light to see the bulging ceiling and long streaks of black mould running down the walls.

Outside, Sharon took great gulps of fresh air, followed by a few draws of her e-cig. She offered it to Christopher. He shook his head.

'Not quite as attractive as the toke? Tempting, wasn't it?'

He looked as if he might deny it for a moment, then he smiled. 'It was indeed.'

*

Christopher visited his mother again, while Sharon waited outside. He wanted her to come in, but there was no point. He asked her if they were all right, as they headed for the airport. She smiled and told him they were. It was just a difficult time for them both.

Chapter 35

Lucy was sitting up the back of the bus with earphones on. She'd refused to sit beside Joe, 'cos he was stinking of drink. He couldn't blame her. Every time the bus went over a bump in the road, his stomach lurched. He had a plastic bag in his pocket, just in case. He hadn't checked it for holes, though.

The bag wasn't needed. By the time they reached town, he thought he might manage a cup of tea in the Castle Restaurant. Lucy left him to it. Half a bacon roll and a cup of tea later, Joe set off for the Clachnaharry Inn. It was a good thirty minute walk. Surely he'd be safe to drive by the time he got there. He dodged a couple of uniforms on Church Street, slipping into a lane until they passed. Soon he was across the Greig Street Bridge and making his way down the river side. He stuck to side-streets until he turned off Telford Road on to Telford Street. Typical – the first car to pass him was a patrol car. They weren't looking.

At the Muirtown Bridge, he took the canal tow path towards Clachnaharry, to give his liver a little more time to do its stuff. There were some fine boats moored in the marina, but they scarcely registered with him. He was too busy beating himself up.

As he neared the locks, he glanced to his right and his stomach turned. In the distance, through the trees, a convoy of tiny cars were crossing the Kessock Bridge. The sun was glinting off the grey metal. It looked so innocuous. And lethal.

At Clachnaharry there were 30mph signs in the windows of the houses. As Joe approached his car, he understood. The wing mirror on the driver's side was hanging off. He'd parked just before the bus stop on the busy narrow road that led north out of Inverness. Idiot. He should have moved the car before he decided to drink himself senseless.

Driving past the station on Burnett Road, he was tempted to go in and ask if Ryan MacRae had seen the light yet, but there was no point. They'd let him know if anything changed, and the only way they could do that for now was on his landline. But he couldn't go home yet.

Either Carla was out or she didn't want to answer the door to him. Maybe she was in bed. Maybe she was ill. As he unlocked her door and stepped into her hallway, he felt certain there was no one at home. In her bedroom, the bed was made, and there were clothes on the bed, neatly folded. Was she planning a trip? Had she already gone? He hadn't expected her to be well enough to leave the house, far less travel.

The doorbell rang. Joe opened the door to a massive bouquet and a pair of skinny legs. The florist had done him proud; just a shame Carla wasn't there to appreciate the gesture. He put the bouquet in a jug of water in the kitchen, then he checked Carla's address book and wrote down the numbers for her mother and Ronald MacKenzie. He didn't want to phone either of them yet; he'd keep trying Carla from his home phone, and come back round later to see if she was in.

Carla's journey had started well enough. Although the plane was smaller and noisier than any she'd been on before, she'd enjoyed the trip as far as Stornoway. It was a good day and she had a clear view of the mountains and lochs of the west coast, and the wee boats in the Minch. The journey from Stornoway to Benbecula was bumpy, with low cloud and no visibility. She saw nothing until the clouds parted on descent, revealing water of the deepest blue, and swathes of white sand. At least they had a proper runway on Benbecula, unlike the island of Barra, where the planes landed on the beach at low tide. Still, the sand would have provided a softer landing.

Benbecula lay between North Uist and South Uist, linking the chain of islands with a series of causeways. The airport was in the village of Balivanich, on the north-west coast. It was the main hub of the island, with a collection of shops, council offices and a police station.

Carla was glad they took a while to open the plane and affix the steps, for she wasn't sure she could stand. She shouldn't have come. It was a stupid idea, running away from the boredom of sick leave and the fear of her results, not to mention wanting to punish Joe for his neglect.

It was so unlike him not to keep in touch, even though his work always came first. He'd been really worried about her in the hospital, so why would he suddenly stop contacting her? She'd given in last night and called him, but it had gone straight to voicemail. She hadn't left a message.

It was breezy in Balivanich, but the air was warm. As she walked towards the terminal building, she saw her cousin standing at the window, and her heart leapt. He was so like her father.

Ronald smelled of soap and grass as he hugged her. 'I can't believe you're here.'

'Me neither.' When they parted, she saw a hint of tears in his eyes. He made her sit down while they waited for the luggage, then he talked non-stop, as if he was scared that any pause would allow the tears to come.

Ronald continued talking as he drove north. The roads had changed a lot since Carla was last here. Part of the causeway to North Uist was 'two-way' now. It was the same on the road between Clachan and Lochmaddy, Ronald said.

'Takes the fun out of driving here,' Carla said. 'Though I didn't think it very funny when Dad sped over blind summits on single-track roads, straight into the path of an oncoming vehicle.'

'There's still miles and miles of single-track – the fun's not over.' Right on cue, he slammed on the brakes, pulling in to the side, as a small bus bore down upon them.

'I see what you mean.'

Ronald turned right onto a narrow winding road that cut across North Uist.

'What's this road called?' Carla asked. 'I remember it had a funny name.'

'The Committee Road. It was built to provide famine relief in the mid-19th century after the crops failed. Rather than give them something for nothing, the men were expected to work for their rations – two stones of Indian maize a fortnight.'

'Sounds like something Iain Duncan Smith would come up with.'

Carla didn't understand Ronald's Gaelic response, but it didn't sound like a compliment.

The road led them across the moor, where many of the peat

banks that had once provided warmth for the island homes now lay unused. There were one or two still worked, Ronald said, but most people relied on oil these days. Not him, though.

The view across to the tidal island of Vallay took Carla's breath. The skyline was dominated by the ruins of a baronial-style mansion built around 1902. 'I'd love to go there. Dad promised to take me, but the tide was never right.'

'If you're up to it, we can go. We'll take the tractor.'

Carla smiled. 'That would be great.'

As they passed the road to the cemetery, she was relieved the graves couldn't be seen from the road. 'I keep it tidy,' Ronald said.

'Thank you. I appreciate it.'

'We'll go whenever you're ready.'

Carla nodded.

Everything in the kitchen was the same. The stove and the easy chair, the lino and the bench, the boots at the door, and the pervading smell of peat. It felt so much like home that Carla cried. Ronald patted her shoulder and took her bag through to the downstairs bedroom that had once been 'the good room'.

By the time he returned, she had composed herself. She was looking out the window, down to the shore. The tide was in and the water was striped in gentle shades of blue and green, the long grass dancing in the breeze.

'Are you sure you won't miss the television?' he asked. 'It would be no bother to get one. I've been thinking about it for a while.'

Carla smiled. 'I bet you haven't.'

'I have, ever since I knew you were coming.'

'I won't miss it. I've several books to read, and I hope I'll be up to going out for walks before too long.'

'And you'll be visiting the neighbours?'

That hadn't been on Carla's agenda. Not that she'd mind, if she knew them, but the people she remembered were gone now. 'Will they expect a visit?'

He laughed and shook his head. 'I'm having you on. Most of them are out working all day anyway. There's always Will, but you'll not get much out of him.' He nodded down the croft to a caravan near the shore. 'He's been living there for a while now, but we've hardly spoken. Walks to the shop and back for his coal in the winter. He won't even take a lift, poor soul. Sometimes I see him sitting outside, huddled by a fire.'

'Who owns the caravan?'

Ronald shrugged. 'I'm not sure. It's been empty for years, since Jessie died. I don't think she had any living relatives, unless there was a distant cousin or two. Maybe he's related to her. Who knows?'

Carla laughed. 'This is not the Uist I remember. Your mother and her pals would have had his full credentials within hours.'

He smiled. 'Aye, things have changed right enough. All too busy working now, and then there's the television and the internet.'

'But not for us.' Carla turned away from the window. 'Will I put the kettle on? You can have a cup of tea and then get back to work. You better get out of those good clothes too.'

Ronald laughed. 'Yes, Mum.'

Chapter 36

There was a fly on the kitchen window. Joe tried to let it out, but it didn't want to go. He hadn't the heart to squash it, so he left it. A bit of company for him. He watched as it made the journey from the sill to the small open window at the top, over and over again. Each time, he willed it to find its way out, but as soon as it neared the open window, it seemed to lose focus, falling back down to the sill, and starting again. Each time it fell, he'd turn and look at the clock on the wall. Time had never taken so long to pass.

His stomach wasn't quite right yet, but it was growling at him, so he made a cup of tea and a cheese sandwich. When he looked at the clock again, he almost cheered. Surely everyone in South Carolina was up and about by now.

Carla's mother sounded just like her, but with a slight American twang.

'Hello. I'm Joe Galbraith, Carla's…'

'Carla's boyfriend. Is she all right?'

He had no idea. He'd gone back to her flat twice, but there was no sign of her. Carla's mother didn't wait for an answer. 'I told her it was a stupid idea but she wouldn't listen. She needs to rest, not gallivant off to the back of beyond. Uist? She could have come here and relaxed in sunshine and civilisation.'

Uist?

'Did she get there all right? Has something happened?'

There was no point lying. 'I didn't know she'd gone. I've been…eh…involved in a big case at work and I've…I've lost my mobile phone, so I haven't been able to contact her. I went round today and she wasn't there. I panicked and thought I'd phone you.'

'Oh, I thought you and she were…well, never mind; that's where she's gone, to see her cousin in North Uist.'

'Ronald.'

'Aye. Do you have his number?'

'Yes. I'd be grateful for Carla's mobile number, though. It was in my phone, and I don't know it…'

'I know. I keep meaning to copy the numbers from my cell

phone down, but I never get round to it. Wait a minute.'

While he waited, Joe googled flights from Inverness to Benbecula. He didn't google the ferries. He knew without looking that it was the same ferry that sailed from Uig to North Uist, and to Tarbert on Harris. He'd journeyed to Tarbert twice last year, and he wasn't quite ready to face the ferry again.

Her mum was back with the number. He wrote it down and thanked her. 'You wouldn't know Ronald's address, would you?'

She laughed. 'No. I've only been there once and I tried to erase everything about it from my memory. There was nothing there; just a straggle of houses right near the sea. And a Co-op. No trees. Desperate weather. The area might have started with 'Sol', or maybe that was the next village. Honestly, you don't want to go there. Just phone. She'll not stay long, trust me.'

He wasn't prepared to trust anyone on that, or to go against his instinct to get the first flight over there. He phoned Flybe. There was a seat on the first leg of the flight from Inverness to Stornoway this afternoon, but no seat from Stornoway to Benbecula. He considered flying to Stornoway and hiring a car, then he realised he would have to drive through Harris, before crossing from Leverburgh to North Uist. He couldn't do it. It wasn't just his dreams and Stephen MacLaren that stopped him. He had family on Harris, and childhood memories that he wasn't yet ready to face. There was a seat all the way to Benbecula tomorrow morning. He booked it.

*

Carla's pal, Louise, was at reception in the station on Burnett Road. She was speaking to an old lady. 'No dear. DC Roberts isn't in. I'll give him a message if you like.'

The old lady passed her a packet of chocolate biscuits. 'Just give him these. He likes them with his tea. And tell him I got everything sorted out. Got my smart television and my iPad. Put the telly on and the first thing I saw was a picture of that other detective on the news, the rude – ' She shook her head. 'Best not to speak ill of the dead, eh? Anyway, maybe Roberts is feeling a bit down about it, though they didn't seem close. These might cheer him up. He's a good lad.'

'Aye, he's not bad, our Nigel.'

161

'Nigel, eh? He kept that quiet.'

Louise looked apprehensive as she greeted Joe. He understood. It wasn't easy to have a colleague in this position, but he wished she'd stop fiddling with the bloody biscuits. There wouldn't be a whole one left for Roberts.

'I was hoping to see DI Black. Is he in?'

DI Black closed his office door and pointed Joe to a seat. 'I shouldn't really be talking to you without Little and Large.'

Joe nodded. 'I know, but I'm going away for a couple of days and I thought I'd better tell you. It's Carla. She's ill and I want to spend some time with her.'

DI Black shrugged. 'Can't stop you, son. You're not under arrest, and I'm bloody sure you never will be. We just need that wee shite to come to his senses and tell the truth. Where will you be?'

'North Uist.'

'Aye?' The DI raised his eyebrows. 'See and don't get stabbed. Have you got a phone number? As soon as there's any news, I'll be in touch.'

Joe took his mobile from his pocket. It was another old one of Lucy's, the one she'd had before the iPhone she'd given him. She'd put the number on a label on the back for him. DI Black laughed. 'That's what the wife did with mine.' He passed his to Joe. 'Get a note of that, and keep in touch. I want you back here as soon as possible. We've got to stop this guy before he kills anyone else.'

There was a knock on the door. A uniformed cop with a memo. The DI read it and shook his head. 'Someone answering Katya Birze's description was seen struggling with a man on Old Edinburgh Road early yesterday morning, before getting in his car. Driver had a walking stick. No make, but we've got a registration number. It's getting checked now.' He looked up. 'That's about thirty six hours ago. If you or I saw something like that, we'd report it immediately. What planet are these people on?'

It was hard to leave the station, knowing they'd just had a breakthrough and he couldn't be part of it. In the car park, he groaned when he saw Tina Lewis slouched against his car, picking at her nails. Before she raised her head, he saw a sheen of grease on her dishevelled hair. She looked up and her face was grey and gaunt, not a scrap of the usual make-up. If only she'd looked like that last night. Joe felt a flush starting at his neck and creeping up his face. 'All right?' he said.

'Not really. Been sick four times. I've had nothing to eat. My head feels like someone's inside banging it with a hammer. You look fine.'

'Hardly. I stopped drinking spirits years ago so I wouldn't ever feel like this again. And I'm off to my folks' house now to try and clean the carpet.'

'Your folks?'

'They're away. My sister's staying there.'

Tina nodded. 'You said that, I think. You didn't drive there last night, did you?' She pointed to his damaged wing mirror. 'I could have sworn I phoned you a taxi.'

'No. Just left it in a stupid place overnight. Was your car at the pub?'

She shook her head. 'I walked down from the house. Listen, Sarge, I'm really sorry. I knew about…that you were spoken for. I…I shouldn't have acted like that. I'm not sure my pride will ever recover from the knock-back. Carla's very lucky.'

It was only the misery on Tina's face that prevented Joe from breaking into laughter and punching the air. He could have kissed her.

'It won't affect our working relationship, Sarge, will it?'

'We don't have a working relationship right now, but if Ryan MacRae ever decides to tell the truth, and I'm back, no, it won't affect anything.'

She smiled, and the grey disappeared from her face. 'Thanks Sarge. I'm glad I saw you. I'm quite hungry now. Fried egg and chips might just about do it.'

Chapter 37

There had been no more texts from Sebastian, and Lucy was glad. He was a spineless git, and he'd treated her like shit. Still, it gave her some satisfaction to know he was sorry. She hadn't replied last night. Joe's arrival had put it out of her head. She decided against texting him now. Nothing he could say would interest her.

She put her jacket on. She was off up to New Craigs with Drew. Mary, the cat strangler, had asked for a solicitor again, anyone but Graeme Freel.

As Drew waited at the Rose Street roundabout, Lucy saw Joe's car passing. Had he been at the station? What was happening? Drew pulled out behind him. Lucy nodded to the car. 'That's my brother.'

'The detective? Joe, is it?'

'Yeah.'

'Did he give you any gossip about the cop that went off the bridge yesterday?'

Did he ever? Lucy was silent.

Drew smiled. 'Sorry. Just being nosy.'

'It's all right. I was the same. I couldn't wait to hear from him yesterday to find out what had happened. He didn't tell me until this morning.'

Drew didn't ask. Joe turned left into Chapel Street, while Drew crossed the bridge. The traffic was at a stand-still on Telford Street. Drew sighed. 'Bloody Muirtown Bridge is open. Gets me every time. We're going to be here for ages.' He smiled at Lucy. 'Any gossip?'

'I'd have to kill you if I told you.'

His laughter was loud and infectious. 'Better not kill me before Mary's Mental Health Tribunal on Wednesday. You can come. And there's the Grounds Hearing on Thursday for the Child Protection Order you did with Graeme last week. I'm sure I can get that kid home.'

That would be something. Graeme's submissions at the court hearing for the Child Protection Order had been dismal, and his representation at the second working day Children's Hearing had been worse. On both occasions, Lucy had been tempted to take the file from him and make a case herself. 'That would be great, thanks.' Although she wasn't relaxed in his company, she was learning a lot from Drew.

The cars hadn't moved. Drew tapped the steering wheel. 'Must be a few boats coming through. We could be here for a while. Any –'

'It was Joe. At the bridge; it was Joe.'

'He was there?'

'He was there and he was accused of pushing his colleague off. But he didn't do it. He wouldn't. He's been suspended.'

'Lucy.' Drew put his hand on her arm. 'That's awful. I'm so sorry for joking about it.'

There could be tears, but she wouldn't let them come. 'Don't tell anyone, please.'

'Hardly. Listen, you don't have to come back in at all if you'd rather be with him.'

She shook her head. 'Thanks, but it's better to keep occupied. I'd probably drive him mad.'

'Is he okay?'

'He wasn't too good last night when he turned up at my folks' house drunk. I've never seen him like that. He was pretty rough this morning. I was going to text him at lunch time, but they took his mobile phone as part of the enquiry. I gave him another one, but it's got an alpha-numeric keypad and he'll never figure out how to text with it.'

'This is your detective brother we're talking about? Solves problems for a living?'

'Suppose so.' She got her phone out of her bag. There was a message. It wasn't from Joe.

Couldn't sleep for thinking about you last night. Can we talk? Sxx

'You all right?' Drew asked, as the cars started to move.

'Aye.' She sent Joe a text.

'That's terrifying, the speed you young ones text at.'

Young ones? Did he think of her as a kid? Bummer. And she didn't want to talk to Sebastian. She had nothing to say.

165

'If Joe needs a criminal solicitor, I could recommend someone good.'

Lucy shook her head. 'He hates solicitors, but thanks anyway.'

'Aye, the polis all hate solicitors, especially the good ones, until they need one. The offer's there anyway.'

The medication must be working. Mary was in cracking form. She apologised to Lucy for the flying incontinence pads. 'I tried my best not to hit you. See that fat bugger? He'll not forget me in a hurry.'

Drew looked puzzled. 'Fat bugger?'

'Aye, that useless arrogant wee shite you sent up here. Wee fat shite.'

Drew looked at Lucy. 'Is he fat?'

Lucy hesitated. She didn't want to be a bitch. Ah, what the hell? 'He is a bit.'

Mary laughed. 'I notice you didn't ask if he was useless or arrogant. We'll take that as a given, shall we?'

Drew winked. 'Right Mary, let's get a look at these papers for the Tribunal.'

She passed over a bundle of papers. He had a quick glance. 'Much the same as last time.'

'Aye, and you'll be arguing there's no risk to me or anyone else again, right? And the necessity test. The order's not necessary. Medication's working. I'm fixed. I'll stay in for a while if they want, voluntary, like. They've got to abide by that minimum intervention thingie – isn't that what you told me?'

'Aye; that's right.'

'So how can granting an order for a patient that's willing to stay in and be medicated be the minimum intervention?'

'Lucy?'

Shit. 'Eh…I guess they'll look at the history. How many admissions have there been? How many times has medication been stopped? Has the patient absconded? Stuff like that?'

Mary laughed. 'You could write the script, love. But I've got an answer for most of that.'

Drew smiled. 'Sounds like you don't need us, Mary.'

'Course I need you. You've done me proud every time.'

'You know what I'm going to say…'

166

Mary took a deep breath. 'Aye; you'll do your best but there's no guarantee and I mustn't get my hopes up and the order's only for six months and it'll soon pass and I mustn't give the panel evils or throw my water at the MHO. Have I forgotten anything?'

'That's about it, Mary. I'll have a good read over the papers and we'll see you at 9.30 on Wednesday morning.'

'We? Do you mean her?'

Lucy blushed.

'Aye,' Drew said. 'Is that a problem?'

'Not at all. I thought for a minute you meant that fat git.' She smiled at Lucy. 'How could a face like that be a problem? She'll charm them into letting me out. I know it.'

No pressure there, then.

Three patients stopped Drew as they walked through the communal area. He didn't seem to mind. One was looking for representation again; he was on a short term detention certificate. There would be a tribunal the week after next, but he was much better and he didn't need to be detained. Aye right, Lucy thought. Maybe when he stopped talking to the invisible person over his left shoulder, he'd be in a better position to prove his sanity.

The other two were past clients who wanted to thank him for helping them. While Drew chatted, Lucy became aware she was being watched. The stern-faced woman was sitting on a sofa. She was well turned out, in a blue dress and cardigan, her grey hair curled and set. When Lucy looked up and caught her eye, the woman didn't flinch. It didn't seem right to stare at her, so Lucy looked away, but not before she saw the woman wink at her.

Those eyes. They took Lucy back to a spring evening in Harris, when she'd thought her life was about to end. And then she knew. The woman was Betty MacLaren, Stephen's mother. And it looked like she knew exactly who Lucy was.

Chapter 38

Sharon was lost. Beside her, his eyes closed as the plane began its descent, was the man she'd loved, no matter what she'd tried to tell herself. The man she'd trusted. He'd given her so much. And it wasn't just the money or the things he'd paid for. They were nothing compared to the understanding, the encouragement, the respect. No guy had ever given her that. And he hadn't battered her. Two nights ago, in the bath, she'd almost told him she loved him. She had never felt so close to anyone.

And it was all shit.

The future terrified her. Ryan in custody. Her and Liam in their dismal council flat, barely surviving on benefits. She felt his hand on her knee. 'You all right, love?'

She nodded.

'Will I come back with you and we can get Liam from school?'

'Do you mind just dropping me off? I need to spend some time on my own with him. And I have to phone the cops, see how Ryan's doing.'

Peter would have battered her for that. Putting the boys before him? That was not on. Christopher smiled. 'Of course. We'll speak later. Maybe do something?'

He didn't mention going to the police, but that was no surprise to Sharon.

They were last off the plane. As they descended the stairs, Sharon was certain it would be the last time she'd fly. Though she'd promised Liam they'd go to Disney World one day, there was no way she could keep that promise.

They followed the other passengers towards the terminal building. Through the glass, Sharon thought she saw DC Roberts. Her heart started to pound. Had something happened to Ryan? She almost reached for Christopher's hand, but she stopped herself.

It was Roberts, with a blonde woman and two uniformed cops. How bad did it have to be to send four cops? Her mouth was dry as she stopped in front of him. 'What is it?'

But Roberts wasn't looking at Sharon. 'Christopher Brent?'

Christopher smiled. 'Yes.'

'I'm arresting you on suspicion of the murder of Katya Birze.'

*

Joe smiled all the way to the garage, and he kept smiling even when they told him they couldn't salvage the mirror and he'd have to get a new one. His mood took a wee turn for the worse as he scrubbed at the stain on his mother's carpet. Lucy had cleaned up the worst of it last night, but the stain was still there. The smell of the cleaner was strong, and his headache was returning. He gave up after three-quarters of an hour. If the carpet had to be replaced, so be it. Home now, to pack.

He didn't go home. When he reached the roundabout at Fishertown, he kept going. It was too good a day to be stuck inside. He needed to walk and think. At Findhorn, he parked in the village and walked towards the bay, his spirits lifting at the tinkling sound of the breeze stirring the masts and rigging on the boats. The curved bay was a sailing and water sports centre, popular with tourists and locals. There were boats everywhere, some moored in the bay, while others had been brought ashore to the gardens of the houses that backed onto the bay. Some of the houses had their own slipways. What Joe wouldn't give to live here, with constant access to the water. He was tempted by coffee in one of the cafes along the water front, but the lure of the sea was too strong. He walked round to the headland, then on to the long stretching sands of Burghead Bay. It was more exposed, and there were fewer people around.

As the soft sand crunched under his feet, he thought of the beaches in Harris with their golden sand and massive dunes. Though this beach was beautiful, there was really no comparison. Something stirred deep inside him, with a whisper of home and heritage. How he wished he could claim it. Let the hurt and the past go. Accept all that should have been his, if things had turned out differently. Maybe someday.

He heard laughter and chattering from the sand dunes. A family had set up camp, with a stripy wind-break and a barbecue. The smell of burgers made Joe's mouth water, and his stomach rumbled. A toddler broke away from his mother. His nappy was only fastened on one side and it flapped around his pudgy thighs before falling to the sand. With a high-pitched squeal, the wee boy made a dash towards the sea. His mother ran behind him, near enough to catch him, but letting him go as far as he safely could. Close to the water's edge, the child stopped and turned. He held out his arms, and his mother scooped him up, laughing as she swung him round, then held him close.

A wave of sadness swamped Joe as he passed the mother and child. He didn't dare look at them, for he feared the mother might see the tears glistening in his eyes.

Tears? Was it the hangover? He remembered hangovers that had made him cry before, especially in the years after his friend Matt was murdered. More than once he'd convinced himself he was suffering from depression, that he'd have to see a doctor, only to wake the next day fully recovered. But that hadn't happened for a long time. Why today?

He looked back over his shoulder, at the mother carrying the child to the dunes, and he knew. For the first time in years, he knew exactly what he wanted.

Chapter 39

Sharon had almost cried out loud at the station when she was shown the photo of Katya Birze; it was the girl in the photos in Christopher's drawer. And the police thought she'd died on Sunday morning, around the time he'd disappeared and claimed to have gone for a drive. Had he been shagging her all along? Every night he wasn't with Sharon? Was that why he hadn't invited her to his house before the day of the shooting? But why would he have killed her?

Alone in her flat, Sharon felt the first stirrings of a panic attack. She hadn't had one since the early days of reducing her methadone. He'd been there every time, with his vitamins and his knowledge and his encouragement. And look where he was now. In the cells. A murderer.

And there was Ryan. He was still in New Craigs and she wasn't allowed to see him. What state was he in? They'd told her nothing. She picked up the small brown bottle of methadone and shook it. Fuck, fuck, fuck. She sank to the floor. If she took it all, she wouldn't get more for three days, but at least she'd feel better. But would she? Why not just call her old dealer, Smish? His number was imprinted on her brain. Gillian had collected Liam from school. He was safe. Ryan wasn't going anywhere. And she was going to hell.

The veins on her arm tingled and she remembered Stephen MacLaren, or Mac, as she'd known him. Last year, the day he'd murdered her neighbour, he'd given her smack to make sure she was out of it. Her last hit. Bastard. He'd reeled her in too. Not with sex or money or false promises. Just friendship and understanding. And it was all an act. If she hadn't lived next door to Moira Jacobs, he wouldn't have given her the time of day. Fucking men. Murdering bastards.

At least she hadn't been detained. She'd told the cops she'd only found out about the links between Todd Curtis and Christopher in London, and that she'd planned to go to the station this afternoon to tell them everything. She gave them details of Christopher's family home and his rented houses. She told them about Dino and Lucas, the email from Todd Curtis and his befriending of Ryan. That Todd lived on Carlton Terrace and was into prostitution and drugs. That was all she knew. She couldn't give Christopher an alibi for early Sunday morning.

She didn't phone Smish. She forced herself to go for Liam. His wee face cheered her up. He'd made a card with a picture of her. She had limbs like sticks and a belly like a Buddha. *To my luvly mam xxx*

'That's fab, son, but you've drawn me with missing teeth.'

'I know, Mam. You've got lovely teeth now, but I liked when you ate bubble gum and blowed huge bubbles through the gaps.'

She helped him with his homework, then they snuggled in front of the telly. He asked when Christopher would be coming round. The thought that he'd never be back gutted Sharon. She took a deep breath. 'His mum's sick just now, so maybe not for a while. We're fine on our own, aren't we?'

He nodded. 'Do you think Ryan will be home soon?'

Sharon's throat tightened. She coughed. 'That's a difficult question, Liam. At least he's safe now, though, eh?'

Liam was fast asleep. Nothing on the telly. The evening stretched before Sharon, and she couldn't see how she'd get through it. Maybe she'd tidy the kitchen cupboards. That might have worked, if she hadn't opened the cupboard beside the sink first, and found a bottle of wine she'd won in a raffle at the community centre.

She'd never liked red wine, but this went down like nectar. Three quarters of the way down the bottle, she decided. Her hands shaking, she phoned Smish.

'Shar, how's it going?' The sound of his oily voice sent waves of nausea through her. 'Haven't heard from you for a while. What can I do for you?'

Butterflies in stilettos danced in her belly as she told him what she needed.

No problem. It would cost her, though.

*

Carla hadn't gone far today. A wander round the croft with Ronald, then she read for the afternoon, before making dinner.

Ronald was apologetic when he came in and found she'd cooked. 'I'm supposed to be looking after you.'

She smiled. 'I don't need looking after. Just a bit of rest, and cooking is restful for me. I don't do it enough.'

'You should; this is wonderful.'

'That's got more to do with your home grown beef and vegetables than my cooking. I should make the effort, but my work patterns don't help, and it doesn't seem worth it when you're only cooking for one.'

'You don't cook for Joe?'

Carla shook her head. 'If we're both off, we usually eat out or get a takeaway.'

'What did he think of you coming here?'

She shrugged. 'I didn't tell him.'

'Ah.'

She took a deep breath. 'It's probably run its course. Wasn't really working out.' With the words came a rush of nausea, followed by despair. The food felt like cardboard in her mouth. She put her knife and fork down, and clasped her hands in her lap to stop them shaking. 'I must have eaten too much at lunch time; I'm not really hungry now.'

Ronald reached for the butter dish. He took his time, cutting off a slab and placing it on his vegetables. Carla watched the butter melt. He looked up and smiled. 'Did I tell you about the escaped cow at the last sale?'

The tale of the rampaging cow that held up the ferry traffic in Lochmaddy for half an hour made her laugh, and then she felt hungry again.

Ronald insisted on washing the dishes before he went to check the beasts. Carla watched him from the kitchen window as she dried up. It was a fine evening, the island bathed in a soft yellow glow. Down at the shore, she saw a figure. It must be Will. She couldn't make out his features, but he looked less decrepit than she'd expected from her cousin's description. The tide was out and he looked to be rummaging around the exposed rocks. He had a pail with him; he must be collecting shellfish.

At the bottom field, close to the shore, she saw Ronald. He'd gone to check the fence for a hole, as the sheep were escaping. The men were only a short distance apart, but Will had his back to Ronald. When her cousin shouted a greeting, she saw Will straighten up, turn and nod at Ronald. And then he eased himself down to pick up his bucket. He had a hand on the small of his back as he shuffled towards his caravan.

When Ronald came in, they drank tea and chatted. She'd been worried he would want to talk about her tests, her prognosis, but he didn't. He talked about the croft he was thinking of renting from a neighbour. He couldn't quite make up his mind if he needed more land, but he hated to see it go to waste. Worse, it might go to one of those buggers that collected crofts like they were going out of fashion, and did nothing with them. By the time he said goodnight, he'd decided; he was going for it.

Carla didn't think she'd sleep. Was it over with Joe? Was that what she wanted? If it was, why did she feel as if someone had taken her heart and shredded it to pieces? She took her mobile phone out of her bag. She hadn't given it a thought since she'd arrived, assuming there was no signal here. Had he been in touch? Maybe she'd switch it on and find there was a signal, and a dozen messages from him, explaining and apologising. And maybe she'd find no messages, and she'd be devastated, and she definitely wouldn't sleep. She put it back in her bag. Maybe tomorrow.

In the bedroom, she stood at the window and wondered why anyone would need a television. The setting sun was descending into the sand dunes on the horizon. The sky was a mass of colours, the fiery orange globe slowly disappearing. It left threads and fingers of light stretching and mingling with the trailing clouds. She watched until the sun was gone, leaving only a faint purple shadow behind the tinted clouds.

Chapter 40

From the plane, Joe looked down on the mountains and moors of North Harris, then the deserted golden sands of the south. The beaches stretched forever, alongside seas of stunning blue and green and violet. He felt his heart lift. No matter how much he tried to avoid it, he knew there was something there for him. One day, he'd go and face the past. He'd take Carla, if she still wanted him.

He avoided looking down at Ceapabhal, the hill that overshadowed the shore where he and Stephen MacLaren had fought, yet still the wound in his chest tingled and an image came to him. He was lying on the rocks, consciousness slipping away, and a shadowy Stephen was walking towards Lucy, the knife in his hand. He shivered.

When he next looked down, he saw that North Uist was nothing but water, with the odd bit of land scattered here and there. It looked so bleak, little ribbons of road connecting fragments of land. There were beaches; he knew that. He'd spent hours on the internet, looking at maps and trying to work out where Ronald MacKenzie might live. There was a place called Sollas on the north coast, with great expanses of sand. That was as good a place as any to start.

When they were close to landing in Benbecula, the plane swept over a massive stretch of white sand, and it looked every bit as spectacular as the golden beaches on Harris.

As he waited for his bag to come off the plane, Joe filled in the paperwork for his hire car. The man handed over the car keys and pointed out the window. 'They'll see you coming.'

Great. A bright yellow Fiat Punto. That's what he got for making last minute decisions. 'Where do I return it?'

'Here. Just leave it open and stick the keys under the visor on the driver's side.'

'Seriously?'

The man shrugged. 'Would you steal it?'

The driving challenges here were the same as those in Harris.

Stretches of two-way suddenly narrowing to single track; blind summits and wayward sheep; road-hogging campervans that crawled along at twenty miles an hour. Joe didn't really mind. Though he couldn't wait to see Carla, he was nervous, and he needed time to decide what to say, and to keep an eye on the route planner he'd printed out the previous evening. Not that there was much scope for going wrong. Once he was on the A865, a couple of miles after leaving the airport, he didn't turn off again for just over eleven miles, when he'd reach the Committee Road. Another six or so miles and he'd be at the Co-op in Sollas. Hopefully someone there would know where Ronald MacKenzie lived.

*

When Carla woke, the house was silent. Ronald must have been very quiet getting up. She couldn't believe she'd slept well. She'd woken once, and felt a hint of worry poking at her. It was vague, a net of gossamer that threatened to capture her. It had almost succeeded, until she heard the faint surge of the sea in the background. She focussed on it, until everything else was gone.

And now, it was a good day, the sky blue and cloudless, the house filled with a wonderful smell that brought memories of a child jumping out of bed and racing to the kitchen for her aunt's scones. She didn't race now, but her mouth watered just as it had then.

Ronald had left the scones covered by a tea-towel on top of the stove. The table was laid for her, a small tea-pot and tea caddy waiting. He'd also put out a frying pan, with a note to say the eggs and bacon were in the fridge, and he'd gone up to Benbecula to take Bessie to the vet.

Carla and her father had always left the island with enough of her aunt's baking to last a couple of weeks, but they'd be gone in a few days. Her favourites were the yellow scones made with maize flour. And Ronald had remembered.

She ate two scones and drank her tea, then she stood at the window and watched the hens pecking in the ground around the old rusted tractor. It was time.

The signal was good. She held her breath as the texts came in. A couple from Louise apologising for not getting back to her. And then a third from Louise.

Shit has hit the fan. Poor J. Hope he's all right.

What shit?

And then several missed calls and three texts yesterday from an unknown number – Joe's, apparently.

I'm so sorry. Don't have my phone. Call me. Please. J xxx

I'm worried. Where are you? xxx

The third was a picture of a beautiful bouquet, sitting in a jug by her kitchen sink. Typical. First time he'd given her flowers, and they were wasting away in her empty flat. She considered answering him, but he'd be tied up in whatever shit had hit the fan. She didn't want to have to wait hours for his response. And she needed time to think.

The smell of the machair was just as she remembered, a salty mix of sea and grass and sand. And it looked just as it had when she'd walked it with her father, except that the hills of Harris had seemed closer and bigger then. It was too far to *Traigh Iar,* the big beach on the other side of the sand dunes, but she was determined she'd make it before she left, even if it was on Ronald's tractor.

She took her shoes off and left them on the grass with her jacket. Though the tide was out, there were rock pools here and there, and the water was warm on her toes.

She wanted to forget about Joe, at least while she was out, but she kept thinking of the flowers. They were beautiful, and at least he'd made an effort, but did it really make up for abandoning her at the hospital when he'd promised to take her home? And why hadn't he called? Even if he'd lost his phone, he could have come round or called her landline. Maybe she should contact Louise and find out what was going on.

Before she knew it, she was almost at the old caravan, and the side of her head had started to ache, nausea seeping through her. She had painkillers in her pocket, but no water to take them with. She was going to have to sit, and she was going to have to face the truth. She could forget for a while, but it was always there, in the background. Sickness; life-threatening sickness. She should face up to it. But how the hell could she, when she didn't even know? She blinked back tears.

'Are you okay?'

The sun was behind him, so she couldn't see his face. Just masses of wild dark hair and a beard. Must be Will. There was no point pretending. She shook her head. 'I came too far. I've been unwell and I'm supposed to be resting; it was stupid of me.'

He held out his hand. 'Here, I'll help you up. Come and have a seat in the caravan until you feel better.'

'I don't want to be a nuisance.'

'You're not; I've nothing else to do, and I can't leave you here.'

Though his clothes had seen better days, they were clean. When Carla took his arm, she could smell wood smoke and soap. Outside the caravan, there was a low circular wall made of stones, enclosing the remains of a fire. A piece of driftwood was balanced on two boulders, making a long shelf for a kettle, some crockery and cutlery, and two battered pans. One of them was full of open razor, cockle and winkle shells.

'The remains of last night's dinner and today's breakfast,' he said. 'Delicious.'

Beside the shelf, there was a rack made of wood, with long pieces of seaweed stretched across it. 'Is that dulse?'

'It is indeed.'

'My dad used to love it.'

'A wise man. Your family come from here?'

'Aye. Only my cousin, Ronald, is here now, though. He has the next croft.'

He nodded. 'He's a good sort; leaves me vegetables and meat. It's all very welcome. You go in. There's a seat by the window. I'll make you tea.'

The caravan was clean enough, but there were dark patches of mould on one wall and a small hole in the roof, above the shoogly table. An empty rusty baked beans can sat underneath the hole. Carla lifted a book about birds and a pair of binoculars from the seat. She put them on the narrow bed beside a rolled up sleeping bag and a black rucksack. There was nothing else in the caravan that gave any clue as to Will's character. Maybe he was a mad axe murderer. Too bad. She didn't have the strength to care. Her

178

headache was gone, though.

Will was crouched at the fire, waiting for the kettle to boil. He looked lean and fit, and nothing like Ronald's description of 'a poor soul'. He glanced over his shoulder and smiled. His teeth were whiter than white. Must have a toothbrush somewhere.

He brought the pan of water inside, with a mug and a spoon. He put them on the table, then he reached for his rucksack, his back turned to Carla while he rummaged. 'I'm sure I've got another somewhere. Aha.' He pulled out a small enamel camping mug. 'It's been there for a while; you're my first visitor.' He used his t-shirt to wipe the mug, then he poured water into the first mug. 'I forgot to say I've no milk. How do you take it?'

'Just as it comes.' She really hoped he wasn't going to give her the camping mug. 'Not too strong, please.'

'I'm sorry I've no sugar. That might help to pick you up.'

'It'll be lovely. Sorry to put you to this trouble, Will.'

He looked a little taken aback, then he smiled and lifted the tea bag out with the spoon, before dropping it into the enamel mug and filling it with water. He passed the first mug to her.

She thanked him. 'I'm Carla.'

'Pleased to meet you, Carla.'

Chapter 41

Sharon's head was banging. Her mouth felt like the bottom of a budgie's cage, and her hands were shaky. She hadn't slept much, too scared to close her eyes. When sleep came, Christopher was trying to throw her off the bridge at Black Rock Gorge, while the Lady of Balconie cried, and her hounds barked. Peter was there. He was holding Liam, as he laughed and encouraged Christopher. And a dark presence in the background, his scent filling the forest, thick and strong and evil. She'd awoken, certain the evil force was in her room. As a shadow moved by the door, she'd screamed. It was Liam, and he was petrified.

Poor wee soul didn't want to go to school. Maybe she'd need him to look after her, he said. That was it. No way was another man going to muck up their lives. He had to go to school, she told him; he had to be clever, become a policeman. That was the best way to look after her.

On her way home from the school, she met Mina. She lived downstairs with her daughter. She was looking rough. Shivering and scratching. And tapping. 'Got a tenner, Shar? No food for the bairn. I'll give you it back on Monday when I get my dole.'

Sharon gave her a tenner, though she knew the bairn had been taken into care weeks ago, and the money was going straight into Mina's veins. Still, if she didn't get it from Sharon, she'd go shoplifting or worse. Sharon watched her go, and she regretted her generosity. Never mind what Mina was going to do with the money. What was Sharon going to do without it? She didn't have much left. Not after giving thirty quid to that skanky bastard, Smish, last night.

Would she get to see Ryan today? They'd told her any visit would have to be accompanied, and that was fine by her. She'd told them everything. No secrets. Well, almost none. She hadn't mentioned the sock or that she'd heard from Ryan after he'd left home. She should have, but she couldn't face a charge and possible detention. She had to be here for them both. She wasn't going to think of Christopher and how he was coping in a cell. It wasn't her problem. She'd thought she knew him. She didn't. She had to move on.

That was easier said than done when the post arrived. It wasn't often she got a parcel. The contents made her cry out loud. Immaculate second-hand copies of six of the children's books her former foster mother, Alison, had written. They'd come from a book dealer in Chelmsford. No one but Christopher had heard the story of Alison and Mark. No one else would think of doing something like that for her. She'd asked in a local book shop years ago if they had any, but they were out of print. She'd told Christopher that too.

Sharon inhaled the smell of the top book, hoping to find a hint of Alison, but it just smelled like a book. She put the books in the cupboard. She would look at them another day, when her heart felt less fragile. She set her mind to tidying up. In her bedroom, the suitcase was still sitting on the bedroom floor, taunting her. When she'd packed it, although Ryan was missing, and her heart was sore, she'd been chuffed to bits, going away with her man. Unpacking it seemed like rubbing it in. She kicked it into the corner. She'd do it later.

When the flat was tidy, she made her way up the town to the Job Centre. There was no getting away from technology these days. The last time Sharon had looked at jobs, they were displayed on little cards on stands, and in the window. Now it was all on computer. She must be learning something, as she managed to access the jobs without too much panic. She could have done it at home on her netbook. Another thing that was going to have to change; Christopher had been paying her broadband subscription. Waste of money; she'd hardly used it. Maybe she'd get a few quid for the netbook.

Could she live on the minimum wage? That was all she was going to get with these jobs. And she wasn't qualified for anything except cleaning. So? She'd been a cleaner at a primary school for a short while after she met Peter. She'd taken pride in doing a good job. But Peter hadn't liked it. Not when she'd mentioned having a laugh with the janitor. That was the end of that. But the minimum wage? No more organic food, and the e-cig would have to go. If others could do it, why shouldn't she?

Next stop was the council's Service Point. It was time to enquire about a transfer. Maybe they should become gadgies. Or maybe

Dingwall was just a step too far.

*

The narrow aisles of the island Co-op were quiet. Just two women with trollies and a young guy filling shelves. Joe smiled at the guy. 'Hi. It's a great day.'

The guy nodded. 'Not bad at all. Can I help you find anything?' He had a strong island accent.

'No, thanks; I'm sure I'll find what I'm looking for. You wouldn't happen to know a Ronald MacKenzie that lives near here, would you?'

He looked blank, shook his head. 'Don't think so, but I'm not from around here.'

'Are you sure? You sound like an islander.' Jeez. As if the guy didn't know where he came from. Lucy always said interrogation was his default mode; he'd been determined not to come across as a cop.

'I'm from the other side.'

Joe nodded. Presumably the other side of the island, rather than anything more sinister. 'Anyone else here who might know?'

'I'll find out. Ronald who?'

'MacKenzie; he's a crofter.'

'A crofter, eh? That narrows it down.'

Was he taking the piss? It was hard to tell.

'Annie,' the guy called to the customer at the end of the aisle, 'you live round here, don't you?'

Annie nodded. 'Aye, for my sins. Why?'

'This fellow's looking for a Ronald MacKenzie. He's a crofter.'

He was taking the piss.

'Ronald MacKenzie?' It was the other woman at the opposite end of the aisle. '*Raghnall Sheonaidh Ailean?*'

The guy looked at Joe in expectation. He shook his head and shrugged. There was a volley of Gaelic conversation, up and down the aisle. The Co-op guy joined in now and again, while Joe waited.

Annie nodded her head. 'Aye, that's who it'll be. He's the only MacKenzie around here.'

The Co-op guy turned to Joe. 'Does that help?'

'Aye, but it'd help even more if I had directions to his house.'

It was the second woman's turn. 'You'll not get him in. He left early this morning, himself and his dog, heading up south, I'd say.'

'Up south?' Joe was intrigued.

'Aye. Up south. I've not seen him pass since.'

But he could have passed while they were in the shop, Annie suggested.

'Aye. That's a possibility.'

Joe smiled. 'Maybe if you could just give me directions, I'll find out for myself.'

The directions were straightforward, and Ronald's house was less than five minutes away. As Joe paid for his coke and crisps, the two women queued behind him. Annie looked him up and down and said something that sounded like 'Polish' to the other. He was pretty certain they hadn't mistaken him for a Pole. He sighed and made a mental note to ask Ronald for the Gaelic for police.

There was no car at the well-kept house, and no answer when Joe knocked on the front door. He opened the side gate and went round to the back door. Still no answer. He glanced around, but no one was watching except two fat brown hens. He looked in the kitchen window. There was a note on the draining board. He couldn't make out what was written on it, but it looked like Carla's writing.

He knocked again, waited, then he tried the handle. The door wasn't locked. It was the done thing in the islands, he told himself as he stepped inside. No one thought anything of you opening their door and walking in. 'Hello. Anyone in?' The smell of her made his heart beat faster. 'Carla?'

It was only two steps to the sink. *Fab breakfast, thank you! Off down to the shore. I won't go far. See you soon. Cx*

Chapter 42

Beneath the beard and the hair there was a good-looking guy not much older than Carla. Will's eyes were blue as sapphires, clear and bright, and full of warmth. His description of life on the island captivated her. The summer days were long and still, he said, the light and colours changing constantly as the earth turned, the height of the sun shortening his shadow on the deserted sands. If he was an artist, he would paint from dawn until dusk. Instead, he tried to hold the changes of the earth in his mind, reliving the colours on days when the land had forgotten.

'Do you write?' she asked.

He shook his head.

'You should.'

He laughed and said he was too busy exploring and foraging. Fish and plants and seaweed, masses of shell fish – he had little need for the shops. He trapped rabbits, but he spared her the details.

Carla smiled. 'I was sure there were more rabbits when I was last here; that explains it.'

'No. Once or twice a week at most; I doubt I'm making much difference. I think many of them died in the bad storms when the machairs were flooded.'

She looked around the caravan. 'I wouldn't fancy being in here in bad weather.'

'No indeed.' He smiled. 'The storms rage across the machair, flattening anything that dares to stand in their way. I lie on my narrow bed feeling the wind tilt the caravan this way and that, the rain battering on the feeble windows, the elements howling accusations and wild threats. Just waiting to be exposed.' His eyes were wide and a little wild, and Carla wondered what he meant. 'I've squatted in the odd barn or ruin when it's been bad, and come back wondering if the caravan might have made it to Harris in the night.'

'You have a fantastic view of Harris.'

He nodded and looked pensive. 'Do you know Harris?'

'We used to go over for the day when I was wee. Beautiful

beaches.'

'Better than here, do you think?'

Carla shook her head. 'Definitely not. Nowhere is better than here, but I'm biased.'

He smiled. 'They're different. I like that the beaches here are hidden. You have to seek them out. Like the beach over the dunes.' He nodded towards *Traigh Iar*. 'It's wonderful. And then there are more little sandy bays before you come to *Aird a' Mhorain*. There's a cemetery down there; the last resting place of the MacLeans of Boreray.'

'I've never been to *Aird a' Mhorain*, but *Traigh Iar* defines Uist for me. I can't wait to get over there, even if it's on Ronald's tractor. What brought you here?'

He shrugged. 'I'd been before and liked it. I needed somewhere to get my head sorted out. This seemed as good a place as any. I'm not too fond of modern living.' The sound of a ping from his pocket made him blush. He pulled out a phone. 'Cheapest model and tariff you can get. I use about 50p in credit every three months.' He read his text, then he put the phone back in his pocket. 'Are you staying with Ronald for long?'

'Not sure. I've been signed off work. I'm…I'm waiting for some lab results.'

'Sorry to hear that. What do you do for a living?'

She hated telling people, but she couldn't lie. 'I'm a police officer.'

He grimaced. 'Demanding job. Doesn't give you much time for a private life, I'd imagine.'

'Not if you're stupid enough to date another cop.'

'Ah. I expect the logistics can be quite difficult. Still, if it's right for you both, I'm sure you can make it work.'

'If it's right for us both; there's the question.' He was such a good listener, she'd have liked to elaborate. But that would be stupid.

'Twitcher alert.' Will reached for the binoculars and looked across the sand, towards the hills of Harris. 'One never knows when a rare species will appear. I like to log them before the townies arrive in their droves.'

Carla looked out the other window. There was a figure on the shore. She wondered if Ronald had come to look for her.

Will lowered the binoculars. 'Nothing interesting.'

'There's someone there. Can you see if it's Ronald?'

Smiling, he raised the binoculars again. The smile faded. When he lowered the binoculars, he looked like a different person, all the laughter and life gone from his face. 'It's not Ronald.' His voice sounded weak.

'Are you all right? Will?'

He nodded and tried to smile. 'It was lovely meeting you, Carla. I better let you get back.'

Disappointed, Carla knew she was being dismissed. At the door, she thanked him. He stood by the bed. 'Bye, Carla. Take care.'

She felt inordinately sad as she walked away. She hardly knew him, but his perspective of the island had been so insightful and refreshing. She was determined to come back.

And then she looked to the shore and saw Joe walking towards her. Her head felt as if it might burst. The phone in her pocket vibrated. She took it out and saw another text from him. It had been sent in the middle of the night.

I love you more than I can say xxxx

They sat at a table in the picnic area as the tide came in. Oystercatchers paraded the last of the sand, pecking and pulling up titbits. Carla had so many questions. 'Why didn't you tell me you were coming? And how could you get away in the middle of a major investigation? Have they got someone?'

Joe didn't know where to start. 'I wanted to surprise you, and apologise. It was unforgivable of me not to take you home from the hospital, not to keep in touch and see how you were.'

'It was. Why didn't you get in touch, Joe?'

He kicked at a clump of seaweed, and wondered how it got over the wall and into the picnic area. Must have been some storm. It had been so hard not to throw himself at her when they met, but she had looked so confused and fragile. She was sitting close now, her thigh touching his, and it felt so right, but would she want anything to do with him when she heard what he had to say?

At the tale of Ryan MacRae's deceit, Jackson's fall, and Joe's predicament, she took his hand. 'No wonder you couldn't call me. I'm sorry I wasn't there for you. I kept trying your phone and then

I got pissed off. I was feeling more than a bit sorry for myself. You must hate me.'

'Never. Carla, you don't know – '

'I've been such a bitch. I've felt like shit for so long, and it all just got to me. I should have made more of an effort to speak to you. I convinced myself you weren't interested, that you didn't care. I couldn't think straight. But you're here now. It'll be good for you. I got your texts, well, two of them, this morning. The flowers are beautiful; I'm sorry they're wasted. And just when I saw you coming towards me, the third text came. Joe, I feel – '

He stopped her, though he didn't want to. How easy it would be just to leave it there, accept her apologies, let her tell him how she felt. But he didn't want to know if she felt the same as he did. If she told him she loved him before she'd heard about Tina Lewis, it would make it all the harder to cope with losing her.

As the tide almost covered the sand, the oystercatchers took off, their mournful cries echoing around them.

'There's something else...'

*

Tina Lewis. The thought of her made Carla feel sick. She'd only met her once, at a wedding dance. Tina was drunk and flirtatious and gorgeous, with trouble written all over her. Carla had refused to allow the faint stirrings of jealousy inside her to grow into anything more. There was no hope for her and Joe if she did that. She knew some of his female colleagues fancied him, but she also knew he wasn't a flirt or a player. Or so she'd thought.

'I didn't know she'd come to the pub alone,' Joe said. 'I was expecting her and Roberts. I only meant to have a half-pint, then I was going to come to the hospital. It was too late to visit, but I thought at least they'd tell me if you were still in. I wanted to speak to you so much, but they'd taken my phone, and I didn't have your number. I'm not trying to make excuses, but I was devastated at what I was being accused of. And I was weak. I could have said no when she bought more drinks, but I couldn't even think straight.'

It wasn't easy watching him tear himself to bits, but Carla said nothing. She couldn't. Not until she knew exactly how weak he'd been.

187

'I could hardly stand. I don't even know how we got to her house. A taxi maybe.'

Her house? Carla stood up. Don't cry, she told herself over and over. 'Why did you come here? Sending those texts and now telling me this?'

'But Carla, nothing happened.' He stood and took her hand. 'I swear nothing happened.'

'So why tell me?'

'Because, and I hate myself for this, I didn't know whether anything had happened until I saw Tina at the station yesterday and she told me. I remember her pouring wine, putting on music, and leaning towards me. The next thing I knew, Lucy was picking me up off the road outside my folks' house, and then I was throwing up on their carpet. I was also desperately searching for the phone they'd taken off me at the station, so I could speak to you. If Lucy hadn't stopped me, I'd have phoned the hospital then. When I woke up the next morning, I had no idea what, if anything, had happened.'

Carla's head was pounding. She couldn't make any sense of it.

'Will you sit? Just let me finish, please.'

Carla nodded and they both sat.

'After I'd checked the hospital and gone round to your flat a few times, I called your mum and she told me where you were. Then I booked the flight, and went into the station to see DI Black. That's when I saw Tina.'

'And she said what?'

'Apologised for coming on to me. Something about not being able to cope with the knock-back. And that you were very lucky.'

Carla wanted to smile at that, but she had too many questions. 'You went back to her house with her. Were you hoping something would happen?'

He shrugged. 'I was so rat-arsed, I haven't a clue what I was thinking. I know how it must look. She's…eh…not bad looking.'

'Really?'

'Carla, I know without a doubt that if she'd told me at the station it was only going to be her, I wouldn't have gone. I hate myself for drinking so much, for going back to her house, for putting myself in a position where I could have hurt you, or ruined our relationship.

'And the last text – I wasn't trying to soften you up before telling you about Tina, I swear. I just wanted you to know that, whatever happens to us because of my stupidity, I love you. I should have told you long ago. So many times I've wanted to say it, but I bottled it. I'd look at you and wonder what the hell you saw in me. I was convinced it wasn't going to last, that you'd find someone better.' He paused. 'It wouldn't be difficult.'

But it would. So difficult. Still, she wasn't going to tell him that. Not now. How had they lasted so long when they both thought the other was too good for them?

'I know you need time to think,' he said. 'I'll find a hotel for a couple of nights.'

'Ronald's got plenty of room.' Though the sun was still warm, she shivered. 'Let's go back to the house. I'm exhausted.'

'Why don't I go and get the car, bring it down here?'

She shook her head. 'I'll be fine.'

Neither of them spoke while they walked, a growing gap between them.

Chapter 43

DI Black looked around the room. This was more like it. A few smiles and everyone looking more relaxed. Exhausted, but relaxed. Progress had been made. It wasn't good that they'd found Katya Birze dead, but at least they had a suspect, and the evidence against him seemed compelling.

'For those of you that were fortunate enough to have had some recent time off, I'll recap. Following a call from a man that saw Katya Birze struggling with someone with a car that's registered to one Christopher Brent, we went to Brent's house at Ness Castle. There were signs of disturbed earth in the garden, and we found the body of Katya Birze buried there. She'd been beaten and strangled. Post mortem's today. We seized Brent's laptop and his emails showed flights had been booked to London for himself and Sharon MacRae. Flybe confirmed they were booked on a return flight yesterday afternoon, at which point Brent was arrested and his car seized.'

'Sharon MacRae confirmed Brent was connected to Todd Curtis and that both men had connections with some dodgy London characters involved in prostitution and drugs. She heard Katya's name mentioned in a club in London. We have some carefully worded emails between Brent and Curtis, in which Curtis mentions having done some business for Brent on Thursday, the day Gordon Sutherland died. And we have some intimate photos of Katya Birze found in a bed-side cabinet in Christopher Brent's house.'

'We also entered James Allingham's apartment at Castlefield yesterday, where we found the belongings of Birze and Danielle Smith. There was a business card for Brent Properties in Birze's purse, and Christopher Brent's prints were on a mug found in the kitchen. Brent has no alibi for between midnight and four am on Sunday morning. His phone shows he received a call around midnight, and he made a call to the same number twice before four o'clock. A spade in his garage had been used recently.'

'We also visited a house near Evanton owned by Brent. There's no suggestion that Birze was ever in that house, but the prints we believe to be Curtis's were everywhere, and signs that he might have been staying there, as well as at Castlefield. Still a lot of unanswered questions, though. Roberts, what did you get from Manchester?'

Roberts cleared his throat and tugged at his tie. 'The DCI in Manchester spoke to the two witnesses in the case again, showed them the e-fit. They couldn't say if it was the guy that had asked about Nancy Connor.'

The troops muttered. A few shakes of the head, and some derogatory comments.

'All right,' the DI said. 'So, it's not our best e-fit. Let the boy finish.'

Roberts' face was scarlet as he continued. 'One of them remembered Nancy Connor saying she had a child in her late teens, not long after she went on the game. A boy. He was adopted. They're looking into adoption records now, but it could take a while.'

'Anything on Danielle Smith?'

'The skin under her nails wasn't Ryan MacRae's.'

DI Black groaned. He hadn't really expected it to fall into place that easily, but still.

'The marks in the lane, above where the body was found, match his trainers,' Roberts said. 'We're waiting for soil analysis, but it's more than certain he was there. Any bets DNA samples taken from the bed in the house in Evanton will match the skin under Danielle's nails?'

DI Black nodded. 'With any luck. Well done, Roberts. Lewis – give us your news about Ali the Bampot's missing girl.'

'I'm waiting for more information from Aberdeen Council, but one Sally MacArthur, eighteen years old, presented there as homeless last year, then she left the area. Intelligence suggests her body may now be somewhere in the Caledonian Canal.'

DI Black sighed. 'It's only sixty miles long. We'll find her eventually. Seriously, though, maybe you could use your considerable charms on the itinerants of Inverness and narrow it down a bit, so we can get the divers in. Good work, Lewis.'

He gave out some tasks, then he went to his office. Not a bad couple of days' work. And that was without his best detective. All he needed now was for Jackson's drugged-up body to come ashore, and for Ryan MacRae to see the error of his ways and tell the truth. With Galbraith back, there'd be more chance of solving this quickly. He remembered Galbraith's suspicions about Alice McGarvie, the SNP councillor. How had she known the details of Gordon Sutherland's shooting? Time for a chat.

*

Typical bloody politician. Couldn't answer a question straight, and if McGarvie didn't like the question, she just answered a different one. Tact had never been Black's strong point. Galbraith would have been much better at this. She was an ugly old bat, right enough. No wonder the grieving widow couldn't take to her. But she knew what she was about.

'Did I say that? Did I really?' Alice McGarvie shook her head. 'I think your officer must have misheard me.'

'Detective Sergeant Galbraith is not in the habit of mishearing people. It's noted here quite clearly. Do I need to remind you where and when you said it?'

She raised an uneven eyebrow. 'DS Galbraith?'

'You haven't forgotten speaking to him then?'

'I forget nothing, Detective Inspector. Nothing. Tell me, is DS Galbraith here? Perhaps we could talk to him and sort this out. If he's not in the station, I'd be happy to come back later, when it suits him.'

She was smirking. The old bitch knew that Galbraith wasn't there. And then DI Black knew, and he smiled too. She had someone on the inside, someone who worked at the station. The son or nephew or second cousin of one of her separatist comrades. Nothing more sinister than that. He stood. 'Thank you for coming in, Councillor. I'll let you get back to your important business. Oh no, I forgot; you're not in power now. It's the other Independents, isn't it?'

Her smile was gracious as she nodded. 'Speaking of important business, Detective Inspector, I hear there's been another death. A foreign girl? Are you any closer to finding out who actually killed Gordon and these two poor girls?'

'I've just scored you off the list, so that's something.'

He was just starting on a cup of coffee when the call came.

Jackson's body had come ashore at Rosemarkie. And wouldn't you know it – there was a wee sealed plastic bag of coloured tabs with smiley faces in his pocket.

*

New Craigs had been five star compared to the police station cells, with a proper room and decent food. Ryan had hoped they'd keep him in for a few days, but he only got two nights out of it. They were nice to him, but he simply wasn't able to convince them he'd seriously considered jumping. He was at risk, they said, particularly given his age and the seriousness of the situation. But the risk was low. He'd be monitored in police custody or a secure unit, if one could be found, but he wasn't sick enough to be kept in hospital.

The psychiatrist, a woman, had asked some searching questions, ones that had made him think. Maybe it was little wonder he was such a fucked-up mess. And maybe it wasn't his fault. Though she'd explained that she couldn't tell the police anything without his consent, he hadn't given much away. Just that he was scared of Todd Curtis, of the future, and of letting his mother and Liam down. He got the impression she'd have liked to keep him in longer to give him some respite from his fears, but she simply couldn't.

'You may not agree,' she'd said, 'but you are a child. And the police and justice system have to treat you, and look after you, as a child. Custody should be a care environment, and they must treat you with respect for your human dignity. I'm sure your solicitor will keep on top of them, but I'm going to get a doctor to visit you tomorrow to check on your condition. Tell the doctor what you're feeling, if you have concerns.'

And now he was back in the care environment, in a cell on his own, with a hard bench for a bed, and a couple of blankets. Respect for human dignity? He wondered if the psychiatrist had even seen the facilities. He had plenty of time to think now. His solicitor had warned him he'd likely be charged shortly. At worst, double murder and rape. At best, perverting the course of justice. Then court. Unlikely to get bail. A secure unit was the probable destination. From what he'd heard, if you didn't know how to be a career criminal before you went there, a secure unit was just the place to learn. Plenty of drugs there too.

So, he was going down, one way or another. Maybe it was time to tell them all he knew. And maybe even time to tell them he might have been mistaken when he thought he saw Galbraith pushing Jackson off the bridge. He'd spent much of the previous night listing possible reasons for his 'mistake'.

- 1. *It all happened so fast.*
  2. *So much shouting and grabbing.*
  3. *Arms and legs everywhere.*
  4. *I was very upset.*
  5. *I was suicidal.*
  6. *I turned away just before Jackson fell.*
  7. *Maybe I didn't see it quite as clearly as I thought I had.*

Aye, right. If he repeated the list often enough, he might start to believe it himself.

*

DI Black checked the blinds were closed. There wasn't the slightest of gaps to give him away. It was just a wee victory dance, his moves imitating the cha-cha dancing baby from the 90s. It was all just too beautiful. Ryan MacRae was ready to spill.

Chapter 44

Ryan hadn't seen these cops before. He'd hoped for Roberts. Despite all he'd said about the officer in the past, he respected him. He seemed honest. But Galbraith had seemed honest too. Still, he'd given that a lot of thought. Of course Galbraith was going to lie to someone who was threatening to kill himself. He was going to say exactly what Ryan wanted to hear. And he'd so wanted to hear that his mother hadn't told Galbraith anything. Had Galbraith been lying about everything? Had he meant it when he'd offered to teach him to sail? Wouldn't happen now.

These guys weren't going to make it easy for him; he could see that from their eyes. Cold and hard as steel. Maybe it was for the best. Keep things real.

He told them he'd texted Todd at the morning break on Thursday, and Todd had picked him up from school. Todd was preoccupied as he'd driven out past the retail park on Telford Street, turning left just before the Muirtown Bridge, and parking at the side of the canal, close to the old boarded up house.

A man parked beside them. Todd told Ryan to stay in his car, while he and the man walked up the slope along the canal bank. They were back before long, and Todd said they were going for a drive in the man's car. Told him to get in the front, while Todd sat behind the man in the back. Ryan had been bored stiff as Todd and the man chatted. Gordon Sutherland had asked him why he wasn't in school, and Ryan had wished he was.

He shivered. What happened next didn't make any sense. Todd told the man to stop on Kenneth Street, and then he shot him in the back. He could have done him in at the canal if he'd wanted to. Ryan tried, yet again, to remember what they were talking about just before Todd told the man to pull in. His mind was blank.

'We're only talking Thursday,' the tall one said. 'And you can't remember?'

Ryan sighed. 'What more can I say? I didn't know what was going to happen. I have no idea why he shot Gordon Sutherland. He was just a boring old man.'

'And you can't remember what they were talking about in the car? You're just sitting there, no idea where the boring old man is taking you, no idea what was going on?'

'Mate, I spend most of my life not knowing what's going on.'

The wee one leaned across the table, a smirk on his face. 'Were you and Todd Curtis having it off?'

The legs of Ryan's chair screeched across the floor. It was only the social worker's hand on his arm that stopped him jumping up. 'What the fuck? That's disgusting.'

'Was Todd Curtis your pimp? Did Gordon Sutherland pay to have sex with you?'

Ryan shook his head. 'No sex, no pimping. What do you think I am?'

'He must have wanted something in return for all he gave you.'

'Not that.'

'So what was it all about?'

Ryan shrugged. 'Youse'll have to ask him. If I was to make a guess, I'd say he was probably involved in my father's death, and he felt guilty.'

The officer opened the file in front of him. 'Peter MacRae. Drug dealer. Wife beater. Junkie. General arse-hole.' He looked up.

Ryan laughed, and saw surprise on the officer's face. 'You forgot 'psycho', but otherwise, you've got him about right.'

'Nothing suspicious about his death. Sounds like he caused it all by himself. Shame he had to take three innocent people with him.'

'Someone was supplying him. I reckon it was Todd.'

'What kind of car does Curtis drive?'

'Mostly a black one, but I've seen him in a few different cars.'

'A black what?'

Ryan shook his head. He'd never been good with cars. Wasn't interested. Different if it was a boat.

'Any distinguishing features?'

Ryan shrugged. 'Don't think so. It's smart; leather seats. Maybe there's an 'L' on the badge. Maybe not.'

'A Lexus?'

'Maybe.'

'Let's get back to Thursday. So you're going along Kenneth

Street. The road's quiet. And suddenly – '

A light bulb went off in Ryan's head. He sat up straight. 'That's it; they were talking about the traffic in Inverness, about the new bypass.' He put his elbows on the table, his hands in a prayer-like pose over his nose and mouth. The room was silent. He sat back. 'That way madness lies.'

The smaller cop scoffed. 'Regular wee Robbie Burns, aren't you?'

'Burns?' Ryan laughed. 'Do you not need any qualifications to be a detective? It's Shakespeare; King Lear.'

'Right, smart arse; what's it got to do with anything?'

'That's what Gordon Sutherland said, right before Todd shot him. That way madness lies. Those were his last words.'

'Apropos to exactly what?' The big one smirked at Ryan.

Ryan grinned. The bugger thought he was going to catch Ryan out with grammar, if nothing else. He clearly hadn't had Miss Campbell for English. 'Apropos their discussion about the different options for the bypass. Todd mentioned a tunnel under the Ness. Gordon Sutherland said, 'That way madness lies'.'

He remembered the ice in Todd's voice when he asked Sutherland to repeat what he'd said. Sutherland repeated it. Todd told him to stop. Bang. Curtis had shouted at Ryan to run, but not to follow him down Fairfield Road.

'Doesn't take us very far, does it?' the tall one said.

Ryan shrugged. 'That's down to you guys. Maybe if you were out there trying to find him...'

'Now that you've had your epiphany, anything else come to you? Like what were you both doing in his car in the first place?'

Ryan nodded. 'Yeah, it's coming back to me. Todd said earlier he was going to see a man about a party. And there was some mention of lunch and then a meeting.'

They didn't believe he had no idea where Todd lived. He'd have liked to know. It would have given him somewhere to go when life and his mother and everyone else was pissing him off, but Todd had never told him.

The taller of the two was leaning across the table. 'Let me get this right. You've been hanging about with this guy for almost a year; he picks you up at school or anywhere else whenever you want; he gives you a phone and money. But you don't know where he lives?'

'I don't. Can I have a break?'

*

DI Black looked over the notes. Didn't take them much further, but at least the wee shite was talking now. Todd Curtis and, perhaps, Christopher Brent, have a grievance against Gordon Sutherland. They try to get some dirt on him by tempting him with call girls, and blackening his name with his council colleagues. That doesn't work, so Curtis uses Sutherland's party and approaches him about a possible donation. Meets with him on the day of a branch meeting, gets in his car to go to lunch, and then to the meeting.

That way madness lies. Why would that trigger Todd Curtis to shoot? Is he mentally ill? Probably, but he's going to have heard a lot worse by way of insult than that. He's certainly got a short fuse, according to MacRae, and he regularly settles scores with people who have crossed him. He's perverted, evil and blatant enough to put that photo through the grieving widow's letterbox on the day of the murder. Some grievance.

He studied the interim post mortem report for Birze. No sign of sexual assault. Beaten and strangled. Some of the injuries were caused by a stick, possibly with a carved metal head. Shame Brent's stick was clean, but he could have scrubbed it well. She'd been buried face down, with signs of fixed lividity on her front, caused by stagnation of the blood vessels after death. Yet there were also faint areas of lividity on her back and buttocks. She had been lying on her back somewhere before she was buried.

They had two sources of evidence that pointed to Brent's window of opportunity being narrow. He'd had four hours at most, to leave Ness Castle, find Birze and struggle with her on Old Edinburgh Road, kill her, have her somewhere on her back long enough for lividity to develop, and then bury her. Did it really add up?

Come on, Ryan, he thought; give us something that makes some sense of all this.

Chapter 45

At the mention of Danielle, Ryan put his head down on his forearms. He felt his solicitor's hand on his upper arm, a gentle stroke. That brought tears to his eyes. He didn't want these bastards to see he was upset. They'd use it against him. They must think he was a cocky little shit. He was. Didn't always mean to be, but he couldn't help himself. There was this well of anger and frustration inside him, and he couldn't stop it from rising up and erupting whenever he felt threatened. It didn't have to be a physical threat. Anything. Anyone. It seemed impossible to control.

He felt something poke his forearm. He looked up. It was a photo of Danielle. She was so beautiful.

'Son, you'll feel better when you've told us.'

Son? I'm not your fucking son. Better? Fucking better? He shook his head, opened his mouth to let the bile out, but it didn't come. He felt as if something was shifting inside of him, the anger melting and draining away.

His voice was steady as he told them about the phone call, the race to Carlton Terrace, the promise to take Danielle to the town. Though nausea threatened to engulf him, he kept calm as he told them of Todd's anger and his offer and the condom. And then he was silent.

'You're doing well, Ryan; we need to catch him. Tell us the rest.'

Ryan looked into a distance of his own, and watched it again, as he had done so many times. 'Todd was watching, waiting to see what I would do. The doors were locked and we couldn't get away. I had to pretend I was going along with it, so I started to open the zip of Danielle's top. She was so scared. I tried to tell her with my eyes that I would never hurt her, but I don't know if she knew.

'He laughed then. Said something about me being my father's son, all right. Then he got out. He didn't lock the car.' Ryan shook his head. 'He must have been so certain that I was just like my father, that I couldn't see what was wrong with it. He walked a bit away, kept his back to the car. I told Danielle we had to get out.

We'd both open the doors really quietly, and she was just to run for the main road, as fast as she could.

'We were just out of the car when he heard us. He came at us, roaring like a maniac. There was a broken branch on the ground and I grabbed it and ran at him. And all the time I was shouting at her to run. The branch was useless; I was useless. He grabbed me by the throat and I was trying to get his hands off me. I think he was angrier at me for betraying him, than he was at her. It was almost like he'd forgotten about her. She could have got away. I thought she had. I thought I was going to die, but at least she'd escaped.

'I kneed him in the balls and he let me go. He was doubled over and I knew I had to run. I looked around for her and I couldn't see her. I swear I couldn't see her.' He put his head down on his arms again.

'Ryan, you came home upset, with bruises and scratches on your throat and your hands. You went into hiding early the next morning. Then you threatened to kill yourself. Can you see how guilty that made you look?'

He looked up and nodded. 'Course I can. He made those marks on me, and I was hiding from him. I was terrified of what he would do to me. And there was the shooting – how long would it be before you lot came back for me? When I left home, I had no idea what had happened to Danielle. I thought she'd escaped.'

'When did you find out she was dead?'

Ryan put his head down again.

'Go on, son.'

He'd go on, as soon as he thought of a way to keep his mother out of it. He looked up. 'Next day. I saw it on my phone, on the BBC website.'

'Ryan, an item of clothing with your DNA on it was found beside Danielle's body. What do you have to say about that?'

As little as possible. He shook his head. 'My DNA? Do you mean my blood? The backs of my hands were all scratched by that bastard. They were bleeding a bit, but I had all my clothes. I don't know what you mean.'

'Take us back to the day of the shooting and what you did with your clothes afterwards.'

'You know I put them in the washing machine.'

'All of them?'

'Yeah.'

'Are you certain?'

Ryan took some time to think, or make them think he was thinking. He shook his head. 'No. There was a sock.' He tried to widen his eyes as if he was surprised. Knowing his luck, he'd just look glaikit. 'No way. Was my sock found near Danielle? I had nothing to do with that. Why would I leave my own sock at a murder scene?'

'Any idea how your sock got there?'

He thought some more, and then he spun a tale that sounded as if it might make sense. He'd found it lying in his room just after he'd had a shower. Todd phoned then and warned him to keep his mouth shut. He'd told Todd about the sock and Todd came straight down, took it and said he'd get rid of it. His mum was in the flat, but she probably didn't hear him sneaking out to Todd's car. That bastard was trying to set him up.

The wee one looked as if he didn't believe a word. 'This phone Todd gave you; where is it?'

'I dropped it off the bridge before Galbraith arrived.'

'Why would you do that?'

He shrugged. 'I was going to jump. Seemed no point in keeping it.' And no, he didn't know the number of his or Todd's phone. In fact, Todd Curtis had more than one phone, and he changed his numbers every couple of weeks.

Another break.

*

Ronald pushed against the fence post, testing it for strength. The half stob Joe had driven into the ground at an angle held tight. 'Not bad for a copper. Where did you learn that?'

Joe straightened up, rubbing his lower back. 'A past life.'

'You were a fencer?'

He shook his head. 'A joiner.'

Ronald smiled and picked up a mallet. He handed it to Joe. 'Quite a career change.'

'Tell me about it. Perhaps I should have stuck to it, and I wouldn't be in the shit right now.'

'But you wouldn't have met Carla.'

Joe nodded. 'True. Listen, I really wouldn't mind finding somewhere else to stay. I don't want to put you out. There's a hotel in Lochmaddy, isn't there?'

'Two hotels and a number of fine guest houses, but you're not putting me out. If Carla's happy to have you here, I'm happy. There's plenty of room.'

'Thank you.' Joe smiled. 'The least I can do is take you out for a meal tonight. Right, what's next?'

'Fit the top wire, then the rylock.'

They continued in an easy silence, the sun warm on their backs. Joe felt as if each breath of fresh salty air was erasing the stress of the last few day, steadying him, grounding him firmly to the ancient rock below. When Ronald muttered in Gaelic, it brought a memory of a summer day in Tarbert, and a small boy on his father's shoulders. Joe turned and looked towards the hills of Harris. The distinctive shape of Ceapabhal stood out from the others. It looked so different from here; a pleasant, gentle hill. He waited for the scar to do its stuff, but it didn't. Smiling, he carried on.

It was some time before the spell was broken by Joe's phone. He put the mallet on the grass, wiped his hand on his jeans, and took his phone out of his pocket. 'It's work; I won't be long.'

Ronald smiled. 'Take your time. Good news, I hope.'

Joe sat on the back door step. He took a deep breath. 'Sir?'

'Ah, Galbraith. Good. Wasn't sure I'd copied your number down properly. Listen, this is probably premature, but Ryan MacRae is spilling his guts as we speak. They've done the shooting. Confirms what you thought; he was in the front, Todd Curtis in the back. Sounds like Gordon Sutherland was taking them to lunch, then the SNP meeting. It was as much of a shock to Ryan as it was to Sutherland when Curtis fired. He has no idea why. Something Sutherland said enraged Curtis; some quote from Shakespeare.'

'What quote?'

He heard the DI scrabbling about. 'Can't find my pad. The way means madness or that way is madness or something along those lines.'

Joe smiled. 'That way madness lies? From King Lear?'

'Aye, smart arse; that's the one.'

Joe kicked a patch of lichen off the step. He smiled as a hen raced after it. 'Sutherland was an English teacher before he retired.'

'So he probably got the quote right, and wasn't shot for crimes against English literature. Who the hell knows except Curtis?'

'Quite. What about Danielle?'

'He says he tried to fight Curtis off to let her escape. He thought she'd gone, then he legged it. Thinks she probably ran the wrong way, further into the lane, and Curtis got her. It fits with the sprained ankle found at post mortem, and the scuffle in the mud – she must have got away and fallen. He confirmed she was wearing a hair clasp just like the one we found. And the signs of a scuffle nearer where her body was found – that would fit with his fight with Curtis.'

'And me?'

'That's what they're doing now. It's been a long session. I'm hoping I might have news for you later today. How's the Hebrides? You haven't been stabbed, have you?'

'Almost got a nail through my hand, but apart from that, I'm in one piece.'

'Good. And Carla's fine, is she? Oh, I almost forgot to say – Jackson's surfaced. Some poor old fella beachcombing at Rosemarkie got more than he bargained for this morning. Post mortem later on today or tomorrow, but, between you and me, it looks like he had ecstasy on him, as well as in him. You didn't slip a wee baggy into his pocket before you pushed him, did you?'

'Aye, I always carry one. Comes in handy for fitting up the junkies, not to mention fellow officers.'

Black laughed. 'Good to see you've not lost your sense of humour, son. Listen, we've had a breakthrough, and an arrest.' He told Joe about Katya Birze and Christopher Brent.

Though it was good they had someone, Joe felt sorry for Sharon MacRae. She didn't have much luck. 'Could Brent have been involved in Sutherland's death?'

'Perhaps. That's what the emails could suggest. On the other hand, Brent may be thanking Curtis for something else entirely. There's a lot of work to be done. SOCO are still at Brent's place. We'll know more later. Keep that phone handy, and no going out to sea; I don't want a repeat of the Harris experience when I couldn't get hold of you or the local police. Sorry if it interferes with your love life, but I want you back here pronto as soon as MacRae spills and these numpties see they've got it all wrong.'

'Aye, sir.'

Typical. As he cut the call, he noticed two texts from Lucy, one sent yesterday, one today.

How r u? Call me

Bro WRU@?

WTF? He took a guess.

North Uist with Carla

He'd hardly pressed 'send' when her response came back. These young ones.

Enjoy. Don't get stabbed

At least she could laugh about it now.

Chapter 46

If only Ryan had done drama at school. He'd quite fancied it, but Miss Campbell had played it all wrong. She should have told him he couldn't do it; that always worked. Instead, she'd been too enthusiastic, tried too hard, and he had walked. He could have done with some acting skills now, as the big detective leaned towards him. 'Let me see if I have this right. Two days ago, you thought you saw Galbraith push Jackson backwards off the Kessock Bridge, but now you think you might have been mistaken?'

Ryan shrugged. 'That's about it. There were arms and legs everywhere, people shouting. I was suicidal. I…I wasn't thinking straight. You know how it was with the shooting. I'm only now remembering what was said. It's shock, isn't it? It does that. In fact, I think I might have heard Galbraith say something like 'Give me your hand, Jimmy, please', but I'm not certain.'

'Really? My difficulty…our difficulty…is that the officers that attended just after DC Jackson fell, they say you weren't showing any signs of shock. In fact, you sounded quite vindictive when you said it, as if you were trying to get DS Galbraith into trouble.'

'They would say that. Roberts and Galbraith are pals, aren't they?'

'It wasn't just DC Roberts. They all said it. And DS Galbraith said you were angry that he hadn't been open with you about what your mother told him.'

'Wasn't open with me? He bloody lied.' Calm down, he told himself. He took a deep breath.

'Quite. And the psychiatrist at New Craigs said she didn't think you were suicidal at all.'

And it had all been going so well. He was sure they believed him about Sutherland and Danielle. Maybe he should have stuck to his original story about Galbraith. But it wasn't fair, was it? Better try a bit harder. 'I honestly can't tell you what I was feeling about Galbraith or Jackson or anyone else. My head was mince. It's only clearing now. Why would I lie about this?'

The tall one slammed his pen onto the table. 'I don't think you are lying about what really happened, but you're lying about lying in the first place. Do you know what this could have done to DS Galbraith's career, not to mention his life?'

Ryan nodded. 'That's been on my mind a lot over the last few days. That's why I asked to speak to you today, because it's all a bit clearer now.'

'Clear as mud to me. So, was Galbraith actually in the cage with you and Jackson, like you said originally?'

Ryan shook his head. 'I don't think so. Maybe he was just leaning in. I'm sorry. My head's all confused.' He looked at the clock. 'We've been talking for a long time.'

*

Carla had tried to nap while Ronald and Joe were fencing. She couldn't. It wasn't just the tap, tap, tapping from outside. Joe's tale was going round and round in her head and it wouldn't stop. Two hours later, she went through to the kitchen. The men looked as if they were getting on well. No strain or forced chatter. They hadn't noticed her.

How was she ever going to make up her mind? Did she even have to make a decision now? Joe was smiling as he worked. He looked as contented as she had ever seen him, until he saw her. He frowned and she knew it wasn't fair to keep him waiting for an answer. But she didn't have one.

She held up a mug and he nodded. Ronald shook his head. Carla knew he was desperate for a cup of tea, but he wanted to give them some time. She made him one anyway, and took it out. Joe followed her in.

'I'm sorry you didn't sleep.' He was washing his hands at the sink. 'It's my fault.'

'Joe...I...'

His phone rang. She watched as he took the news. He nodded and glanced at her from time to time. 'Thank you, Sir; I'll check with the airport. See if I can get back tomorrow.' He cut the call, closed his eyes and took a deep breath.

'Good news?'

He opened his eyes and she thought there might be tears lurking in the blue depths. 'Yes...and...and no.'

'Ryan MacRae's told the truth?'

Joe nodded. 'And Jackson's body's been found – I heard that earlier, when you were resting. Post mortem's about to start, but they found drugs on him.'

Carla smiled. 'How could this not be the best news you've ever had?'

'Because I don't want to go back. Not without knowing. I better call the airport.'

There was a seat on the flight.

*

There were birds singing in the trees outside Langass Lodge as soft colours bathed the island. Beyond the trees, Eabhal, the highest hill on North Uist, rose from the rugged landscape, its craggy contours sharp against the evening sun.

The food was good, the conversation easy. Carla seemed relaxed. When Ronald left them to go and speak to someone, Joe put his hand on hers. She didn't pull away. He was about to ask, when an elderly woman approached them. She'd been at school with Carla's grandmother. Carla's eyes were bright as she listened. Then Ronald came back, and it was time to go.

At the house, they had tea, then Ronald went to check the beasts. Joe took a deep breath, and the phone rang. It was Carla's mother.

He stepped out into the warm night and watched as three oystercatchers hurried past, their shrill sound filling the night. Along the horizon, the sky was streaked with stripes of red and purple and blue. A good day tomorrow, no doubt. And he'd be gone. Through the kitchen window he saw Carla's serious face. Was she telling her mother what he'd done?

A movement caught his eye. An owl gliding past on broad, golden wings, its flight seductive. It turned its head and looked at Joe, its chiselled features almost human. Perhaps it had a secret for him. Perhaps it knew. He laughed at himself. Probably just as well he was going back to real life. But the night wasn't done with him. Halfway down the field, he saw Ronald speaking to someone. The gate was open, and he felt as if the sunset and the sea were drawing him down the track towards them. As Joe got closer, Ronald looked up and smiled. His companion turned. He had bushy dark hair and a beard. He muttered something and took off.

'That's Will,' Ronald said, as the man made his shuffling way down the croft towards the shore. 'Stays in that caravan. A bit of a poor soul, really. He took Carla in earlier, when she felt unwell. She said they had a good chat, but this is only the second time I've ever spoken to him. The first time, he just said his name.' Ronald paused, then he smiled. 'You know, he might not have been telling me his name at all. He could have been about to ask me any number of things that began with 'Will', like will anyone mind if I stay in that caravan? I must ask him next time I see him. I don't know what takes these people here, but we attract our fair share of eccentrics.'

Joe looked around. 'It's certainly very beautiful. I wish I could stay longer.'

Ronald nodded. 'You'll just have to come back when you've solved your crimes.'

As soon as Joe and Ronald went into the house, Carla said she was going to bed. 'I'm sorry, Joe; I'm shattered. We'll talk in the morning?'

Joe nodded. He'd be up at the crack of dawn waiting for her.

Chapter 47

Lucy made herself a cup of tea and sat down to check her emails. There was one from her mum attaching two photos from Lanzarote. Her father at Fire Mountain, eating chicken cooked over a hole in the ground using natural volcanic heat. Her mother on a sun lounger at the hotel pool. They were having a lovely time, she said. There were many more photos, but they were taking too long to upload. Lucy would just have to look forward to her father's usual endless slide-show when they got back. Anything doing at home? If only you knew, Mother.

There was an email from her friend, Millie, asking if she'd met anyone interesting in Inverness. She wanted to tell her friend about Drew, and today's developments, but maybe she needed to get it straight in her own head first.

They'd been discussing the Permanence Order case in the afternoon, when her phone had beeped in her bag. She should have had it on silent. She'd ignored it.

'Go on,' Drew had said. 'It might be Joe.'

It was. 'That's a relief. He's in Uist with his girlfriend. I thought I was going to have to get the bus through to Nairn to see if he was still alive. A box set and a large glass of wine is called for.'

Drew smiled and put his pen down. 'You've had a rough few days.'

'Not as rough as Joe.

'Still, it hasn't been easy for you. Do you fancy going out for a meal tonight?'

Lucy had stopped trusting her judgement on men after Sebastian and Stephen MacLaren, so much so that she hadn't gone out with anyone since last year. Not that she'd been swamped with opportunities, but there had been one or two. Millie said she was giving off seriously daunting vibes that were keeping any interested guys away. Clearly not daunting enough.

Was Drew blushing? She was. 'Eh…'

'Sorry. I've put you on the spot. Forget I asked.'

'No. I mean, yes; I'd like that.'

'Good. I'll pick you up. About seven? We could have just gone after work, but I've…I've got something I have to do first.'

After work? That didn't sound like a date. That was good. For the best. Aye right. Who was she trying to kid?

When she'd opened the front door to Drew at seven, he'd looked a little awkward, and she'd wondered if he was regretting it already. She was. It was going to make her last few days at the law centre difficult. Still, not much she could do about it now.

'You look lovely, Lucy.' His eyes were distracted. He looked over his shoulder to his car. 'Listen, this is difficult, but I've got my daughter with me. She insisted.'

Maya was seven and full of attitude. Beautiful, and she knew it. She wanted to go to MacDonalds, but he insisted on the Mustard Seed. He could always take her home. Maya shook her head. No way. She'd come.

She pretty much ignored Lucy until they'd finished their starters, while Drew tried his best to divide his attention between them. It wasn't easy. The conversation kept coming back to Wookies and Darth Vader, light sabres and Stormtroopers.

'How old do you think Chewbacca is?' Maya asked Lucy.

Lucy hesitated. Should she admit she'd never seen a Star Wars film? She reckoned her level of street cred with Maya had started with a minus figure, so she really didn't want it going any lower. But which one was Chewbacca? 'I reckon he must be pretty old.'

'Two hundred years. Dad, is your car two hundred years old?'

Drew laughed. 'No. It's twenty years old. It's a classic.'

'Mummy says it's a clapped-out old banger. What does clapped-out mean?'

'Your mother should know.'

'Okay, I'll ask her.'

What was with the mother? Were they together? The 'clapped-out' comment suggested otherwise, but maybe it wasn't meant to be as insulting as it sounded. Maybe he was very happily married, and always took his students out for a meal. Maybe she'd got entirely the wrong idea.

Or maybe not. When Maya insisted she would go to the toilet on her own, Drew was profuse in his apologies. 'This isn't what I had hoped for. I'm so sorry.'

Maybe he was both happily married and available. It wouldn't be the first time, would it?'

'Don't apologise. She's lovely. A bit young for Star Wars, though.'

'That's what her mother says. My irresponsibility knows no bounds, and if I even dream of letting her watch Harry Potter, well…there will be consequences.'

But what kind of consequences? Banished to the spare room? Divorce? Lucy smiled. 'That's a shame. I can talk endless Harry Potter, but I've never seen Star Wars.'

'Philistine. Oh, here she comes. I was about to ask if you were doing anything this weekend.'

She'd been hopeful that he'd drop Maya off first, but he hadn't. And now, she didn't know what to think. Deciding not to answer Millie's email tonight, she closed down her laptop, finished her tea, and made for bed.

*

Todd was weary. Tired to the bone. Head like mince. It was never clear these days. What was it that drugged up whore, Nancy Connor, had said to him all those years ago in Manchester? *There's a time bomb inside your head, just like mine; looks like it's about to explode.*

It had exploded all right, after he heard what she had to say. It had chased the malice from her eyes and the venom from her voice. There was only terror then, her blood-shot eyes wide, painted lips pleading. He couldn't do this to her. Yes, he could. Skanky whore. In her fifties and still on the game. How she'd pleaded. Sometimes her voice woke him, as if she was lying beside him, whispering, then screeching, until he couldn't get back to sleep, and only a cold shower would stop it.

There was still no photo of him on the internet. He'd wondered if they'd find one at Chris's place. He'd hummed *Watching the Detectives*, as he saw them turn the place upside down, dusting for prints and searching for evidence. They hadn't found any of the cameras yet.

They were crawling all over the apartment at Castlefield and the house at Evanton too. With no picture yet circulated, he'd be safe enough going to a hotel for now. But that would mean mixing with ordinary dull little people. Having to be nice to them, to smile, to pretend to give a fuck. He was all out of fucks to give.

He'd made too many mistakes. No proper planning. Making it all up as he went along. He should just go. He could have another car and a passport within an hour. By tomorrow afternoon, he could be on a beach somewhere. Far away from Chris and all the shit that had come with him.

But he hadn't done all he'd vowed to do. He hadn't finished. One more day. That was all he needed.

Chapter 48

Joe didn't see the crack of dawn, but he saw every hour before that, aware that Carla was sleeping, or not, in the room directly below him. It was eight when he woke. He had to be away before nine.

Carla was in the kitchen. She apologised. 'I slept in. I didn't think I'd need an alarm, but I didn't sleep well. I was just going to shout you when I heard you in the shower.'

'I couldn't sleep either. What are we like? I really don't want to go. We need to talk.'

Carla nodded. 'Not much time for it now, but – '

Joe could have cried as the back door opened and Ronald came in. He looked taken aback. 'Joe, you're here? I thought I'd missed you. What have you done with the yellow submarine?'

It seemed that car thieves in North Uist weren't that fussy after all.

Ronald drove to the airport, a little too fast for Joe's stomach. 'It'll not be a thief, as such,' he said. 'Someone will just have borrowed it.'

Joe smiled. 'Oh, that's all right then. And there's absolutely no problem with some toe rag sneaking into your house in the night and taking the keys off the kitchen table?'

'When you put it like that…I wonder why they didn't just take my car. The keys were in the ignition. Maybe it's time I started locking the car and the house. It might help if I could find the house key.'

'What do you do if you go away?'

'I leave the door open, and nothing has ever been disturbed. It's a different world here.'

Joe nodded. 'It's the same in Harris. And we all know nothing bad ever happens there.'

From the back of the car, Carla put her hand on his shoulder. It was only for a moment, but it felt so good.

The car hire man didn't look too put out. Neither did the cop Joe had arranged to meet at the airport. 'It didn't go on any of the ferries this morning,' she said. 'I've checked with Lochmaddy, Lochboisdale and Berneray. And we'll monitor the next crossings. Someone will have borrowed it. It'll show up.'

Borrowed it? What were they like? 'I presume you'll be speaking to the neighbours, taking prints from Ronald MacKenzie's front door handle, from the kitchen. You might even want to take prints from the car, if it 'shows up'?'

She nodded and smiled. 'You just leave it with us. We'll do all that's necessary. Now, I'll just get a few more details.'

She paled a little when she heard he was a detective. She looked at her notebook again. 'Galbraith? Detective Sergeant Joe Galbraith? From Inverness? Really?'

He nodded. 'Really.' Had she heard about his role in Jackson's death or was it last year's stabbing in Harris? Probably both.

'Thank you, Sir.' The pallor was replaced by a pink flush. 'We'll do everything we can. Everything. I promise. Now, have I forgotten anything?'

The flight had been called, and Ronald had said goodbye. It was just Joe and Carla. Joe took her hands. 'Please, please, keep in touch.'

'Of course. I'll let you know about the car, if we get any news. We'll talk properly, soon. Take care, Joe.'

He felt warmth in his chest, as he always did, when she used his name. To hug or not to hug?

'You better go.'

Their eyes met and he pulled her close, breathing in her smell. 'I love you, Carla. And I'm so sorry.'

She pulled away, and he saw tears in her eyes. Was that a good sign?

The sun was shining on the windows of the airport lounge. As the plane began to taxi, he thought he could see her standing watching, but maybe it was just a tall plant.

*

It almost felt as if he'd never been away. If it wasn't for the funny looks from his colleagues, Joe would almost think it had all been a dream. His first task was to speak to a man who had turned up at the station. A man who had just returned from a holiday in Australia and couldn't get into his own home.

Joe studied the man opposite. Intelligent. Well-dressed. Rich. And seriously pissed off. 'Mr Allingham.' Joe nodded at him. 'I'm Detective Sergeant Galbraith. This is Detective Constable Roberts. I understand you've been to your apartment.'

'I have been to my apartment, as I've already told several of your colleagues.' His eyes were cold and grey. A scar ran from his eye to his chin, and it was twitching. 'Not one of them saw fit to enlighten me as to the reason I cannot access my apartment.'

Joe took a long drink from a bottle of water. When he was done, he screwed the top back on and put the bottle on the table. He stared. Saw Allingham's scar going mental, his rage threatening to erupt. If Joe didn't have so much to do, he'd draw this out for longer, but time was short. 'Todd Curtis.'

'I beg your pardon?'

Joe pushed the bottle aside and leaned towards him. 'Todd Curtis. He is the reason you can't access your apartment.'

He looked a little less cocky now. 'I...I'm afraid I don't understand.'

'How long have you been away, Mr Allingham?'

'Two months.'

'And were you aware Todd Curtis was staying in your apartment?'

The rage was gone, but there was still a lot going on behind those eyes. Caution, cunning, perhaps a hint of fear. At last, he nodded. 'I understood he might occasionally stay there while I was away.'

'Is that a regular occurrence?'

He shrugged. 'I have a spare room. Todd comes and goes. He's a bit of a nomad.'

'He drives a black Lexus – is that correct?'

Allingham nodded. His eyes avoided Joe's. 'The Lexus is mine. I allowed him to drive it while I was away.'

'Really? You must be close friends.'

He shook his head. 'I wouldn't describe us as close.'

'Are you work colleagues?'

'No.'

Partners in crime, undoubtedly. No proof, yet. Joe pushed a

picture of Katya Birze across the table. 'Do you know this woman?'

That scar. What a giveaway. Allingham rested his elbow on the table, his hand covering the scar. 'I've met her.'

'Professionally?'

His pupils contracted with anger. 'Absolutely not. I believe she's an acquaintance of Todd's.'

'A dead acquaintance of Todd's. As is this girl.'

Allingham stared at the picture of Danielle Smith.

'And this man.'

A picture of Gordon Sutherland.

He shook his head. 'I have never seen either of these people before.'

'What about these people?'

Allingham looked at the pictures of Ryan MacRae and Christopher Brent. He shook his head.

Joe gathered up the pictures. 'Mr Allingham. Todd Curtis is wanted in connection with three murders, possibly more. At least one of the victims has been in your apartment, and the belongings of two victims were found there. We also found a significant quantity of cash. We would like to take a full statement from you. You are, of course, entitled to have a solicitor present, but it would be helpful if you would tell me now when you last heard from Todd Curtis.'

He sat back, his hand still on his face. He looked smaller, far less sure of himself. 'It was before I left for Australia. I haven't heard from him since.'

'Do you know where he might be?'

He shook his head.

'Do you have a phone number for him?'

He took his phone out and gave Joe a number. 'That may no longer be in use. He...he changes his number from time to time.'

'And why would he do that?'

Allingham shrugged. 'I have no idea.'

'Do you wish to have a solicitor present?'

He nodded, then he made a call to a solicitor in Glasgow. Joe knew of him; he represented the seriously rich and the seriously guilty. Allingham's voice was sharp and his tone imperious. He didn't care if the solicitor was busy. He wanted him to set off for Inverness now.

Chapter 49

DI Black was pleased. 'Good work. I'll take his interview, with you or Tina Lewis?'

'Don't mind, Sir,' Joe said. 'I've got some questions for Ryan MacRae. Little and Large might think they're hotshots, but they've missed a heap of stuff.'

The DI frowned. 'Will we get someone else to do it?'

Joe shrugged. 'It's up to you, but I'll be professional.'

'Okay, take Tonto with you.'

Roberts almost rolled on his back to have his tummy tickled. As they walked down the corridor towards the interview room, he coughed and tapped Joe's arm. 'Sarge, I just want to say something.'

Joe stopped. 'Aye?'

'I would never have told anyone what you said about Jackson the other night. Never. I hope you know that.'

Joe's feminine side was taking a real beating these last few days. He patted Roberts on the shoulder. 'Appreciate that,' he said, making an effort to lower his voice.

'So we're sound?'

'We're sound as a pound, Nigel.'

For once, Roberts didn't grimace at the use of his hated first name. He smiled all the way down the corridor.

At least Ryan had the decency to look a little shame-faced. It didn't last. 'Not you two. Don't even think of asking me about Jackson's 'fall'. I've told those other tossers everything.'

Joe smiled and wondered if there was a little less animosity and rage than before. He was probably just imagining it. 'I'm not here to ask you about that, Ryan. I've read over your statements about Gordon Sutherland and Danielle Smith. I just want to tidy up a few loose ends.'

Ryan rolled his eyes. 'I doubt there's anything else I can say.'

'Let's see. We didn't get any of your prints on the outside handle of Gordon Sutherland's car. How is that possible?'

'He held it open for me.' Ryan looked sad. 'He was a nice man.'

'And only a partial thumb print inside. How did you manage to open the door without leaving prints?'

Ryan shrugged. 'Dunno. I used my hand.'

'That's very odd, Ryan. Were you wearing gloves?'

'In June?' Ryan shook his head.

Anne Morrison, the social worker, leaned forward. 'Can I say something?'

Joe nodded. Anne put her hand on Ryan's arm. 'Were your hands like they are now?'

He had pulled his sweatshirt sleeves down over each hand. He studied them and nodded. 'Thanks Anne,' Joe said. 'You told the others you don't know where Todd Curtis lives. Did he ever take you to Carlton Terrace before the day Danielle Smith died?'

Ryan shook his head.

'Castlefield Apartments?'

Ryan shrugged. 'Where's that?'

'Up near Asda, off the distributor road. Fancy flats with glass fronts and balconies.'

'Definitely not.'

'Did he ever give you any hints about where he might live?'

Ryan was certain he had never been to Todd's house. Yes, he'd been to flats and houses; he'd waited outside, but there was nothing to make him think Todd lived in any of them. 'If there was no one in, he'd come out and say he'd get them later.'

'Get them? What did you think he meant?'

'I think he meant he'd half kill them when he got hold of them.'

'Was he ever injured when he came out? Any signs of a fight?'

Ryan laughed. 'Have you seen him?'

Stupid question. 'That'll be a no, Ryan; we haven't seen him. But we'd very much like to. What did you mean by that?'

'He's enormous, terrifying; no one is going to stand up to him. Not without a baseball bat or a gun.'

'You did.'

Ryan looked down at the table. 'For all the good it did.'

'It was a very brave thing to do.'

'I wasn't brave when I ran off, was I?' He looked up and his eyes were full of pain and regret. 'I could have called the cops; I could have stopped it. I thought she was gone. She was, but I don't know where. Couldn't have been very far when he got her. If only she'd ran the same way I did. It all happened so quick. Bastard.'

'Did you suspect he was capable of that?'

'Of murdering a young girl? No. Even when he was angry with her in the car, I didn't think that would happen. I thought he was just going to give her a fright and let her go. What kind of sick bastard does that?'

'So you'll understand why we want to find him, before anything else happens?'

There were tears in Ryan's eyes. He nodded. 'Of course I understand. I wish I could help you more, but I've told you everything.'

He'd never met Kat before the day Danielle was killed, he said, but he'd heard Todd speak to her on the phone, giving her names and times, or telling her to look after someone well. He didn't remember any of the names.

'Do you know Christopher Brent?' Roberts asked.

Ryan sighed. 'Yeah. And before you ask – and you probably won't believe me – I don't know much about him either. I don't know where he lives. He's posh. Rich. He's…he's good for my mum. Almost got her off the methadone. All she eats now is organic chicken, hummus and carrot juice. And a shit load of vitamins.'

'Do you know how she met him?'

Ryan shrugged. 'No idea. It's been a while, though. Nearly a year.'

'Is he acquainted with Todd Curtis?'

Ryan nodded. 'Curtis said to me in the car at Portland Place that Brent was involved in Gordon Sutherland's death. And I heard them speaking on the phone a couple of times.'

'Was Brent out and about with you and Curtis?'

'Never.'

'Did you ever hear Todd say anything about Brent and Kat?'

Ryan shook his head. He looked so tired, his face drawn and thin. Joe smiled at him and saw a hint of shame in his eyes. 'Thank you, Ryan. Just one more thing – you said you were parked at the canal the day Gordon Sutherland and Curtis met up. Did Curtis say anything about the canal that made you think he might have disposed of someone's body there?'

Ryan shook his head. 'Do you think I'd have stuck around if he had?'

'No, but you might not have realised what he was saying.'

Joe saw it come to him, a slight widening of his eyes. Ryan nodded. 'He did. The day we were waiting for Gordon Sutherland. He'd parked facing the canal. He said something about the crap they'd find on the bottom if they drained it. 'Worthless shit', he said. He kept saying it, over and over.'

Joe wanted to punch the air. 'Well done, Ryan. And this was beside the Muirtown Bridge, in the car park by the boarded up house?'

Ryan nodded. There were tears in his eyes. He wiped them away with the back of his hand. 'He's a fucking animal.'

Ryan cheered up when he saw their e-fit. 'Whoever helped you with that was having a laugh. Curtis is less Shrek and more Michael Chiklis on stilts and steroids.'

Soon they had a picture approved by Ryan. 'That's him.'

As Ryan was leaving the room, Joe thanked him again. 'You've been a big help.'

Ryan looked helpless, like the child he was. He shook his head. 'I haven't, and I'm sorry. Really sorry. I was scared and I panicked.'

Joe smiled. 'I know.'

Ryan looked at his feet, then he looked up. 'Thank you.' He almost smiled. 'For…for everything.'

'What's that all about?' Roberts asked, when Ryan had gone.

Joe shrugged. 'Who knows?'

'Mmm. I bet you do. Probably offered to help him out, if he ever sees the light of day.'

Chapter 50

There were two phone numbers on the pad in front of DI Black. He tried the number Allingham had for Todd Curtis first. Straight to voicemail. The second number belonged to the person that had called Christopher Brent on Saturday night, the person Brent had called back twice. He'd tried it before, with no response. It was a pay as you go, and there were no registered details for the owner. It had to be Curtis. It rang for a time, then went to voicemail. The second time he tried, it rang once before going to voicemail. He left a brief message.

Within five minutes, his secretary put a call through to him. The voice made something shiver inside him. He was glad they weren't in the same room.

*

The sun slid behind the clouds as the diver came to the surface and held up his thumb. He was close to the steps by the car park. It was a while before the wrapped bundle was lifted from the murky waters of the Caledonian Canal. Joe shivered when he saw the shape. It could be nothing other than a body. And such a small body, the thick black plastic encircled with duct tape around the neck, the waist and the ankles. The head and feet looked distorted. There was something else in there. Something heavy, no doubt.

Despite the efforts of the police to clear the area, there was a small group of bystanders huddled together on the other side of the canal. Most of them had dogs; their daily walk would never be the same again. They weren't for moving on, though. Maybe they expected to see the SOCOs opening the top of the bundle for him, like they did on TV, when the detective never wore protective clothing and always recognised the deceased. It would be some time before this bundle was opened.

*

Roz Sutherland looked better. The PF had released the body, and she'd buried her husband this morning. Now she had people back at the house. She seemed more positive. Joe had often seen that.

A sudden and temporary respite. The act of laying a loved one to rest somehow made everything seem much better. For a time. When the stark and lonely reality hit home, there was often another deeper slump. For now, Roz was upbeat and talkative. Joe got her alone for a moment and asked about money. He'd gone through their bank statements, and found nothing, but he wondered if there had been any problems. Not that she knew of. Gordon looked after the money, but she'd met with someone in the bank at the end of last week and it seemed he'd left her well provided for.

'He was a good man,' she said. 'There were so many people at the church, from all parties. He'd have liked that. He tried to avoid being too partisan. That wasn't easy over the last couple of years. He understood the desperate fears of the other side, and he hated that the referendum divided Scotland so bitterly. The lies and scaremongering of Better Together frustrated him, but he understood. The Party needs people like him. Fighting and division just won't do it. People need to be persuaded rationally. He was just the man to do it. I've lost count of the people that have told me what a wonderful councillor he was. You know – '

'Detective Sergeant Galbraith.' It was the lovely Alice McGarvie. She looked Joe up and down. 'You're back. That must be a relief.'

Joe smiled. He wouldn't give her the satisfaction of a response. DI Black had told Joe of his suspicions that she had a mole in the Force.

'Perhaps you'll catch this killer now. Another two deaths, I hear. How many more?'

Joe still didn't answer. He hadn't wanted to tell Roz Sutherland of the other deaths, but Alice McGarvie clearly had no such qualms about upsetting anyone today.

'Roz.' She put her hand on the widow's arm. 'What a lovely send-off for Gordon. He'd have been so proud to see you and the children so composed. You know, he told me, oh it must be ten years ago...in fact, it is ten years ago next month, isn't it? He told me then how it was only the thought of you and the children that helped him escape the darkness and chaos of that dreadful day. He said...' She paused and wiped an imaginary tear from her eye. 'He said he didn't think you would have coped without him if he'd died. I hope he was wrong.'

Bitch. But what darkness and chaos? What dreadful day?

Roz gave Alice McGarvie a smug wee smile. 'We'll cope. We have each other. It would be much harder for someone on their own, like you.'

'Did I not mention it?' Roz looked puzzled. 'I thought I did, but my head's been all over the place. Gordon was on the London Underground on 7th July 2005. He was going to the second day of a teaching conference. He was very lucky; the bomber was in the carriage next to him. He took a long time to recover emotionally, as you might imagine. So many deaths and horrific injuries, and he escaped with only minor cuts and bruises. That's why he decided to take early retirement. He'd glimpsed just how fragile life is. He wanted to make the most of the time he had left.'

Joe nodded. He'd seen a documentary recently. Some of the survivors were interviewed, and they'd met up over the years. 'Did Gordon keep in touch with any other survivors?'

Roz shook her head. 'He'd have hated that. He wasn't one for looking backwards. He had the opportunity to participate in the official reports, when they wanted to interview survivors, and he refused. He wouldn't even read them. I did, and I wished I hadn't. The suffering was horrific.' She stopped for a moment, remembering. ' Remarkable stories of courage too.'

'Did Gordon speak about it much?'

'Not with me. I don't believe he discussed it with her, either.' She nodded towards Alice McGarvie, who was in conversation with Roz's son. 'No matter what she says. Sergeant, are there really two more dead?'

Joe nodded.

'Is one of them the other girl in the picture? I heard there was a body of a foreign girl found at Ness Castle.'

'I'm afraid so, but we've arrested someone in respect of that murder.'

'But not for Gordon's murder, or the other girl?'

'Not yet. I'm sure they're all linked, though.'

Roz shook her head. 'I can't see what Gordon has to do with any of this. It makes no sense.'

*

DI Black was looking pensive. 'So London's the only link we have? And a random quote from Shakespeare. This Curtis doesn't sound like a literary buff to me.'

Joe nodded. 'I know, it's not much. Would it be worth getting the names of those that were in the same train as Sutherland?'

'Can't do any harm. Listen, I called those numbers. Nothing from the one Allingham gave us.'

'And the other one?'

He had a dreamy look about him. 'Elena Conti. She lives in London. Sounded foreign; well-to-do and plausible. Very helpful. She and Brent have been friends for years, though they hadn't been in touch since he left London. She said she was also a friend of Katya Birze, but they'd lost touch. Katya called her in hysterics on Saturday night. Said she was somewhere that sounded like Balloon Road, and she was scared and needed help. Elena Conti says she called Brent and asked him to look for Katya. Brent phoned Conti twice to say he couldn't find her. And that was that. The Met are taking a full statement from her.' He paused, his brow wrinkled. 'Can't make sense of it all. Listen, the plods from Teuchterland have been looking for you. Some news about the stolen hire car, apparently. What is it with you and the islands, eh? Unlucky or what?'

The yellow Fiat had been abandoned down a track near Sponish Bridge in Lochmaddy, the constable from Uist told Joe. No damage. And a neighbour had seen the man that was living in a caravan down by the shore leave the village in the hire car around 6.30 a.m. She'd thought it odd he was driving a car, when he didn't seem to have two ha'pennies to rub together, but she'd seen the car the previous day at Ronald MacKenzie's house, and his was the nearest house to the caravan, so she'd thought no more about it. The police had been to the caravan and he was gone. Had Joe met him?

'No. Carla did, and Ronald. You'll have spoken to them?'

'Yes, Sir. PC MacKenzie said he gave no hint of intending to leave, but Mr MacKenzie said, on reflection, he may well have been saying his farewells when they spoke last night. He didn't say as much, but he was very grateful for the food Ronald had given him. Wished him all the best for the future. We've seen the passenger registration cards from Lochmaddy. There's one with a 'W Hill', which might have been him.'

'Will Hill?'

'Yes, sir. Sounds odd, I know. Anyway, there was someone matching his description on the ferry and on the Inverness bus from Uig. The driver thinks he got off at Cluanie Inn.'

'What about prints?'

'We're waiting for those. Chances are he's not on the database, but we'll be in touch as soon as we have anything more.'

Chapter 51

The wind was ruffling the feathers of the short-eared owl perched on the post. It held fast, its head tilted to one side, watching Carla with a quizzical gaze. Perhaps it wondered at the tears that trickled down her face unchecked as she stood at the kitchen window. The phone was still in her hand, her fingers clutching it tight as the words turned over and over in her head. There were gulls in the sky, fluttering like windswept paper, pulled this way and that by forces they couldn't control. Just like her.

But the owl knew. Carla saw it in the golden eyes, wise and ancient. One final long gaze, before it spread its mottled wings and took off. As she watched the pale grey of its underwings flashing in the morning sun, she remembered to breathe.

She dialled again, expecting no answer. His voice startled her. She rubbed away the tears. 'Joe?'

'Carla, are you all right?'

There was noise in the background. Voices. The hum of printers. Phones ringing. A room full of people trying desperately to piece together a puzzle that felt so far away from her, it was almost unreal and unimportant.

'Joe. It's…it's my results.'

'Wait a minute.' The sound of talking faded. She pictured him in a corridor, his face pale, his blue eyes troubled. 'Carla?'

'My bone marrow…it's normal.' And then she was crying again.

*

Joe felt as if his legs might give way in the corridor. He forced them to the nearest toilet, and slammed the cubicle door. A virus, he heard Carla say. There were more results to come, but the doctor didn't expect to find anything sinister.

'Joe, are you still there?'

'Yes.' He swallowed. 'Carla, that's fantastic.'

'I know. Listen, my head's all over the place. I was going to phone you anyway, before the doctor called. You've heard about the car? About Will?'

'Yeah. It's weird. He didn't give you the impression he was

about to leave?'

'No. He loved it here. Sounded like he was set for life. Until he saw you coming.'

Joe's stomach plummeted. 'What?'

'There was a change in him when he looked through the binoculars as you were walking along the shore.'

'Probably fancied you and was disappointed when he saw you had such a fine specimen of a boyfriend.'

Carla laughed. 'He didn't know you were my boyfriend at that stage, and I had no idea you were there.'

Am I still your boyfriend? Joe had to know. He had to ask. But that wasn't the question that came out.

*

Betty MacLaren was bored stiff in New Craigs. Maybe it was time to go home. She was feeling better and had been for a while. She'd talk to the doctor. She was a voluntary patient. They wouldn't want to detain her if she said she was leaving. They needed the beds for the real dafties.

She was sick of the other patients. That Mary. Thought she was a cut above them all with her minimum intervention nonsense, but Betty had seen her at her worst. Throwing used incontinence pads at her own solicitor? If she'd even saved them for the doctors. No, that Mary had nothing to be superior about.

And there was Big Aggie watching the Jeremy Kyle Show, and giggling like a lunatic. Betty had no time for Aggie, and even less for Jeremy Kyle. Exploiting the dafties, he was. Why did people find that amusing? It was beyond her. Ach, probably best to just go home to her own house. All on her own. No son, no Stephen.

It wasn't an attractive thought, but she couldn't stay here forever. Maybe she should take more trips into the town first, ease herself in gently. There were clubs for senior citizens, things she could do. She'd look into it.

She left Aggie with Jeremy, and went to her room to read her book about the travelling folk in Scotland. She'd have liked their life. Nothing to tie you down. Just an open road and a tent. Or a horse-drawn carriage – even better. Pearl fishing and picking the berries. Sleeping in a barn when the weather got rough, listening to the cows chewing the cud. Why hadn't she gone her own way, done her own thing, instead of tying herself to a man, and one that didn't deserve her? She put the book down, and lay on her side. Ach, she couldn't regret it, could she? Not when she had her Stephen.

She didn't think she'd slept, but she was drowsy, right enough, when she heard tapping on the window. She turned over and the sight made her heart pound. There was a wild man at her window, with great bushy black hair and a long beard. She almost screamed, and then she looked into his eyes.

'Stephen!'

He put his finger to his lips.

Betty checked her bedroom door was locked, then she opened the window as far as it would go. It wasn't far enough to let her out or him in. Heaven forbid that she might try and kill herself by jumping three feet to the ground. Stephen was smiling as he took her hands. Those eyes. And now they were filling up with tears, and so were her own. 'Mum, it's so good to see you. How have you been?'

'Never mind me. Look at the state of you. Wild man of Borneo.'

'Can you get out and meet me along the road? Go left when you come out the main entrance. Just follow the hedge along a bit. I can't stay long. I'll have to get out of Inverness as soon as possible.'

'Then just go, son, go. You've seen me; I'm fine. You get off.'

He shook his head. 'I can't go without a hug, can I?'

Betty was certain no one saw her leave the ward, except a couple of visitors, and they probably thought she was a visitor too. She was much better dressed than the other patients. Shower of scruffs and simpletons.

She followed the hedge until it became a low drystone wall. As she neared a gap in the wall, she felt a hand on her sleeve, and then they were in each other's arms and she was breathing in his smell. That smell hadn't changed since he was a boy. Her boy. How she'd missed him. They'd kept in touch by phone, though they didn't often speak. It was too risky, in case someone heard her. He'd given her the phone with plenty credit on it before he left. Told her to keep it hidden, and she'd done that. No one knew she had it, or that she could text just as fast as the youngsters.

Sometimes she played the dafty and asked stupid questions about their fancy phones, in front of the staff. That way, if anyone ever came asking, the staff would tell them there was no way Betty could use a mobile phone to keep in touch with her boy. There was only one number on her phone. Well, until recently. Two now.

'My darling boy.' He probably didn't hear her with all that hair, but never mind. He felt robust enough, and when they pulled away from each other, she saw that his skin and his eyes were clear, and he looked as healthy as she'd ever seen him. If only it wasn't for all that hair. She shook her head.

'Don't worry, Ma; it's going soon. My mate gave me a lift up; I'm going back to his to chop it off. A couple of people to see, then I'll have to leave the town. I'm on a kind of a…a secret mission. Undercover sort of thing.'

'Aye, son.' Think your old mother's daft, do you? 'I always said you'd go far.'

'It'll be further this time. Maybe America. What do you think? You can come and see me when I get settled.'

She nodded. 'Sounds like a plan.' She'd heard the young ones saying that. 'I'm thinking of going home. It's no use in there.'

'Are you sure, Mum?'

'What else can I do? Can't stay there forever. I'm doing well.'

He smiled. 'I can see that.'

Such love in his eyes as he stroked her face. She didn't really deserve his love. She'd been a hopeless mother. He wouldn't be in this situation now if it wasn't for her. 'You better not come to the house, son.'

'I know. But we can keep in touch by phone. If you're home, you'll be able to speak to me any time. No one listening in.'

'Aye, that'll be great. You better get off.' She put her hand in her pocket and pulled out a bundle of notes. 'You'll be needing that.'

He shook his head. 'I can't take your money. You'll need it yourself when you go home.'

'There's more where that came from. Just you let me know if you're running short. Maybe you'll have an address that I can send money to next time.'

'Thank you, Mum. I love you.'

'I love you too, son.'

She was walking away when he called out to her. 'Lucy? How was she?'

'She looked lovely, son. Bright and happy. Don't you worry about her.'

As she passed the bus stop, Betty turned and blew her son a kiss. He looked lonely as he walked away.

She didn't want to go in, so she sat on a bench behind the ward. Though she liked to look out over the town, today she didn't see it. She was remembering Stephen as a boy. He'd been such a good boy, always looking after her when she was so drunk she couldn't look after either of them. And he was always honest. Not today, though. On a mission, indeed. She wasn't that daft. He was on the run, had been ever since he'd killed that Moira Jacobs and tried to kill those Galbraiths last year. Couldn't blame him. Moira Jacobs was a nasty piece of work, and those Galbraiths…she shook her head. Lucy might be a beautiful wee girl, but it didn't bear thinking about what that family did to her and Stephen. He deserved a medal, her boy. They'd tried to tell her he'd killed her sister, Jean, but she didn't believe that. That old bitch was rotten inside; her death was nothing to do with Stephen.

Chapter 52

DI Black's eyes were mournful, his great long jowls shivering as he invited Joe into his office. He was miserable at the best of times, but now he looked as if he was about to tell Joe that Todd Curtis had massacred and eaten every member of both their families. He shook his head and said nothing.

Joe frowned. He had things to do. 'Sir?'

'Son, sit down. This is going to come as a shock. I'm sorry.'

Joe didn't sit. He'd had a few shocks in the last few days. What now?

DI Black took a deep breath, and exhaled in a loud sigh. 'The car, the prints: they're Stephen MacLaren's.'

Joe laughed and shook his head. That was impossible. Stephen MacLaren was dead, drowned. He must be. No one could have survived in that water. Lucy wouldn't have lasted much longer if the local PC hadn't rescued her. His legs felt a little weak, so he sat. 'He can't be, Sir; it's a mistake. I saw that man last night; it wasn't him. And how could he have got to Uist last year, when all the ports were monitored?'

'Look.' He passed the report to Joe. 'See for yourself.'

Joe read the report. Prints in the car and on the door handles and kitchen table.

And he remembered Carla's words: *there was a change in him when he looked through the binoculars as you were walking along the shore.*

Nausea rising in his throat, he looked up. 'MacLaren was in Ronald MacKenzie's house last night?'

The DI nodded.

'But he could have…'

'Aye, but he didn't. Had to leave clues, though. He couldn't just go quietly, take someone else's car. He had to let you know just how close he was. Typical nutjob. I've sent Roberts and Lewis up to New Craigs. MacLaren's had a few hours on the loose. He probably got off the bus at Cluanie to throw us off the scent, but he could be in Inverness by now. Maybe he's been up to see his mother.'

Someone said her name and Betty jumped. It was that detective, the nice tall one that came to see her last year, when they were looking for Stephen. He had a blonde piece with him, a tart if ever there was one. Talk about full of herself with her purple suit and her glittery sandals. She wasn't going to catch many criminals wearing those, was she?

'Betty?' the tart said.

Betty ignored her. She smiled at the detective. 'I can't remember your name, son.'

'Roberts; DC Roberts, Mrs MacLaren.' He frowned at the tart. 'This is DC Lewis.'

Betty nodded. 'Have you got any news for me? Have you found my Stephen? There'll not be much left of him.'

She saw the shock on the tart's face, followed by a tight smile. 'That's just it, Betty,' the tart said, 'we have reason to believe Stephen's not dead.'

Betty's howl was loud enough to waken the dead. She glanced in the direction of Tomnahurich Cemetery, just to make sure. All quiet. Her hands covering her face, she rocked back and fore until she felt a touch on her shoulder. Better not be that tart, or she'd bite her hand off. It was Roberts.

'Mrs MacLaren, I'm sorry to upset you. It's just that Stephen's fingerprints have been found in a caravan and a car in North Uist. And we're pretty certain he left Uist by ferry this morning and got on a bus. We think he got off before Inverness, but he could be making for the town.'

'No, no, no.' Betty shook her head. 'You're just trying to mess up my head. If my boy had been alive, he'd have been in touch with me long before now. He wouldn't do that to his mother. This is just a cruel trick.'

'No, Betty.' The tart crouched in front of her. 'It's not a trick. I know it's – '

Betty pushed her and she fell on her backside. 'Keep her away from me. I don't like her. She's telling lies.'

The tart was standing now, rubbing at the seat of her trousers and giving Betty evils. Roberts nodded at her to get out of the way and let him in. He sat beside Betty, and took her hand. 'I know it's hard to take in. We think he's grown his hair, and a full beard.'

'Never. Not my boy. Hates facial hair, he does. No. You've got the wrong man.'

'Perhaps you're right, Betty. We'll look into it further. But if he does get in touch with you, you will let us know, won't you?'

Betty shook her head. 'He won't get in touch unless it's through one of those dafties on the TV. They pretend they can speak to the dead. Con artists, they are. Charlatans.'

'A psychic?'

'Whatever. My Stephen will have nothing to do with the likes of them. I tell you, he's dead and gone. A mother knows.'

How long had she given Stephen to get away? Not long enough. Another howl and more rocking. A plea for them to get someone to help her. Some muttering and mumbling to Roberts, while the tart went to find a nurse.

When the nurse arrived, Betty clung to Roberts' arm. 'Don't leave me, son.' And the good boy that he was, he came back into the ward with her, the tart trailing behind, her little heels clip-clopping all the way along the corridor.

Betty managed to stretch it out for a good forty five minutes. Anything for her boy. She managed to avoid a sedative too. She wasn't taking any more of that junk.

*

No way had Betty had any contact from Stephen, Roberts told Joe and the DI; he'd bet his life on it. She was more lucid than she was last year, and the staff had said she was doing really well, but she was still fragile. The staff hadn't seen anything untoward and they confirmed she didn't have a mobile phone, and wouldn't know how to use one.

The DI frowned. 'What do you think, Lewis?'

Tina Lewis shrugged. 'Hard to say. I'm not as convinced as Roberts that she wasn't playing us, but I guess he knows her better than I do. There was something odd about it.'

'There was nothing odd about it,' Roberts said. 'Except that she didn't like you.'

'That's very odd, isn't it?' Tina winked and Roberts blushed.

'Lewis', DI Black said, 'you're coming with me. Allingham's brief has arrived. Galbraith, you need to see your sister.'

Chapter 53

Lucy hadn't achieved much today. The office had been quiet and she'd spent most of the day reading appeal cases from the Mental Health Tribunal, but nothing had gone in. She liked Drew. He was smart and funny. Older than her, probably by about ten years or so. But what was going on? If he didn't live with Maya's mother, why not drop the child off first last night, instead of her? And then there was the text from Sebastian. It had come mid-morning.

Lucy, please get in touch. I really need to speak to you. Sxx

She'd typed a response telling him he was the last person she wanted to speak to, but she'd deleted it. Much as he'd hurt her, she didn't want to be rude. Blocking his number was probably the best thing to do. She'd do it later.

She looked at her watch. It was almost home time. And then another text arrived. It was Joe. Could they meet?

She'd hoped to see Joe looking much better. She knew his trip to Uist had been cut short; he'd texted her this morning to say he was back at work. He wasn't as green around the gills as he had been when she left him the morning after the night before, but he was looking very worried. She put her hand on his arm. 'Is Carla okay?'

For a moment, his face relaxed. He almost smiled. 'I think she's going to be fine.'

'Brilliant. And the investigation's been dropped – that's fantastic.'

He nodded. 'Aye, it's good.'

'So what's wrong? When did you ever ask to meet up during a major investigation?'

'A major investigation that's going nowhere, while the bodies pile up.' His shoulders were slumped as he stirred his coffee.

'Bodies?'

'Another two.'

'Grim. Were you hoping to pick my criminology brain? I got

the highest mark in the class for my dissertation.'

He smiled. 'You're all right. Listen, I've got some bad news. I'm really sorry.'

Lucy felt her stomach plummet. Their parents were leaving Lanzarote today, due home tomorrow. 'What? Is it Mum and Dad?'

'It's Stephen.'

Her heart was racing. 'His body's been found?'

Joe shook his head. 'Not exactly. He's not dead.'

Lucy's coffee went cold as she listened. When Joe finished, she put her hand on his. 'He could have killed you last night.'

'He didn't. I'm more worried about you. Be careful, Lucy. I don't know if he came to Inverness. He could be miles away already.'

Lucy glanced out the window, just as Drew was passing, on his way back from a meeting. He looked at her hand on Joe's. He smiled, but it didn't reach his eyes. Flustered, Lucy took her hand away. And then her phone rang.

Joe nodded at the phone. 'Are you not going to get that?'

She shook her head and rejected the call. 'It's Sebastian.'

'What does he want?'

Lucy shrugged. 'He's sent a couple of texts but I haven't answered. I'm going to block his number.' She looked at her watch. 'I better let you go.'

'I'm coming to stay at the house tonight, and until he's found. Keep the doors locked when you get home. I'll speak to the DI about having the house watched.'

*

Was she being watched? The town was busy, everyone hurrying home from work. He could be anywhere. Lucy had intended to go straight home, until she realised she'd left her jacket at the office with her house keys in the pocket. As she passed Drew's room, she could hear him on the phone. She'd get her jacket and leave as quickly as she could. Maybe she'd get a taxi. Home didn't seem all that attractive on her own.

Her phone rang again. Bloody Sebastian. She'd had enough of this. 'What the hell do you want? Haven't you got the message? I'm not interested.'

Only it wasn't Sebastian.

Drew stuck his head round the door. 'Have you not got a home to go...Lucy, are you all right?'

She shook her head.

'What is it?' He sat beside her and put his hand on her arm. 'You look terrible. Do you want coffee?'

'Please.'

She could hear him clattering about in the kitchen next door, and all she could think was that the coffee would be too strong, he'd forget to put the milk back in the fridge, and he'd leave a trail of splashes and dirty spoons that would annoy the admin staff tomorrow.

She took the mug from him. Sure enough, the coffee was far too dark and there were drips running down the side. Under her notepad, she found a coaster.

'Do you want to talk?'

Lucy shrugged. 'I really would have to kill you if I told you this.'

'Damn. Was that a local crime lord I saw you with earlier? He looked a bit dodgy.'

Lucy laughed, and shook her head, but she didn't tell him. Why shouldn't she have secrets too? She shook her head. 'No, but I have some information that would be of interest to the police, and I don't know what to do about it.'

'Tell your brother?'

'Yeah; that's what I should do.'

'But?'

Lucy took a sip of her coffee, then she looked out the window. 'By delaying, I'm already compromising myself. Perverting the course of justice.'

'How long have you delayed?'

She looked at her watch. 'About ten minutes, although if I wasn't such a numpty, I'd have worked it out days ago.'

'And every minute counts?'

She nodded.

He stood. 'I'm not going to keep you talking, for obvious reasons – you need to decide what to do, Lucy. If you want any help, you know where I am.'

As soon as Drew closed the door, Lucy called Joe.

*

The suitcase was eyeballing Sharon from the corner. And it wouldn't stop until she'd emptied it. Wimp; she'd faced up to everything else. Accepted that her life was going to be shit again. Accepted the mood swings that had taken her up and down several times today, as she waited to hear from Smish.

She had packed carefully, soberly, for London. Though she hadn't imagined for a minute that his family lived in a four storey villa with a spaceship in the attic, she'd known it was going to be somewhat upmarket of her flat in the Ferry. What wasn't?

As she took out the most modest of her clothes, the ones she'd packed just in case he'd managed to persuade her to accompany him on a visit to his mother, she felt like throwing them out the window.

More tears. She had to get a grip. He was a chancer and a liar. A murderer. Don't think about it, she told herself. He's made his bed. You have to move on.

When she saw the envelope at the bottom of the case, she thought it was from Ruby. The child had been inconsolable when Sharon and Uncle Chris left that morning that seemed so far away now. She'd asked them to come straight back, with Sharon's boys. She was waiting for them.

It wasn't from Ruby. It was a letter from Christopher, and it broke Sharon's heart.

Chapter 54

Just as well Liam was going to play with his pal, Jody, after school. Sharon would have hated to have him see her like this. He'd seen enough in his short life, wee soul. He always knew when she'd been crying, even a couple of hours later. Maybe if she had a walk, she'd get rid of the red eyes and the blotchy face. She was just leaving the flat when Galbraith phoned. Ryan wanted to see her.

Sharon stopped off at Jody's mother's flat in the next block. 'Elaine, I've got to go somewhere. I thought I better let you know in case I'm late in picking Liam up.'

Elaine smiled. 'No worries. He can stay as long as he wants. They always have a great time. He's a wee darling.'

'Sound, that's great. It's…' Maybe she didn't have to let on where she was going. Or maybe she could just start telling the truth, like a normal person. 'Did…did you know that his brother, my boy, Ryan, well…he's in custody?'

Elaine put her hand on Sharon's arm. 'That's awful. I saw in the paper they were looking for him. I just thought he'd run away from home.'

'Aye, he did, for a while. He's at the station now and he's asking to see me. I don't know how long it'll take.'

'It doesn't matter; take as long as you need. Liam will be fine. If you're too late back, he can stay here.'

*

Ryan's hair. What was he like? Sharon hardly recognised him. And he looked small and lost. He barely glanced at her before he sat. To anyone else, it would have seemed like he didn't care, but Sharon knew. He was ashamed.

Anne Morrison nudged his arm. 'Ryan, I think your mum might like a hug.'

'Too right I would.' Sharon looked up at Galbraith. He was standing at the door. 'Is that allowed?'

He smiled and nodded. Ryan felt so thin as he clung to Sharon. Tears were welling in her eyes and she could hear him sniffing. And then a whisper in her ear, as he started to pull away: 'Don't mention the sock.'

He was staring at her. She looked at Galbraith. He was looking at his phone. Sharon nodded.

Ever the big man, Ryan had little to say. He wasn't about to tell his mum how he really was, but she knew. 'I heard you've been helpful,' she said. 'That's the best way, son. Tell them everything you know.'

Ryan raised his eyebrows at that. Sharon smiled. She chatted about Liam and his weekend trip, then she told Ryan about her visit to the Job Centre. And through it all, he barely indicated he was listening. Until she mentioned the possibility of a move to Dingwall.

He straightened up. 'No way, Mam. That would be well minging. I'd rather be in here.'

Galbraith laughed.

Ryan was taken away, and it was just Sharon and Galbraith. He sat down opposite her. 'How are you doing?'

Sharon shrugged. 'So so. Thanks for letting me see him. He looks so thin and tired. Do you think he's okay?'

'He's like you, Sharon; he's strong. I haven't told him – don't want to get his hopes up – but there's a chance he won't go down for this. The psychiatrist thinks he's suffering from post-traumatic stress disorder, as a result of seeing what his father did to you. A good report to the court, or the Children's Hearing, and he might be home again, with restrictions.'

Sharon closed her eyes and felt as if her heart might soar through the roof. Though Christopher's letter had left her as raw as she'd ever felt in her life, her boy might not go down.

'Sharon, can you…will you talk about Christopher?'

She opened her eyes and nodded. 'I swear we were in London before I knew anything. I tried phoning you, but you weren't available. I was going to come to the station whenever I got back.'

He nodded. 'You must have got a shock at the airport.'

'Too right. I can't believe Christopher would kill anyone. He's gentle, and…' Her voice tailed off. 'But I've no idea where he went that night. Those pictures in his bedroom, and now she's dead. It's horrible.'

'Did you ever suspect he might be having a relationship with someone else?'

'No. Yes.'

Galbraith looked confused. Sharon wasn't sure she could explain it, but she tried. 'My heart would say no, absolutely not. He was kind and loving and attentive. I didn't see him every night, but he always phoned, and I had no reason to doubt him. But that didn't stop my head telling me he must have someone else, someone better, someone normal. Why wouldn't he?'

Galbraith's hand moved towards hers, but he didn't touch her. He shook his head. 'Don't put yourself down.'

She shrugged. 'Doesn't matter now. I've got to put Ryan first, and you've got to find that bastard, Curtis. I thought Christopher would help you with that. He said he was going to come and see you, tell you everything.'

Galbraith smiled. 'That was before he was arrested for murder. Even if he wanted to talk, his lawyer would advise against it. Can't blame him, really. I don't want to worry you, Sharon, but do you think you might be at risk from Curtis? He's a very dangerous man.'

'I saw how scared Ryan was when he went to meet him. You will keep Ryan safe, won't you?'

'Of course we will. I'm concerned about you, though. Do you think Curtis would have it in for you?'

She shrugged. 'I doubt it. I've never even met him.'

'Would he have it in for Christopher?'

'I don't know. Probably not, after all they've been through.'

'What do you mean?'

The letter was in her pocket. She'd been turning it over all the way down to the station, and several times since she arrived. It was her letter. It was deeply personal. She pulled it out and threw it on the table, then she stood. 'I can't...I don't know what to think about anything. Tell me a killer wrote that letter and I'll accept it. I trust you. Just tell me.'

Chapter 55

Sharon, I can't sleep, so I've been watching you. You look so beautiful. I shouldn't have asked you to come here while Ryan's still missing. You must have felt so torn, but you came anyway. You're a brilliant mum, and you've given me so much. I don't deserve you, and I'm worried about us. I'm sorry for taking you to that place, and not keeping you safe. I wasn't thinking straight. I should have insisted on keeping you beside me.

I wanted to tell you more tonight, but it's not easy to talk about this, and you looked so tired. However, if you and I are going to have a future, you need to know everything about that day, and afterwards.

In London, you learn not to see anyone else, especially on public transport. That day, ten years ago, I was too busy thinking about the relationship I'd ended, and how upset she was. I was feeling sorry for myself, wondering if I'd ever settle with anyone. I don't remember being aware of anyone else in the carriage.

I didn't see the bomber, though he was sitting opposite me. Others saw him; they said he was fiddling with his rucksack. I remember the sound, like a giant balloon popping. This amazing bright white light, and I was dragged into a vortex of black smoke, tearing metal and flying glass. I was aware of the others then. I can still hear them. Not their voices, but their screams and groans and swears, desperate prayers and pleas.

The medics tried to tell me I was imagining it. I was right in the centre of the blast; my hearing must have been affected; I couldn't possibly have heard anything. But I knew. No one's imagination could create what I heard.

My theory is that the pain forced me into a heightened state of consciousness. I couldn't see my injury, but I knew the bone had been crushed, and shards of glass or metal were pinning my leg to the floor, and my life was draining away. And it was such a shit life, Sharon. I'd done nothing good. Nothing bad, either. Just nothing.

I worked for my father in his property business, but I didn't work very hard. I didn't have to. There was always plenty of money and no need to do too much. It's not good for your self-worth when you don't really have to work for your money, when things come too easily.

So I knew my life, my useless life, was seeping from me. And I wanted so much to keep it then. I wanted to be something. Something good. A husband and a father. I wanted it so much. There was someone lying beside me. A pretty young woman. She wasn't conscious, but I started talking to her. She didn't open her eyes or answer, but I felt she could hear me; I was helping her to hang on. And then I lifted my head and saw the lower half of her body was missing. There was worse than that, Sharon; much worse. Things that could, and probably did, drive people to madness, to drugs, to God knows what.

I became aware of this battering noise, endless banging and grating. I thought it must be the emergency services. When it stopped, I saw him. Hair standing on end like something you'd see in a cartoon, and his face covered in dirty great streaks of smoke and blood. He had a huge smile. A smile? In the middle of such carnage? I thought I was hallucinating. He took off his belt and tied it round my leg to stop the bleeding. The pain was excruciating, so I knew it was real. Then he started chatting. Every time I drifted off, he'd bring me back with more chat. I told him things I'd never told anyone, and he just listened and kept smiling.

When he took my hand, I felt a surge of power, of goodness, of healing. It reminded me of John Coffey in 'The Green Mile'. I knew I was safe, and I was going to live. And it was all because of him. A passenger in the next carriage, a stranger that could have run for safety, had heard my cries and smashed his way in. He didn't have to. Others ran, and no one would have criticised him for following them. If he had run, I would have died.

It took the emergency services ages to come. I guess they were stretched pretty thin, with bombs going off all over the place, and so many wounded. By the time they reached us, he had saved my life and my leg.

I've seen references to an old Chinese proverb that states if you save a life, you are responsible for that person forever. Another version, in books and films, is that someone whose life is saved by another owes that person a life-long debt. Whichever version one prefers, the outcome is the same – a bond between two people that cannot be broken.

I can hardly believe I'm writing this now, but I want that bond broken. Though he gave me my life, I feel like he has held me back for almost ten years, stopped me from moving forward. It…he…has become a burden. And saying that makes me feel guiltier than I've ever felt before.

If you haven't guessed, it was Todd that saved me. Ordinary likeable Todd. A civil servant, he'd moved back home with his father a few months before the accident, after his mother died. He was on his way to work that day, and he saw things no one can safely live with.

He needed counselling. God knows I had enough of it – two years, and I was still a mess. But Todd wouldn't accept my father's offer of help. He'd saved someone's life. That was all he needed. He went back to his work, but he couldn't stick it. He said it was too ordinary; he was meant for something better.

The Todd I met in 2005 was gentle and kind and simple. I have clung to that memory for ten years, ignoring the obvious. Even today, I found it impossible to believe he could be involved in the things you mentioned. But I have to face it now; the guy that saved me is gone, and has been for a long time.

Shortly after the accident, Todd's father died. He discovered he'd been adopted. He was devastated at first, then he convinced himself that his real parents were special; they must have given him up for some great cause. He started to look for them, through an agency. He thought his mother might be in Manchester, but after a while he told me the trail had gone cold. It was then he seemed to change. His ideas grew more and more grandiose. He believed he was special, better than others.

I told you the truth that I no longer ask what he's involved in. He scares me now, the way he talks, the way he treats women, the mania that sometimes seems to stalk him. A few months ago, a young girl on drugs approached us in the street, offered us sex. He went mental, shouting and swearing at her. I had to drag him away, or he would have hit her. The Todd that saved me would never have done that. Is it my fault? Did I create a monster?

Sharon, this is one of the hardest things I have ever had to face,

but I know what I must do. If we don't find him tomorrow, I'll
go to the police. I owe it to you to do what's best for Ryan.
I'm going to put this letter at the bottom of your suitcase, so you
don't see it until you're on your own. I know I should have told
you all this before, but I was scared and confused. I still am. But
one thing I'm not confused about is you.
Sharon, I love you. I hope you can forgive me. I want you in my
life always.
With all my love
Christopher xxxx

Joe's head was bursting. It was already full of Stephen
MacLaren, but he wasn't allowed to investigate that. Ten
years…the ten years Todd mentioned in his emails. He should
have known as soon as Roz Sutherland mentioned the London
bombings. He asked Sharon to wait. He didn't have to go far.
Roberts was hurrying down the corridor with the information
from London. Todd Curtis and Gordon Sutherland were in the
same carriage that day, sitting side by side. 'And there's more,
Sarge. There's more.' He could hardly get his words out with the
excitement. 'Guess who was in the next carriage, where the bomb
went off?'

He should let Roberts have his moment. He didn't.
'Christopher Brent.'

The disappointment on Roberts' face. 'How…?'

Joe shook his head. 'What else did you get?'

'Gordon Sutherland was one of the first to escape. Todd Curtis
broke his way into the next carriage and saved Brent's life. He was
recommended for a bravery award, but he couldn't be traced.'

Joe held out the photo Sharon had found in London. 'This is
probably Curtis eight years ago.'

Roberts shook his head. 'Looks like a decent guy. Doesn't bear
much resemblance to the e-fit, does he? Speaking of which, we
had a call from a woman on Fairfield Road, about ten minutes
after the e-fit went up. She was in her garden when he ran past on
Thursday afternoon, around the time you saw Ryan on Kenneth
Street.'

Chapter 56

Galbraith hadn't said much to Sharon after he read the letter, but it had certainly got him wound up. He wanted to keep it as evidence. Sharon had shrugged. If she took it home, she'd only keep reading it, over and over, tormenting herself with wishing and doubts and useless speculation. She was tormenting herself anyway, as she crossed the Black Bridge. Turning it all over and over in her head until she was so mixed up, she didn't know what to think. He loved her. Wanted to be with her always. Fucking typical.

Another sentence kept coming back to her: *It's not good for your self-worth when you don't really have to work for your money, when things come too easily.* She had taken so much from him, without a thought for her self-worth.

She almost asked for fags in the shop on Grant Street. Her hands shaking, she paid for her milk and chewing gum. All she could think of as she walked down the road was lighting up and inhaling, and how good that would feel.

On Thornbush Road, a fancy blue convertible was coming towards her. The driver slowed down. He was wearing dark glasses and a baseball cap. He smiled at her. Less than a minute later, she heard a car slowing behind her and stopping. It was the convertible; he must have turned. The passenger window came down. The driver was still smiling as he leaned across the passenger seat and removed his sunglasses and baseball cap. 'Hi Sharon.'

It took a while for her to recognise him. He looked so different. His eyes were bright and his skin was brown and healthy. He had a neat beard, and his hair was shorter. He almost looked like a caricature of the pale man that had reeled her in last year. 'Mac, what the fuck?'

'Can we talk?'

*

She needed her head seen to, sitting in a car with a killer, at the old ferry point. But he'd been a good friend, Mac or Stephen, or whatever he was calling himself now, until he gave her smack and murdered her neighbour. Still, she knew she was in no danger from him. He was staring at her as if he couldn't believe his eyes. 'Sharon, look at you; you're gorgeous.'

'Thank you. Don't even think of coming on to me.'

'Wish I could, but that ship sailed long ago. Probably around the age of eleven.'

'What do you mean?'

He shrugged. 'Relationships are not for me. Maybe if my childhood had been different…Who knows?'

'You and me both. Why did you kill Moira Jacobs?'

'I didn't mean to. I just wanted some answers, but she hit me first and I lost it. It all goes back to when I was eleven. The defining chapter of my life. Without her, things would have been very different. Sharon, I'm sorry. I shouldn't have done what I did to you. Giving you that shit. It was unforgivable.'

'Aye, it was, you bastard. But guess what? I haven't touched it since. And apart from the last two days, I've hardly even thought about it.'

Her phone rang. It was Smish. All he could tell her was that Todd was an evil bastard, and she should have nothing to do with him. No one knew where he lived or what his surname was, but the rubbish he was selling had killed two people in the last year.

Sharon rolled her eyes. 'Smish, I could have told you most of that, and given you his surname. That wasn't really what I was looking for. Is that it? Thirty quid's worth?'

'I'll throw in a couple of wraps. It's good stuff. I'll bring it down now, if you like.'

'Nah, you're all right. Save it for some other mug.' She shook her head as she ended the call. 'Tosser. So, last I heard, you'd jumped into the sea after stabbing Joe Galbraith. That's not on. He's a good guy.'

Stephen nodded. 'He probably is. Have the cops been down to see you yet?'

She smiled. 'Aye, once or twice. I'm on my way back from seeing Galbraith at the station now. But not about you. So you didn't drown. How did you manage to stay hidden this long?'

'You know how they say truth is often stranger than fiction?' He smiled and shook his head. 'I still can't believe it worked. I did want to die, but it just wasn't happening, so I swam ashore. I had clothes and camping gear in the boot of my hire car. I walked to Leverburgh while the emergency services were battling to save the Galbraiths. Hitched a ride to Uist inside a roll of carpet in a van bound for a village hall sale. The cops gave that van a good going over; they just didn't think to look inside the carpet.

'I spent two months in the hills with only a tent, a fishing line, a box of matches, and some purification tablets. I didn't emerge until I'd grown a massive beard, then I acted the role of village idiot, which I did rather well. I'd be there now if Galbraith's girlfriend wasn't related to the nearest crofter.'

'That's some story.' Sharon ran her hand over the black leather dashboard. 'How have you managed to afford a motor like this?'

'As if. It belongs to a pal. Well, not really a pal; an acquaintance who's scared of what I know about him. A quick call to Davie today and he couldn't do enough.' He stared out across the Firth. 'I'm leaving Inverness tonight. I didn't want to go without seeing you. I went round to the flat just now. I wanted to tell you how much you meant to me. I was too messed up at the time to treat you like the good friend you were.'

Sharon shrugged. 'Story of my life. I met someone nearly a year ago, first guy since Peter. His name's Christopher, and he's…he's been fantastic.'

Stephen nodded. 'Liam looked happy to see him just now.'

'What?'

'At the play park. He just picked Liam up in his car.'

There was a rushing sound in Sharon's ears. She shook her head. 'He didn't pick Liam up; he can't have. What was this guy like?'

'Didn't see his face. Big, bald. Driving a black Lexus.'

Chapter 57

Lucy didn't go home. Drew took her to the police station to give a statement, then they went to Riva for a meal, and back to his house. It was a single man's house if ever she'd seen one, and she'd seen a few. No sign of a wife, and the only ornamentation was a few photographs of Maya. A single man with a cleaner, she suspected, as she flushed the clean toilet and washed her hands in the sparkling sink.

She'd told him a bit about Stephen and the Harris experience. Not everything, but enough for him to insist that she wasn't going home to her folks' house, not unless Joe was there. He said he knew he'd heard the name Joe Galbraith before, and then he remembered the press coverage and the search for Stephen MacLaren. She didn't tell him she was no longer scared. Stephen had said he would never hurt her, that he was sorry for all he'd done. He was a different person now, and he meant her no harm. And she'd believed him. If Joe hadn't almost exploded when she told him that, she'd have gone home alone without any worries.

Drew smiled when she came into the living room. He was sitting on the chair. There was a glass of wine for her on a small table beside the sofa. 'I hope you don't think I've hijacked you?'

She shook her head. 'It was good of you. I'm sure I'd have been fine at home, though. They'd have arranged protection for me, but I guess they're a bit stretched at the moment. When I had coffee with Joe this afternoon, he said they'd found another body today. They're still looking for the killer.' She stared at Drew. 'And you're smiling why, exactly?'

'Sorry. I hope they get the bastard soon.'

There was still a hint of a smile on his face. She frowned. 'You're freaking me out now. Next you'll be telling me you're the killer. It's par for the course where I'm concerned. Fly paper for freaks, that's me.'

'Lucy, don't say that. Look at you; of course you're going to attract guys. It's just bad luck that one of them happened to be a psycho. You weren't to know.'

'I didn't exactly attract him, as such. There was a reason he targeted me, and it wouldn't have mattered how I looked, but I don't want to go there just now. So why were you smiling?'

'Because you said you met your brother this afternoon, and I'm hoping it was his hand you were holding in the café.'

Lucy blushed and nodded.

Drew's smile spread across his face. 'He didn't look at all dodgy; I lied. How about watching a film? Take your mind off things? I'll drive you home when you hear from Joe.'

'I'll get a taxi – you can have some wine. Or Joe can pick me up here.'

He shook his head. 'I need to keep my wits about me.' He lowered his voice. 'Maybe we were followed.'

She threw a cushion at him, then they watched the first of the original Star Wars trilogy. But it wasn't really the first, she said; hadn't they released two prequels later? Drew rolled his eyes. This was the first, and that was that.

*

Sharon grabbed Stephen's arm. 'When was this?'

He looked at the clock in the car. 'Ten minutes ago. Not long before I saw you. Liam looked really happy, so I didn't think anything of it. I didn't want to speak to him, in case I gave him a fright. What is it?'

Her hands shaking, she took her phone from her pocket. 'Police. I've got to phone the police. He's going to kill Liam.' Her hands wouldn't work. She dropped the phone on the floor of the car. It rang. She didn't recognise the number.

Liam sounded so happy. 'Hi Mam. Your friend Todd's taking me to a Harry Potter place. He says I'll meet my dad there. I'm in his car now.'

'Son. Liam.' Sharon closed her eyes. What could she say? He's going to kill you? Get out of the car? There was nothing she could say.

'Todd says you can come too, if you can find the bridges, but you've got to keep it a secret. Remember Mam, a big big secret. You can't tell anyone.'

In the background she heard deep laughter.

'See you soon, Mam. I love you.'

The line went dead before she could tell him just how much she loved him back.

Sharon stumbled out of the car. On her knees, she vomited on the ground. Nothing there but coffee. She wanted to cry out, but the lump that had stopped her from eating earlier was growing in her throat, stopping her breathing. Her whole body was shaking, her head spinning, and she couldn't stand.

She felt Stephen's hand on her shoulder. He was crouched beside her. 'Breathe, Sharon; just breathe. Tell me what I can do.'

'Nothing.' She could hardly get the words out. 'You can't do anything. He's going to kill him.'

He grabbed her by the elbow and tugged. 'Get up, Sharon. Quick. In the car. Do you know where they're going?'

She nodded. 'Evanton. Black Rock Gorge.'

He helped her to the car, pushing her down into the seat. He closed the door and ran round the other side. He started up the engine. 'I know where the gorge is. Do you want me to phone the police?'

She shook her head. 'He said it's a secret. I can't tell anyone.'

Stephen nodded. 'Okay. Just keep breathing. When you're up to it, tell me what's going on.'

They were on the Kessock Bridge before Sharon spoke again. 'Do you believe in God?'

Stephen shrugged. 'Probably not. You?'

'Dunno. Do you think a prayer would help? A silent one.'

Stephen put his hand on her arm. 'Go for it.'

Chapter 58

There were questions tumbling round in Joe's head, as he paced back and fore. It wasn't just the letter. Brent's prints weren't on the photos of Katya Birze. Only Sharon's. Unless she had printed them, someone had wiped those photos before they went in the drawer. And the mug they had found in Castlefield didn't match any of the crockery in that flat. It matched a set of mugs at Ness Castle. Did Curtis have access to Brent's house? How difficult would it be for Curtis to plant the business card, the photos and the mug? Joe had passed a note to DI Black asking him to check the mug with Allingham.

Roberts was watching him. 'Penny for them.'

Joe sat. 'I'm not convinced about Brent. The post mortem results don't tie in with the timescale we've got from Sharon or the guy that reported seeing Katya.'

'The walking stick? The number plates? Pretty compelling.'

Joe nodded. 'I know. Listen, I can't help thinking Curtis must hate Sharon because she's taken Brent away from him. She doesn't think she's in any danger, but I'm not convinced. I'm going to have a quick word with Ryan, then we'll go down and see Sharon, ask her to stay somewhere else for a few days.' He was leaving the room when the phone rang. He listened and nodded. He cut the call and shook his head.

Roberts looked impatient. 'Well?'

'Someone has been watching Brent. Cameras in his house, and they're covered in Curtis's prints.'

Roberts' eye widened. 'Looks like you might be right about Brent. Maybe he'd talk now, if all this was put to him.'

Joe nodded. 'Maybe. I'll have a word with the DI when we get back. There's more. Nancy Connor's baby was adopted by William and Ann Curtis. They lived in London.'

Roberts grimaced. 'Curtis killed his birth mother.'

The little colour that remained on Ryan's face drained as he remembered. 'Curtis had photos of Liam. The day we were in his car. I forgot. How could I forget that? You have to keep them safe; both of them.'

The early evening traffic was quiet. They were on Grant Street when the call came. Roberts answered. 'Aye. On our way to see Sharon MacRae. Liam? When?'

Joe pulled into a bus stop. Roberts' face was ashen. 'Harry Potter place? What the hell does that mean? Can you find out? I don't know. Try Google – Harry Potter, Inverness – something like that? Yes, I'll hold.'

'What is it?' Joe asked.

'I think Curtis has Liam. A neighbour's child has just come in and told her mum that a bald man in a big black car took Liam away from the play park about twenty minutes ago. Said something about taking him to a Harry Potter place and then he was going to see his dad.'

'See his dad?' Joe's heart started racing. He heard a tiny voice from the phone.

Roberts nodded. 'Yeah. Still here. Still waiting. Filming? Yeah, good idea. No, it's not going to be the viaduct at Glenfinnan. Have you any idea how far that is from here? Keep looking. Anywhere else they filmed? Evanton?' He looked at Joe and rolled his eyes. 'Why would they film anything in Evanton? Oh. Black Rock Gorge? Right, we're on our way. Find out exactly where it is. And tell DI Black or DCI MacBain we need an armed response unit. Now.'

Joe had already turned the car. 'Get you, Sergeant Roberts – well done.'

Roberts blushed. 'Aye, but how the hell are we going to find this gorge?'

'Anywhere near Brent's house on Glenglass Road? You were there when they searched the house, weren't you?'

Roberts nodded. He put his head down. 'Think, think, think. There was a sign. Near the house. A sign that might have said Black Rock Gorge.'

He called control and told them to look on the map near Brent's house for the quickest way to Black Rock Gorge.

Chapter 59

Was this sprog really Peter MacRae's? Todd doubted it. Just like the tart to be putting it about. Brother or half-brother, there was little resemblance to Ryan. Like his father before him, Ryan was a sullen, unpleasant toe rag, who thought the world owed him something. He didn't think he'd ever seen Ryan smile, but this sprog was different. Smiling, laughing, chatting, doing his head in.

'Are we nearly there yet? Is it down that way? Which film was it? Do you think my mam will come?'

She fucking better. Not easy for her with no car, but if she cared enough, she'd find a way. 'Sure she will. Has she got any friends with a car?'

'Linda's got a car, but she might be away at work. She's my mam's best friend and I love her. She makes biscuits with me.'

'And does she stay close to you?'

Liam shrugged. 'Not too far.'

'Maybe Linda will take her.'

A smile. Quite a cute one. He felt an unfamiliar pang, a hint of something that felt like remorse. It didn't last.

It was risky getting this close to the Evanton house. The cops might still be there, but what the hell? Not much point in being alive if you didn't take risks. You might as well give in, lie down and die. He wished this kid would quieten down. Should have given him something and put him in the boot.

He'd thought he might like children at one time. That was before. Everything mundane was before. If it wasn't for the actions of those four deluded martyrs nearly ten years ago, maybe he'd be a father now. An uninterrupted journey to work that day and everything would have been different. Promotion, marriage – maybe Jenny in Procurement? And children. He laughed.

'Why are you laughing?'

'Nothing gets past you, does it? Just thinking of something silly; that's all.'

Liam's eyes sparkled. 'I like silly things. Where do bees go to the bathroom?'

'I don't know, Liam; where do bees go to the bathroom?'

'At the BP station.'

'That's quite funny.' He left the main road and drove down a track.

'I know lots more, but Mam says they're annoying.'

'That's what mothers are like. No fun.' Good. There was no one else in the car park, and nobody on the path that led to the gorge.

'Have you got a mam?'

Todd didn't have a mother. He'd had two. One of them, a dear simple soul, had made him who he was before. The other, a drug-addled whore, had made him all he'd been afterwards. He shook his head. 'No, I haven't. No mum, no dad, no brothers, no sisters. I had a good friend…once.'

'I might be getting a new dad. Christopher – '

'No.' Todd shook his head. 'No new dad. Peter MacRae was your father. Not Christopher. Never.'

Liam shrugged. 'I've got a brother. He's called Ryan. He's not at home just now because a bad man got him into trouble. I'm never going to be friends with a bad man.' He looked up, his eyes so innocent. 'Why are you laughing? It made my mam cry.'

'C'mon; we're here.'

*

Where did kids get their energy? Must be near his bed time, but the sprog was full of life, jumping up and trying to catch the thin branches of the trees that lined each side of the narrow path.

'What was the film?' At his shout, three wood pigeons rose from the trees. With strong wing beats, they headed away from the forest, across the fields.

He was back. Jumping up and down. 'What was the film? What was the film?'

'The Goblet of Fire. Remember when the Hungarian Horntail chased Harry?'

'Yeah, I remember. And Harry won. He always wins. Is Mam here yet?'

He looked back. 'Doesn't look like it. No other cars in the car park.'

'Okay.' And he was off again.

Liam peered through the wire on the bridge and shook his head.

'It's very narrow. I don't think a Hungarian Horntail would get in there. Are you sure this is where it was?'

'Definitely. They can do anything in films. And it's broader at the next bridge. It's amazing, isn't it?'

Liam nodded. 'It's cool. I'm going to find some stones to throw down there.' He ran up the steps towards the forest, still laughing, still talking.

The boy's chatter faded, and Todd heard only the water rushing through the gorge, the sound constant and calming. He liked it here. Chris had brought him first. He'd looked out a map showing the route of the river, from Loch Glass to the Cromarty Firth. He'd talked of how the gorge was formed. Something about rapids and sediment and ice sheets. Not that Todd had been interested, but it felt good with Chris, that easy way he'd thought they would always have.

He should never have encouraged Chris to move up north. But he'd been worried about him. His friend had been shrinking, losing strength, fading away. The accident, the pain, the family, the indebtedness: they were stealing Chris from him. So he'd saved his friend. Again. Twice.

Fucking twice. His hands gripped the wooden rail until his knuckles turned white and his thoughts turned red. He should have run with the rest of them ten years ago. He should have followed that cowardly bastard, Gordon Sutherland. Maybe Sutherland had been right to refuse to help him break through to the next carriage. How he'd pleaded with him, but Sutherland was having none of it. *That way madness lies.*

Those words had never left Todd. They taunted him endlessly. Was Sutherland right? Had breaking into the carriage and saving Chris made him mentally unstable? He shook his head, but it wouldn't clear. *There's a time bomb inside your head, just like me; looks like it's about to explode.*

No, it wasn't saving Chris that did it. That had been a good thing. The best. It was all down to that Nancy Connor. What a mistake he'd made, searching for her. Thinking he was going to find someone special, someone like him. The disgust on her face when she heard who he was. Jesus. How could you look at your own son like that? She'd laughed when he asked about his father.

255

Take your pick, she'd said; you might not like what you get.

He'd had the best mother and father ever. That should have been enough. But they should have told him, as soon as he was old enough to understand. His real mum and dad, the only ones that mattered, they should have told him. They could have avoided all this.

And he hadn't even tried to find Sutherland. He'd just needed to get out of London and make a new start. Jimmy Spaz had suggested Inverness. The capital of the Highlands, gateway to a host of towns and villages and islands full of desperate people. It had been fine at first. Until Chris came, and started going out with that skank.

And then Councillor Gordon Sutherland had smiled at Todd from the front page of the Inverness Courier. Patron of a charity to help the disadvantaged? Him? The coward that wouldn't consider helping anyone else? The plan had been to bring him down slowly. Expose him as a fraud and a cheat and a coward. But the time bomb inside his head had other ideas.

None of it really mattered. It was right that Nancy Connor should pay. And Sutherland. Now they were all going to pay.

'Liam, where are you?'

He came like the eager little puppy he was. 'I came back twice before and threw stones down there, but you were like a zombie. Are you all right?'

He nodded. He was fine. 'C'mon. I want to show you something.'

Beyond the second bridge, the trunk of the fallen tree that bridged the gorge was parcelled in soft green moss, adorned with saplings and ferns. It was a gift from the gods. On the other side of the gorge, where the tree had once stood tall, there was a great tangled gnarl of exposed roots, covered in ferns. It looked to be holding steady enough. 'See that?'

Liam nodded.

'That's a special bridge. Only special people can cross it.'

'Did Harry?'

'Of course he did. Will you?'

Liam's smile slipped a little. 'It's just a tree trunk.'

'A very special one. Remember I said you could meet your dad?

He's going to meet you on there, right in the middle of the bridge.'

'But my dad's dead. How can I meet him?'

'Harry saw his parents, and they were dead. You can sit down to cross it. You don't have to walk it. Here, take my hand.'

Chapter 60

Stephen pulled up beside the black car. Sharon glanced inside and saw Liam's Spiderman figure on the passenger seat. She wanted to throw up again. She looked at Stephen. His brow was creased with worry. 'How far from here?'

'Minutes.'

'What are you going to say if he asks how you got here?'

Sharon shrugged. 'A mate?'

Stephen nodded, then he hugged her. 'A real mate. Are you sure I can't come with you? I could stay in the background. He'd never know I was there.'

'I can't risk it. I appreciate it, though. Take care, Mac.'

As she ran along the path, Sharon could hear the soft cooing of pigeons echoing through the trees. It made her shiver. They sounded as if they were trying to warn her. She reached the first bridge and there was no sign of them. Her feet thumped on the wooden slats as she ran across it. She didn't look down. At the end of the bridge, she turned to her right. The path split, and she followed the lower path towards the second bridge.

The smell of Curtis came to her on the breeze, and she remembered the flat in London and the house at Evanton. This man would leave an imprint of evil wherever he went. His laughter rang through the trees, rising above the sound of cascading water. She saw him leaning against a crooked tree, looking straight ahead. Looking at Liam. Her boy was half way along a tree trunk that stretched across the gorge. He was sitting with his back against two twisted branches that rose from the trunk, giving a hideous two-fingered salute to the sky. How had Liam managed to get past those branches without falling?

Sharon forced herself forwards, her mouth dry and her heart racing. The gorge was wider at this bridge. She was half way across before she could see Liam's face, and his look of utter terror. Then Todd looked at her.

He was nothing like the picture of Christopher's curly-headed friend from 2007. Nor was he much like the e-fit picture Galbraith had shown her. It was just an outline of a large bald man. It hadn't shown the cruelty etched in the lines around his mouth, or the hint of madness in his eyes.

'Sharon.' The sound of his voice made her shake. 'You made it.'

Liam turned his head towards the bridge, and the movement unsteadied him. Sharon gasped and shook her head.

'Mam.' Liam's voice was weak. 'Mam, how cool is this? It's a special bridge. I even managed to get over the branches.'

Sharon forced her lips to smile. 'Look at you. My brave boy.'

'Did Linda bring you?'

She nodded. 'In her new blue car – wait until you see it.'

Todd sounded bored. 'Where is this Linda?'

'Gone to see her mate in Evanton. I said I was going up to the house to get some things for Christopher. Said I'd phone her to come for me.'

'Get some things for Christopher.' Like a child, he mimicked her. He pushed himself away from the tree and she saw how big he was. 'It's Chris. Not Christopher. It's always been Chris, until you came along.'

Liam tried to look round again. His body wobbled, and he grabbed a slender branch in front of him, knocking off a piece of dead bark. It spiralled down into the gorge.

'Liam, don't look down, son, and don't look round. Stay still. Okay, honey?'

He nodded, his legs tightening on the tree trunk. 'I don't really like this, Mam. I don't care if it's a special bridge. I don't even care if I don't meet my dad. I think I'd just like to get off now.'

Todd's laughter shook the trees and silenced the birds. The sound poured through Sharon, sucking her breath from her. He was bouncing on the balls of his feet, as if a current of excitement was running through him. 'You ever seen what happens to a melon thrown from a height?'

Sharon couldn't answer. She was standing on the edge of a loss so unbearable, she would rather throw herself into the gorge, than have to watch anything happen to Liam.

'Splat.' Todd smiled. 'Not much left. So, Sharon MacRae, why are we here?'

She shook her head.

'Come on; surely you can guess?'

'Did you…did you hope Christopher would come with me?'

'Christopher? Don't be so fucking stupid. I've made sure that's not going to happen. He's going nowhere for a very long time. Did you find the pictures?'

Sharon nodded.

'What did it do to you thinking of Chris with that tart? Did you ask him to kill her?'

'I don't believe he did it.'

He laughed again. 'Aw. Bless. Such faith in him. Of course he didn't. He's too soft, too good for that. Or he was, until you came along. You are such a fucking tart. What did he see in you?'

'You'd have to ask him, 'cos it's beyond me.'

'It's beyond me.' That mimicking voice again. 'This is beyond you too.' He sprang forward and planted a massive foot on the end of the tree trunk. He bounced a little and the trunk moved.

'No. Please, no.'

'You've taken everything from me. You? Peter MacRae's missus? His skanky tart? The one he boasted about raping, about turning into a junkie? The things he made you do. I know them all. Have you no shame? Don't even bother answering that. We both know. But you'll never have Chris. Neither of us will, and you are so going to pay.'

Chapter 61

At the Tore roundabout, they got a call on the radio from DCI MacBain to say the local police had found a black Lexus in the car park off Glenglass Road, the closest entrance to Brent's house and the gorge. There was a child's toy on the passenger seat. 'Caused a bit of confusion here,' the DCI said. 'When the local cops called the registration number in, turned out to be Brent's number. But we've got his car. This bugger has been using cloned plates.'

'Sunday morning, the struggle with Katya,' Joe said. 'It wasn't Brent.'

The DCI sighed. 'You're probably right.'

A patrol car was blocking the narrow track towards the gorge. Joe showed his card to the two officers, and asked if they'd heard or seen anything. The female shook her head. 'Nothing. Waiting for the armed response unit.'

Joe nodded. 'Do you know the area?'

'Yeah. The gorge runs along this edge of the forest. There are several ways in and out. Dingwall and Fortrose cops have sealed off the other main entrances.'

'How close can we get without being seen?'

'Depends where they are.' She unfolded a map. 'We're here. The Black Rock bridges are there. Not very far, and the path's good. If he's on one of the bridges, he's not going to see anyone until they're almost there, but if he comes to the edge of the forest, he can see as far as the car park. It's possible to go in one of the other entrances. You can take vehicles in, to a point, but it would take time.'

Roberts was pacing around the Lexus. 'What if Liam's in the boot?'

'What if he's not?' Joe said. 'The alarm on that thing will alert Curtis.'

Roberts shook his head. 'So we just wait here, while he kills Liam?'

'We don't know he's going to kill Liam.'

'He said he was taking him to see his father. What else could he mean?'

Joe nodded. What was it all about? Was it to get at Sharon? And where was she? She'd been due to pick up Liam when she was finished at the station, but no one had seen her since. Did Curtis have her too? Joe would have loved to open the boot of the car. He expected to find a walking stick just like Brent's, and DNA from Katya Birze.

Roberts sighed. 'Can we not just take a look along at the bridges? We don't even know if he's armed.'

Joe raised his eyebrows.

'Okay, Sarge; that was stupid. But I can't just stand here and do nothing.'

Neither could Joe.

The crack of every twig beneath their feet was too loud, but surely the sound of rushing water would provide some cover and let them get close. When they neared a fork in the path, they stopped and listened. Nothing but the water, and a chorus of birdsong. They took the path on the left, and it led them to the first bridge. Though the female cop had said you couldn't see one bridge from the other, they crouched as they crossed. When Joe looked down through the wire on the side of the bridge, he felt his stomach and his head falling. It looked as if the land had been sliced in two by a giant sword, the edges of the wound gaping, then narrowing and meeting in a dark channel far below.

At the next fork, they went left, upwards through the trees, away from the edge of the gorge. The trees were sparse and there was little cover. Joe looked down and saw Sharon standing on the bridge. A little further up, and he saw Curtis, his back to them. What were they looking at?

And then he saw it, a desperate tableau of innocence and fear. Liam was sitting on a fallen tree trunk, his back towards them, his little shoulders shaking. They were too far away to hear anything above the sound of the water. Roberts pointed to a broad tree on his left, a little lower down. Joe nodded. That was the only way. Move from tree to tree, as quietly as possible.

He could see Curtis's left hand by his side. It was shaking. The other was in his pocket. He saw Liam try to turn his head. Joe's stomach lurched as the boy's body wobbled.

*

Sharon's heart missed a few beats. 'Remember what I said, son.'
She tried to keep her voice firm. 'Don't turn. Just keep looking
ahead. It's all going to be fine.'

'But I don't like it, Mam.'

'I know, son; I'm going to get you off there.'

Todd laughed. 'And how are you going to do that?'

'Let me help him off. He's done nothing. I'll call Linda and
she'll pick him up at the road end, and he'll be fine.'

'Will he? Without a mum and a dad?'

Sharon nodded.

'Suppose you're right. What good is a whore for a mother? I
should know. So, how's this going to work?'

'I'll do anything.'

He had such an evil laugh. 'That skank Danielle Smith said the
same. *I'll do anything, Todd.* And she would have done anything,
and I would have made sure she never breathed a word to anyone,
and we'd all be fine, if it wasn't for your stupid son. Who the fuck
does he think he is, trying to get one over on me? Choosing to
help her escape, after all I've done for him.'

His whole body seemed to be shaking with rage. And then he
was still, his face composed. He smiled. 'Thanks for the sock, by
the way.'

'How?'

'Poor wee Chris had such a sore leg that day. Lucky I was at his
house when you rang. Being the good mate I've always been, I
drove him down to yours. He comes out with the sock, tells me
Ryan's been in a bit of trouble.' He shrugged. 'What could I do
but offer to take care of it? I'm not sure that was what Chris had
in mind, but hey, you've got to take your chances where you can.
So, how are we going to take care of this?'

'I'll…I'll go on there and help him off.'

He laughed and shook his head. 'You are a skinny bitch, but do
you really think that can take your weight as well as his?'

She shrugged. 'Can't see I've got much choice.'

Liam started to wriggle himself backwards. 'No, Mam. Don't!
It'll break.'

Todd's shout stopped him. 'Don't you fucking move, Liam.' He pulled something from his pocket and turned to Sharon. It was a gun, and it was pointed at Liam's back. 'You'll walk it.'

The excitement on Todd's face was chilling. He nodded towards the trunk. Sharon slipped off her shoes, her bare feet stirring fallen leaves as she walked towards him. At the end of the trunk, there was a branch sticking up and she steadied herself by holding onto it. She put one foot on the trunk. The moss was soft and a little wet. She didn't look down; she couldn't. To get to Liam, she was going to have to let go of the branch, and there was nothing else to hold onto before she reached the gnarled branches in the middle of the trunk.

She took a deep breath and looked round. Todd was still grinning. Could she break the branch and hit him with it? It was too firm, and Todd would shoot them both before she managed to break it.

There was a movement beyond Todd. Was it just the leaves of the trees, or was someone there? Had Mac followed her?

'What's keeping you?' Todd gestured to the trunk. He waved the gun at her. 'Fucking hurry up.'

'No, Mam. Don't. Don't. Don't. You'll fall!'

Sharon turned. 'I'm not going to fall, honey. I'm not. But you have to promise me, Liam; promise me whatever happens, whatever you hear, you won't turn round. You have to stay very still. Okay? For me?'

Liam nodded.

Sharon looked into Todd's eyes. They were dark grey. Cold and hard, like the gun. 'Why are you doing this?'

His eyes widened in surprise. He shrugged. 'Because I can.'

Chapter 62

Joe pointed to a rock lying on the ground close to Roberts. He nodded to his right, towards the other bridge. 'That way, but wait until I signal.'

Joe crept downwards, until he reached a massive tree close to Curtis. Sharon hadn't moved.

'Hurry up, you stupid cow. I haven't got all – '

Joe gestured to Roberts. As the rock landed with a thump several feet away, Curtis spun towards the noise. Joe sprang forward. He saw Sharon throw herself at Curtis. He staggered backwards, the gun still in his hand. It was pointing upwards into the trees when Joe smashed a rock against Curtis's head. A shot exploded in the trees before Curtis dropped the gun. He fell into the leaves, and Joe leapt for the gun. Roberts got there first.

Joe heard a roar. He turned to see Curtis on his feet, blood running down his face. His eyes were enormous. Hands outstretched, he lunged for Joe. Above the gushing of the water, and the sound of blood rushing through Joe's head, he heard Sharon. 'Stay still, Liam! Stay still. I'm coming. Don't look round.'

'No. Sharon – ' Curtis's hands stopped Joe's words. His eyes were bulging as he squeezed. Though his vision was blurring, and black stars were falling in front of his eyes, from the corner of his right eye, Joe saw Roberts. 'Let him go, or I'll shoot.' He was walking towards them. He held the gun steady, and Joe remembered that though he'd had no formal training, Roberts had been shooting with his grandfather since he was a child.

Curtis laughed and squeezed harder. As Joe's legs lost all feeling, Roberts ran at Curtis and pressed the gun into his shoulder. Joe felt the impact of the blast running down Curtis's left arm, and then he was free.

Joe dropped to the ground, gasping for air, his head spinning. For a moment, as the blood rushed through his ears, he couldn't grasp where he was. He looked up and saw Curtis stagger to his feet. He stared at Roberts, at the gun, looking bewildered as he clutched at his shattered shoulder, blood pouring through his fingers.

'On the ground. Now!'

Curtis ignored Roberts. He took his hand from his shoulder and looked at the blood. He turned towards the gorge, to where Sharon was sitting on the trunk, edging herself closer to Liam. Curtis started walking towards them. 'Stand up, you fucking bitch. Stand up!'

'Stop.' Roberts' hand was shaking a little. 'I'll shoot again.'

There was no emotion on Curtis's face. It was blank, as if he couldn't hear Roberts. He wasn't going to stop.

'Roberts –'

But Joe didn't have to say it. Roberts was aiming and firing. As his right knee exploded, Curtis let out a howl that echoed through the trees, and he dropped to the ground.

Sharon reached out a hand and almost touched Liam. 'It's all right, honey. Don't worry. Roberts and Galbraith are here. They've stopped him.'

But they hadn't. Again, Curtis struggled to his feet. His shirt and his lower right trouser leg were dark red with blood. His gaze focussed on Sharon, he started hobbling towards the gorge, grunting and moaning as he went.

Roberts raised the gun again, and Curtis fell. There had been no shot, just enough blood loss to knock him out. His body was slumped against a tree, his face pale, his breathing shallow. They cuffed his hands around the tree, then Roberts pulled off his tie. He looked at it and shook his head. 'Breaks my heart; Jill gave me this.' He tied it round Curtis's leg, above the wound, using a stick to twist the tourniquet until the bleeding stopped. He took a hankie from his pocket and pressed it against the wound on Curtis's shoulder. Joe left him to it. He saw that Sharon had almost reached Liam. She was still talking. 'Honey, I'm nearly there. I'm going to get you off...'

Her words were stopped by a loud creak, then another. Joe rushed to the edge. Sharon turned and her eyes were wild and desperate. 'It's going.' She tried to keep her voice low as she pointed at the trunk between her and Liam. 'It's going.'

'Sharon,' Joe said. 'Shuffle backwards. Now.'

She shook her head. 'I can't leave him.'

'If we get your weight off it, it'll hold. Liam weighs nothing. The roots are on the other side. It's much more secure. Come on. You have to do it now.' He lowered his voice. 'Or we'll lose you both.'

With every inch Sharon gained, the creaking grew louder. She spoke all the way. 'Don't worry, son. It's going to be fine. Keep looking ahead. We're going to come round the other side and get you. Remember that time we went to the circus and you loved the trapeze artists? You're just like one of them now. I reckon if you weren't so keen on being a policeman, you could join the circus. You are so brave. Wait 'til we tell Ryan. He's going to be so proud of you. He's going to – '

As the trunk broke, Joe grabbed Sharon and pulled her backwards. They fell into the leaves. Sharon was first to her feet. 'Liam, don't look round. It's fine. We'll get you.' She ran for the bridge.

The tree was still creaking. Liam was crying. Joe saw movement on the other side of the gorge. Was that Roberts, inching towards the fern-covered roots of the tree? Joe turned round and saw that Roberts was still with Curtis. The guy on the other side looked up. As their eyes met, Joe felt as if his scar had been tazered, as if it might just burst open. It was Stephen MacLaren. He was sitting on the gnarled mound of roots. Joe ran across the bridge.

Stephen reached out a hand to Liam. 'Hey Liam. Do you remember me?'

Liam was clinging to the tree. It was at an angle now, sloping down behind him. He nodded. 'Mac?'

'That's right. I'm your mum's friend and I'm going to help you. You've been such a brave boy. Your mum's fine. I need you to move towards me. Just a little bit, and then I'll have you.'

Liam shook his head. 'I can't.'

'Aye, you can. One hand at a time. Which hand do you write with?'

'This one.' He lifted his right hand a little and wiggled his fingers.

'See, you can move. Just a little bit closer to me. That's good. Now the other one.'

Liam was bending forward.

'Now you just need to shuffle your bum along towards your hands.'

Liam shook his head. 'I'm stuck.'

Stephen laughed. 'You're not. I promise. Try.'

He tried and he moved. Just an inch or so. In his rigid shoulders, Joe could see the tension. Stephen moved forward until he was sitting on the trunk. The creaking was louder. It could only be seconds before the whole thing went. Stephen stretched out his arms to Liam. 'You need to reach out to me. You're safe, Liam. As soon as I have your hands, I can lift you. Galbraith will catch you.'

'Honey, do what he says.' Sharon's voice was firm. 'Go on.'

Though the leaves beneath Joe's feet shifted, the ground was firm. He watched the concentration and trust on Liam's face as he reached out to Stephen. With a loud groan, Stephen grasped Liam's arms, lifting him above his head and passing him to Joe. Liam's body was shaking. He made no sound as tears poured down his cheeks.

'Well done, Liam. You were very brave.' Joe passed the boy to Sharon. She held Liam and sank into the leaves, holding and hugging and crying.

A loud crack reverberated through the gorge. Joe turned as the remainder of the tree crashed downwards, leaving nothing but a tangle of broken roots.

Chapter 63

The young trees that lined the gorge grew in all directions. Some sprouted upwards, others inwards, stretching towards the trees on the other side. As Joe sidled towards the edge, a slender branch twitched. And again. He looked down and saw a hand clinging to the branch, the skin scratched, the knuckles white. Joe lay on his front in the leaves and grasped Stephen's wrist with both hands. There was no great weight, and Joe knew he must have his feet on a ledge. He heard a voice behind him. 'Mam, will Mac be okay?'

'Course he will, Liam.'

'Sharon,' Joe said. 'Go and see if anyone else is in the car park.'

Stephen's eyes were huge. Joe tightened his grip. 'Give me your other hand.'

Stephen shook his head. 'I can't…my shoulder.' His arm was hanging at an awkward angle, the shoulder dislocated or broken.

Joe nodded. 'Okay. We'll have help soon. Keep your feet where they are. Try not to move.'

Stephen closed his eyes. His breathing was fast and shallow. In his wrist, Joe could feel his pulse; it was rapid and weak. His eyes still closed, Stephen spoke. His voice was soft, and Joe had to strain to hear him above the sound of the water below. 'Let me go. Please.'

Joe didn't answer. He tightened his grip.

'No one will know.' Stephen's eyes were still closed. 'Please. I won't survive prison. You thought I was dead. It'll be easier this way.'

As the birds of the forest called to each other, Joe felt the dampness of the ground soaking through his clothes. Stephen opened his eyes. There was no trace of the madness of last year. Just desperation, determination, and the faint remnants of the boy Stephen had been, before he and Joe, their lives and their families, had collided so brutally.

'Going to take my feet off the ledge. Don't want to take you with me. Let me go.'

Joe understood. There was a strong fresh scent rising from the earth. It smelled of freedom. He watched Stephen pull it into his lungs, as if for the last time. Wouldn't it be easier for them all just to let him go? A hero's death. No trial. The family secrets safely kept. Easier, perhaps, but impossible.

'Stephen, I can't.' Joe had failed to save Jackson. It wasn't happening again. And the dreams, they would never stop if he was responsible for Stephen's death. Pain tore through the muscles in his shoulders as he felt the full weight of Stephen, a stronger, heavier man than the one he'd fought last year. He felt his body start to slip through the leaves.

'Joe, I'm sorry, so sorry for everything. Tell the others. My mum. My dad. Lucy.'

Joe groaned. It was hard to get the words out. 'You can tell them yourself.'

Stephen kicked against the wall of the gorge, forcing momentum into his body. The agony of cramp in Joe's fingers, and the weight on his wrists, was almost unbearable. The chilling damp was soaking through his body, weakening him. He couldn't hold on for much longer.

Stephen kicked again, swinging his body outwards. 'Please. Better for everyone.' His voice was getting weaker. 'Better this way.'

Joe felt his fingers start to lose their grip. It was going to be just like his dreams; it was going to be his fault. Maybe there was no point in resisting.

But he wasn't the only one that would be affected. Joe had no idea how it had come about, but Stephen had risked his life and his liberty for Liam. 'Stephen,' Joe said, 'how will Liam live with it?'

Stephen groaned and tried to shake his head. When their eyes met, Joe knew he had won. The struggle stopped. 'Bastard,' Stephen said, but there was no venom in it.

And then Roberts was behind Joe, holding him and pulling. There was a man gripping Stephen's wrist and another loosening Joe's grip. And two people to his side, on ropes, and they were lowering themselves down towards Stephen.

Chapter 64

As the van driver waited for the barrier to rise, the steady thumping beat from the back of the van grew louder. He looked at his companion. His face was pale. The constant sound had accompanied them from the prison. Not that the prison was far. It was only a few minutes, but the journey seemed to have lasted forever. There was only one prisoner in the van, and four guards. Two of the guards had sustained injuries getting the prisoner into the van. Nothing serious; a sore foot for one, and a tender cheekbone for the other. Enough to make them all dread opening that compartment, when they reached the Castle.

The prisoner's hands and legs were cuffed for transport, a step only taken with prisoners exhibiting a high level of violence. He would be further hand-cuffed on arrival, to two lucky officers. He shouldn't have needed this level of cuffing. His leg was in plaster, and his shoulder in a sling, the joint and nerves having suffered extensive damage. He was scheduled for another operation next week.

But he needed cuffed all right, and the process must have caused him excruciating pain. No one would have known. Anger, definitely, but no sign of pain. The cuffs hadn't stopped him stamping on one guard's foot, and elbowing another in the face.

The barrier rose, and the van creaked its way up towards Inverness Castle, and the court. It was rumoured the court was to move to a purpose-built justice centre in the next few years. For now, the Castle was where it was at. They passed the main court building, turning left into the area between that and the North Tower, where the prisoners were unloaded and led to the cells.

There was a van already there. The driver parked behind it, then he phoned the court. They were ready for him. That was a relief. They could take the prisoner straight into court, and back again, bypassing the cells and the prospect of more trouble.

There were four police officers waiting. They frowned at the steady beat coming from the back of the van. A quick discussion about strategy and they were ready.

The driver banged on the compartment door. 'Mate; we're here.

There's eight of us. You can come quietly or you can fight. Up to you. It'd be a shame to damage that shoulder even more. I'm opening up now.'

An increase in the tempo of the beat and the sound of laughter made his hands shake. Was this bugger even fit to plead? Not that he'd be pleading today. It was the first appearance on petition, in a closed court, where the procurator fiscal would set out the charges and ask for the court's approval to investigate the crime. The prisoner would be committed for further examination, and the question of bail would be addressed. There would be no bail for this monster.

The compartment was small, and when the guard saw the prisoner sitting there, he thought of a huge stuffed toy, squeezed into a box. He backed off, keeping eye contact with the prisoner. 'Come on, mate; time to go. You couldn't just make it easy for everyone and come quietly?'

The prisoner sighed. He got to his feet, his back crouched to clear the doorway.

'Gently, okay? No need for any aggro.'

The prisoner stamped his foot, and the guard jumped backwards. There was a shout. 'Bastard!' It wasn't the prisoner. The guard had landed on the injured foot of his colleague. Behind him, it sounded as if a few toes had been stepped on. It amused the prisoner. His laughter was deep and loud, like his voice. 'Just having you on, guys. Relax.'

The two biggest guards each had a set of handcuffs. They closed in on either side of him, their backup behind them. The prisoner descended the steps of the van. He turned and looked up towards the row of houses in the Crown, above Castle Street. It was a warm day, the sky blue and cloudless. 'Guys, can you give me a second? I'm not going to be any bother. Just want to feel the sun.'

*

The men took a step away. Just a step, but it was enough. Todd smiled and glanced behind him; there was no one there. He closed his eyes and lifted his face, then his arms, his hands together, as if in prayer. There was a buzz of pain from his injured shoulder, and he welcomed it. Pain made him stronger; it always had done. He breathed into it, allowing the sensation to surround him, to swirl through him, and to float from him. He was strong, invincible, exceptional. No court, no trial, no prison. Not for him. Up and up his arms went until they were above his head and his chest was exposed. He took a deep breath, then he nodded, smiled, and fell.

*

Joe had never slept so well. He'd expected the dreams to escalate as his mind dredged up all the new possible scenarios involving him and Stephen MacLaren at Black Rock Gorge. But they'd stopped; there was nothing. Stephen had pleaded guilty to the culpable homicides of Moira Jacobs and Jean Henderson, a hit and run, and assault to the severe injury of Joe and Lucy. Sentence had been deferred for reports.

As for Todd Curtis, his DNA matched that found under Danielle Smith's nails. They'd found blood and DNA from Katya Birze, and an identical walking stick to the one Brent used, in the boot of Allingham's Lexus, along with a selection of number plates. Curtis's gun matched the one used to kill Gordon Sutherland.

Enquiries into Curtis's death were ongoing. He'd been killed by a sniper, situated on the flat roof of an extension of a house on Ardconnel Terrace. A professional killing, but who was behind it? James Allingham? Curtis's former associates in London? Joe was in no doubt they all had plenty to lose if Curtis had decided to talk.

The guards and police officers at the Castle were certain Curtis knew it was coming, had even welcomed it. Had he begged someone to do it? Was it Brent? The end of the life-debt? Joe doubted it. He didn't think Brent had it in him, and there was no record of any contact between the men since Curtis was captured. Still…

Epilogue

The deep blue sky was reflected in the rock pool, the clouds opaque and shimmering. The warm, gentle breeze carried the scent of sand and wild flowers. It left a crust of salt on Joe's lips. The caravan was gone and he was glad. He'd been here yesterday and only the low circular wall surrounding the fire remained. He'd sat on the wall and thought about Stephen. He couldn't help pitying him. There were reasons Stephen had done what he did. Those reasons didn't excuse the appalling crimes he'd committed, but the Stephen that rescued Liam was a different person from the one that had stabbed Joe; he was certain of it. How must he feel being incarcerated after living freely here for so long? The thought made Joe shiver.

He felt someone touch his shoulder. It was Roberts. 'Will we get on? Lucy and Drew are waiting with Jill at the picnic area. They've got the wellies.'

Joe looked at his watch, then he stood. 'Suppose we better. What do you think of Drew? Might have known she'd fall for another solicitor.'

'He's all right, for one of them.'

Joe followed the others across the shallow ford. They skirted round the sand, heading for the track that would take them over the dunes to *Traigh Iar*, Carla's favourite beach.

Joe had been there yesterday too. He'd gone on his own, while Carla rested. She was much stronger now. Still not back at work, but her doctor expected her to make a full recovery. They hadn't been able to identify the virus. There were a list of possibilities, but no positive matches.

Joe had looked down on the stretching white sands of *Traigh Iar*, and for the first time in a very long time, he had felt that all was well in his world. It wouldn't last; he knew that. He was too uptight, and too prone to stress. But he'd enjoy it for now.

Lucy stopped and turned. 'Is it this way?'

Joe nodded, and followed them along the path between two fields, towards the steep sand dune. In the field on the left, a large brown cow was chewing the cud, watching them with lazy eyes. The sound of a tractor distracted the cow. Joe looked behind. The tractor was crossing the ford. Lucy laughed. 'Relieved?'

'A bit.'

They were at the bottom of the dune. Drew opened the bag he'd carried on his shoulder, and they all swapped their wellies for shoes. Drew held his hand out to Lucy. Joe watched him pull her up. He followed, Roberts and Jill behind him.

At the top of the dune, Joe stopped. The beach looked different today. Yesterday, he'd been alone as he'd walked its length, his soul at perfect peace. Today, there was a cluster of people on the sand, as a warm breeze skimmed across the waves. Joe smiled when he saw his mother rest her hand on his step-father's shoulder, as she brushed sand off her high heels. 'I'll just wait here,' he said.

Roberts looked at the beach and whistled. 'This is something else, Sarge. Thanks for asking us.'

'It's Joe. And how could I not ask you? You saved my life.'

Roberts smiled. Was that a tear in his eye? 'Hardly, Joe. You'd have fought him off if I hadn't been there. No sweat.'

They both knew that wasn't true.

'We'll get off down, then. See you on the other side.'

Joe smiled and patted him on the shoulder. As Joe turned to watch the approaching tractor, Roberts spoke again. 'Oh, Sarge, I mean Joe – I forgot to tell you, I was invited to a wedding party tonight, in the Phoenix.'

'Aye?'

Roberts nodded. 'Bumped into Sharon MacRae yesterday. She and Christopher Brent are getting married in Belladrum Chapel today.'

There was a lump the size of a small rock in Joe's throat. 'That's fantastic. How are the boys?'

'Doing well. Enjoying Ness Castle and their new schools. Ryan's on an electronic tag from the Children's Hearing. Sharon said something about you and him going sailing? Not sure what she was on about. She also said to give you and Carla her regards, and she'll not let you forget your anniversary.'

Joe laughed. He'd never forget. Never.

The tractor stopped below the dunes. The sun was shining on the windows and Joe couldn't see inside. Ronald got out, his kilt lifting a little in the breeze. Joe held his breath. What if Ronald was on his own, come to tell Joe she couldn't go through with it? Ronald looked up at Joe and winked. As he went round to the other side of the tractor, Joe felt his chest relax.

Carla was wearing a short lace ivory dress. Her long legs were tanned, and the sun was glinting off her dark hair, dancing and shining in highlights of copper and gold. She held a bunch of light pink roses in one hand. She looked to her left, across the fields, to where a cluster of gravestones rose from the machair. They would take her flowers there after the ceremony.

Carla looked up. When their eyes met, every hurt, every doubt and every loneliness Joe had ever known was gone. He was home.

END

About the Author

Helen Forbes

Helen Forbes is a civil litigation solicitor in her home town of Inverness, specialising in social welfare law. She has also lived and worked in Edinburgh, Fife, and the Outer Hebrides, where she edited Am Paipear, an award winning community newspaper. Prior to studying law at the University of Edinburgh Helen was a veterinary nurse in Inverness and at the Royal (Dick) School of Veterinary Studies in Edinburgh.

A member of the Highland Literary Salon and the Edinburgh Writers' Club, Helen has had short stories published in Northwords Now and the Global Shorts Anthology. She has also had success in national and international writing competitions, having been highly commended by the Highland and Island Short Story Association, Neil Gunn Writing Competition and Scottish Association of Writers.

Also from Helen Forbes

In The Shadow Of The Hill
Helen Forbes
ISBN: 978-0-9929768-1-1 (eBook)
ISBN: 978-0-9929768-0-4 (Paperback)

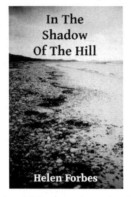

An elderly woman is found battered to death in the common stairwell of an Inverness block of flats.

Detective Sergeant Joe Galbraith starts what seems like one more depressing investigation of the untimely death of a poor unfortunate who was in the wrong place, at the wrong time.

As the investigation spreads across Scotland it reaches into a past that Joe has tried to forget, and takes him back to the Hebridean island of Harris, where he spent his childhood.

Among the mountains and the stunning landscape of religiously conservative Harris, in the shadow of Ceapabhal, long buried events and a tragic story are slowly uncovered, and the investigation takes on an altogether more sinister aspect.

In The Shadow Of The Hill skilfully captures the intricacies and malevolence of the underbelly of Highland and Island life, bringing tragedy and vengeance to the magical beauty of the Outer Hebrides.

'...our first real home-grown sample of modern Highland noir' – Roger Hutchinson; West Highland Free Press

More Books From ThunderPoint Publishing Ltd.

The Oystercatcher Girl
Gabrielle Barnby
ISBN: 978-1-910946-17-6 (eBook)
ISBN: 978-1-910946-15-2 (Paperback)

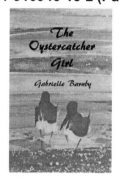

In the medieval splendour of St Magnus Cathedral, three women gather to mourn the untimely passing of Robbie: Robbie's widow, Tessa; Tessa's old childhood friend, Christine, and Christine's unstable and unreliable sister, Lindsay.

But all is not as it seems: what is the relationship between the three women, and Robbie? What secrets do they hide? And who has really betrayed who?

Set amidst the spectacular scenery of the Orkney Islands, Gabrielle Barnby's skilfully plotted first novel is a beautifully understated story of deception and forgiveness, love and redemption.

With poetic and precise language Barnby draws you in to the lives, loves and losses of the characters till you feel a part of the story.

'The Oystercatcher Girl is a wonderfully evocative and deftly woven story' – Sara Bailey

The House with the Lilac Shutters:
Gabrielle Barnby
ISBN: 978-1-910946-02-2 (eBook)
ISBN: 978-0-9929768-8-0 (Paperback)

Irma Lagrasse has taught piano to three generations of villagers, whilst slowly twisting the knife of vengeance; Nico knows a secret; and M. Lenoir has discovered a suppressed and dangerous passion.

Revolving around the Café Rose, opposite The House with the Lilac Shutters, this collection of contemporary short stories links a small town in France with a small town in England, traces the unexpected connections between the people of both places and explores the unpredictable influences that the past can have on the present.

Characters weave in and out of each other's stories, secrets are concealed and new connections are made.

With a keenly observant eye, Barnby illustrates the everyday tragedies, sorrows, hopes and joys of ordinary people in this vividly understated and unsentimental collection.

'The more I read, and the more descriptions I encountered, the more I was put in mind of one of my all time favourite texts – Dylan Thomas' Under Milk Wood' – lindasbookbag.com

Changed Times
Ethyl Smith
ISBN: 978-1-910946-09-1 (eBook)
ISBN: 978-1-910946-08-4 (Paperback)

1679 – The Killing Times: Charles II is on the throne, the Episcopacy has been restored, and southern Scotland is in ferment.

The King is demanding superiority over all things spiritual and temporal and rebellious Ministers are being ousted from their parishes for refusing to bend the knee.

When John Steel steps in to help one such Minister in his home village of Lesmahagow he finds himself caught up in events that reverberate not just through the parish, but throughout the whole of southern Scotland.

From the Battle of Drumclog to the Battle of Bothwell Bridge, John's platoon of farmers and villagers find themselves in the heart of the action over that fateful summer where the people fight the King for their religion, their freedom, and their lives.

Set amid the tumult and intrigue of Scotland's Killing Times, John Steele's story powerfully reflects the changes that took place across 17th century Scotland, and stunningly brings this period of history to life.

'Smith writes with a fine ear for Scots speech, and with a sensitive awareness to the different ways in which history intrudes upon the lives of men and women, soldiers and civilians, adults and children' – James Robertson

Dark Times
Ethyl Smith
ISBN: 978-1-910946-26-8 (eBook)
ISBN: 978-1-910946-24-4 (Paperback)

The summer of 1679 is a dark one for the Covenanters, routed by government troops at the Battle of Bothwell Brig. John Steel is on the run, hunted for his part in the battle by the vindictive Earl of Airlie. And life is no easier for the hapless Sandy Gillon, curate of Lesmahagow Kirk, in the Earl's sights for aiding John Steel's escape.

Outlawed and hounded, the surviving rebels have no choice but to take to the hills and moors to evade capture and deportation. And as a hard winter approaches, Marion Steel discovers she's pregnant with her third child.

Dark Times is the second part of Ethyl Smith's sweeping *Times* series that follows the lives of ordinary people in extraordinary times.

'What really sets Smith's novel apart, however, is her superb use of Scots dialogue. From the educated Scots of the gentry and nobility to the broader brogues of everyday folk, the dialogue sparkles and demands to be read out loud.' – Shirley Whiteside (The National)

The False Men
Mhairead MacLeod
ISBN: 978-1-910946-27-5 (eBook)
ISBN: 978-1-910946-25-1 (Paperback)

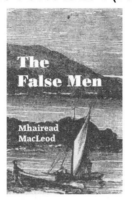

North Uist, Outer Hebrides, 1848

Jess MacKay has led a privileged life as the daughter of a local landowner, sheltered from the harsher aspects of life. Courted by the eligible Patrick Cooper, the Laird's new commissioner, Jess's future is mapped out, until Lachlan Macdonald arrives on North Uist, amid rumours of forced evictions on islands just to the south.

As the uncompromising brutality of the Clearances reaches the islands, and Jess sees her friends ripped from their homes, she must decide where her heart, and her loyalties, truly lie.

Set against the evocative backdrop of the Hebrides and inspired by a true story, *The False Men* is a compelling tale of love in a turbulent past that resonates with the upheavals of the modern world.

'...an engaging tale of powerlessness, love and disillusionment in the context of the type of injustice that, sadly, continues to this day' – Anne Goodwin

Dead Cat Bounce
Kevin Scott
ISBN: 978-1-910946-17-6 (eBook)
ISBN: 978-1-910946-15-2 (Paperback)

"Well, either way, you'll have to speak to your brother today because...unless I get my money by tomorrow morning there's not going to be a funeral."

When your 11 year old brother has been tragically killed in a car accident, you might think that organising his funeral would take priority. But when Nicky's coffin, complete with Nicky's body, goes missing, deadbeat loser Matt has only 26 hours in which to find the £20,000 he owes a Glasgow gangster or explain to his grieving mother why there's not going to be a funeral.

Enter middle brother, Pete, successful City trader with an expensive wife, expensive children, and an expensive villa in Tuscany. Pete's watches cost £20,000, but he has his own problems, and Matt doesn't want his help anyway.

Seething with old resentments, the betrayals of the past and the double-dealings of the present, the two brothers must find a way to work together to retrieve Nicky's body, discovering along the way that they are not so different after all.

'Underplaying the comic potential to highlight the troubled relationship between the equally flawed brothers. It's one of those books that keep the reader hooked right to the end' – The Herald

The Wrong Box
Andrew C Ferguson
ISBN: 978-1-910946-14-5 (Paperback)
ISBN: 978-1-910946-16-9 (eBook)

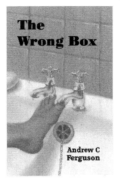

All I know is, I'm in exile in Scotland, and there's a dead Scouser businessman in my bath. With his toe up the tap.

Meet Simon English, corporate lawyer, heavy drinker and Scotophobe, banished from London after being caught misbehaving with one of the young associates on the corporate desk. As if that wasn't bad enough, English finds himself acting for a spiralling money laundering racket that could put not just his career, but his life, on the line.

Enter Karen Clamp, an 18 stone, well-read wann be couturier from the Auchendrossan sink estate, with an encyclopedic knowledge of Council misdeeds and 19th century Scottish fiction. With no one to trust but each other, this mismatched pair must work together to investigate a series of apparently unrelated frauds and discover how everything connects to the mysterious Wrong Box.

Manically funny, *The Wrong Box* is a chaotic story of lust, money, power and greed, and the importance of being able to sew a really good hem.

'...the makings of a new Caledonian Comic Noir genre: Rebus with jokes, Val McDiarmid with buddha belly laughs, or Trainspotting for the professional classes'

Toxic
Jackie MacLean
Shortlisted for the Yeovil Book Prize 2011
ISBN: 978-0-9575689-8-3 (eBook)
ISBN: 978-0-9575689-9-0 (Paperback)

The recklessly brilliant DI Donna Davenport, struggling to hide a secret from police colleagues and get over the break-up with her partner, has been suspended from duty for a fiery and inappropriate outburst to the press.

DI Evanton, an old-fashioned, hard-living misogynistic copper has been newly demoted for thumping a suspect, and transferred to Dundee with a final warning ringing in his ears and a reputation that precedes him.

And in the peaceful, rolling Tayside farmland a deadly store of MIC, the toxin that devastated Bhopal, is being illegally stored by a criminal gang smuggling the valuable substance necessary for making cheap pesticides.

An anonymous tip-off starts a desperate search for the MIC that is complicated by the uneasy partnership between Davenport and Evanton and their growing mistrust of each others actions.

Compelling and authentic, Toxic is a tense and fast paced crime thriller.

'...a humdinger of a plot that is as realistic as it is frightening' – crimefictionlover.com

The Bogeyman Chronicles
Craig Watson
ISBN: 978-1-910946-11-4 (eBook)
ISBN: 978-1-910946-10-7 (Paperback)

In 14th Century Scotland, amidst the wars of independence, hatred, murder and betrayal are commonplace. People are driven to extraordinary lengths to survive, whilst those with power exercise it with cruel pleasure.

Royal Prince Alexander Stewart, son of King Robert II and plagued by rumours of his illegitimacy, becomes infamous as the Wolf of Badenoch, while young Andrew Christie commits an unforgivable sin and lay Brother Brodie Affleck in the Restenneth Priory pieces together the mystery that links them all together.

From the horror of the times and the changing fortunes of the characters, the legend of the Bogeyman is born and Craig Watson cleverly weaves together the disparate lives of the characters into a compelling historical mystery that will keep you gripped throughout.

Over 80 years the lives of three men are inextricably entwined, and through their hatreds, murders and betrayals the legend of Christie Cleek, the bogeyman, is born.

'The Bogeyman Chronicles haunted our imagination long after we finished it' – iScot Magazine

Mule Train
Huw Francis
ISBN: 978-0-9575689-0-7 (eBook)
ISBN: 978-0-9575689-1-4 (Paperback)

Four lives come together in the remote and spectacular mountains bordering Afghanistan and explode in a deadly cocktail of treachery, betrayal and violence.

Written with a deep love of Pakistan and the Pakistani people, Mule Train will sweep you from Karachi in the south to the Shandur Pass in the north, through the dangerous borderland alongside Afghanistan, in an adventure that will keep you gripped throughout.

'Stunningly captures the feel of Pakistan, from Karachi to the hills' – tripfiction.com

QueerBashing
Tim Morriosn
ISBN: 978-1-910946-06-0 (eBook)
ISBN: 978-0-9929768-9-7 (Paperback)

The first queerbasher McGillivray ever met was in the mirror.

From the revivalist churches of Orkney in the 1970s, to the gay bars of London and Northern England in the 90s, via the divinity school at Aberdeen, this is the story of McGillivray, a self-centred, promiscuous hypocrite, failed Church of Scotland minister, and his own worst enemy.

Determined to live life on his own terms, McGillivray's grasp on reality slides into psychosis and a sense of his own invulnerability, resulting in a brutal attack ending life as he knows it.

Raw and uncompromising, this is a viciously funny but ultimately moving account of one man's desire to come to terms with himself and live his life as he sees fit.

'…an arresting novel of pain and self-discovery' – Alastair Mabbott (The Herald)

A Good Death
Helen Davis
ISBN: 978-0-9575689-7-6 (eBook)
ISBN: 978-0-9575689-6-9 (Paperback)

'A good death is better than a bad conscience,' said Sophie.

1983 – Georgie, Theo, Sophie and Helena, four disparate young Cambridge undergraduates, set out to scale Ausangate, one of the highest and most sacred peaks in the Andes.

Seduced into employing the handsome and enigmatic Wamani as a guide, the four women are initiated into the mystically dangerous side of Peru, Wamani and themselves as they travel from Cuzco to the mountain, a journey that will shape their lives forever.

2013 – though the women are still close, the secrets and betrayals of Ausangate chafe at the friendship.

A girls' weekend at a lonely Fenland farmhouse descends into conflict with the insensitive inclusion of an overbearing young academic toyboy brought along by Theo. Sparked by his unexpected presence, pent up petty jealousies, recriminations and bitterness finally explode the truth of Ausangate, setting the women on a new and dangerous path.

Sharply observant and darkly comic, Helen Davis's début novel is an elegant tale of murder, seduction, vengeance, and the value of a good friendship.

'The prose is crisp, adept, and emotionally evocative' – Lesbrary.com

The Birds That Never Flew
Margot McCuaig
Shortlisted for the Dundee International Book Prize 2012
Longlisted for the Polari First Book Prize 2014
ISBN: 978-0-9929768-5-9 (eBook)
ISBN: 978-0-9929768-4-2 (Paperback)

'Have you got a light hen? I'm totally gaspin.'

Battered and bruised, Elizabeth has taken her daughter and left her abusive husband Patrick. Again. In the bleak and impersonal Glasgow housing office Elizabeth meets the provocatively intriguing drug addict Sadie, who is desperate to get her own life back on track.

The two women forge a fierce and interdependent relationship as they try to rebuild their shattered lives, but despite their bold, and sometimes illegal attempts it seems impossible to escape from the abuse they have always known, and tragedy strikes.

More than a decade later Elizabeth has started to implement her perfect revenge – until a surreal Glaswegian Virgin Mary steps in with imperfect timing and a less than divine attitude to stick a spoke in the wheel of retribution.

Tragic, darkly funny and irreverent, *The Birds That Never Flew* ushers in a new and vibrant voice in Scottish literature.

'...dark, beautiful and moving, I wholeheartedly recommend' scanoir.co.uk

Over Here
Jane Taylor
ISBN: 978-0-9929768-3-5 (eBook)
ISBN: 978-0-9929768-2-8 (Paperback)

It's coming up to twenty-four hours since the boy stepped down from the big passenger liner – it must be, he reckons foggily – because morning has come around once more with the awful irrevocability of time destined to lead nowhere in this worrying new situation. His temporary minder on board – last spotted heading for the bar some while before the lumbering process of docking got underway – seems to have vanished for good. Where does that leave him now? All on his own in a new country: that's where it leaves him. He is just nine years old.

An eloquently written novel tracing the social transformations of a century where possibilities were opened up by two world wars that saw millions of men move around the world to fight, and mass migration to the new worlds of Canada and Australia by tens of thousands of people looking for a better life.

Through the eyes of three generations of women, the tragic story of the nine year old boy on Liverpool docks is brought to life in saddeningly evocative prose.

'…a sweeping haunting first novel that spans four generations and two continents…' – Cristina Odone/Catholic Herald

The Bonnie Road
Suzanne d'Corsey
ISBN: 978-1-910946-01-5 (eBook)
ISBN: 978-0-9929768-6-6 (Paperback)

My grandmother passed me in transit. She was leaving, I was coming into this world, our spirits meeting at the door to my mother's womb, as she bent over the bed to close the thin crinkled lids of her own mother's eyes.

The women of Morag's family have been the keepers of tradition for generations, their skills and knowledge passed down from woman to woman, kept close and hidden from public view, official condemnation and religious suppression.

In late 1970s St. Andrews, demand for Morag's services are still there, but requested as stealthily as ever, for even in 20th century Scotland witchcraft is a dangerous Art to practise.

When newly widowed Rosalind arrives from California to tend her ailing uncle, she is drawn unsuspecting into a new world she never knew existed, one in which everyone seems to have a secret, but that offers greater opportunities than she dreamt of – if she only has the courage to open her heart to it.

Richly detailed, dark and compelling, d'Corsey magically transposes the old ways of Scotland into the 20th Century and brings to life the ancient traditions and beliefs that still dance just below the surface of the modern world.

'...successfully portrays rich characters in compelling plots, interwoven with atmospheric Scottish settings & history and coloured with witchcraft & romance' – poppypeacockpens.com

Talk of the Toun
Helen MacKinven
ISBN: 978-1-910946-00-8 (eBook)
ISBN: 978-0-9929768-7-3 (Paperback)

She was greetin' again. But there's no need for Lorraine to be feart, since the first day of primary school, Angela has always been there to mop up her tears and snotters.

An uplifting black comedy of love, family life and friendship, Talk of the Toun is a bittersweet coming-of-age tale set in the summer of 1985, in working class, central belt Scotland.

Lifelong friends Angela and Lorraine are two very different girls, with a growing divide in their aspirations and ambitions putting their friendship under increasing strain.

Artistically gifted Angela has her sights set on art school, but lassies like Angela, from a small town council scheme, are expected to settle for a nice wee secretarial job at the local factory. Her only ally is her gallus gran, Senga, the pet psychic, who firmly believes that her granddaughter can be whatever she wants.

Though Lorraine's ambitions are focused closer to home Angela has plans for her too, and a caravan holiday to Filey with Angela's family tests the dynamics of their relationship and has lifelong consequences for them both.

Effortlessly capturing the religious and social intricacies of 1980s Scotland, Talk of the Toun is the perfect mix of pathos and humour as the two girls wrestle with the complications of growing up and exploring who they really are.

'Fresh, fierce and funny…a sharp and poignant study of growing up in 1980s Scotland. You'll laugh, you'll cry…you'll cringe' – KAREN CAMPBELL

29727345R00166

Printed in Great Britain
by Amazon